# Gordon Skene

Our motto – *In order that a good story may be told* –
reflects our belief that tomorrow's literary heritage depends on investment in today's writers.

First published in Great Britain 1998 by
The Malvern Publishing Company Limited,
32, Old Street,
Upton-upon-Severn,
Worcesterdhire,
WR8 0HW
England.

email Malpub123@aol.com

British Library Cataloguing in Publication Data

A catalogue record for this book is available
from the British Library


ISBN  0 947993 79 7

Printed in Malta by Interprint Limited

FOR PAT AND SHERMAN

# PROLOGUE

## WALK RIGHT IN - WALK RIGHT OUT

"Ray ban, is the mouse on tight?"

I gaze at the face shouting at me and think; what he really meant to say was,

"Hey man, are you all right?" Only it's not coming out that way.

Okay, how do I work this?

I've been hit by a bus. At least, I think that's what's happened because all I can see is the smiling front grille and the bright letters RTD. I'm lying in the street, reeking of radiator steam, and my head feels like it's going to explode.

Another face yells at me and I don't understand a word of it this; it's like somebody put a tape on fast rewind.

I try to move my mouth to ask if somebody will help me up; it's hard to stand up on my own. In fact, I can't. Swell. Nobody is listening to me; they quiety gawk.

I don't know. I was having a good time up until now. I honestly think I was having a great time. I was happy as hell about something but can't seem to remember what about. I feel myself being lifted onto a stretcher. A woman leans over me; she has a warm face and green eyes. She looks efficient and business-like, studying my face with the scrutiny of an office building being surveyed by a wrecking crew.

"Nelson?" The woman pulls my wallet out of my pants and flips through it. "Is your name Nelson Rivers?" I nod my head, pleased that someone is actually talking to me.

"Nelson, can you understand me?"

She looks through me and turns to her partner, nonchalantly shrugging her shoulders. It is not a confidence inspiring gesture. Next thing I know I'm being shoved into an ambulance. I think the young woman has given me a shot because I feel a stupid smile seep across my face. My lips feel like airplane tires. At least my headache has gone away.

The young woman studies my driver's license. She glances periodically over at me. "So that's what he looks like." She looks at it again for a moment and quietly chirps to herself. "June 23rd. I've got a cousin born on the 22nd."

9

"Nels, I think you better sit this dance out."

I know that voice. I've heard it thousands of times, only I don't know where it's coming from. The best I can do is move my eyes around, trying to focus past the ambulance attendants.

Sitting on the edge of my stretcher is Buzz Jordan. He's one of my best friends. I've known him forever. He sits on the edge and lights a cigarette, inhaling deeply and blowing out a cloud of white-blue haze that quickly envelopes the tiny enclosed area. I'm worried the attendants will see him and throw him off, but they don't pay any attention to him; they don't even know he's there. Buzz is sixteen. His thick, curly black hair is parted on the side which he tries to comb straight, running the risk of having his hair sticking up in all the wrong places. He's wearing the same black velvet cape, lime - green Edwardian shirt with four-inch paisley-print cuffs, knee-high brown suede boots with fringe laces and thick grey corduroy pants that he's worn for years. The cape hangs loosely over his right shoulder and there are big patches of worn spots where velvet used to be.

"Buzz, what am I doing here?"

He drags on his cigarette again before stubbing it out on the ambulance floor. He blows a giant ring of smoke out and smiles. "You're looking for the man who reimagines things. If I were you I'd fade."

He raises his hand and does a long, slow wave, making a 180 degree arc with his hand. As he does, he slowly begins to disappear. By the time his hand has completed the arc, he has vanished.

Just what I need: a cryptic message and a disappearing act. Funny thing. Seeing Buzz has reminded me of another place and time. I guess it's the past, but I'm not so sure. I'm mixed up in all this confusion. But if I was to stake my life on it, I could swear it's 1964. What other year can it be?

I'm fighting to stay awake, but it becomes harder and harder to. I feel a warm wave of surrender flowing up from my spine, rushing past my ears. As if someone were trying to spare me the reality of the moment. I decide the best thing to do, under the circumstances, is to let go and see where all of this takes me.

# CHAPTER ONE

## A HEAD FULL OF DYNAMITE - A MOUTH FULL OF BLASTING CAPS

Jesus, I've become the missing link. I'm physically grotesque. I've never considered myself a particularly handsome kid, but this is unbelievable. Over the last few weeks my nose has gotten so big it's threatening to take over my entire face. Hair is appearing in places where no hair has ever grown before. Bad enough the hair on my head is taking on a life of its own and sticking straight up - there's enough hair spilling out of the other parts of me to make me wonder if I have done something to reverse my evolutionary state and am about to become an attraction at the Griffith Park Zoo. Even my voice is cracking. The brand new me is so frightening that I spend most of the time staring at the ground when I walk. I'm unfit for human recognition.

Only three months ago I was basking in the heady glow of being the hot-shit in my sixth grade class. Now I'm a notch above mildew.

\*    \*    \*    \*

*"Has he stabilized?"*
*"His pulse is eratic."*
*"What about the other vitals?"*
*"Blood gases are stable."*
*"Good. Order a brain scan as soon as possible and call the OR."*

\*    \*    \*    \*

One thing for seventh graders, no matter how well-adjusted or maladjusted we are, there are new and horrifying rituals facing all of us. Take gym and the showers for example. Okay, everybody's body is changing, but not everybody's body is changing at the same rate. The cruel humiliation some pimple-encrusted freshman feels, sloshing out of the shower cold, wet and naked, only to be asked in a bellowing yell, "Hey, didja lose something in there?" is more than enough ammunition to fill up a lifetime's worth of confusion. The only person I know who doesn't take this razzing indifferently is Buzz Jordan. If seventh graders have the misfortune of being the new kids in school, Buzz has the greatest misfortune of being the newest

11

kid period. He arrived at Pasteur three weeks into the new semester and doesn't know a soul. He keeps to himself and doesn't say anything to anybody except people who speak to him and then it's a one or two syllable reply.

We don't have any other classes together; our nine a.m. gym class is the only one. Six laps around the track, fifty-two push ups and an assortment of other sweat-inducing exercises - then the march to the dreaded showers. The eighth graders have gotten in there five minutes earlier and are waiting for us.

"It might grow if you didn't play with it so much," yells Mike Marmer, a tall, bony kid with marsupial features and a mouthful of aluminum braces. In most cultures he would be the last to point out the shortcomings in others, but his friends, an equally geeky batch of maladroits, howl approval. So Mike knows no fear. Standing under the alternating hot and cold taps, I turn my head to see Buzz, Mike's target of the day, making his way calmly toward me at the end of the bank of showers, the only spot where there's a space. He steps in beside me.

Mike's still standing at the entrance, sporting a five foot smirk on his face, readying up another salvo. Buzz stays under the shower only long enough to rinse himself off, then shuffles calmly out and pads back up the bank to the towel dispenser. I hear Mike mutter something; then a dull, smacking thud echoes through the tiled room.

*    *    *    *

*"Has anyone contacted next of kin?"*
*"Social Services are locating the address on his drivers license."*
*"We've got a stable pulse."*
*"Is there any sign of motor reflex?"*
*"Nothing so far."*

*    *    *    *

Mike is doubled over in the shower, screaming blue murder, holding his nose as blood sprays through his fingers and splashes on to the shower floor, turning the water pink and rinsing into the drain.

Buzz continues walking on to his locker as if nothing has happened. Judging from the thick blanket of silence that has fallen over the gym I would imagine the teasing's going to stop now. And it's at this point I realize Buzz Jordan is okay.

Nobody has it easy, though. Seventh grade girls have their own share of problems. Most of them are round and unformed, so in order to make their presences known to guys in the eighth and ninth grades, they have to come up with some serious, and often very creative make-overs. The knee socks, plaid skirts and saddle shoes soon head straight into the trashcan and out pops a whole sub-culture of thirteen year-old girls who look, walk and talk just like Tuesday Weld. The ratty page boy hair is replaced by lacquered bouffants that stay frozen in place, even during field trips to wind tunnels. The baggy, starchy cotton blouses become form-fitting cashmere sweaters worn with pleated tweed skirts or, if they're willing to get roasted by the Girl's Vice-Principal, skin-tight painted on dresses so snug only the skinniest girl on the planet ever looks good in them. Eyebrows suddenly appear, black, thick and arched. And by the time the first month of school is over, every seventh grade girl is wearing a bra of some kind; whether she needs one or not. Kleenex is a hot commodity at Pasteur Junior High. At thirteen, deception is rife.

Life has become one big Indianapolis 500 of agitation and frustration. The guys are in heated competition for the few girls who stoop to look sideways at them and the girls are busily studying Teen Magazine and Glamour for any tips and inside leads on the race to womanhood.

In the midst of all this I feel pretty uneasy about my own changes, but I've found sanctuary, at least for a few hours. Most Saturdays, at eleven in the morning, I take the Fairfax bus to the corner of Hollywood and Vine and head to Wallich's Music City down on Sunset. It's a huge store; taking up almost an entire city block. It stocks every record imaginable and the perimeter of the store is lined with soundproof listening booths where you can submerge your mangled psyche for hours on end under a bulky pair of headphones, with no obligation to buy, and sit in a molded pink plastic chair with a view out to Sunset Boulevard. The people who work there hate you for it, but it's a downpayment on your own private heaven. Anyway, who cares what some idiot salesman thinks?

\*       \*       \*       \*

*"Hi Nelson - I'm Sidney Roth. I'm with Social Services. We're trying to contact your wife. Are you comfortable? Do you know where you are? Can you understand me? . . . Nelson?"*

\*       \*       \*       \*

Sidney is one of the Wallich's salesmen and like all the employees, he wears a white shopcoat that makes him look like a lab technician or dental assistant.

Sidney works the 45 section of the store. He has a face like the surface of the Moon, wears grimy grey glasses and prays for the day murder will become legal.

"Probably want the new releases, don't you?" Sidney sneers and grimaces, showing his greenish-yellow teeth. My musical taste up to this point has been Classical, with five years worth of piano lessons to show for it. Since my transformation though, it's taken a slight detour. Maybe it has to do with hormones, or the desire to fit in, but I'm spending more time listening to The Beatles than to Brahms. In the month I've been coming to Wallich's, I've only bought one record: *Soul Serenade* by King Curtis. Today, I decide I'm going to buy *Good Golly Miss Molly* by The Swingin' Blue Jeans, but I want to hear what else is new. Sidney works on commission. He and the other employees of Wallich's fight over customers if they look even remotely like they have money to spend. One look at me indicates to Sidney that he isn't going to retire off my sixty-nine cent purchases during this lifetime. He stands behind a raised counter overseeing the listening booths. In front of him sit racks of new releases. It must've been a good week because there are over fifty new records sitting there. I scoop up a copy of each and head off to my sanctum. Sidney gets down from his pedestal every few minutes and walks by the booths, hovering by mine in particular, snarling at all of us. Each of the occupants is under the age of sixteen and the thought of making only two dollars for the day is probably turning his stomach. But as far as I'm concerned, Sidney could be on Mars.

*A World Without Love* by Peter & Gordon fills my headphones as I look out on Sunset where people move painfully slowly on the sidewalk; they have every good reason to: the temperature tower on the bank building across the street cheerfully announces it's 107 degrees, and it's only twelve-thirty.

A red and white Tanner/Grey Line Tourbus pulls to a stop in front of my window. Thirty large and out-of-place tourists spill out, led by a sweat-soaked bus driver, who does his best to shuttle the group across the street to the NBC Building where there is air conditioning and a game show to watch.

Every one of the tourists is suffering. From the look of their gabardine suits and ties, they have to be from some religious group that actively practises discomfort and self-flagellation. Their faces are pale, bleached white and sweating in economy-sized portions. I can't imagine why people have to dress like that if they know they are going to be miserable. Just looking at them makes me conjure visions of dying, going straight to hell and being forced to wear a wool suit for eternity.

There's a tap on the window of the booth to the right of me. I turn around and see Buzz waving at me. I'm a little surprised. I haven't seen him since the shower episode. He's doing the same thing I am, sitting with a stack of new releases in front of him, listening and looking out at Sunset Boulevard. Buzz seems older than most of the guys in my grade. Maybe it's because he's fashion conscious. He's the only one in school who wears a Beatle jacket, your basic sport coat with collar missing and a thin line of black velvet where the collar used to be. The thing that lets Buzz down however, is his hair which says a lot about where you are on the hip ladder of life. Straight hair is in. Brian Jones of the Rolling Stones is the guy everybody wants to look like. Buzz can't. Buzz has kid hair; a tangled mess of curls and cowlicks that he keeps plastering down, hoping to train in some direction, which he never seems quite able to find.

Buzz is the only kid I know who smokes. He's smoking now, engulfing his booth in a blue haze. But not for long. Sidney spots him and comes storming over, banging on the door with his fists and screaming loud enough to be heard down the street.

"Hey, moron, can't you read the fucking sign? No Smoking!"

Sidney probably thinks his lung power will impress the store manager. It backfires because all he manages is to attract the attention of everyone in the store, who stop what they're doing and watch him convulse. The pimples on his face and the veins in his neck look like they're all going to burst at the same time. Buzz gets banished from his booth, probably for life, or at least until Sidney gets another job.

Not satisfied with chasing Buzz out, Sidney now focuses his attention on me. He shoots a sadistic leer, but I'm not going to give him the satisfaction of leaving. He keeps staring, hoping he'll burn a hole in the side of my head. I sit back in my chair and adjust my headphones, pretending Sidney doesn't exist. I watch the bus driver, who's now sitting in comparative peace and quiet on his empty bus, reading an issue of Playboy and adjusting a small fan that blows a breeze on him.

I notice Buzz is still hanging around outside. He catches my eye and cocks his head in the direction of his former booth. I see that Sidney is busily cleaning it. Buzz raises his finger and motions for me to watch. He turns around, pulls his pants down and presses his pale ass against the window of Wallich's Music City. Sidney is bent over picking up some candy wrappers. He raises his head and comes face to face with Buzz's butt, like pressed ham on the window pane. I can't hold it in. I blow a gasket and start screaming with laughter.

Sidney comes tearing into my booth howling,

"Get the fuck out of my store, you little piece of shit!"

It isn't his store, it's Clyde Wallich's store. He says so every week on the radio, but I'm not going to quibble over it. Sidney is taller, older and a lot uglier than me and right now he just wants to terrorize someone. Seeing as I'm the likely candidate, I bolt out of the booth and race to the safety of the street.

I meet up with Buzz, who's standing safely on the corner, well out of the sight of Sidney and the rest of the Music City staff, lighting up another cigarette. He looks back at Wallich's and sighs.

"Too bad about Pizza-face. Somebody musta kicked him out of bed this morning." Buzz takes the whole thing with a deadpan expression on his face. I think he's one of those guys you never quite know if he's pissed off about something or not. Buzz has a long fuse, but it's definitely attached to an explosive devise; when the fuse blows, I'm sure it has a Yucca Flats quality to it.

We walk slowly down Sunset.

"So you hang out at Wallich's?" Buzz asks. I nod. "Bitchin' place. I used to live six blocks away - came here all the time. That was before Pizza-face showed up."

"How come you moved?"

15

"Got evicted. They tore the building down. My mom wanted to move anyway. Said she wanted me to go to relatively okay school." He looks at me and snorts.

The idea of Pasteur Junior High being an okay school seems kind of funny. Buzz explains his mother does hair for a living. She owns a shop, Renee's House of Beauty, on Beverly and Crescent Heights in West Hollywood. Her claim to fame is having been an extra in most of the movies made at the Republic Studios in the 1940's. Buzz is the only child and, apparently, the only male in the Jordan household. I don't ask him where his father is and he doesn't come racing out with answers.

Buzz isn't dressed for the heat. He's wearing herringbone pants with black patent leather boots and Cuban heels. He wears a powder blue shirt with oversized cuffs and silver cufflinks in the shape of rectangles. I've never seen him with his sleeves rolled up; it's considered uncool. Sweat pours off Buzz's attempt at straight hair, which he parts on the side, allowing a large burst of jet-black to sweep across his forehead. Patches of sweat form on his shirt in big blotches. It doesn't seem to bother him though.

I'm still dressed in modified kid clothes; the one exception being my candy-apple green Dobie Gillis shirt with button-down collar, and sleeves that only go halfway up my arm - my mother's token gesture towards my becoming fashion conscious. My blue jeans are too long and have to be rolled up (my mother keeps assuring me I'm going to grow into them) and my feet are stuffed into brown Hush Puppies.

Buzz flicks his cigarette butt onto the sidewalk, reaches into his left boot and pulls out a slightly crushed pack of Camels. He taps the pack and pulls one out. He points the pack at me. "You smoke?"

"Yeah, sometimes," I tell him, passing off the remark with a shrug. The truth is; I've never even looked at a cigarette until now. But I don't want to blow my burgeoning image as one of God's own outcasts so quickly. To be completely honest, being thirteen, with a foot long nose, a face you can sink an oil well into and hairy fingers, smoking just doesn't seem that bad a vice to jump into at the moment.

Buzz makes a jerking motion with the pack and a cigarette magically pops up. I pull it out and gaze at it for a second. It has no filter and I have no idea which end is supposed to be lit. I decide the end with the word Camel printed on it is the right one, so I foist it to my mouth.

Buzz pulls a bulky Ronson lighter out of his pocket. It's smooth and shiny silver. He has lighting it down to a single-motion science. He flicks it open and strikes the flint all in one snap. I press my cigarette to the flame and, bingo, it's lit.

Now what?

I drag deeply, maybe for five minutes. At least it feels that way. I don't know what to do with the smoke once it gets into my mouth. I blow a little out and that seems to work. It feels like I'm on to something; this is easy. However, I look down at my cigarette, clutched in my hand and it doesn't look right, not like on TV. I'm holding this thing like it's a communicable disease. Buzz lets his lay casually between his fingers, flicking it every once in a while with his thumb. I try to act more at home with the cigarette, but

I notice I've reduced the lip end to a soggy stump. The paper is sopping wet from hanging out of my mouth and tobacco is flaking out all over the place.

Buzz glances over at me as we walk down Sunset. "Don't inhale yet, do you?" I've been busted.

"Uhh, well," I stammer, searching for a good, or even stupid excuse.

"It's okay, it took me a month to figure it out."

I'm relieved. Like me, I guess Buzz needs a friend, so he tolerates my bungling in uncharted territory. We see each other as kindred souls. We're stuck in situations we really don't understand. Changes bigger than just waking up in the morning, finding it raining instead of sunny like the weatherman said. A lot of things that were important a week ago aren't important now. And likewise; things that weren't important a week ago have now become the most important things on earth.

We continue walking. You can get bored really quickly wandering around like a zombie or getting chased out of stores because the sales people know you aren't going to buy anything; or worse, are convinced you're going to steal everything that isn't nailed down. Wallich's is one of the few places where we can actually hang out.

By one-thirty the cheerful news from the Time and Temperature Tower in front of the KFWB studios on Hollywood Boulevard is that it has become 109 degrees. A hundred and nine baking, frying, burning degrees. My nostrils are like blow torches from the heat and I'm feeling dizzy.

\*     \*     \*     \*

*"He's running a fever - hundred and three."*
*"He's going into shock."*
*"His blood pressure's gone erratic again."*

\*     \*     \*     \*

"Hey, you wanna go to the beach?" Buzz asks, combing his hair in front of the window of Sy Amber's. Hollywood Boulevard is empty. Nobody with any brains would be caught dead in this furnace; except us. I don't know why, but the idea of going to the beach doesn't strike me as such a good one. True, I haven't been there since I was nine when my father stopped dragging us off to Playa del Rey every Saturday.

It isn't that. I just have this weird feeling some ominous event is going to take place that has our names written all over it. To top it all, my stomach is getting nervous. I feel a sudden sharp jolt in my jaw. I run over to a nearby trashcan just in time to bury my head in it and heave.

\*     \*     \*     \*

*"Jesus, get a cleanup - the guy's blowing everything in his stomach!"*
*"He's in shock."*
*"Make sure he doesn't choke."*

\*     \*     \*     \*

"I didn't get sick the first time I smoked."

"It's probably the heat."

"Yeah, the beach sounds like a good idea."

"Uh-huh." Anything is better than standing around in this frying pan. So we dig in our pockets, pull out quarters and dimes and head for the bus stop. Like somebody said: "That which doesn't kill you makes you strong." Oh, bitchin.

# CHAPTER TWO

## THE FUGITIVES FROM STATION EIGHT

The Number Seven bus groans to a halt on the corner of Pico and Ocean Avenue, the last stop before Santa Monica beach. We've been stuffed like sardines on a bus that has no air-conditioning for almost an hour. Technically it's only spring and the buses aren't geared for summer yet. The air-conditioners probably won't work until sometime late in June, when the average day gets barely above 67 degrees, air-conditioning comes in handy then.

It seems like everybody else in Los Angeles has the same idea as us. You can hardly see the beach for bodies taking up every square inch of sand. Row after row of swimmers standing waist deep in water, dodging the occasional surfboard that careens out of control. Between people nearly drowning and people getting bashed in the head by flying wedges of fiberglass and wood, the lifeguards and ambulance drivers are working overtime.

Buzz and I take up posts on a concrete wall overlooking the sand, halfway between Pacific Ocean Park (the only amusement park I've ever been to where the rollercoaster actually careens out over the water) and the Santa Monica Pier, where the din of pinball machines, pellet rifles and the Merry-Go-Round drown out the sound of the ocean a few feet away. Behind us is a city parking lot, jammed with cars and families, and beyond that, a sloping hill leading up to Ocean Avenue. This is a quieter stretch of beach than the others, although the air is filled with a hundred tiny transistor radios, all tuned to KFWB. The breeze alternates between warm and cool and smells of salt and Coppertone Suntan lotion. We sit feverishly admiring the wonderful sights. Blondes, tans, cleavage and all of them completely unapproachable. Buzz chain smokes and tries not to give any indication that he is dying for one small sign that any of these girls has noticed him. He lets out a sigh after each one walks by. He's sighing constantly.

"Hey man, you better get off the beach or you're gonna get your asses kicked!"

I turn around at the sound of the hostile voice. It whines out behind us between the asphalt walkway and the parking lot. A kid our age stands on the walkway. He's skinny and gawky and has a head too large for his body. He wears green plastic zorris, bright red baggies and a grimy tee-shirt, four sizes too big for him, spattered with mustard and suntan oil. He has a big blotch of zinc-oxide on his nose and his hair is a mixture of blonde-red-carrot streaks. It looks like something he tried to do on his own, with the help of his mother's Clairol. Across his tee-shirt is a painted cartoon character from the Burgermeister Beer commercials; a little guy with huge eyes and a crooked smile.

"What for?" I ask. I don't know anybody on the beach. Why would anybody want to kick my ass? Stupid me.

"Nobody likes greasers on our beach asshole!" the kid yells back.

Buzz is less enthusiastic about the warning. "Go fuck yourself, peckerhead!"

I look up and down the beach and then I look at Buzz and I realize we don't resemble anybody anywhere near us.

A small group gathers around the kid. They all have blotches of zinc-oxide on their noses and tee-shirts with everything from Rat Fink to Chiquita Banana printed on them. One kid wears a plastic German Army helmet. They look more pathetic than threatening and probably don't know why they're being hostile, other than it seems like the right thing to do.

Buzz, however, isn't fazed by them. "So what're ya gonna do? Beat us with your sandals?"

From somewhere in the crowd, a Pepsi bottle flies through the air and lands a foot away from Buzz, smashing into a million pieces. The hundreds of tiny transistor radios become suddenly, eerily, silent and I feel a destructo coming on. Everybody is watching us. At the moment I miss Sidney and the comfort of a Wallich's Music City soundbooth.

Buzz decides to handle this situation in the most diplomatic way. His fist flies out and lands square in the kid's face with a sharp smacking thud. When Buzz draws back, his knuckles are covered in a mixture of blood and zinc- oxide. The kid crumbles over and smacks the ground head first.

I'm now jumped from fifteen different directions and a serious number of fists land all over me.

Never having actually been in a fight in my life, I have no idea what I'm supposed to do. I know one thing; I am getting the living crap beaten out of me. So the only choices I have under the circumstances are pull a hair-out and run, or pull a crazy and stay. My brain stops sending soothing, rational messages like don't kill, don't stomp into a bloody pulp, and come, let us reason together. Instead it goes on strike and Gorilla Monsoon comes leaping out.

I go nuts and start slugging wildly at anything that moves. I can hear kids howling and running. But I'm not content to stop. I'm on a rampage and I want blood.

*    *    *    *

*"He's convulsing."*
*"Watch it; he's pulling out his IV."*
*"Keep him restrained until we finish!"*

*"Blood pressure's 120 over 170."*
*"Hang on!"*

\*    \*    \*    \*

The kids I have pounded into space-dust go running off to get fresh reinforcements. They come barrelling down the walkway, right at me. This new bunch are a lot older and they are really pissed off.

Buzz has his own problems. He's getting kicked to the ground by the remaining pint-sized surfers. Meanwhile the kid who started it all is lying near a parked Chevy Impala, trying to get his nose to stop bleeding.

It's looking like early death for me. The logic portion of my brain switches back on and the first thing it does is to send a bulletin to my feet: Run, you idiot!

As I turn, I realize that coming toward us, having just pulled into the parking lot, are three, count 'em, three Chevy Impalas loaded with the guys we were mistaken for - Greasers.

Greasers used to refer to Mexicans, mostly Mexicans in gangs; but lately the term Greaser has begun to imply anybody who isn't a surfer. Casual surfers, or people who look the part but really haven't gotten into surfing seriously, are known as Ho-Dads. The term Greaser also applies to guys who hang out in Hollywood who are into the music scene. It comes down to a matter of taste. If you're into Dick Dale and His Del-Tones or The Beach Boys, you're simpatico with the surfer ethic. But if you like The Beatles, Dave Clark Five, or worse, The Rolling Stones, you're definitely Greaser and heading straight to hell.

The kids pummeling Buzz to the ground vanish as the bigger, meaner replacements arrive. It's one thing to get caught up in a fight with a bunch of thirteen-year-olds, but it's something else to get stuck in the middle of a war between hardcore seventeen and eighteen-year-olds who are used to this sort of thing.

The kid who started it looks scared now, real scared. He has every right to be; he's suddenly on the wrong side as the Greasers swarm over the Impala he's lying against. He starts to cry. He's still holding his nose; and blood has spattered all over his Burgie tee-shirt and he's shivering as if the temperature has suddenly dropped forty degrees.

The calm and peaceful crowd on the sand responds by tossing Coke, Pepsi, Nehi and Coppertone bottles at the brawlers. The brawlers respond in turn by pulling out baseball bats, chains, knives, tire irons and beer cans and hauling ass on each other. Above the cacophony of yells, howls, screams and the booming sounds of The Four Seasons singing *Big Girls Don't Cry* over somebody's car radio, I can hear the faint wail of Police car sirens coming from the cliffs above us.

I run over to the kid and help him up, telling the hostile crowd of bloodthirsty seventeen-year-olds that it's okay, he's my little brother, even though we look the same age, and don't look anything like each other. Buzz staggers to his feet, spitting blood from his upper lip and nose as we

21

scramble to comparative safety at the outer fringe of the parking lot. We've escaped and we've managed to survive.

Don't ask me why I helped the kid. The little shithead started it. If it wasn't for him it would've been a pleasant Saturday afternoon during a heat wave in May. Instead, he triggered a brawl and probably deserved whatever he got. But I wasn't looking at it that way. I hate it when people cry; it always seems like the last resort of hopelessness. And this kid is pretty hopeless.

We stumble up to a park overlooking the beach. We're far away from the skirmish, which is finally winding down to an occasional bottle or can toss and the swinging of a police nightstick. The sun begins to dip low on the horizon and the people on the beach, from one end to the other, are beginning to leave. Meanwhile, at the parking lot, there are eight squad cars and two patrol wagons. The warring armies are being separated and booked while Police confiscate various instruments of destruction.

I sit on a wooden park bench looking down at P.O.P., Pacific Ocean Park, or 'Pay One Price' as the ads put it. I hear muffled shrieks of people being hurled around on the rollercoaster and the dull patter of Arnie And His Amazing Trained Seals performing to a crowd in the amphitheater. I gaze over to the Pier and hear the faint sounds of the Merry-Go-Round and the occasional ping of a pellet hitting a target, bringing the owner of the lucky shot a stuffed dog or six more chances. Occasionally, I catch faint whiffs of French fries and corn dogs. All the smog has blown out to sea and a thin brown layer lines the horizon for miles.

Buzz has his head submerged in the water fountain, trying to get his lip to stop bleeding and the swelling of his nose down. His clothes are a mess. His powder blue Sy Devore shirt has been almost completely torn off and even the white tee-shirt underneath is shredded. His oversized cuffs flap lifelessly into the fountain, becoming drenched with water. His cufflinks are a memory. His herringbone pants are ripped at the knees and sand-caked scraped skin pokes out. Every few seconds Buzz picks his head up from the fountain, trading off with his hands, running them under the cooling water, hoping to bring the swelling down.

I look down at myself and it hits me that I'm not much better off than he is. I've got some serious explaining to do to my parents. My brand new candy-apple green Dobie Gillis shirt with continental spread collar is ripped with holes big enough to fly a 707 through. The same goes for my pants. As the adrenalin begins to leave me, the pain comes crashing in. My sides start to throb, my stomach is a pulsing knot and my jaw is numb. I can feel my left eye swelling to the size of a grapefruit.

I look over at the kid. He's rolled up in a ball on the grass, his chin touching his knees, shuddering and spasaming and making a feeble attempt not to let on that he's weeping like a baby. He buries his head, lets out a bark, and follows it with a series of phlegmy wheezes. He finally lifts his head and I can see that his nose resembles a purple basketball.

"My dad's gonna kill me," he says, trying to touch his nose, which cascades snot and dried blood. He looks over to Buzz, who has gone back to dunking his head in the fountain. "You didn't have to hit me so hard, fuckhead!" he whines.

Buzz picks his head up from the fountain and snorts, "Aw shut up, pencil-dick . . . you started it!"

"I was trying to warn you, goddamit! I didn't wanna start a fight!"

Buzz cuts him off. "That's 'cause you fight like a girl."

The kid looks hurt and humiliated. "I didn't even throw the fucking bottle and you go ploughing into me."

The kid doesn't seem like the violent type. He's too skinny to fight with anybody. Maybe he was trying to show off for his friends.

"Why's your dad gonna kill you?" I ask. I'm starting to feel sorry for him. I figure the war's over and the least we could do was be civilized.

"He's a cop."

"Color you lucky!"

I can see his point. No matter how much screaming and yelling my parents are going to do at me, it won't hold a candle to what's in store for him.

"What's your name?" I ask. He points at his tee-shirt, to the cartoon figure partially obscured by the smears of type-O.

"Burgie."

"Yeah, but what's it really?"

"Ernest. Nobody calls me that though."

"Can't say I blame them."

Burgie flashes a grin and winces in pain.

The longer we sit there, the more Burgie calms down. He starts talking about himself and I realize that he's just as mixed up as we are. He's the same age, stuck in a strange new school, and largely invisible to most of the world; just like us.

He lives closer to Santa Monica than we do and goes to Palms Junior High which is on the border between West L.A. and Santa Monica. It's easier for him to hang out at the beach, just like it's easier for us to hang out in Hollywood. Burgie likes the ocean and he likes surfing. But the older kids don't like him because he's thirteen and the younger ones are into the social part of the surfing scene, which has little to do with actually surfing, but more with being seen, wearing the right clothes and having the correct attitude - which means, basically, being an asshole.

Buzz is hard to re-orient once he gets into the search-and-destroy mode. But after a while he gets over the idea of Burgie as a little prick and actually expresses envy for Burgie and the surfing scene. He confesses a deep down love for the ocean, but it's tempered with fear. When he was ten he was hit by a surfboard, which landed him in the hospital for a week. He still has the scar on the back of his neck, which is largely covered by hair. The accident has made him wary of the sea, but it hasn't stopped him from going to the beach, sitting on the sand and staring out at the water. He just never, ever goes in.

Buzz strikes me as a cynic. You can tell it in the way he says things. Round - about ways of saying how he feels, but not actually coming out and saying he's happy or scared. Looking at girls passing him on the beach, all he can do is sigh. He watches them, and if they look back he turns away out of shyness.

Burgie, on the other hand, is an optimist. "Hey, at least it was a nice day out," he honks through his swollen nose. Any guy who can find something nice about our recent episode is either crazy or a lover of life.

We sit on the bluffs overlooking the beach; swollen, shredded and blood-stained. The sun has almost set and we have to figure out what to do about home. Getting there isn't the problem, it's what we're going to say once we get there that has us worried.

The Number Seven Blue Santa Monica Bus sits on Pico and Ocean Avenue, waiting. We all limp on. The bus is as packed on the return trip as it was coming out. Wall-to-wall, floor-to-ceiling people; all coming from the beach. They're red, tanned and happy and smell of a mixture of salt-water, suncream, cigarettes and beer.

The bus driver, a middle-aged black guy with horn rimmed glasses, looks at us with a combination of curiosity and disgust. "Been fighting?" he asks.

I nod to him with my one good eye. He shakes his head, smiles slyly and motions us to get on. "You kids look fucked up good." He waves us on and doesn't charge us.

As he pulls away, the bus is almost broadsided by a two-toned green 1956 Plymouth Suburban station wagon. Brakes jam and tires squeal and all the occupants of the bus lurch forward. They laugh. At this point, a bus accident would be more like an amusement ride than a trip to the hospital. The driver leans out his window and shoots the fried beachgoer and his puffy family a look.

"Make up what you got left of your mind!" he yells at full lung-power.

The woman in the passenger seat of the car has a baby-oiled face; she wears flared pearl glasses and her head is covered in a flower-print scarf. She waves the bus driver to calm down, as her husband negotiates a speedy getaway. Two small children, climbing around in the back of the station wagon, peer out at us. The boy wears a striped tee-shirt, has scarecrow hair, freckles and a mouth covered with chocolate goo; he sticks his pink tongue out at the bus driver; meanwhile his sister pulls her white sun dress up over her head to reveal no underwear. Just plain folks.

The bus starts down the street again. Buzz, Burgie and I turn to face the crowd and attempt to find a place to sit. It's like parting the Red Sea. People immediately make room as we stumble down the aisle. The busload of beachgoers stare with horror and shock and turn away, trying not to draw attention to the fact that we look like war-ravaged mutants. It's the first time in my life that I get a major sympathy vote from so many strangers.

The sympathy vote only goes as far as looks; since nobody gives up their seats. We stagger to the back. There are three black guys sitting there, spread out over the rear row, one guy on either side of the open window, smoking Kools. They have enormous pompadours and wear impenetrably dark glasses. The guy in the middle has a transistor radio in his hand tuned to KGFJ. *Heat Wave* by Martha And The Vandellas wafts out through the bus. They don't really look at us, but somehow an all-clear signal is given and the guy in the center moves over to let us sit with them.

The bus lumbers slowly down Pico. As the crowd starts to thin out with each passing stop, Burgie, Buzz and I begin to worry. Burgie tries distracting himself.

"You know, I gotta confess, I really don't like The Beach Boys," he says.

This strikes me as a little funny. The black kid wearing a white terry-cloth shirt, looks over at us with a squint. "You in that fight?"

Buzz leans over, pointing his finger at Burgie. "This stupid fuck started it!"

The black kid starts to laugh and shakes his head as if it was the silliest thing he'd ever seen.

It was silly, and from the looks of us, nobody won.

Burgie confesses, "It's been going on all year; surfers and greasers - fights all the time. A kid got killed a couple of weeks ago. A bunch of greasers stabbed the shit out of him."

The black guy at the left window glances over at the three of us for a second. He has no expression on his face. He returns to his window view as we pass by the miniature golf course on Pico and Westwood.

Burgie lives near by in Rancho Park. It's a pretty plush neighborhood. More plush than the one I'm living in. Burgie's lip starts to quiver as he reaches up and signals he wants off at the next stop. The blood on his shirt has dried and it looks like somebody has doused him with a creepy shade of brown paint. The bus pulls over to the stop.

I get up and motion Buzz to do likewise. I tell him we're going to Burgie's house. Buzz looks at me as if I'm insane. I'm sure he's contemplating forgetting he ever met me.

I lean over and tell Buzz, "Hey man, I'd do it for you."

Buzz shoots me a look of complete disgust, but reluctantly gets off the bus with us and we walk the rest of the way to Burgie's house. Buzz refuses to say a word to anybody during the five-block walk.

Burgie's father, Ralph, is built like a brick, he acts like a brick and, I am sure, he thinks like a brick. He wears wire-rimmed glasses and looks as though he hasn't smiled at anything for most of his adult life. He's standing in the front yard with a hose, watering the lawn. He looks up at the three of us wandering towards him and says nothing.

I decide I'll break the ice. "Hi, I'm Nelson Rivers, this is my friend Buzz."

Ralph doesn't react. His mouth and jaw are clamped shut. He shows no emotion. He just stands there, square faced, square jawed, malevolent.

"Dad, a fight broke out on the beach and I got caught in the middle of it," Burgie lies feebly.

"It wasn't his fault," I chime in. "We were surrounded - we tried to get away, but they were hitting us from all over." I make things up as I go.

25

Anything to get Ralph to unlock his jaw. Finally, he reaches over and turns the hose off.

"Ernie, tell your little friend to shut his yap," Ralph tells Burgie.

*    *    *    *

*"What's the status on his internal bleeding?"*
*"He's stabilized."*
*"Is he conscious yet? Is he saying anything?"*
*"Incoherent stuff - he keeps asking about somebody named Otto."*
*"Who's Otto?"*
*"No idea."*

*    *    *    *

"Dad, these guys saved my life, they helped me out. I'd probably be dead if it wasn't for them," Burgie pleads.

"Get to the medicine cabinet," Ralph instructs Burgie, who dutifully marches in. Ralph slowly turns back to face us and, almost as an aside, and hardly moving his lips, says, "I'll call a cab."

Ralph remains surprisingly absent of emotion. Buzz says nothing; he probably doesn't want to be the one to bring the old man's wrath down.

Ralph doesn't invite us in the house, but he doesn't not invite us either, so we follow him in. He points a thick index finger to the front room and we assume that's where he wants us to go.

We sit. I glance around the room, puzzled by the obligatory prints of paintings of the Bay of Naples and Vermont in Winter on the walls. Everything in the house is white with gold trim. It reminds me of a hospital, or the Haven Of Rest Sanitarium where my Uncle Milton used to live before he died.

Burgie mentioned earlier that Ralph really wasn't a cop in the conventional sense. His job was to write tickets on cars in front of expired parking meters. It figures he'd have a rotten attitude; puttering around Rodeo Drive all day on a motorscooter, getting yelled at by socialites from hell who don't feed the meter, or let it expire. It's only natural he should take his frustrations out on his family.

A Yellow Cab pulls up to the house and honks its horn. By magic, Ralph appears in the doorway of the front room and motions with his portly index finger for us to follow him to the waiting car. We watch as he hands the driver a ten dollar bill and tells him to take us home. He turns and walks back into the house and doesn't say a word to us. I mumble, "Thanks," but he's already slamming the door closed. The porchlight clicks out.

I look out the cab window at the sights on Pico Boulevard. It's a strange street that doesn't seem to belong to anyplace or in any time. It's always empty.

Buzz lives the closest, so he gets dropped off first. It's dark when we pull up to his house. I offer to go in with him, but he declines. "It's okay, my mom's never home anyway," he tells me as he shuts the door to the cab. Buzz trudges up the steps of his duplex.

That leaves just me, going home and knowing my parents will be there. They'll be sitting around the TV watching Jackie Gleason.

I have my house keys and open the front door slowly, trying not to draw any attention. When I hear the faint sound of the TV in the living room, I think I'm safe. I quickly head to the bathroom, hoping at least to get cleaned up before I face them.

"Oh my God, what happened to you!" my mother shrieks. Even from the dim light of the TV set in the living room, she can see I've got lumps the size of cantalopes on my face and a bowling ball where my eye used to be.

All the lights in the room flash on and the inspection begins. "What did you do?" she keeps screeching over and over.

Clearly, I didn't smash myself in the face with a rock, push myself through a plate glass window or beat myself senseless with my fists. Somebody did it for me. But the way she was makes it sound, I'm the one responsible. For the next few minutes I'm subjected to a steady stream of verbal abuse peppered with phrases like: "You're gonna wind up in prison some day." All the while, she slathers one of the more disgusting poultices ever concocted by a human being, all over my skin: Wonderful Dream Salve, a thick sludge of caramel-colored goo with a label that claims 'it's good for man or beast.' I doubt that well-intentioned proclamation because, judging by the smell, no human being will come near me while I have it on and no dog within a five mile radius will leave me alone.

My father is busy watching Jackie Gleason, oblivious to my plight. To him, if I'm not dead or in a coma, I'm okay.

"And your shirt! I paid five bucks for that three days ago at the May Company and now it's ruined! Am I made of money or something?" She's on a rampage. It's not bad enough I'm beaten to a bloody pulp. My shirt, which cost less than the junk she's smearing on my face, will probably live out its life as a dust rag and I'll be stuck wearing an itchy cordoroy shirt I could fit three of me in. My mother is only concerned that I have 'grown up the wrong way' and that she has, somewhere in my upbringing, made a terrible, horrible, unforgivable mistake. She's convinced I'm one of those kids destined to make the newspapers as either a statistic or a disclaimer.

I'm shuttled off to bed and denied all kid privileges for a week.

I peel off my shredded clothes and lie down, trying to forget the putrid aroma of Wonderful Dream Salve hanging over me like a cloud. The only light that comes into my bedroom is the glow of the living room lamps under the door. I reach over and flick on my bedside radio. The dial slowly illuminates and I hear the gradually increasing volume of the slow movement from the first piano concerto by Tchaikovsky. It's the closing theme from *The Gas Company's Evening Concert Of The World's Finest Music*.

The music fades as the announcer proclaims brightly, "KFAC AM and FM, Prudential Square, Los Angeles."

I love classical music, but I'm not in the mood tonight. The strains of Tchaikovsky and Brahms aren't doing it for me. I need something with angst. Some raw emotion. Something teenage. I twirl the dial looking for it. I come to KFWB and *Louie, Louie* by The Kingsmen. It's as angst-filled as I'm going to get on this Saturday night. The song ends, so I flick the radio off and stare at the ceiling. Just me and the darkness and the subtle, muffled words "And awaaay we go!"coming from the TV in the living room.

The phone rings. It rings three times before anybody answers it. My father never answers the phone if he doesn't absolutely have to. He figures it's either bad news or somebody selling something he doesn't want. I can hear my mother coming towards my room. She opens the door and holds her hand over the receiver, looking in to see if I'm asleep.

"It's some little girl with a strange name . . . did you want to talk to her?"

I can't figure out which little girl it is, let alone one who could be calling me on Saturday night. It has to be a joke, but I nod and mumble, "Sure," and she drags the phone in. We don't have extension phones in the house; my parents don't believe in them. My mother claims the electricity generated by a telephone is enough to kill you if the house is ever hit by lightning. So we have only one phone and a hundred foot cord that is always tangled into a rat's nest of twisted cable when anybody tries to take a call in another part of the house other than the dining room. On the rare occasion when I do actually get a "personal call", I have to drag the phone to a safe part of the house which is never really safe because the cord is so thick and tangled it makes it impossible to shut any doors for privacy. I used to think my mother spent hours tangling the phone cord so I couldn't get any privacy in my life. She had a strange reaction when I finally hit puberty; a mixture of dismay, dread and looming curiosity.

"Nelson, it's Burgie." Burgie was the 'little girl' in question. I'm disappointed, having hoped by some bizarre stroke of fate that I was getting a call from a lovesick female classmate. But then I wonder, How did Burgie get my phone number?

"Oh . . . hi, Burgie. What's up?" I ask. With my swollen face it sounds more like, "Ny, Nurgie. Nud's ub?"

It turns out he's checking on me, to see if I got in any trouble. From the muffled, cheerful sound of his voice, I can tell he came through the episode with no parental reprisals or emotional scars, even though his nose is bandaged up. Me, the great peacemaker, gets grounded for a week and encased in putrid glop. Clearly I'm not playing my cards right.

We don't say much on the phone. There isn't much left to say that hasn't been seen or said earlier in the day. Burgie keeps apologizing for the riot. I keep telling him to stop worrying; it happened and nobody died. He wants to hang around with us some time. I tell him I'm grounded, but maybe in a couple of weeks we will. I put the phone down and try to go to sleep.

28

*    *    *    *

*"How is he?"*

*"He just got out of surgery. He should be coming around in a couple of hours. You're his wife?"*

*"Yeah, the police called. I wasn't home. I just got the message. Is he going to be okay?"*

*"We don't know just yet. He had some pretty bad head injuries. We just have to wait until he comes out to see what happens next."*

*"So . . . you don't know if he'll be okay."*

*"Not yet."*

*    *    *    *

Burgie is persistent. He calls me every afternoon after school to check on how I am. I'm rotten.

To be honest, teenage disfigurement at Louis Pasteur is a popular fad. Some of the girls have gotten into the habit of nicking their wrists with razor blades and bandaging them up to look like suicide attempts. It's usually connected to some guy they just broke up with or some guy who wouldn't give them the right time of day. Guys, on the other hand, often show up at school looking like five foot abreviations of the Sonny Liston/Cassius Clay fight, from Liston's point of view. They're always fighting, and it's always about nothing. But most every Monday morning, some kid in the eighth grade comes limping in with his hand bandaged and his face black and blue and it has a certain air of respectability to it. In our own misguided, self-inflicted way, we want desperately to be noticed and taken seriously. A swollen face gotten in a fight is a serious badge of distinction.

But my face looks like it's been sprayed with red paint, or worse, like I have measles. Every blood vessel, from my forehead to my chin, is broken in some ugly blotch. I not only don't win respect, the entire student body goes into fits of laughter when they see me. I'm given the nickname Impetigo.

Buzz is the only one who doesn't stare or laugh, except of course Burgie. But it doesn't count with him; he goes to another school. Neither of them have to face the hordes of roaring students starting every mid-morning at Nutrition. I want only peace, and the chance to eat my L.A. City Schools' wad of deep - fried, sugar-coated dough and drink my cup of greasy hot chocolate without some geek slapping me on the back, shrieking, "What happened, did you implode?" I have become the origin of a new word in the Louis Pasteur Junior High lexicon of slang. Anything that is completely screwed up, or ugly beyond belief is Nelsified.

I decide it's probably best for me to disappear, and go to the place where all the other misfits and pariahs go: the school orchestra.

# CHAPTER THREE

## THE LAW OF AVERAGES IT AIN'T

I'm standing in one of the practice rooms. There are three of them, all opening out to the main room where the orchestra members sit amidst a jumble of chairs, risers and music stands. They're looking back at me; a sea of weirdos and wild ideas. I realize the rumors about orchestra class are true. Louis Pasteur is a small school, and it's possible to see everyone at least once in a day, but I've never seen any of these people before in my life.

\*     \*     \*     \*

*"I keep waiting for him to wake up, but he doesn't."*
*"We really have to wait and see."*
*"You think he'll be all right?"*
*"I'm sure he will. The next twelve hours ought to give us some sign where he's heading."*
*"But you're not worried?"*
*"I've seen a lot of these cases. It just takes time."*

\*     \*     \*     \*

Having some experience in elementary school with piano, I've volunteered to learn the string bass; an unwieldy mass of strings and wood that towers two feet above my head. It's just about big enough to hide behind and, for that reason, I like it. It's also the only instrument the orchestra has a need for. Only one other guy, a seven foot ninth grader with pernicious dandruff, named Harvey, plays bass; he's graduating at the end of the semester. I feel like I'm finally someplace where I'm needed, even though I can't let on that I have no idea what I'm doing.

The practice room is soundproof, with acoustic tiles surrounding the walls and ceiling. Lining the walls of the room are framed pictures of Haydn, Brahms, Beethoven, Mozart and Bach. They're supposed to serve as an inspiration. But my guess is they're letting us know just who's music it is we're mangling up.

*    *    *    *

*"So, I heard you play violin?"*
*"Yeah, I do."*
*"Me too. Mostly college though. Then I got accepted to Nursing school. I miss it a lot. I still play sometimes."*
*"How far did you go?"*
*"Second violins."*
*"Me too."*
*"I just love Beethoven."*

*    *    *    *

"I just love Beethoven, don't you?"

I shouldn't have turned around so quickly. Standing behind me, looking cow-eyed, is one of the strangest manifestations of a human being I've yet to meet this lifetime.

I'm assuming it's female, but I really can't tell for sure. It's short, very short, with wild, ratty clumps of greasy hair. It's got a mouthful of braces, and glasses so thick they make its eyes look like frying pans - big, grey frying pans. It has no neck, and it has the longest, hairiest arms I have ever seen up close without being separated by a wire cage. I have the distinct feeling I'm in the presence of the missing link.

It's name is Fern Straubinger and it plays the flute.

Fern waits for my response with open mouth. In fact, her mouth never really closes. It stays open and fills the tiny, soundproof room with the gamy aroma of Oscar Meyer Bologna and Miracle Whip

For months I've fantasized that some girl would find me appealing; only not a girl who looks anything like this.

The practice room door is closed. Having gone through my own humiliation from the battle of Station Eight, I know what it's like to be looked upon with disgust by people. I want to get out of here, but I also feel a sense of compassion. Big mistake.

Sitting on top of a file cabinet, next to a pile of sheet music, is a book: What We Hear In Music by Walter Damrosch. I sense an opportunity. I'll pretend I'm looking for the book, find it, get quickly out of the room and live happily ever after.

I succeed in as far as picking up the book and turning to the door. Less than ten steps to freedom, but I have this completely idiotic urge to turn around and say: "Yeah, I kind of love Beethoven, too."

Not too smart. Fern instantly assumes I've handed her a neon sign saying 'I'm interested,' and nothing in the universe is going to persuade her otherwise.

There's a storage shed by the shop classes. It's a dilapidated brown stucco building that seems abandoned but isn't. The rear of the building faces out to the alley. Between the alley and the shed stands a formidable twenty-foot fence. The area between the fence and the shed is covered in junk, pieces of sheet metal and rusted fifty-gallon drums. The custodians toss stuff back here where it sits, gathering dust and creating a wonderful shelter for burgeoning untouchables like me and Buzz. We gravitate to this little haven when we want to cut a class and smoke. We aren't the only ones. We once had a stare-off with some ninth grade hoodlums until they realized we're back there doing the same thing they were. A truce was declared and we agreed to take turns standing watch in case a teacher or custodian ambled by and smelled tobacco.

I seriously believe I'm safe here from Fern, or Bugly, short for Butt Ugly as Buzz calls her. The bliss doesn't last long. She finds me trying to light a Viceroy. She starts yammering, in her high-pitched, steel-reinforced, concrete-piercing whine, about Beethoven; the string Quartets; the deep inner meaning of the Eroica Symphony.

Buzz doesn't feel sorry for her. And neither do the low-lifes behind the storage shed. I'm banished until I get rid of her. I try. My brain is working overtime, thinking of ways I can. I go so far as to pop an Alka-Seltzer in my mouth and chase her through the crowd at Nutrition with foam exploding out of my cheeks. She laughs. There is nothing I can do to convince her she is not the girl of my dreams. Bugly isn't taking no for an answer.

"Nelson, there's a little girl here to see you," my mother burbles enthusiastically, as she stands in the doorway to my room. It's a cloudy, damp Saturday afternoon and Burgie is hanging out with me, listening to records. We're alternating between The Beatles' Second Album, *Glad All Over* by The Dave Clark Five and *Big Band Bossa Nova* by Stan Getz, playing them on my crummy little Voice Of Music hi-fi with a dime taped to the tonearm to keep it from skipping.

Burgie's eyes light up. He's beginning to cultivate the image of being a ladies man and is interested in meeting this specimen of femininity from Louis Pasteur. A sick feeling races through my stomach, but being something of an optimist, I hope that maybe, by some strange miracle, it's somebody else who wants to see me.

No such miracle. Sitting on the living room sofa, surveying the house like an auditor from the IRS, is Bugly. She has tracked me down, and worse, my mother has actually invited her in. Burgie stands next to me and I can hear him gulp from disbelief when he sees her. I am now convinced that what esteem I'm trying to cultivate among my friends is being chopped into dogfood.

32

My mother stifles a laugh and cheerily announces, "I've invited your little friend to stay for lunch."

"For God's sake; what ever you do, don't tell her you like Beethoven," I warn Burgie.

My mother must have sensed Fern ate with her mouth open, because lunch consists of tomato soup, bacon, lettuce and tomato sandwiches and carrot sticks. Any one of these foods in Fern's mouth can make enough noise to empty a room. Together, they create a cacophony of smacks, slurps, chomps and spray.

"The Beatles? Ucchk. Who listens to that junk?" Fern has an opinion on just about everything. "Is that real wood or plastic?" she asks my mother, flicking her fingernail into the crack of the dining room table, peeling off a chunk of Formica coating. "My dad's working on a cure for cancer you know."

This brings a mumbled comment from Burgie; "Yeah, and it looks like he's not doing so hot."

I have no appetite. It walked out the second she walked in the house. Fern eats everything on her plate and asks me if I'm going to eat what's on mine. She inhales my lunch and eats half of Burgie's.

She babbles non-stop, about everything. But she's inconsistent. First her father's a scientist, then he's a dentist, then he works for the city. Her mother's a movie star who spends six months out of the year in Rome. Then she slips in that her parents are divorced. At one point she announces her mother's dead, and a few minutes later blurts out that her mother wants her to live with her in London and that she's been accepted to study with Jean Pierre Rampal, the famous flautist in Paris.

Burgie gets up to leave. He makes up an excuse about promising his dad he'd mow the lawn. But I know his father has a gardener. I want to go with him, but I know if I do, she'll follow us to his place, and it doesn't seem fair to heap Fern on his unsuspecting household.

Bugly stays for hours, rummaging through everything and commenting. I am constantly moving from room to room, because everytime I stay in one place for longer than two minutes, she follows me in, closing the door behind her and breathlessly croaking, "Alone at last!"

As much as I'm intrigued by the opposite sex, and want desperately to explore, there is no way in hell I am going to do it with her.

Finally, around seven o'clock, my father comes home from work. He's an engineer at a local radio station, and this is his first week as Saturday afternoon announcer. He's in the mood to celebrate, and he wants to take us out to dinner. But not with Fern.

He takes one look at her, then points to me and says, "Gunther, I want to talk to you for a second." My father has devised a series of nicknames for me ever since I was old enough to be potty-trained. Gunther is the latest one and that's good, because before that I was Chowderhead.

My dad shuttles me out to the front porch. He puts his hand on my shoulder and looks at me with complete seriousness etched across his face.

"Gunther, is that the best you can do?"

I shake my head violently. "No, dad. She's been bothering me for weeks. I can't get rid of her. She doesn't take no for an answer."

My father assesses the situation. "This isn't somebody you're serious about, I take it?"

Again I shake my head, trying to underline the point that Fern foisted herself on me, and definitely not the other way around. He nods his head and we walk back into the house.

Fern is sitting in the living room, rummaging through my father's prized collection of Martin Denny and Stan Kenton records, spreading them all over the floor, muttering "God, who listens to this junk?"

"So Fern, where do we drop you off?" my father asks. He's probably holding back the urge to pick her up and bodily toss her out of the house - nobody, but nobody speaks disparagingly of Martin Denny or Stan Kenton in the Rivers household. Fern looks up with a mixture of dread and disappointment on her face. It's at this exact moment that I realise something I've been suspecting all afternoon. Forget that Fern is ugly, rude and has the table manners of a tree sloth. Fern doesn't want to go home for a reason - and it has nothing to do with me.

"It's okay," she mutters, "I don't live far from here anyway. I'll walk."

It's getting dark out and my mother doesn't want to entertain the possibility of Fern getting attacked, molested or kidnapped on some dark street, even though it could be an answer to my problem.

So we pile into my dad's red MG Roadster, which is a two-seater. I always ride in the back because I'm small enough, and Fern scrunches next to me. She sits silently as we drive down to Venice Boulevard. For once, her mouth is completely closed and, in the orange-yellow glow of the passing streetlamps, it's just possible to imagine that some day she might by chance look so-so.

We get to Venice and turn right, heading to La Cienega. We drive past the KHJ transmitter tower and a block further, past a motel with the unlikely name Sand n' Surf. Fern looks back at the motel, concentrating on it, even a half block after we pass it. We get to La Cienega and turn right, heading north.

"Turn left at the next street," she blurts out suddenly. We turn onto Eighteenth Street and drive a block further to Garth Avenue before she says, "It's here, on the corner." We slow down at a bigger-than-modest Spanish style house of beige stucco with a large picture window in the living room. It's a nice place; a lot nicer than ours.

She jumps out of the car and thanks my mother for lunch. My mother is polite, giving the obligatory, "It was very nice meeting you, dear." Fern thanks my father for giving her a lift, and my father nods his head, a sure-fire sign he's only too glad to get rid of her. She smiles and waves at me, then turns to walk up the path to the house. My father puts the car in gear and speeds quickly away.

I don't know what makes me do it, but I turn my head to watch her walk to her house. Just as I suspected, she takes a few steps and turns, crossing the street and runs down Eighteenth.

"Boy, that kid went for a swim in an empty gene pool," my father exclaims as we drive away.

My mother cocks her head back at me and cracks a saccharine smile. "Nelson, we don't really mind you having a little girl friend, but, well . . . you know." My mother doesn't come right out and say it, but it's on everybody's mind; Fern is a real piece of work.

The rest of Saturday night we celebrate my dad's promotion to announcer. It's something he's wanted to do ever since we moved to L.A. from Cleveland in 1958. As with all celebrations, we do it at Ollie Hammond's Steak House, a sprawling brick eatery on La Cienega, in the middle of Restaurant Row. We celebrate there often, even if there isn't anything to celebrate. There's a ritual to it; my dad slaps Smitty, the Maitre-D', on the back and engages in small talk while we wait for our table at the bar. It's a dark, plush, quiet place with faint, barely audible sounds of Mantovani wafting through speakers hidden in planter boxes.

Being thirteen, I can't exactly sit on a stool and order a Martini, so my parents always get a table and order the same drinks: a dry Martini with two olives for my dad, a Grasshopper for my mother and a Hopalong Cassidy for me. My mother never drinks, so the Grasshopper sits ignored until our table is ready and then she forgets to take it with her, or motions to Smitty not to bring it. I always drink my Hoppy and long for the day when I can order a White Horse scotch on the rocks. Not because I like scotch, or have even ever tasted it; but because I love the label; yellow and black with a drawing of a white horse wrapped around the bottle.

For me, dinner at Ollie Hammond's means The World's Thickest Small Steak and Spaghetti Platter and a bowl of split pea soup. It is a custom I look forward to unlike any other.

When we finish, we always go for a walk up La Cienega, past Melrose, to an area known as Gallery Row, where all the art galleries bunch up in a two-block stretch and the dealers hawk their latest discoveries.

My dad is in a good mood this particular night. He tells my mom they should start collecting art. They have this conversation every week, but it never goes anywhere. My father's taste in art leans towards the football paintings of LeRoy Neiman and my mother's hovers around Hawaiian travel posters.

I can't help thinking about Fern Straubinger. No matter how repulsive she is, there's something sad and strange about her. She was so fascinated by the motel on Venice Boulevard that it had to be a clue. I decide to play a hunch.

The next day I drag my bike out of the garage and go for a ride down to Venice Boulevard. I turn right and head toward the Sand n' Sea Motel. There's an alley behind the motel, so I cut across, up Hi-Point Avenue, a half-block away, and continue down the unpaved alley to the rear of the motel.

The Sand n' Sea consists of a series of bungalows, all painted a pale shade of aqua. It's run down and will probably be demolished before too much longer, but there is still something interesting about the place. On each door, next to the number of each bungalow, sits a brass seahorse. And over each door knocker, hangs a small life preserver. In all the times I ever rode past this motel, I never saw the lot occupied by more than one or two cars, and the No Vacancies sign was never lit. Each bungalow has a parking space, and the ground around each bungalow is overgrown with weeds. The motel must've sold off it's extra land because the sign pointing to the Pool leads directly to a printing plant next door.

I skid my bike to a halt and get off, and walk it the rest of the way, trying to be quiet. I'm not sure what I'm doing here, or what I'm expecting to discover. But my hunch quickly pays off when I hear the sound of a flute coming from one of the bungalows. I park my bike next to a fence and walk slowly in the direction of the music. It's coming from Number Four. The front door is closed, but all the windows are open. I dart around to the rear of the place, hoping to get a better look.

From the rear of the bungalow I can look inside, although it's hard at first; the screens are thickly brown with rust and haven't been cleaned in years. I cup my hands over my eyes, trying to block out the sun. Fern sits in the front room. She doesn't see me, and I'm glad, because I have no idea what I would say if she found me. The last thing I want Fern to think is that I'm actually following her.

From where I stand, it looks like the bungalow has been hit by a tornado. The floor is covered with clothes, newspapers; junk all over the place. The walls are a tobacco-stained sienna, probably white a couple decades earlier. The plaster is chipped and there are cracks from the floor to the ceiling. There's a bed against the wall, but the sheets and blankets are strewn over the floor. A single bare bulb hangs from the ceiling. A car drives down the alley and I quickly pull away from the window and pretend I've lost something. I stare at the ground intensely as the car slowly passes, stirring up clouds of dirt and dust. I don't raise my head until I'm sure it's safe. The car stops before it turns onto the street, just as I glance up to see it drive away. I feel my body relax and I let out a sigh. I find another window at the side of the bungalow, but it's covered over by tree branches and the ground under the window sill is overgrown with weeds. I inch my way over and separate the branch of the tree just enough to look in.

I can see the hallway and what I imagine is the living room. It looks the same as the bedroom, only instead of the bed against the wall, there's a threadbare sofa, stained in so many places it seems like part of the pattern. There is no TV, not even a radio. Just a bookshelf and a coffee table and an end table on which sits a small lamp. It's a tiny lamp; a kid's lamp. It has a small gleaming white porcelain base and a tiny shade with blue windmills painted on it. You could go blind if you had to read by it. But it sits on the end table, and all around it is clean and neat.

The music stops and I quickly dart back from the window. I run down the alley to my bike and jump on it, pedalling away as hard and as fast as I can.

Monday morning it starts all over again. Fern catches up with me on my way to school. She tells me how nice she thinks my parents are and how she looks forward to spending weekends with me. I'm convinced the only way Fern is going to stop bothering me is if I kill her.

"Buzz, is murder legal in some states?" I ask as we stand under the shower in the boy's gym. It's the only place Bugly can't try and find me.

Buzz shakes his head. "Can't dump the Pygmy, can you?"

On the one hand, I feel sorry for her. But on the other hand, she's made my life miserable and there doesn't seem to be any end in sight.

Then there's Tuesday. It starts off like all the other days. Fern appears like clockwork in front of my locker before first period. She hangs around and waits for me and then follows me off to class, then to orchestra.

We are in the process of assassinating the Triumphal March from Verdi's Aida. Harvey, the seven-foot bass player, keeps jabbing me with his bow, while Fern stares holes through me from a pocket mirror she has devised on her music stand. It is, by all accounts, a typical day.

Just as we're about to hit the climax, the door to the music room opens and three official-looking people walk in. Mister Delatore, the haggard and partially deaf orchestra teacher, calls the musical auto da fe' to a stop. One of the newcomers is Mrs. Rosenthal, the Girl's Vice-Principal, a rotund woman a little over five feet tall and, probably, five feet wide, who likes to wear bright, flower-print dresses and lots of costume jewelry. She is accompanied by two men I've never seen before; they wear identical dark blue suits and look casually around the room and show virtually no expression on their faces.

Mrs. Rosenthal whispers something loudly in Delatore's ear. Delatore turns around to address the flute section of the orchestra.

"Fern Straubinger? Mrs. Rosenthal would like to see you."

Fern turns the color of a stop sign. She slowly reaches down, packs her flute into its case and picks up the books lying under her chair. She gets up, walks to the front of the room and leaves with Mrs. Rosenthal and the two blue suits.

I have the feeling this is the last I'll be seeing of Fern Bugly Straubinger.

According to the L.A. Times, Maurice Straubinger, Fern's father, isn't a scientist, dentist or city employee. He's a bank robber who's wanted in five states, including California. He's been on the run most of the time, but would occasionally send his daughter enough money to pay the weekly motel bill and to buy herself food and whatever else she needed, including braces for her teeth. Fern's parents were divorced and, according to the newspaper, Maurice didn't exactly have custody of Fern.

Six months earlier, he took the kid out on his customary weekend visit and didn't bring her back. Fern's mother, the report goes on, wasn't available for comment, being between engagements in Kansas City, working as 'Patty Waggin.' So it turns out Fern has been on her own since the beginning of the semester. And if it wasn't for a suspicious motel manager, and Maurice trying to pass off a marked twenty-dollar bill in Fresno, she probably would've stayed at the Sand n' Surf for years.

Consider me relieved. But I still feel sorry for her.

# CHAPTER FOUR

## KNOWING EVERYBODY LIKES YOU . . . BUT NOT LIKE I DO

"Nelson, what are you doing?"

The question comes from Mister Brundage. Brundage, or Mister Transistor as we call him, has the distinction of having not one, but two hearing aids strapped to his head. He also has the distinction of being one of the most boring geography teachers in the history of Molino High School. It's no secret. He knows it, the class knows it and even the Board of Education knows it. But nobody wants to admit it. Everybody feels sorry for him, except the poor slugs who have to take his class. He always wears the same charcoal grey suit with gravy stains on the elbow and is one of the last people on earth to continue wearing bow-ties. He doesn't seem to realize it's 1967.

The greatest wish in my life is to prove to someone in authority that I can do something extraordinary without any effort whatsoever.

So I've decided I can fly.

It's pretty easy once you get the hang of it. I just sit in my chair and close my eyes. I hold my breath and count to three. I float up from my desk, several feet off the ground, come dangerously close to getting stuck on the ceiling, but then I make a quick turn and sail straight out the window. Dead simple.

I'm floating above Robertson Boulevard.

It's pretty amazing considering, but I don't want to think about how it works. I'm afraid if I do, I'll lose the power and like Icarus, I'll come crashing to earth.

So I make a quick right turn and float over to a retaining wall that surrounds the roof of the school and sit there for a while, smugly watching the street below me. I feel fearless and extraordinary and capable of almost any superhuman feat. That is, until I look over my shoulder and see someone else sitting on the same retaining wall, peering down at the street below.

Leslie Noritake.

Leslie is this girl I have known since elementary school. She's Japanese and has one of the warmest, most wonderful personalities of anybody on the planet. Every semester, from the third grade until we graduated and went to separate schools, Leslie was always voted most popular of everybody in our class. People just like her, even teachers.

So what is she doing on the roof of Molino High?

"I'm in Home Economics, making a chocolate layer cake, so I imagine I'm here right now. I am, you might say, dying of boredom. Pretty groovy, no?"

I haven't seen Leslie in over three years. She hasn't changed. She still has a beaming smile, just like she had in third grade. But the kid-oriented clothes I remember her wearing, the white cotton blouses and plaid skirts, have been replaced by a purple velour mini-skirt and suede boots with fringe around the edges. Leslie's hair is a lot longer since I last saw her. In grade school it was short and curled, probably from one of those Toni Home Permanent kits that were the staple of every American home. Now her hair is parted in the middle and cascades in a thick straight line halfway down her back.

"So, we're imagining this?" I ask her.

"'Fraid so," she answers.

I feel a tugging at my shirt. Some unseen force is pulling me over the side of the building. I'm afraid I'm about to fall.

*    *    *    *

*"He's crashing!"*
*"What happened!?"*
*"I don't know - he was stable ten seconds ago!"*
*"No pulse!"*
*"Get him on a respirator. Where's the crash cart?!"*

*    *    *    *

"Well, Mister Rivers? What's the answer?"

Brundage stands over me, stone faced; the thin beige wire attached to the earpiece on his right hearing aid droops lifelessly over his starched shopcoat pocket. Everyone in class focuses their attention on me with an assortment of smirks, muffled laughs and rolled eyes. I blurt out an answer, the first thing that pops into my head.

"Tigress and Euphrates?"

"Very good, Mister Rivers. I thought you were sleeping."

Mister Transistor gives me a snide look and walks back down the aisle to the front of the class. As he turns to address us, the bell rings. It signals bedlam because it's the last period and school is over for the day. I scoop up my books and gallop out the door.

Because of my dream I'm not surprised to see Leslie walking toward a row of waiting school buses. I instantly break into a run, catching up with her just as she is about to get on.

"Leslie?"

She turns. When she sees it's me her face lights up. "Nelson!" she lets out a yell and drops her books on the ground and wraps her arms around me.

"I was just thinking about you!" she beams.

"Yeah, so was I. How long have you been at Molino?"

"Since Monday. I got transferred."

We hold on to each other like long-lost relatives. We used to talk to each other on the phone, but lost touch somewhere around the eighth grade. I've really missed her.

The Blue Santa Monica Bus starts its engine. It's a signal for Leslie to get on. We stand in the doorway while students jam their way around us. Neither of us wants to leave.

"I have to ask you something. I just had this weird dream. . ."

"And I was in it?" she interrupted.

"Yeah! On the roof?"

"Uh-huh?"

"Flying?"

"Yeah."

"Wow! Pretty wild, wasn't it?"

Leslie nods her head and gives me a wide grin. I feel an unexplained racing in my heart and a lightness in my head.

*    *    *    *

*"Okay - Mrs. Rivers he's coming back. Can we sit down for a second?"*

*"What happened?"*

*"He's having trouble stabilizing. I need you to sign a consent form to put you husband on life support."*

*" Life support?"*

*"His vital organs have to stabilize."*

*"I thought you said he was going to be okay?"*

*"He is, but he needs some help."*

*"Do what you need to do. I'll sign."*

*    *    *    *

Leslie leans over and kisses me gently on the cheek. She hugs her books and walks up the steps of the bus, which is threatening to close its doors any second.

She disappears among the people behind them, while I stand there, trying to figure out why my hands are so moist and why I feel this insane urge to burst out laughing. She opens the window near the rear of the bus and calls out to me.

"Hey Nelson! If you want, meet me at the Infinite Mind tonight around eight."

She waves as the bus pulls away. I wave back. We don't take our eyes off each other. The bus turns left on Robertson, heading north and disappears from sight.


"Man, the idea of white side-walls with a poof of shit on top depresses me."

Buzz and I are waiting for Buzz's turn for a trim in Cosmos Hairstyles on Crescent Heights and Sunset. He's paranoid about getting cornered by the Boy's Vice-Principal. Still a slave to fashion, he comes here every two weeks for the same thing; just enough to keep the dress-code enforcers off his back, but not enough to be considered uncool.

I decide now might be a good time to tell him about the episode with Leslie on the roof.

"You can do what?" Buzz raises an eyebrow.

But Buzz is the last one to judge bizarre behavior. He has taken to wearing big green suede boots and an oversized black velvet cape. He refers to himself as Harry on occasion, in honor of Harry Houdini, a person he holds in high esteem and who, one day, he wants to emulate by doing the great disappearing act. Periodically Buzz wears a Civil War-styled cap to school with the words Surgeon, Bellvue Hospital embroidered in gold across the front. He carries a tambourine around with him most of the time and launches into a rhythm when the whim strikes him; whether there is any music playing or not.

"So, this chick flies too?" he asks suspiciously, flipping through the latest issue of Playboy.

"Yeah, I saw her."

"Uh-huh, well, like where did you go?" There's a skeptical tone in his voice.

"Uh, we were just sitting on the roof, looking down at traffic on Robertson."

Buzz pulls a cigarette out of his leather pouch and lights it, scratching his thumbnail against the blue-tipped match. He takes a drag and blows out a smooth white cloud.

"Your mom's been putting shit in your Wheaties again, right?"

Buzz is a regular at my parents' house. He knows my mother is obsessed with health food. Lately it's gone past mere wheat germ. Now she's buying fifty pound bags of carrots every week, turning them into juice and making us drink it religiously, three times a day. My skin has turned orange and I'm convinced my skull is going to sprout green leaves soon.

Buzz, on the other hand, has a fixation for Cracker Jacks, which he claims he's only interested in because of the prizes. "I gotta get a new decoder ring, the last one I melted with a 'rette butt."

Buzz has been putting on weight. He's not bad looking, at least Burgie and I think so, but then, we aren't girls. His hair is getting longer and he's pretty vain about it. Every time we walk past a store window he stops to look at himself and remarks, 'Man, it's getting good in the back.' If he weighed a little less, girls would probably fall all over him. Instead, they are tripping over him on their way to somebody else.

Life at Molino High is considerably different than it was at Louis Pasteur. For one thing, my two best friends are now going to the same school. Buzz and Burgie finally, after almost two years, are friends. We spend weekends hanging out on the Sunset Strip. Despite the infamous riot between the cops and the kids in November, the Strip is still the place where everything is happening, even though in most places you have to be eighteen to be part of the happening scene. It helps to know somebody whose father is a cop. Burgie knows somebody who makes fake ID's. We used them once; to get into the Crescendo to see The Byrds. We were so paranoid over getting caught we hardly saw the show, especially as the waitress kept hawking us for drinks. None of us had more than two dollars, and a lukewarm Coca-Cola with no ice was going for a buck seventy-five!

The only place that lets us in without ID is Dave Hull's Hullabaloo Club. Hullabaloo is wonderful. In the 1930's it was Earl Carroll's Vanities, and the place still has that Hollywood essence oozing up from the red velvet carpets. By the 1950's it had become the Moulin Rouge and it was one of the first places I went as a kid when we moved to L.A. They served the worst spaghetti in the world but it was the first place in my life I saw real, live bare breasted dancers on stage (tastefully, mind you). Lately it's become a rock n' roll club. It has a revolving stage, so that when one band finishes their set, they ride off and are followed by the next band. Very quickly we become aware of who is fab and groovy on the L.A. scene and who isn't.

Along with our fascination with the Strip, Buzz, Burgie and I hitch out to Malibu on the weekends where Buzz sits for hours; boots, velvet cape and Surgeon Bellvue cap, staring at the water. I think he believes that everything going on in the world begins somewhere under the sea and filters up to land. Everything: wars, peace, change of weather, birthdays, love; the whole deal. It all begins in Neptune's world.

In terms of women, he's a doubter and it doesn't do any good trying to convince him otherwise. Buzz doesn't see a future between me and Leslie.

Burgie, on the other hand, sees tons of possibilities.

"Get rubbers," is his advice.

Buzz, Leslie and I sit in the blacklight room in the back of the Infinite Mind, behind a set of tie-dyed curtains, engulfed in a big cloud of incense. The Infinite Mind is a kind of store, but I can never figure out if they actually ever sell anything or not. There are a few racks of books, some very old magazines and a couple of beat up records: *I'm A Vulture for Horticulture* by Jimmy Durante and *Mission To Moscow* by Benny Goodman. The walls are covered with posters of everybody from Che Guevara to W.C. Fields. And then there's the incense, which burns in large brass pots in every corner, making it hard at times to see one end of the store to the other.

On the street you can always tell you're near the place; you can smell it a block away. For that reason it doesn't make the neighbors particularly happy, especially on this block of the Fairfax district; the part of town casually referred to as The Borscht Belt. It's Kosher City and every opportunity is taken by the residents to voice disdain over the creeping degenerates who are gaining a toe-hold. Up the street is another counter-culture conclave known as the Free Press Book Store And Kazoo (nobody can figure out what the Kazoo part actually means), and the old codgers, glancing in and quickly looking heaven ward, shake their heads and mutter, 'Such a bunch of chaloshes,' and slog by.

It's gotten so bad an unofficial war has broken out, in the form of a musical skirmish. One of the guys from the Infinite Mind plays *7 and 7 Is*, the new single by Love, full blast, and it's countered across the street at the Mount Zion Kosher Meat Market by *Weddings, Bar Mitzvahs and Brisses* by Micky Katz. It goes on for hours and then it stops, at least until somebody starts up again. Tonight, fortunately, it's quiet.

The stereo in the front room plays a Ravi Shankar album. Buzz is busy waving his hand in front of his face, following imaginary trails of colors each time his fingers pass. Leslie gazes at the cloud of incense, watching threads of smoke spiral up to the ceiling. I sit watching her completely dumbstruck, hopelessly in love.

"Do you want to smoke some dope?"she asks quietly. I'm stunned at first and try not to show it. It never occurred to me that Leslie would want to do something like that. It just wasn't in keeping with how I remembered her. Being the proverbial innocent and all, I've never smoked dope before in my life.

Leslie reaches into an Army surplus gas mask bag from World War 1 that she uses for her purse. She pulls out a small French lozenge tin, an elegant little box, ornately designed in golds and reds and shows me a neatly rolled joint.

Buzz stops waving his hands and turns around, a wide-beamed smile spreads instantly across his face.

We leave the Infinite Mind and walk down Fairfax towards Wilshire. We decide the best place to celebrate is the LaBrea Tarpits. The air is cold and damp; typical for February. Fog and low clouds hang over the city like wads of unwanted dough, muffling and making dull the noise of passing cars. The air is a thick mixture of ocean kelp and diesel exhaust. Tonight, however, it smells the sweetest on earth.

My hand brushes against Leslie's and stays there. We hold on to each other, her fingers wrapping tightly around mine. I squeeze and she squeezes back. Her hand feels incredibly warm and soft and it doesn't let go. We stay that way until we get to the tarpits. My mind races all over the place. Is this my imagination? She has to suspect something; I have a dewy-eyed gawk of amazement plastered all over my face. She grins and squeezes my hand harder. She knows that I know that she knows that I know.

We pass Park LaBrea Towers. We joke about the people who live there; the geezers on Fairfax who complain about everything and the old ladies with their bloated ankles, waddling up and down the street. It's easy to joke about these things; they're never going to happen to us, at least not until some distant, unforeseeable day in a future we can't imagine yet.

We finally make it to the tarpits. I completely forget that we are in post-curfew time, that grey period after ten o'clock on a school night when everybody under the age of eighteen is supposed to be home and in bed, at least that's what the police department claims. It's past midnight, it's Wednesday and I could care less.

The LaBrea tarpits take up most of a city block, although they share space with the L.A. County Art Museum, which opened a couple of years ago. What was, a million years ago, a giant pool of stinking goo has now been transformed by civilization. Even though parts of the museum are in the process of sinking, after only two years, with big globs of tar oozing up to the sidewalks, it's still a nice place to go and hang out.

The main building sits on much of the tarpit and an archaeological dig goes on behind the building. The nice part about all this progress is that the park is pretty much left alone. Partially obscured by the museum, it's a cluster of trees and wonderful hiding places; especially at night, since no one is ever around. In the middle of the city, it's a small slice of heaven.

We sit under a footbridge, a tiny wooden span that extends over a stream that never has any water in it, except when it rains, which is seldom. The lights of the city glow a pink-orange-grey in the distance, illuminating the low - hanging clouds, making them seem like wads of rolled up silk. Across from the park, on top of a four-story office building housing the radio station my dad works at, is an enormous billboard advertising Cadillac. Like the cars themselves, it's bright and flashy and blue with gold iridescent colors, casting its luster on the park like a surreal midday sun.

Leslie, Buzz and I sit in the comfort of our hideout. Leslie opens her bag and pulls out the lozenge tin. She flicks it open and two joints appear. She digs back in her bag, looking for matches. But Buzz, the man with the five-pound Ronson lighter within fingertip reach, pulls it out of his satchel and produces a shooting flame with one quick snap. "Allow me," he intones in a voice suddenly four octaves deeper than usual. Leslie holds the joint to her lips, while Buzz scorches the tip until it lights. She drags deeply and holds her breath for a long time. The faint glow of the cigarette casts a shadow across her face. It makes her completely enchanting and exotic. We share the joint; solemnly passing it around, each taking turns, inhaling deeply and blowing out dense clouds of blue-white smoke. In a matter of minutes, the first joint is gone and the second one becomes a microscopic blemish on the end of Buzz's thumbnail. Buzz keeps his thumbnail long so he can use it as a roach holder. His thumb and forefinger are stained an orange-brown from all the practice.

"So, maybe we should . . ."

I forgot what I was going to say. We all start to say things, but stop in mid- sentence. We have become stupid. Worse, when we actually try to say something, it sounds like we've eaten a box of chalk.

Communication seems to be out for a while. Nevertheless, we manage to wander out from our hiding place and fall over like dominoes on the ground, rolling around on the grass thick with dew. I feel like one of those bumper cars at P.O.P. We keep banging into each other and falling over, laughing. After a while we're soaking wet.

I decide to lie still, face-up and stare at the sky. The orange-pink-grey clouds roll in, touching the tops of the higher office buildings, deadening the sound to a phlegmatic thud. And just then a hole appears right above me. I can see a faint glimmer of a star as the hole gets bigger and as the clouds separate and the black night sky emerges. I point my hand up. "Look, here comes heaven."

Leslie rolls over and lies next to me, resting her head on my stomach. Buzz follows and put his head on her stomach. The three of us don't say anything, we just watch the light show taking place above our heads.

I have no idea how long we're lying here. It must be a long time, because I can feel dew on my eyelids and a clammy feeling in my back from my wet clothes. As the clouds slowly dissipate, a magnificent moon appears, bringing with it a clean white beam that bathes the park and the city in its light.

I start to laugh, even though nothing is particularly funny about this moment. I'm laughing out of astonishment. And as I laugh, Leslie's head bounces up and down on my stomach. Then she starts laughing and Buzz's head bounces up and down. After a while, our heads are bobbing up and down like corks and nobody can seem to stop.

"Say uh, I don't know about you, but I could go for an economy-sized plate of French Fries right now." Buzz says the magic words. They signal the start of a ravenous, stomach- churning hunger.

"Whadaya kids want?" Belle, the waitress at Canter's, bellows at us in our booth. She is big and brassy, like a dented horn nobody wants to play, or cares to learn. She has leviathan hips and a mammoth ass, which she stuffs into a bright yellow uniform like ground pork in a sausage casing. On top of her head she's arranged an immense beehive of bleached blonde hair, lacquered into a position that no hurricane of a hundred miles an hour or more can budge.

There is no love in this puffy face, nothing but a zombie-like glint in her eyes that focuses dispassionately on an order pad. Her thick, bloated fingers are wrapped snugly around a well-chewed pencil. She knows we aren't going to be big tippers. She takes an instant dislike to all of us.

"Large Fries," Buzz orders.

Belle is unimpressed. So far the check is a grandiose seventy-five cents. She points her note pad to Leslie.

"Large Fries," Leslie orders.

Belle is unmoved. "You?" barking in my direction.

"Large order of Fries. . . and a cup of coffee," I say proudly.

Belle snaps up the menus with ferocious efficiency, then vanishes behind the kitchen door.

I look around the restaurant and see two tables of people watching us. They are probably in their sixties or seventies: five old ladies and three old men who smoke big, rancid cigars. They don't seem particularly happy we are sitting in their section. We have landed in enemy territory.

Buzz looks like he wandered out of a hospital thrift-shop; Leslie is wearing a patchwork quilt jacket, olive-green fringe knee-boots and purple velour mini-skirt which, if you look the right way, can allow a clear view straight up to her white cotton panties; and I'm wearing a bright red marching-band jacket, complete with dangling epaulets, gold buttons and an embroidered shoulder patch with the words Loyal Order Of Moose scrawled across my left arm. All of us have red eyes and frozen stupid smiles on our faces. It's no wonder we're getting stares. But we don't look any different than the waves of people promenading up and down Fairfax, hanging out in doorways, coming in and out of the Infinite Mind or the Free Press Bookstore.

Dinner arrives and is inhaled quickly. We run through two bottles of ketchup before Leslie discovers mustard actually tastes good on French Fries. We leave the table smeared with blobs of red and yellow.

Leaving Canter's, we wait for the last known bus going south on Fairfax to arrive. The three of us sit on a bench with Leslie in the middle.

"Boy, isn't it amazing what they can get potatoes to do?" Buzz says, breaking the silence. Leslie and I are holding hands and resting our heads on each other's shoulders.

"Yeah, but you can't get them to take out the garbage," I answer.

Buzz gets up from the bench and leans over to Leslie and I. "Look, would you two stop all this hooey and make out?" Buzz has wandered halfway down the block by the time Leslie and I stop laughing and lock lips.

I don't know who is more surprised, her or me, when we find ourselves wrapped up in each other's arms, not letting go for anything. 'Gee,' I think, 'ain't love grand?'

I spend a lot of time at the Noritake house. Leslie and I become inseparable. It's also because I like the house so much. Leslie's father, Ken, likes to work in the garden; he's the one who does the magic. He owns a used car lot on Figueroa and it's a high-stress situation. He comes home at night and works in the back yard turning it into something you'd have dreams about - a surreal landscape of amazing and ornate designs. The harder the day or week is at work, Leslie's mother tells me, the longer he stays in the garden.

Dale Noritake is a strikingly youthful looking woman with coal-black eyes and hair. Where Ken is the outdoor-type, Dale is the indoor equivalent. The house is always filled with music. She loves Bach and is enormously proud of the harpsichord she's built from a kit and which she plays often. Leslie gets her appreciation of music and curiosity of life from Dale; and her feet firmly planted on the ground from Ken.

The whole concept of sex is still pretty vague for me, even though I'm fifteen, going on sixteen. I know about it, see the pictures, have the fantasies, think about it all the time and run off to the bathroom whenever the latest issue of the Sears Catalogue is dropped into the mailbox. But I haven't actually been there, or to put it more directly, been in there.

Leslie and I are both new to this game, even though we know what the game is. At first it's simple kissing, with tongues, roughing up each other's hair and lots of panting. We realize quickly there's a lot more to this; we're getting sweaty and bothered. Then we start pawing around. And before long we get experimental.

Thank God Burgie has his driver's license, and his father, Ralph, the jarhead whom nobody particularly likes, bought him a VW van! What nirvana! Burgie's first car of any kind, and it's the best of all possible cars on earth.

It's 1967, but a 1963 white and Burgundy two-toned 'loaf of bread', as we call it, is a serious status symbol. It means, among other things, that you are no longer tied down, or dependant on other people to get you where you need to go in life. It's our first sweet taste of freedom, and Burgie has gone to great lengths to turn his symbol of freedom into an Arabian Nights on wheels.

He's outfitted the entire rear half in paisley curtains, a kind of muted musty brown with light purple and gold highlights; and the floor is one big mattress dotted with overstuffed pillows. This van has sex written all over it.

Burgie sees no reason not to take advantage of his new-found freedom. Armed with whatever elaborate excuse he can come up with, Burgie regularly cuts school now and drives out to the beach and spend the entire day, from early morning until the last fatal rays of sundown, in search of perfect waves.

Burgie is glad we want to use the van, too. He likes the notion of love being spread around and he feels sympathy for our plight, even if it means we have to come up with our own elaborate excuses to cut school and hitch a ride on Pacific Coast Highway past Malibu at eight in the morning to get where Burgie is surfing, going the wrong way from the traffic flow. Who said love is easy?

It's all good, clean, dirty fun at first. We take turns lying on top of each other, nude except for Leslie's Sears Roebuck panties; I know those panties well, I've seen them thousands of times in the catalogue. They're white cotton and pretty shapeless. Sexy underwear is something you only see in *Playboy, Knight, Dude* and most every other 'Art Magazine' being published.

Leslie has small breasts that are smooth and firm. She has a long torso and perfect navel and breathtaking skin. The pudgy kid I used to know has vanished. It feels as if her body is wrapped in silk and my fingers go into excited shock each time I touch her. We spend hours making out, taking turns on top, dry humping and in no time we're drenched in sweat and panting breathlessly. After a while she takes my dick in her hand and presses the shaft against her stomach, rubbing it back and forth. I don't know where she got this idea, but it works.

*   *   *   *

*"The catheter's not working"*
*"The line's blocked."*
*"Try another one."*

*   *   *   *

And then it happens. We're rolling around. Leslie gets on top and I feel myself slip inside someplace I've never been before. The warmest and most mysterious of places. Leslie becomes wide-eyed, with an 'uh-oh' expression on her face when she realizes what has happened. She lets out a small yelp. It's like a change of gear, and I wonder, what does this mean?, as I cautiously and slowly move in and out.

This wild and incredible sensation races to the top of my head and back down to my toes. I must be reacting because Leslie starts to smile as if she's surprised me. Truth is, she has. We've surprised each other. I feel light-headed and wonderful and very serious all at the same time.

But in a few seconds it's over. Not completely sure what has happened, or if there's supposed to be more, I lie back on the mattress and feel instantly very good about life, and a little smug at the same time. I quickly realize how amazing this power is that we both have. Somehow I know that from the moment Leslie opened up and I climbed in, our live's have changed; there's no going back.

However, it's the blood on Burgie's sheets that has me a little freaked out. Leslie isn't upset.

"Didn't you read about that?"

"I must've missed a chapter."

"Are you gonna be sick?"

"Me? . . . No."

There's nothing like it; nothing I can compare it to. Making love with Leslie reminds me of every good feeling I've ever had in my life up to this point. I want to remember everything. Every move, press of skin, curve of arm, drop of sweat. I want to be ninety and still remember exactly what Leslie Noritake's hair smells like.

The sun heads west as it always does at three in the afternoon. It looks like the time we'd be leaving school. I wonder how I'm going to make up a sick-note for school the next day. I'm getting really good at forging my mother's signature. But the thought quickly comes and goes. We lie gazing at the ceiling. Burgie dyed a bedsheet a dark night-sky blue and dotted it with hundreds of tiny gold stars; some no bigger than pin-pricks. It's a makeshift sky.

"Leslie, I love you. I've never said that to anybody before in my life."

A smile spreads over her face. It isn't a kid smile this time. "Nelson, I think it's only fair to point out that it's not going to last."

"Why not?"

"It just doesn't. It never does. I'm being completely realistic here."

"So, what are you saying?" I feel a twinge of paranoia racing around my rib cage. Is this a trick? I am really, honestly, completely in love with her. I've wanted to tell her since the night we sat on the bus bench in front of Canter's.

"I'm just saying that people change their minds, that's all. Don't get all huffed-out and strange. I'll probably be in love with you until I'm, maybe seventy. But after that though, I'm really not so sure."

Leslie and I look at each other for a moment and then we start roaring with laughter. Leslie, I've come to realize, has a very dry sense of humor. She will often say something with complete mock seriousness, only to reverse herself a minute or two later with a slap on the shoulder and the cheerful admonishment, "Are you nuts?"

The way I figure it, we have roughly fifty-five years before we'll break up, and even then, it isn't for certain. Fifty-five years is somewhere in the next century, and thinking about how I will feel around 2022 doesn't seem nearly as important as how I'm feeling in 1967.

But I'm sure I'll feel wonderful by then too.

# CHAPTER FIVE

## A POT FOR EVERY LID . . . A FISH FOR EVERY BICYCLE

'Easter Sunday. The Griffith Park Merry-Go-Round. Somewhere around 5:30 in the morning. The gathering of the tribes.' That's what it says on the flyer they've been passing out in front of the Infinite Mind, The Free Press Bookstore, even the Hullabaloo Club. This is the first Easter Love-In ever to take place in Los Angeles.

Burgie, Buzz, Leslie and I stay up all night Saturday; we're too excited to sleep. We're also pretty wired from the Preludin Burgie got hold of. When we get to Griffith Park, around five in the morning, it's already filled with people. You can't see them. It's pitch dark out. No moon, no street lights, no candles. Just wall to wall people milling around clouds of incense. The tinkling of lots of little bells fills the air. Some people bring sleeping bags, spread them out on the ground by the Merry-Go-Round and crash peacefully, while most everybody else treats the occasion like a giant slumber party. Tambourines, bongos, flutes, guitars; anything musical. It's one big jam session, with no particular tune in mind. The hit of the morning is the impromptu raga being played on an honest-to-God sitar and tabla.

Buzz gravitates toward a group of people known as The Bongo Kings where his services as tambourine player are put to good use. Burgie is pressed into service passing out flyers advertising a benefit concert for Radio Free America, a project that involves setting up a pirate radio station three miles off the coast of Southern California. They need to raise money in order to buy a ship they can sink so they can build a platform in the middle of the ocean. It seems far-fetched, but Burgie enthusiastically hands out the flyers, while Leslie and I wrap ourselves in a blanket and discreetly make out.

The early morning chill nearly freezes half the campers. A blue haze hangs over the meadow. It has the heady aroma of frankincense, strawberries, Marlboros, dope and burning garbage. A few people start fires in nearby trashcans, fifty-gallon drums that make excellent places to stand around and get warm. From one end of the meadow echoes the sound of a group of people, about fifty, all chanting "Om".

From the other end of the meadow, a group of Indians gather on a platform. They're humming and beating on drums.

As the sky changes color, we can finally see how many people are here. The meadow is packed and people keep coming. The hills surrounding the meadow are covered with little tribes of painted faces carrying banners and wearing peace symbols. The roads surrounding the meadow, however, are filled with police who stand idly by, looking on, barely speaking more than one syllable, even when spoken to.

Everybody gets their turn to welcome the morning. A group of Hopi Indians perform a sun ceremony, a Catholic priest performs a group blessing. A band of self-proclaimed Druids in robes with hoods walk through the crowd, intoning spells of peace and fertility. Then the Hare Krishna Temple followers show up and everybody starts jumping around. The love-in has started.

A group of people calling themselves The Diggers Free Society set up several rows of picnic tables and spread out thousands of peanut butter and honey sandwiches. The line to receive free food snakes around the meadow as the shivering Easter Morning participants shake themselves out of their blankets, hangovers and sleeping bags.

A couple of people dressed as white rabbits and wearing tuxedos wander around the meadow, handing out Easter Eggs. A makeshift stage is set up and the white rabbits join a cast of other characters, including an assortment of Queens and Mad Hatters, and an impromptu free-for-all Alice In Wonderland begins.

Leslie and I stand in the food line, like everybody else. We're really hungry but we're too excited to think about food. To us, or me at least, this is more fun than camping. Especially since it has nothing to do with my parents and we're with a few thousand people we don't even know, many of whom keep coming up and, for no reason at all, keep telling us they love us, smiling like Cheshire Cats and handing us flowers, sticks of incense, beads, Easter Eggsand bells.

Buzz is in heaven. He's been promoted from mere tambourine player to unofficial Bongo King. He sits on an orange crate, straddling a huge conga drum, and pounds out rhythms with six other guys; while four women, dressed in brightly colored costumes belly-dance around them, clinking tiny finger-cymbals.

When I spot Burgie standing by an elm tree, I think he's hugging it. It's completely possible; there are more exclamations of love going on this morning than I have ever seen in my lifetime. Moving closer, I realize he's hiding behind the tree, peering quietly out at something going on just beyond him.

"God, she's beautiful," Burgie mutters over and over like a mantra. She is the only one out of thousands with white-blonde hair cut blunt to her shoulder and parted in the middle, dressed completely in black. She sits in the Lotus position, eyes closed, holding a stick of incense in one hand while her other hand is correctly placed on her knee, palm up, thumb and forefinger touching. She sits with another girl, who chain smokes and seems bewildered by the whole thing.

"Have you said anything to her?" I ask Burgie.

I'm sure I heard several blood vessels burst after I make the suggestion. It's clear he hasn't.

Leslie walks up, armed with a sandwich that she offers to share.

"Burgie's in love," I tell her. He slaps my arm out of embarrassment, giggling hysterically.

"Oh yeah? Who with?" Leslie peers around at the crowd sitting nearby.

"That one," I tell her, pointing at the blonde.

"Jeanie Nurstrom, are you serious?"

Leslie says it loud enough to attract Jeanie's attention. She opens her eyes and turns her head in the direction of the voice. Burgie darts behind the tree, dragging Leslie with him. That leaves me standing out in the open, recipient to Jeanie's smoldering gaze. She has extremely large, dark blue eyes and a face chiseled out of marble. Her mouth parts slightly in an ethereal, far-away smile. The exchange lasts two or three seconds. It could've lasted longer, but I turnaway, because Burgie nervously laughs so hard, it's reduced him to a bubbling, pre-pubescent bowl of Jell-o.

Leslie tells us that Jeanie also goes to Molino and is in the same grade as us. What luck, if you want to call it that. Leslie disappears into the crowd before either Burgie or I can see where she went. The next thing I know, she's sitting talking to Jeanie.

"Burgie, I've gotta be honest, I've never seen you like this before."

Burgie lets out a deep sigh. "Yeah, I know. It's embarrassing, but I've never seen anybody like her before."

Call it chance, call it fate; Jeanie is stranded. Her friend, the bewildered chain-smoker, has to leave, and since she drove there, Jeanie either has to go with her at noon, or try and hitch a ride back home later, with several thousand other people bunched up on Griffith Park Drive, trying to do the same thing.

For some reason, Jeanie must have thought Leslie was talking about me when she comes over to meet us. I can feel a sense of disappointment from her when Leslie wraps her arm around me and drags me off to check out the rest of the goings on at the love-in. I have the feeling Jeanie is going to be trouble, but I don't tell Burgie that. He's too busy being infatuated and nervous to think about anything else.

Even Leslie doesn't care for her that much. Apparently the only class they share is gym. She never actually participates, but instead always has a note excusing her because she is convinced the showers are a breeding ground for 'all kinds of bacteria.' Jeanie is obsessed with venereal disease and can speak at great length about the various types of syphilis and gonorrhea to be had. And at even greater lengths about some of the cures. I'm sure we'll be hearing a lot more about Jeanie in the coming months.

Buzz, on the other hand, has been swept off his feet by one of the belly-dancers. Leslie and I are walking behind the Merry-Go-Round when we see them, curled under a blanket on the ground. Darcy Ostroff appears to be a good five years older than him. She has a frenzied mass of curly dark brown hair, and dark brown dots for eyes. She's slightly pudgy, and all her front teeth are crooked. She has large boobs and is the only woman I've ever seen with a tattoo. On her foot, just above her ankle, is a small drawing in blue and red of Pegasus, the winged-horse. She bears a faint resemblance to Shetland Pony, and is all over Buzz, alternately making out with him and putting surgical tape on his swollen fingers, now that Buzz has become an official Bongo King.

By three in the afternoon, the love-in starts to wind down. We start the process of rounding everybody up. Burgie and Jeanie are wandering around the old Zoo, a place which has been abandoned for the new zoo facilities, but which still has some great cages and pathways to sanctuaries that no longer exist. It must appeal to Jeanie enormously because they are firmly wrapped around each other by the time we get ready to leave. Buzz hints that he would like to drop Darcy off at her place; she's staying in Silverlake, just east of Hollywood. He adds that he can hitch home from there, even though he's inherited the large Conga drum he's been playing all day.

Jeanie has taken an almost instant dislike to Buzz, but nobody dislikes Darcy. She works at a radio station and that's considered very cool.

Jeanie sits in the passenger seat next to Burgie in the front of the VW van. Leslie and I are just behind them, in the Arabian Nights room. Burgie's recently installed an eight-track tape machine and *Between The Buttons*, by The Rolling Stones pounds over the speakers . Buzz and Darcy cover themselves in blankets, and roll around in the far back of the van. Darcy is certainly no novice at the finer points of heavy-petting; she rubs her hands over some pretty strategic spots on Buzz, while the eight-track plays *Cool, Calm, Collected*.

The passion-wrestling stops long enough for Darcy to give Burgie directions to her place. She lives above Silverlake Reservoir in a small guest house. It's tucked in the back of a large gated Spanish mansion surrounded by Eucalyptus trees that tower fifty feet above the ground. Every breeze, no matter how small, sends Eucalyptus leaves rustling and slapping against each other, some of them showering to the ground. The smell is aromatic and intoxicating.

"You guys want to come in for some wine or something?" Darcy asks. She has a drawl to her speech; a Texas lilt to certain words. "Guys want" sounds like "Gahs won't."

Buzz nods his head excitedly. "Absolutely," he says. He looks over at me, hoping the rest of us will decline. I get the hint.

"Hey, maybe next time for us," I tell Darcy. I have the feeling we'd be less than welcome.


"I got this . . . little problem," Buzz confesses when he shows up at my house a few days later.

"Can I uh, use your bathroom?" I nod and open the door. He knows where it is; he's only used it a few hundred times. Buzz motions for me to follow him. I don't get it at first, but Buzz turns to me, "I gotta show you something."

53

Inside the bathroom, he digs his hand into his shorts and starts scratching. He pulls his hand out, bringing with it a fistful of pubic hairs, and holds them up to the bathroom light. "See that?"

I don't quite get what he's looking for at first, but when I get closer, I realize his hand is full of tiny moving dots; barely visible with lots of legs.

"How do you get rid of 'em?" Buzz asks. I have no idea; neither of us do, and we don't know anybody who does either. Still, I don't think it's anything deadly, so I tell him I'll ask my mother over dinner. Being the health food fanatic, she has a home remedy for just about everything.

Major mistake. Apparently, Buzz has crabs and they're a little more serious than we think.

When my mother finally stops screaming, "Where the hell have you been?" she grabs every piece of clothing from my closet and boils it. Everything goes into the bubbling cauldron. And when she finishes with my clothes, everything I have ever touched, or am ever going to touch is boiled. Sheets, pillow cases, throw rugs, towels, kitchen utensils; if it isn't imbedded in concrete or impervious to germs, it is boiled or otherwise sterilized in some way. To add further insult to a non-existent injury, she runs out to the local pharmacy and buys several bottles of something called Blue soap.

Wonderful Dream Salve can't hold a candle to this. Not trusting me to do an adequate job myself, my mother has me lay in the bathtub, face up, while she dumps an entire bottle of this putrid smelling potion on me. I look at the instructions: 'Use sparingly: enough for twenty-five applications.'

If anybody in my house smoked, we would've exploded from the fumes. I become lightheaded, which is great, because I need something to get my mind off the unendurable incinerating going on just below my navel.

My entire reproductive and discharge system is on fire. I have the appalling image of my balls being burned so badly they fall off in the tub and rinse down the drain. My asshole is so singed with scar tissue that it's likely to stay shut and never work properly again.

My mother keeps mumbling, alternating between; "I knew we should've sent you to Catholic school when we had the chance," and "You're gonna wind up in prison some day."

The episode comes and goes and no one has died. Most of my clothes shrink, which is a good excuse to check out a new hip-clothing store on Sunset, The Great Linoleum Clothing Experiment, which Burgie has discovered, now that he has turned into a 'Dedicated follower of fashion,' to paraphrase the Kinks. Buzz has the same excruciating experience as me. The only difference is, he has a reason to and his mother won't go near him with a barge pole.

After making the fateful phone call, informing her of the news, Buzz hasn't heard from Darcy Ostroff again. She's left her guest house in Silverlake, her job at the radio station and has moved to Virginia City, Nevada, a semi-ghost town with a vast hippie population near the California border. Buzz is distraught at Darcy's vanishing act and is convinced he's the cause of her leaving. And even though he pretends he doesn't care, every five minute interval between periods at school sees Buzz hovering inside the phone booth on the first floor of the main building; calling the radio station, trying to find out what's happened to her, and if there are any messages for him from her, and did they make sure she got his address.

He keeps asking Burgie if he feels like driving up to San Francisco during summer vacation and: "Hey, man, did you hear about those ghost towns in Nevada?" Darcy Ostroff is going to be a sore point with him for a while.


Burgie is staying in L.A. for the summer. Jeanie Nurstrom has become a hot item, hotter than any of us imagined. And the more we know about Jeanie, the more concerned for Burgie we become. Jeanie is a head-case, but she is also stunningly beautiful: a major-problem combination.

Burgie is hopelessly in love with her. Jeanie has a free, crazy and on-the-edge aura about her. She is a marathon person and completely impulsive. Everything in life is either the best of all possible worlds, or the worst of anything that will ever happen. With Jeanie there are no in-betweens. It's only natural that she would be a drama major.

Jeanie lives with her mother in Rancho Park. Her parents are divorced and her father lives in Boston, working on a research project at MIT. Her mother is hardly ever home, and if she is, nobody can tell. Burgie spends a lot of nights at Jeanie's. In fact, he's spending more time with Jeanie and less time with the rest of us.

Jeanie is intriguing, there's no denying it. Recently, I went to her house, looking for Burgie. She answers the door wearing only a bra and panties that I had never seen in any issue of a Sears Catalogue. The panties are snug fitting pop-art bikinis resplendent in a series of brightly colored circles, with a big red dot at the center. Kind of an - X marks the spot - type thing. The bra is a low-cut black satin number that barely kept two impressively developed boobs from popping out. Jeanie has skin whiter than a nurse's uniform and I can't help but stare at the road-map of blue veins that crisscross each breast. Once Jeanie realizes I'm not looking her in the eye, she starts to tap her feet in some unknown rhythm, making her boobs jiggle. She likes being a tease. She stands in the doorway long enough to let me know what the package really looks like before feigning embarrassment and darting behind the door. She peers winsomely out again with an innocent smile to tell me Burgie has gone to the market and is on his way home.

I don't know why I'm worried about Burgie. If happiness at sixteen can be gauged on how often you're getting laid, I would say Burgie is ecstatic. But Jeanie is very possessive, so we hardly see him without her.

Jeanie has annoying habits. She has a sigh you can hear a block away and an ear-piercing whine that makes your skin crawl. It's like Wilma Flintstone from Hell. In fact, Burgie has given Jeanie the nickname Wilma.

It's not that any of us decided we should 'Get Jeanie'; Leslie and I have nothing against her - only Buzz, who listens to her tirades and announces, loud enough for her to hear, "That chick makes my sphincter pucker."

Burgie's in love and that's good. Jeanie just has an attitude problem. She's spoiled, opinionated, and vocal about what she doesn't like. More importantly, Jeanie isn't a deep-down happy person. She pretends she is, but she occasionally stares off into space and her face suddenly changes. There is something very sad about her.

Burgie and Jeanie can't be separated with a crowbar. She has convinced Burgie to take Stage Crew, a class that covers the technical part of putting on plays by the drama department. Burgie, not wanting to be alone in this new adventure, asks me to take the class with him. He also asks Buzz, who surprisingly agrees, thinking there are infinite possibilities in the hanging of lights, hammering of nails and stretching of muslin over flats. "Hey, man, this place has serious potential!" Buzz exclaims the day we sign up. But I can't picture Buzz with a tool belt strapped around his waist. But what Buzz likes most about the class are the enormous hiding places to be had in the auditorium - vast, expansive dressing rooms; an entire attic, practically the size of a football field; a projection room that is hardly ever used; and exit doors that lead out to the street.

I am convinced Buzz has become so eccentric that no woman in her right mind will ever think about him for more than half a second, like between a shopping list and a sneeze. But I could be wrong about that.

# CHAPTER SIX

## INSTANT EVERYTHING

*"So what do you think?"*
*"I don't know."*
*"I hear rumors."*
*"Like what?"*
*"Like the operation didn't take."*
*"Don't believe everything you hear Burgie."*
*"Yeah, but what if it's true?"*
*"Don't think like that."*
*"Is he gonna die?"*
*"I don't know."*
*"Where's Stoika?"*
*"Eating lunch."*
*"Lunch? What time is it?"*
*"I dunno . . . Lunchtime."*

\*     \*     \*     \*

It's pouring rain. The lunch bell just rang, but nobody wants to go outside. Normally we sneak off campus and venture over to Poochie's, a fast-food joint just under the freeway overpass on Robertson. But Burgie doesn't own anything that resembles a raincoat. His only jacket is a brown velvet Edwardian Tunic with a fitted waist and oversized sleeves. Burgie can't get this thing wet; it'll shrink, or worse, disintegrate. Buzz makes the huge mistake of wearing his new Landlubber's; thick corduroy pants that, when wet, smell like a sheep ranch. They probably do wonders for rams, if there were any wandering the halls, but they do nothing to impress girls, who hold their noses in unison as Buzz walks by. Leslie is safely home in bed with the infamous Hong Kong flu, sleeping, or throwing up, or watching Search For Tomorrow on TV. Jeanie hasn't come back yet from Boston. She's supposed to return to L. A. sometime this afternoon. Burgie doesn't seem too bent-out-of-shape though. Going together for almost eight months, they're starting to wear on each other like old shoes on a pair of feet they never fit.

The halls are packed. Students wander around looking like victims of boating accidents. The air is clogged with the smell of wet hair, wet clothes and L.A. City Schools lunch-food. There is always some hapless kid who has the gross misfortune of having packed a liverwurst sandwich; the bouquet creeps through the halls and classrooms and hangs in the air for hours.

On days like this we take refuge in the auditorium, where we can ingest two joints or half a pack of Viceroy's before the end-of-lunch bell rings. Today, however, the auditorium is open to the rest of the student body; and the other members of the stage crew are sprawled out in the dressing rooms. The only safe haven is a place seldom inhabited by students, unless they're forced: the school library.

The room, as usual, is mostly empty. The polished oak tables are sparsely dotted with students who don't say a word. Buzz, Burgie and I pick a table close to a window. We look out on to Robertson Boulevard and watch it turning into a river. Burgie gets up and stands over the steam heater that encircles the perimeter of the library. He opens his jacket, hoping for some warmth to creep inside. Buzz becomes infatuated with the ceiling.

"Do you know a palm reader you can trust?"

Burgie turns away from the heater. Buzz slowly drifts his gaze downwards. Standing next to him, staring at him with two of the largest and most piercing dark eyes I've ever seen is Stoika Foley.

Stoika is half Russian and half Irish. She looks as though she's made out of porcelain. You have the feeling if you touched her the wrong way, she'd break into a million pieces. But she never will. Her expression suggests she knows something of earth-shattering importance may happen any second.

Stoika doesn't mean to make people uncomfortable, she has no axe to grind. She just looks at things with more interest than the norm. She doesn't appear to have any friends; I've never seen her hanging out with anyone. She stays pretty much to herself.

Buzz looks at her for a moment and I know some magical connection is taking place. I can almost hear his brain spinning around as he tries to come up with something clever to answer her with. Nothing comes out. Buzz, the man with a million retorts, sits dumbfounded at the sight of Stoika Foley. Finally, he shakes his head and says "Like, who can you trust these days?"

That's all he needs to say, because she instantly sits down next to him and proceeds to tell him all about palm-reading. She holds out her hand, palm up, pointing at the lines.

"I'm really not sure if this is my life-line, my future, or my past. I have this really screwed up past, unfortunately." Never missing an opportunity to press flesh of the opposite sex, Buzz slowly runs his fingers over her hand and scrutinizes the mysterious eyes that are observing him.

Buzz has never been attracted to conventionally pretty women. Stoika is not conventional, but in her way, she is extraordinary. She is rail thin, but average in height. She has remarkably clear features; an angular face with sharp cheekbones, a soft nose and deep-set eyes. She has a beautiful mouth and full, sensual lips. Her hair, a deep red, hangs straight and covers her ears, but barely touches her shoulders. She wears bangs that go halfway down her forehead, but don't cover her eyebrows. She is notorious for wearing the same clothes for days at a stretch - a white, oversized cotton blouse and dark grey felt skirt. On days like this, when it rains, or when it's cold, she wears a bulky beige three-quartered jacket with large pockets and a hood to cover her head. The jacket hasn't been cleaned in some time.

Stoika gets off school an hour earlier than we do. She's on a work/study program, the same one Burgie took advantage of. Burgie landed a job at Chicken Delight, working in the kitchen and making deliveries. But the job didn't last long. The place blew up after closing from a gas leak in the kitchen. His job vanished in a pile of rubble, but now he has an extra hour of freedom in the afternoon, which usually means hanging out at Wilma's.

Stoika works at a bakery on Pico. She makes doughnuts. Unlike Burgie, she likes her job and loves the idea of making things with her hands. Buzz and I go over to Constantine's Bakery and hang around the alley at the rear of the place, smelling the intoxicating aroma and waiting for Stoika to take her break.

"So, is she incredible or what?" Buzz asks, flipping the butt of his Marlboro into a puddle of rainwater.

I like Stoika, even though I don't know her very well. From what I can tell, I think she's deep-down a good person. It's taken Buzz a long time to get over the episode with Darcy Ostroff, the 'older woman'. He's needed to meet somebody to turn his head around. There is no doubt that Stoika does.

"She's great, Buzz. I think you two definitely have something." We pace around the alley until four o'clock when Stoika takes her break. She comes out of the bakery with a small bag of doughnuts. They just came from the oven.

Across the alley from the bakery is an old apartment building surrounded by a small brick wall. It's barely three feet high and is dotted with graffiti and missing chunks of mortar. We sit on the wall and Stoika passes the bag around. We each scoop up a doughnut and listen to the Greek music coming from a jukebox at the Metropolis Gyro House next door.

Stoika's hands are crusted with flour. She wears a large white apron that covers her blouse and skirt. It's spattered with flour and stained with doughnut filling. Her hair is covered in a white Babushka, tied tightly so it won't fall off at an inopportune moment. She looks like a tractor driver on a collective farm, working on another five-year plan.

Buzz and Stoika don't say much. Whatever exchange that is taking pace happens with eyes and hands. After a few minutes, they fall into their own world. I hear Stoika giggle and, by the time I turn around to hear the joke, they are wrapped around each other.

It doesn't leave much for me to do except stare up at the sky and admire the clouds breaking up the afternoon sun. I stare down at my doughnut, and try to think of some easy exit I can make while Buzz and Stoika lock lips. Let's face it, it's embarrassing to be third party in a situation where all you can do is watch a couple slurp, smack, and come up for air every couple of minutes.

They stay that way until Constantine peers out the rear of the bakery and clears his throat. Stoika recognises the signal and reluctantly breaks away from Buzz. Constantine's bald head, looking like an enormous egg in a nest of black feathers, glistens in the afternoon sun. He motions Stoika to get back to work. She hops off the retaining wall, still holding Buzz's hand. Buzz promises her he'll see her after work. They kiss again and walk slowly across the alley to the rear door of the bakery. Stoika finally disappears inside, leaving Buzz speechless and out of breath.

It's midnight when I hear my mother banging on my bedroom door. I'm peacefully laying in bed. *See Emily Play* by Pink Floyd is shattering my eardrums from the bulky headphones that clasp my skull. My room is pitch dark, except for the Miller High Life 'bouncing bubbles' sign casting faint shards of green, red and blue light around the room. I slowly remove my headphones, reacting to the dull thuds I can feel through the floor.

"It's Buzz's mother; she's looking for him."

Mom stands in the doorway, waiting for an answer. I don't know where Buzz is, but I have my suspicions. He said he was picking up Stoika from work at ten, but I can't exactly tell Mrs. Jordan, seeing it's past midnight and Buzz is obviously spending the night with her. I have to come up with another excuse, fast. I take the phone from my mother and start making up a story that springs into my head.

"Hi, Mrs. Jordan. Buzz went with my father to the radio station. Something about a job after school." My mother stands in the doorway with squinting snake-eyes. I am absolutely lying through my teeth. Buzz is nowhere near my house. My father has been home from work since six. He's busy watching Johnny Carson in the living room. He has no idea he's about to become implicated in some bizarre lie.

Mrs. Jordan, or Mommy-Monster, as Buzz calls her, is satisfied for now. She asks if my father is going to give him a ride home. Like an idiot, I assure her he will. I'm digging myself deeper and deeper into this. I hang up the phone and get dressed. I have three problems to deal with: Buzz's mother, my mother and "Can I borrow the car?"

There's no time to get the speech from my mother about the virtues of honesty, Karma and the whole what-we-send-into-the-lives-of-others-comes-back-into-our-own mumbo-jumbo. What I need right now is to find Buzz. And of course, there is no way I am going to get the car. I am cheerfully reminded that I only have a learner's permit and it's past curfew and, as my mom is quick to point out, a school night.

I grab the phone book and look up Foleys. There are over fifty of them. Luckily, they don't all live in the same neighborhood. I finally find one: Carl Foley, who lives on Cattaraugus, less than two blocks away from school. It has to be her.

The phone rings ten times before anyone answers.

"Nyelllooo?" It sounds like Stoika, but she is either dead-asleep or on another planet.

"Stoika? It's Nelson. Is Buzz there?"

The voice on the other end takes days to answer. "Uhhhhh . . . gezzo," is the thick-tongued answer.

"Can I talk to him?" Another year-long pause. The phone suddenly goes dead. She hung up. Something is wrong.

Buses in Los Angeles run on an if-and-when basis. Sometimes they show up every ten minutes and sometimes they show up every ten days. The bus running on Venice Boulevard is semi-dependable. Venice is two blocks south of my house and, as Cattaraugus crosses Venice, it's the best chance to take. I tell my mother I'm going to sleep and go through all the motions of yawning and going to the bathroom. When it's safe, I throw on my clothes, roll up some blankets and stuff them in bed to look like me sleeping, then quietly unlatch my bedroom window and slide out to the night air. I run two blocks to the bus stop and hope, the bus, for a change will be on time.

A little after one in the morning the pale green MTA bus pierces the quiet and lumbers to a stop in front of me. I am the only passenger and sit nervously behind the driver, tapping my feet. The driver is in nothing resembling a hurry. He whistles along to the Ray Charles tune playing on the transistor radio sitting beside him.

Stoika lives just south of Venice Boulevard, in a block of modestly run-down homes with overgrown lawns. When the bus finally wheezes to a stop, an hour later, I race down the block looking for the address and, when I finally find it, uncover another piece in the puzzle called Stoika Foley.

You have to look very closely to see there actually is a house. It's been overtaken by vegetation and is almost impossible to spot from the street. Sitting in what looks like a jungle plantation, obscured by towering palm trees, wild bushes and vines, is a modest wood-frame house. It certainly isn't a new place; the vegetation that runs amok didn't just spring up overnight.

The house is dark; with not even a porch light burning. The best I can make out, it's a dirty, off-beige-white. A narrow dirt path leads up to the front door. I walk slowly up the path, trying to figure out the most diplomatic approach to take. It's dead quiet now. A clear and moonless night, with no cars, no people. Only the faint aroma from Helms Bakery, and the heady smell of next day's baked bread wafting down the street.

I hear laughter coming from the rear of the house. I try fixing my eyes in the darkness to see how I can get back there. The dirt path trails off and curves around the side of the house to an overgrown driveway. I walk down the path until I reach a rusted, sagging fence. Trudging through this jungle, I push my way through and come face to face with the backyard.

The back yard is in much worse shape than the front. Somebody has let nature go insane back here. Four huge palm trees spiral toward the sky, their fronds jutting out like the arms of a giant burdened with too many responsibilities. In the distance, toward the rear of the yard is an old greenhouse. Next to it sits an ivy-covered garage, too small to fit any car built since the nineteen- twenties. The roof sags from the weight of the palm fronds resting on it. One side of the garage door is split and broken off its hinges.

Sitting on the rear porch, rocking back and forth in a jerry-rigged swing are Buzz and Stoika. They are completely, totally shit-faced drunk. Stoika has obviously passed out and is spread across the swing, her head resting in Buzz's lap, her legs dangling over the side. Buzz is hypnotized by the night sky, staring glassy-eyed at the stars. Perched precariously on Stoika's hip and about to slide off any second, is a gallon jug of Red Mountain Wine. Only a small amount is left, swirling and sloshing against the side of the bottle.

Buzz doesn't recognize me. I have to convince him I am someone he knows. I keep saying, "Buzz, we gotta get you home." But he doesn't budge. I'm pissed off at myself for making up a stupid story in the first place and worse, implicating my father, who is probably going to get a verbal blast from Mommy-Monster once the dust finally settles.

"There's like, millions of stars out," Buzz babbles kinetically. He breathes deeply, and every time he exhales, he blows a pungent wine-scented cloud in my direction and I nearly gag.

I think seriously about leaving him here, and I probably should, but I am neck-deep in this and have to get out of it somehow. So I carefully remove the gallon jug of wine, pry Buzz loose from Stoika and drag him up. Stoika doesn't budge. She continues to sleep peacefully on the back porch swing.

Buzz is a little taller than me and a lot heavier. I drape his arm over my shoulder and limp toward Venice. He feels like a sack of steel-reinforced concrete. I am exhausted by the time the bus stop comes into view, but fortunately the cold night air is starting to work on Buzz. He gains consciousness long enough to let out that tell-tale groan that indicates something of major importance is just about to take place. We call it 'Looking for Huey.' And within seconds, Buzz is looking for Huey with a vengeance. Everything he drank, along with everything he ate all day and probably all week goes flying all over the sidewalk. It's difficult to keep walking; he just keeps throwing up, but we only have a few more steps to go. We finally get to the bus stop where Buzz buries his head between his legs and gushes like a freshly tapped oil well.

There is nobody around, but I still feel badly for the guy. There is something pathetic about hearing somebody moan and mumble "Oh Jesus" every few seconds and blow vomit all over his new suede boots.

We sit at the bus stop for a long time. Naturally, no bus comes. I have the feeling we are going to be stuck here until after dawn. Buzz lifts his head up and looks around the empty street and down at his ruined shoes. He breathes heavily and keeps saying over and over, "I'll be okay, yeah, I'm okay," just as he slumps back over and resumes the search for Huey.

A beat-up Volkswagen bug comes ambling down the street. It slows to a stop in front of us. The driver, a guy in his early twenties, leans over and yells out the open passenger window.

"Is he sick?"

"Yeah, a little," I tell the driver.

"Does he live around here?"

"A couple blocks north of Pico."

"Come on, I'll give you a lift."

He introduces himself as Rick. He has long, straight dark hair and a neatlytrimmed Walrus moustache. He's naked from the waist up and has all the windows in his car rolled down. He is breathing with a loud, asthmatic wheeze. He tells us he's heading for his pre-induction physical for the draft, which is taking place at six a.m. He's been driving around all night, trying to get his asthma to act up so he'll be rejected. From the sound of him, it's working. He's shivering from the pre-dawn cold, but he's determined not to get warm until he gets the 4-F he's hoping for.

Buzz is folded over in the backseat like a month-old newspaper in a rainstorm, trying to get the world to stop spinning. Luckily for Rick, Buzz has yacked up everything he's going to for the night. I sit in the front seat, while Rick quivers from near-frostbite and flips the dial on his Blaupunkt, looking for a good station to listen to.

He tells me he's the bass player in a band called Lessons In Ventriloquism. I've heard of these guys. They play all over town; mostly at Pandora's Box and The Hullabaloo. I read something last week about them getting signed to a record deal. At the moment, it seems like the furthest thing from Rick's mind.

We reach Buzz's house and stop. I get out and move my seat over for him to stumble out. I ask him if he's okay for the walk up the stairs. He mumbles, "Yeah, I'm okay, I can maintain." He reeks of stale wine and fresh vomit and I hope his mother is asleep. I get back in the VW and we continue to my house.

When we get there it's almost five in the morning and I'm exhausted. Rick still has another hour to go before his physical. He stops the car. I thank him for helping me and Buzz and shake his hand. He reaches over and pulls a string of brightly colored beads down from his rear-view mirror and hands them to me.

"Here, these are good luck."

I look at them for a few seconds. "Maybe you should keep them," I tell him. "You could use the luck right now."

He turns to me and smiles. "I got asthma. That's better than luck."

I stand on the curb, holding the beads and watch Rick drive off to the Draft Board. I hope for his sake he's right about his luck. I turn and walk up the steps to my house and, as quietly as I can, open the door and tiptoe in. The only greeting I get is from Dolores, our half-Dachshund, half German Shepherd mutt, who gives out a muffled growl from the kitchen. At the ripe old age of ten, she couldn't care less if someone was actually coming in to rob the house. She only growls because, for some reason I can never figure out, she loathes me.

I collapse in bed and pass out. A minute later, my alarm clock rings. It has gone from being five a.m. to six-thirty a.m. in a remarkably short period of time.

My mother doesn't say a word to me. Her disgust is amply apparent in what I get for breakfast; a glass of parsley juice and a lemon.

I make it to school in automatic, but at least I make it to school. Buzz doesn't show up at all.

Stoika does, however. I must've missed something. I find her standing in the cafeteria line, sipping hot chocolate and chewing one of the doughnuts from work. She looks completely normal. A few hours earlier she was passed out, sloppy drunk on her backporch swing. I don't get it.

"Have you seen Buzz?" she asks cheerfully. Cheerful for Stoika is two raised eyebrows. When she speaks, her forehead wrinkles and she giggles, self-consciously. She can't control it. It adds to her intensity and certainly part of her charm.

"You don't remember anything about last night?" I ask her.

She looks at me, perplexed. "I did have this dream and you were in it. You were riding a motorcycle in the ocean and you told me you made earthquakes for the government."

Obviously, Stoika doesn't remember. I find out last night is a common occurrence for her. People have hobbies; they collect stamps, they embroider, they roll up bits of tin foil into monolithic balls. Stoika drinks. She goes out for it in a big way.

Unlike Buzz, Stoika never has a hangover the next day. She can get roaring drunk and, along with it, funny, mean, completely emotionally unglued, morose, euphoric and, no matter what happens that night, the next day she is completely fine, except she can't remember a thing that happened. But because she treats it as a hobby, she never lets it get in the way of other things. She has laid down her own ground rules. She never drinks at school, never comes to school drunk. Never drinks at work and never comes to work drunk. She only drinks red wine and, ironically, she hates other drunks.

So why does a sixteen-year-old who drinks herself into oblivion get involved in this complicated lifestyle? None of us know for sure, but we suspect it has something to do with her homelife.

Five months have gone by and it's the last day of school before summer vacation. The semester is officially over at noon. Buzz, Burgie, me, Leslie and Stoika are sitting on the auditorium steps, contemplating the next three months.

"Wow, three months of instant everything," Burgie remarks.

"Yeah, kind of frightening," I chime in.

We watch the multitudes of kids pile on to waiting buses, their rides to freedom. We're waiting for Jeanie to finish auditioning for the summer stock group sponsored by the Drama Department. She is one of fifty finalists chosen throughout the city. It does wonders for her ego and makes us miserable in the process.

A car pulls up to the bus stop on Robertson, about a hundred feet from where we're sitting. The driver hits his horn and it roars out *Tumblin' Tumbleweeds*. We all look up. All of us except Stoika.

The car is an old Cadillac convertible, painted the hottest shade of pink ever dreamed up in a laboratory. The seats are upholstered in cowhide. The hood has a large pair of steer horns mounted on top of the radiator cap. The detail around the door handles and wheel wells is chrome. The door handles are white mother-of-pearl pistol grips.

The icing on the cake is the guy behind the wheel. A fugitive from Marlboro Country. He wears a gleaming white ten-gallon Stetson hat on his head and a waxed brown-grey handlebar moustache on his tanned-leather face. He'd probably be shooting a six-gun if it wasn't a misdemeanor. I half-expect him at least to pull a weather-beaten guitar out of thin air and start singing. Instead, he keeps hitting his horn.

Stoika rolls herself into as small a ball as she can. Leslie turns to her, smiling as she peers down at her rapidly shrinking friend.

"You're missing this guy," Leslie cheerily informs her.

"No I'm not," Stoika mutters, barely above a whisper. "I'm related to him." She clears her throat. "He's my dad."

We turn in unison and look at Stoika in stunned silence. The hot pink Caddie and Cowboy Carl Foley are attracting a lot of attention. A crowd forms. Stoika finally gets up, burying her head in her looseleaf binder, and runs through the crowd, jumping into the waiting Caddie. To her, this nonchalant parental lift from school has all the drama of an FBI dragnet.

"Kind of makes you wonder about the paint job," Buzz comments, in typical nonsequitur fashion.

"Yeah, but I dig his moustache," Burgie adds.

It turns out that Carl Foley lives somewhere in the Old West. The Old West of his mind. But that's only half the story. There's also Ludmila. Ludmila is Stoika's mother. The Russian half. The Russian half who adores Dorothy Lamour movies and the South Sea Islands. She is the one with the green thumb run amok. She loves palm trees and thick underbrush and vines. She is a big, buxom woman with a roaring laugh and a gold front tooth. She spends most days wearing khaki shorts, a khaki military shirt and a pith helmet; tending vines, spraying weeds and planting jungle foliage. She has the biggest smile on the face of the earth. Stoika invented it, but Stoika rarely uses it.

Country Joe and The Fish have a song. One of the lines goes; *"Some people, they find each other."* That's Carl and Ludmila in a nutshell. They found each other in a probable-improbable place: somewhere near the Brandenburg Gate in post-war Berlin.

Carl was in the Quartermaster Corps and Ludmila was a Red Army Traffic Officer. They were both sergeants. The exact circumstances and conditions of their meeting remain a mystery, and even the shreds of information about them come begrudgingly from Stoika, who never likes to talk about them. She showed us a picture of Ludmila taken during her Red Army Occupation days and it was crystal clear why Carl fell for her; she was adorable if you can use 'adorable' to describe an eighteen-year-old girl in a Russian Army uniform, with a Kalashnikov sub-machine gun slung flirtatiously around her shoulder. She had a face like the moon: round, bright and beaming. Her eyes were clear and dark. She was encased in a bulky uniform and her hair was cut modestly short. She wore a stiff-brimmed military hat with a Red Star emblazoned across the front. She was laughing; laughing about something or someone just out of camera sight. The smile, then as now is a killer.

Two months after meeting Carl, Ludmila defected to the western zone and, after Carl's discharge, they married. Carl grew up in Boston, but Ludmila was starstruck by Hollywood. Part of the deal Carl made, while smuggling her across Checkpoint Charlie to the Allied Zone, was to promise they would settle in Los Angeles, and a deal was a deal.

Because Carl and Ludmila have very strong personalities of their own, there isn't too much room for Stoika's to come out. So Stoika exists in a void of her very own. Occasionally she'll say that, if abortions were legal in 1951, she would've been a sanitation problem, or part of a landfill somewhere in Encino.

As Buzz describes it, the Foley house from the inside is a bizarre testimony to The Old West. "Uh, you may not believe this," he tells us, "but there's a stuffed horse in the living room."

There is. An Appaloosa named Charlie, who died in 1958, standing at attention in the living room, with glass brown eyes that follow you everywhere. He is the biggest ghost-like presence in a room packed with ghosts. Deer antlers hang on the walls everywhere. And where there aren't deer antlers, there are Indian blankets of red and turquoise hung up or draped over every available surface. Even the table lamps have their own ominous touches. Cattle skulls and rawhide lampshades. It's like falling into a time-warp. Inside it's the O.K. Corral and outside it's Bora-Bora.

It's no small wonder that Stoika keeps her room locked all the time. She is jealously guarding the twentieth century within the confines of her own four walls. It's also the only room in the house where the walls are painted every bright, shocking color imaginable.

Carl and Ludmila aren't your typical parents. They really don't mind the way you look and they certainly aren't judgmental, being, I imagine, from the those-who-live-in-glass-houses-shouldn't-throw-stones school. Still, they are the first parents I've ever met, aside from Leslie's, who are actually fun to be around. But fun isn't what Stoika is after. Stoika wants her own personality. Left to her own devices, the device she's discovered, and fits most comfortably with, is boozing.

Stoika has her share of problems. Buzz figures prominently in them.

Summer is just beginning.

# CHAPTER SEVEN

## SOMETHING'S COOKING AND IT MIGHT BE YOU

We're sitting in our usual eighth row seats at The Bing Theater, watching *The Wedding March*, by Erich von Stroheim, with rapt attention. Midway through the film, which is shot in glimmering black and white, the screen blazes into color. It's a jolt to the audience because it looks so gorgeous. I glance over at Stoika who, more than anybody, would be impressed. However, her head is buried in her hands and I realise she's sobbing. Buzz has his arm around her and is trying to calm her down. He shoots a look over at me. In a second, Stoika bolts out of her seat and runs to the lobby. Buzz follows.

After a while Buzz comes back. He whispers to me that Stoika is crying hysterically in the Ladies room. He doesn't know what's wrong with her or what to do. We decide we'd all better leave the movie.

Stoika doesn't let up during the ride back to her house. She sits in the back of Burgie's van and wails. The only thing Buzz can do is wrap himself around her and hold on to her. We still have no idea why she's carrying on like this. We try talking to her, but all the circuits are down: she doesn't hear us. She keeps mumbling over and over that it's nothing, she's all right.

We pull to a stop in front of Bora-Bora on the range. The fog and low clouds gumming up the skies start drifting in, licking the tops of the skyscraper palm trees. Buzz nudges Stoika and leads her out of the van. She doesn't say anything to anybody; no goodnights, get losts, drop deads. She just walks out, dazed. Buzz turns to close the van door.

"What's happening, is she okay?" Silly question, but I have to ask it.

"Man, you got me,"Buzz answers with a long sigh, stubbing his cigarette out on the curb. "Don't stick around, I'm staying." He turns around and shuts the van door and follows her around to the back of the house, where he climbs through her bedroom window.

Buzz usually calls me on Saturday morning to check in. But on this particular Saturday nobody's heard anything from him or Stoika. Whenever something is wrong, Buzz takes a ride to Santa Monica Pier. He'll go to the furthest point closest to the ocean and look out, watching the water. He'll do it for hours. Looking maybe for Catalina, looking to make some sense out of life, or an answer somewhere. We decide to look for him there.

Burgie comes by my house at eleven to pick me up. Leslie's promised her mother to go shopping with her, so she can't come and Jeanie doesn't usually wake up till noon during the summer.

We find Buzz alone at the pier. He tosses a cigarette butt over the edge to the water and automatically lights another. "Guess what, my life just got complicated," he announces to Burgie and me. He looks awful, like he hasn't slept in days. His eyes are red and puffy. His normally neat and hip appearance has been traded in for crumpled and disheveled. "She's pregnant. Surprise."

A thick soupy silence envelopes the pier. About the only thing we can do is join Buzz, draped over the railing and gaze out at the calm, peaceful ocean. The sky has become appropriately grey and overcast. And a thick fog floats in, obscuring the beach and the palisades overlooking the pier. Only the occasional creak of wooden beams suspended from the water and the sounds of fishermen's rods casting off break the dull, congested atmosphere around us.

Buzz flicks another Marlo into the ocean and watches it float for a few seconds before it dissolves and sinks into the green frothy water.

"Kinda makes you want to go out dancing, doesn't it?" He forces a smile and it breaks the silence. His teeth are stained brown from all the cigarettes. He confesses he's gone through three packs since the night before.

"What's gonna happen?" I ask him. There's no point tap-dancing around the ubject.

"I guess I better get used to being called Pop or something." Buzz speaks in is usual off-handed way. He pops another Marlo out of its pack and lights it, letting out a good hack as he sucks in a cloud of smoke. It's raspy and loaded with phlegm.

We go through a whole list of scenarios. He'll marry her, she'll get an bortion. She'll put the kid up for adoption. He'll give her money and never see her again. He'll pretend it never happened. They'll get an apartment and he'll get a job. He'll drop out of school. She'll drop out of school.

It goes on all day. We're walking around on egg shells. Nobody knows what's going to happen next. When we meet up with Stoika later in the day we find she's become a space cadet. In the middle of a conversation she drifts off, staring blankly at a wall, or down at her hair, which she's let grow to the point where she can put several strands of it in her mouth and chew on it.

Buzz has developed a nervous tick. Every twenty seconds or so some uncontrollable urge sends a periodic spasm from the right side of his neck to the right side of his mouth. It looks like he's smirking.

Everybody is hoping for a small miracle.

A place called The Free Clinic just opened on Fairfax, about two blocks south of the Infinite Mind. Rumor has it it's a place where people can go to get their lives sorted out, at least in a medical way. For that reason, it's always crowded.

Stoika gets counselling; a whole list of pro's and con's and, finally, the name of a doctor if she wants to get an abortion.

"I decided to have the baby and I'm going to keep it and you don't have to do anything." Stoika is completely sober. She has mysteriously stopped drinking for a few weeks now. She's jumping head-first into mommy-mode and nobody can stop her.

The grand announcement comes just as Leslie is blowing out the candles on her birthday cake. It's July 20th, and Leslie Noritake has turned seventeen. I'm glad we're together. Glad for a lot of reasons. Glad I'm not Buzz. Glad I'm not Burgie. They've gotten involved with insane women. At least Leslie is normal, more or less. As normal in a sea of babbling screwballs as one can be, while still having a foot firmly planted somewhere in the clouds.

Leslie's birthday has fallen on a Saturday this year and her parents have thrown a party for her. They set up tables in the backyard where we're sitting around on wooden lawn chairs, eating hot dogs, drinking Hawaiian punch and secretly wondering what Stoika's kid will look like.

It's a big family affair, lots of aunts and uncles, and even Leslie's grandparents from Japan. Even Leslie's sister Stephanie shows up. Stephanie is the older one, by three years, and though they bear a close physical resemblance, they bear no emotional resemblance to each other whatsoever. Stephanie is the straight one; today she's wearing a Nixon's The One button on her blouse. At one point she almost made me forget it isn't a good idea to slug a woman when she proclaimed, loudly, after hearing our discussing the anti-war demonstrators getting beaten up in front of the Century Plaza Hotel, "They should've shot a bunch of them." For obvious reasons, she stays only long enough to sing "Happy birthday," give Leslie a twenty-five dollar gift certificate to Robinson's Department Store, and splits.

Stoika's announcement brings an audible gulp from Buzz. He gazes at the moss creeping over the vines that dip into the water of the Koi pond. I think he's reluctantly decided fatherhood won't be such a bad thing after all. At least his nervous tick has disappeared.

By sunset we decide to leave the party and drive downtown to the Shrine Expo Hall near the USC campus to see The Jeff Beck Group, Fleetwood Mac, The Outlaw Blues Band and Clear Light.

The Shrine Expo Hall is the single greatest bargain on earth. Two dollars and fifty cents for five hours of non-stop music. It's a huge cavern. No seats, no permanent stage, just a vast empty area, the size of a football field. Every week a concert is put on. Bands make the circuit, coming down from San Francisco, where they play the Fillmore on Friday, and the Shrine Expo on Saturday.

Because there are no seats, everybody sits on the floor. There are thousands of people, a sea of them; sitting, sprawled-out, or standing and dancing; one huge, happy family. The thing that's legendary about the Expo Hall is the boast that you can't walk from one end to the other without getting stoned from just breathing the air. And it's true. The air is a wonderful mixture of oranges, which are always sitting in fifty gallon drums for people to eat, Delicado cigarettes and dope; mostly dope.

We get inside around eight-thirty, just as the first band sets up. The Hall is nearly filled, but we find a clearing strategically placed between the restrooms and the light show and stake out our claim.

Burgie fumbles around in his jacket pocket and hands Leslie a small round ball of tin foil. "Happy Birthday." He smiles widely.

It's a small chunk of hashish. Buzz looks over, eyeing the goodies, and instantly produces a small, bronze pipe from his pouch. He grins and waves it at us, handing over the pipe and his Ronson lighter. Leslie unwraps the foil, breaks off a small piece of hash, puts it in the pipe and lights it. We pass it back and forth and to the people sitting near us, who smell the unmistakable aroma of hash and light up at the prospect.

Buzz wraps his Harry Houdini cape around Stoika. I guess he's more protective of Stoika, now that she's made her decision to keep the kid. And you know, by looking at them, that he's going to be in love with her for a very long time. Even if she is a little nuts, has started drinking carrot juice like a fish, reads The Spirit Of The Upanishads so much she can quote from memory: 'That which is not to be shall never be; that which is to be shall never not be,' and thinks about life after death all the time. Buzz is hers and he puts his arm around her and tries to keep the world, and all its particular looniness, at bay for as long as possible.

We start to realize that Stoika hasn't been sitting with us for some time. Earlier, she excused herself from Buzz and wandered off to the bathroom. The best we can remember, it must've been an hour ago.

In a completely unexpected show of concern, Jeanie volunteers to go off searching for her. She gets up, stepping lightly over the limp bodies that litter the hall, and staggers to the restroom.

A few minutes later, Jeanie races back in a panic. The crowd has jumped to their feet, stomping and shouting as Mick Fleetwood decimates his drum kit during a solo on *Shake Your Money-Maker*. Buzz is the only one who isn't watching. A look of dread sweeps over him as Jeanie gets his attention. He jumps up and quickly follows her. Along with the rest of us.

Stoika is in the bathroom. We can hear her from outside the door, even though the sound of the audience stomping their feet and yelling for an encore is shaking the auditorium. Jeanie and Leslie run in, followed by two women who work for the concert promoter. Buzz stands outside, freaking out and helpless.

I get a quick glance inside. There is blood all over the place. Stoika is being led out from a stall, by Leslie and the two women. Her hands are covered in blood.

One of the women, a petite ticket-taker, who wears a black armband and has jet black hair, tells Leslie that Stoika needs to get to the Free Clinic as soon as possible. She grabs a towel from the office and hands it to Stoika who holds it between her legs while we get her out of the Expo Hall. She lays in the back of the van as Burgie races us to Fairfax and Beverly Boulevard.

It's midnight and we're discovering that the Free Clinic is one of the least fun places on earth. Stoika has been taken to an examination room, along with a girl who shot up speed earlier and got it into her head that shooting up milk was a good antidote.

We have interesting company in the waiting room: two bad acid trips and a woman freaking out on Peyote.

The woman on Peyote keeps clawing at her face, screaming, "It really doesn't mean what it says!"

And the acid trips slap each other, yelling "Ha! I've got your mind and it's dead!"

Leslie stays with Stoika the whole time, while Jeanie stays in the waiting room, talking to the Peyote casualty. Burgie, Buzz and I get up and go outside. Burgie and I pace back and forth in front of the building, while Buzz sits on the curb, submerged in grief.

All in all, it's a fun and rewarding experience which no amount of money will ever get me to repeat again. It's the first time I've ever seen Buzz cry. He's crumbled over and sobbing like a baby. There is nothing Burgie or I can do or say to make him feel any different or any better. We all know Stoika has lost the baby.

I wonder what the kid would've looked like. Buzz has a large nose. Stoika has a small, yet pronounced nose. The mathematical probabilities of the kid having a proboscis the size of a city block was better than good. Buzz has insanity in his family. Stoika has insanity in her family. I heard all the stories about the aunts and uncles who popped their corks in either Russia, Ireland or, in Buzz's case, France and Egypt. The kid would've been a whack-job from the word go.

To paraphrase Tennessee Williams, God was playing God tonight. And the operative phrase is 'Wait a minute!' Cruel as it seems, it was probably a blessing.

Dawn creeps up and the crisis has passed. Stoika doesn't want to go home, so we drive to the top of Mullholland, where the paved road ends and the dirt road goes off to Topanga, eventually emptying out at Pacific Coast Highway. Burgie stops the van on a ridge. To the north sits the San Fernando Valley. To the south, Los Angeles. The sun starts to rise over the silent houses that spread endlessly out to infinity.

The view of the city this high up doesn't make you feel particularly powerful or important. It makes you hear all the little things in life. You can hear the faint sounds of dogs barking, pissing off some pigeon who has most likely been sleeping on a car someplace; and the abrupt sound of lawn sprinklers turning on automatically, dowsing the grass and the newspaper some guy got up at two in the morning to deliver.

I turn to look at Leslie, one year older, lying beside me, sleeping peacefully. Burgie and Jeanie have gone outside and are lying in Burgie's sleeping bag. Stoika sleeps across from Leslie. Buzz has disappeared. I get up, gently moving Leslie's arm from my shoulder and on to the rolled up jackets we're using for pillows. I gingerly creep over the sleeping bodies and open the door of the van. I feel a blast of hot air rush inside and up my nose.

Outside, I find Buzz sitting on a rock, staring over the valley. A pile of cigarette butts have collected around him. His eyes are still red and puffy from crying the night before.

"I don't know what it is with all those bungalow-ranch-style houses. I wouldn't be caught dead in any them," Buzz mutters as he takes a deep drag off his fortieth or fiftieth Marlo, letting a cloud of smoke fly out.

He flicks the ash to the ground and taps it around his feet, mixing it into the earth. He rests his elbows on his knees and looks down at the ground.

"Look, uh, don't tell anybody, but I think I'm gonna disappear for a while." He takes another drag and turns his head to face me. "I decided to split to San Francisco and check out the Haight. The summer's only half gone and I'll be back before September, maybe. I gotta get out of here." He stubs the cigarette out on the ground and I can tell he has mixed feelings about leaving, but he's made up his mind.

The sun comes barelling over the ridge frying everything in sight. It's going to be over a hundred today. Burgie and Jeanie are snugly enclosed in Burgie's sleeping bag; zipped up the side and snapped at the top. The scorching rays of the sun hit the bag and it begins to twitch and gyrate like a mummy with St. Vitus' Dance. Burgie pokes his arms out of the top, searching desperately for the zipper, gasping for air. He unzips the bag and lies there for a minute, trying to get his bearings. Jeanie's not a lot of fun to be with in the morning; even Burgie admits it. She let's out an unintelligible bark and punches Burgie in the head, trying to get him to turn out the light. Burgie stumbles out of the bag, clad only in his BVD's: big, baggy kid-shorts. On anybody they look strange, but on Burgie they look eerie. He's been losing a lot of weight lately and his shorts don't seem to fit at all. They keep falling down.

He stumbles over to the van and pulls his pants and shirt out of the front seat and slaps them on. He's bleary-eyed and incoherent. He finds his shoes and hobbles over to the rock where we're sitting. He gazes out at the valley and then shoots a look of disgust at Buzz.

"How the fuck can you smoke first thing in the morning?"

Buzz gazes back at him. "Who said anything about this being first thing in the morning?"

"You've got to have lungs like prunes by now," Burgie mutters, tying the laces of his shoes.

"Oh shit! Oh shit!" Jeanie wakes up with a shriek. The sun has hit her square on the face and the sleeping bag is now a furnace. She tosses the top layer off of her and lays there, panting for cool air. She doesn't realize she's naked but we do. Jeanie has the most perfectly shaped breasts of anybody; even Leslie, I hate to admit. She never goes out in the sun and doesn't even own a bathing suit. Burgie lives for the beach and Jeanie is revolted by it. Love is not blind; love is near-sighted.

"Mommy, what big eyes you have," Buzz comments, watching Jeanie's boobs bob back and forth, as she breathes in deeply. Jeanie, realizing she's putting on a show, submerges herself back in the bag and fumbles around for her clothes.

Leslie and Stoika pile out of the van. Stoika limps a little, but she seems bright and cheerful. Maybe it's the calm before another storm or maybe she's relieved the ordeal is finally over.

We're starving and we have, between us, three dollars. Burgie's gas gauge is on empty and he needs a dollar to get us all home. That leaves two dollars for the five of us.

The best we can haggle is a jar of Skippy Creamy Peanut Butter, eight day-old dinner rolls and a half gallon of Hi-C Imitation Orange Drink. That leaves us with fifty cents, so we send Jeanie back to the market for a jar of Welch's Grape Jelly.

We sit in the parking lot of the Shopping Bag Market on Ventura Boulevard and consume our feast. We dip our fingers in the peanut-butter and jelly jars and lather rolls with brown and purple goo. We take turns sipping out of the Hi-C can and, with each subsequent sip, we leave a peanut butter and jelly ring around the opening.

Buzz is silent the whole time. He won't look at Stoika or talk to her. He quietly munches his way through his breakfast and gazes, trance-like, at the ceiling.

Leslie finally corners him at the gas station, where Burgie is busy getting his ration of regular gas and everybody else raids the bathrooms.

"I think it's lousy what you're doing to Stoika. She really needs you Buzz."

Buzz sits on the running board of the open van door. He lets out a long sigh and runs his fingers through his matted, uncombed hair. He really wants to light a cigarette, but the No-Smoking-Turn-Off-Your-Engine signs are plastered all over the place.

"Look, it's all my fault. I feel like shit about the whole thing and I would really like to crawl into a hole someplace and disappear."

Leslie doesn't realize that a disappearing act is exactly what he has in mind. I mean, what else would you do if you wanted to be Harry Houdini? This is the opportunity of a lifetime.

Armed with a Wilson Bowling Ball Bag full of clothes and twenty-five dollars, plus thirty-five dollars he's carefully lifted from his mother's jewelry box, Buzz plants himself on Pacific Coast Highway and sticks his thumb out. Heading north. North to Paradise.

Unfortunately, it leaves me to handle the switchboard of insane phone calls from Mrs. Jordan.


"Burgie, I promised somebody I wouldn't tell anyone where they were going, but everybody wants to know where they are." I sound like an Indian Guru publishing his first book in English.

We're sitting in the back of Aron's Records on Melrose, taking turns playing the twenty-five-cent used albums on the turntable. I feel guilty that I'm hiding important information from people who are worried.

Burgie slowly lifts the tonearm, placing it down on *Music to Listen To Barney Kessel By*. He turns and cocks the headphones away from his ear.

"It's okay, I know Buzz is in San Francisco. He told me he was going."

All this time I think I'm keeping a deep, dark secret. Afraid someone will hold a hot poker to my face, or string piano wire around my earlobes to get a confession out of me. I'm being loyal to Buzz, and Buzz goes and tells Burgie. I feel like an idiot.

"Okay . . . who else knows?"

"Stoika, I told her. Jeanie knows and Stoika told Leslie."

My frustration quotient has been reached. I slap my forehead loudly over and over with a copy of *Days Of Future Passed*. The cardboard cover makes a sharp, piercing smack and everybody in the store stops and stares at me.

"But he told me not to tell anybody!" I yell.

"Well, he didn't tell me not to," Burgie replies nonchalantly, tapping his fingers to *Love Is For The Very Young*.


As long as Buzz is in San Francisco, with flowers in his hair, why are we sitting around in heat-scorched, smog-impacted L.A.?

Every parent in every suburb and city in the world is convinced San Francisco is the closest thing to Sodom in modern-day culture. There is no convincing the mother and father of a seventeen year-old that sending him or her to hang around the streets of Haight-Ashbury is a fun and enlightening thing. The newspapers are jammed with stories of kids freaking out on acid and jumping off bridges, buildings, buses; anything anybody can jump off of, there is a story that some dope-crazed kid did it.

So, faced with the overwhelming odds that our parents will give the proverbial thumbs-down to our little adventure, we do what every other seventeen-year-old kid who wants to get to San Francisco does. We lie.


"Mom? Dad? I'm going to Yosemite with Burgie." My father nods passive approval.

Mom, however, squints into her now infamous Nancy Rivers Reptilian Gaze and purses her lips.

"Oh? Who's going with you besides Burgie?"

I sense the time has come to break out the parent-child tap-dancing shoes. Maybe she knows something, or maybe she's bluffing. I can never actually tell with her. But after years of falling into her traps, I decide it's better to give no information at all than dribs and drabs that can lead to lots of trouble. I play dumb.

"Nobody."

"Stoika called." Trouble. She does know something, and if anybody is going to slip, it'll be Stoika. Her parents think it's a wonderful idea to go to San Francisco. So great, in fact, that Ludmila is busily cooking half a dozen chickens for us to take on the trip. They can't wait for their red-haired, dark-eyed manic-depressive daughter to get out of the house.

"Now, Nelson," Mom revs up for a speech; she tilts her head to one side and becomes wildly authoritarian. "don't get me wrong, I think it's nice you have a little girlfriend" (note the emphasis on 'little'; like a speck of lint or ball of dandruff) "but I don't think it's such a wholesome idea to go off on vacations together. Not at your age."

I'm stunned. After all these months, my mother is completely unaware I'm seeing Leslie and Stoika is Buzz's girlfriend. I sense she doesn't know exactly what is going on. I feel light at the end of the child-parent tunnel.

"Stoika's looking for Buzz. He went to Seattle to visit his grandparents." I'm having to think on my feet now. I just hope I can remember my stories later so I don't get tripped up during the cross-examination.

Everything is okay as long as it's just me and Burgie. The reason my mother likes Burgie so much is because his father is a cop. And children of policemen don't go running off to San Francisco to smoke dope, lay on sidewalks and play tambourines. Burgie is a  good influence. Buzz, on the other hand, is a one way ticket straight to hell. I can't figure how she's arrived at this bizarre assessment, unless she and Mommy-Monster are busily comparing notes. With Buzz  in Seattle and Stoika  not coming with us, the road is clear and I'm free to go.

But then she proceeds to pack for me.


"Hey man, you're going to San Francisco, not Mars."

Burgie is looking at two suitcases, a four-foot duffel bag, a pup tent, Coleman four-burner camping stove, a Kerosene lamp, pots, pans, enough canned goods for a four-month stay in the Himalayas, two cots and a battery operated Zenith TransOceanic multi-band shortwave radio. He grimaces.

"I couldn't talk her out of it," I tell him. "She said yes and she went berserk." Burgie holds up two fishing poles and a wicker bait-and-tackle bag. The pained expression on his face reverberates all over his body.

"She, uh, thought we might go fishing," I mumble.

Stoika has a pea-coat, a handbag and carries a half-dozen chickens, neatly wrapped in tin foil under her arm. She is a big believer in travelling light. Leslie and Jeanie are less modest with one suitcase each. I'm the only one with two tons of luggage.

It's four o'clock Friday afternoon by the time we finally head west on Pico, all the way to Pacific Coast Highway and points north. Nobody looks back.

"I was worried for a minute. My mom said you called."

Stoika, Leslie and I are sitting in the back of the van, pulling at Burgie's new shag carpet. Stoika unrolls her pea-coat and produces from her handbag a bottle of Cherry Kijafa Wine, a sickeningly sweet alcoholic syrup capable of producing an instant diabetic coma. Her brush with health food and carrot juice lasted about as long as her pregnancy. She unscrews the cap and takes a quick slug.

"Oh yeah. I called 'cause I didn't know what the weather was going to be like in San Francisco and I figured you'd know since your dad works for a radio station." My eyes start to bug out of my head. "It's okay, she said it would be cold up there, but it would be very hot in L.A. by the time you got back. Your mother is very strange. Does she work for a clairvoyant or something?"

No. But I can feel the ominous clouds gathering on the psychic horizon. World War Three is going to break out the second I get home. Still, a week is a long time. Anything can happen in a week. The entire world can change in a week.

I'm hoping it will.

# CHAPTER EIGHT

## THE CHILDREN OF OOFTY- GOOFTY AND EMPEROR NORTON

*"Any sign?"*
*"No. You'd think after playing all these albums he'd respond to something."*
*"Burgie, honest; Dan Hicks And His Hot Licks?"*
*"Yeah, he really likes that album."*
*"Do me a favor and don't play Saucer Full of Secrets again."*
*"I think I saw his finger move. Look."*
*"You're imagining things."*
*"Did you call Leslie?"*
*"I left a message."*
*"How are you feeling?"*
*"Like a thick white cloud."*

\*       \*       \*       \*

We arrive at the outskirts of San Francisco at five in the morning. We pass Oakland and head to the Bay Bridge. It's dead quiet out. We're only one of three cars on the entire freeway. The fog has rolled in hours earlier and The City is engulfed in a thick white cloud. We don't sleep, we can't. It reminds me of Christmas morning. We're too wired from anticipation to do anything as mundane as sleep. If we did, we'd be afraid of missing something, and we don't want to miss anything.

We're also afraid if any of us goes to sleep, it'll be a signal to Burgie, who is trying desperately to stay awake, to pass out.

Slowly, slowly, slowly, as we creep across the bridge, into what seems like a void of swirling outer space, the city begins to appear. Burgie has his window rolled down, trying to get the cold morning air on him to keep him awake. The breeze that blows in is a heady mixture of salt-water-fishy dampness and the sweet aroma of roasting coffee beans from the Hills Brothers Coffee plant a half-mile away. Through the fog we can make out the Hills Brothers sign; the motto, Good To The Last Drop, emblazoned in ornate script underneath. The red neon pierces through the fog, turning the air pink along with it.

Everything about this place has an air of magic to it; the mystery of some great unexplainable event just about to happen around every corner. There is a mythic luster to this city, it glows like no place else on earth. Not that I've been to every city on earth, L.A. and Cleveland being the only two. But I believe San Francisco is the logical appointee to the 'heaven on earth' mantle.

And I have good reason to believe it. The upper floors of office buildings vanish, swept into a grey, murky void. Streets reach endlessly up high hills, straight into oblivion, with no indication of ever coming back.

It's unbelievable, even as a bus roars up behind us, switching lanes quickly and thundering past. Its diesel engine spews exhaust into a large, vaporous black cloud which quickly fill the van, even as Burgie vainly rolls up the window to avoid getting dosed. It is, after all, still a city.

We really don't know where we're going. Burgie has a map, but Jeanie gets carsick if she reads anything while we're moving. Stoika has downed her bottle of Cherry Kijafa and passed out a few hours earlier around Fresno. As the sky starts to change color into morning, she slowly wakes up from her alcohol-induced sleep and sits up, peering out the rear window, singing Kurt Weil's *Alabama Song*; The Doors version, or maybe Lotte Lenya's. It's hard to tell with her voice.

Burgie has the presence of mind to take the 101 offramp north to the Market Street exit. Haight Street is just a block or so away.

We drive down Haight Street and it's your typical San Francisco neighborhood at first. It's not until thirty or so blocks later that we realize we've found Mecca. Most of the stores are closed, but people are hanging around anyway. We're driving past places we heard about in L.A. Fabled places. House of Richard, The Blushing Peony, The Print Mint, The Straight Theatre.

Burgie starts to nod out at the wheel.

"Burgie! You're gonna miss everything!" Jeanie keeps yelling, slapping his arm.

Burgie turns to her, beyond exhaustion. "Come on, Wilma, we got a whole fuckin' week to go sightseeing."

We continue trundling down the street as the darkness gives way to a slowly brightening shade of grey. More people surface. They come from nowhere, maybe from all the disappeared office building tops, all the vanished streets. The street is beginning to come alive. Even if it is people going to work.

We get as far as the entrance to Golden Gate Park before Burgie pulls the van into the first empty parking space he can find. He stops the engine and slumps over in the driver's seat. He stays that way, and starts snoring loudly.

We're parked across the street from the Panhandle; a grass and tree covered strip of land that runs to the entrance to the park. A line of people forms. They run the gamut in costume from wild rainbows of flowers and robes and ecstatic hair to thick Mexican serapes, somber grey trenchcoats and olive drab Army jackets. Everybody's wearing beads. Everybody keeps some kind of rhythm with their feet.

Jeanie rolls her window down and sticks her head out. We get a blast of cold, crisp morning air and hear the unmistakable sound of drums, percussion instruments, tambourines and finger cymbals. Anything that can make a musical noise.

A short guy, about five-foot-two, with a walrus moustache, thick dark hair and bushy eyebrows, traipses by the van and sticks his head in Jeanie's open window. He's smiling like he's just learned how. She shrieks.

"So, you guys going?" he asks. "It's breakfast time."

He turns and heads off with his friends, another guy and a girl who both look like they've been up all night, towards the Digger Feed; a once-every-once-in-a-while free food giveaway that happens on the Panhandle. We see notices stapled to telephone poles:

**FREE FOOD - HEALTHY CEREAL - FRESH BREAD - FRESH FRUIT**
**BRING A BOWL AND SPOON TO**
**THE PANHANDLE AT ASHBURY STREET.**
**SUNRISE - SUNRISE - SUNRISE - SUNRISE - SUNRISE**
**IT'S FREE BECAUSE IT'S YOURS!!! - THE DIGGERS**

We leave Burgie unconscious in the front seat and pile out of the van. My feet hit the concrete, the first solid ground I'd been on since we left L.A. and it feels sensational. I'm tingling all over. The air is brisk and heady in its jabs of cold. Row after row of stately Victorian homes line the streets, all looking incredibly clean and bright, with polished facades and windows.

Leslie and I walk arm in arm. Stoika's already ahead of us. Jeanie, as usual, straggles. We stop and wait for her to finish putting her sweater on. Jeanie isn't comfortable here. She really didn't want to come to San Francisco in the first place. But since she's possessive of Burgie, and he wasn't going to stay at home, she wasn't going to be left out. Particularly with all the free love she's been hearing about lately.

The crowd at the Panhandle quickly swells to several hundred. Eating seems like a secondary thing. Several huge cardboard boxes are being foisted around. They look like the boxes you'd pack a refrigerator in. They're loaded with all kinds of bread. Dinner rolls, French rolls, torn up loaves of rye, Italian, sourdough, Wonder Bread, pumpernickel. Everybody takes a few pieces, then passes the box on to the next person. The fresh fruit and healthy cereal from the flyer never seem to materialize, but nobody seems to care.

"We just got here from Wichita man, and this place just fuckin' melts my mind, man!" a bubbly short girl with pressed-flat mousy brown hair and fire-hydrant eyes announces to the people in front of us. She keeps clacking her teeth together. Her whole body seems to vibrate. She tells us she hitched out from Kansas with her boyfriend and his sister. She hasn't slept in four days and, as she puts it, "Man, I don't fuckin' think I'm gonna fuckin' sleep at all, man, it's so fuckin' beautiful here, man!"

I realize, looking around at the crowd, that most all of the people here are from someplace else; some other city or town. Like us, they're hot on the search for Mecca. It's hard to tell if they're going to find it or not, or what their idea of Mecca actually is.

"So, what do you think these do?" Stoika asks, holding seven capsules of different shapes and colors in her hand. She's run off and already made friends with some of the locals, including a guy named Humphrey who wears a double-breasted pinstripe Tommy Dorsey suit, suspenders and a huge tie painted with flowers. Around his head he's wearing a turban and dark Jean-Paul Belmondo shades. The lapels of his suit jacket are dotted with buttons; the largest one says: 'Kiss me, I'm Irish'; the next says: 'I passed the Acid Test.' He looks like he has expert written all over him.

"He said to share these," Stoika adds enthusiastically. She hands us two of each. She bolts hers in her mouth and juts her head back, trying to get it down dry. Leslie and I do the same.

Jeanie is, as always, the lead weight. "What if it's rat poison?" she wonders, peering circumspectly at her pill.

Leslie shoots her a face. "The worst it can probably get is aspirin or No-Doz."

Jeanie keeps her eyes fixed on the pill. After a few minutes of us staring at her like a wax dummy, she reluctantly agrees to take it. But first she needs water.

We go looking for water.

I'm walking in the park looking for a water fountain and I come across a brilliantly white porcelain bowl sitting on a pedestal. I turn to Jeanie and the others and say, "There it is." All of a sudden, my brain disengages from my body and the world becomes this wonderfully soft, sponge-like flickering presence filled with endless colors. Not just the usual palette, like the kind you get with the jumbo box of Crayolas. We're talking about more colors than God. The air and the world in general are full of them and they are rushing at me, all dying to meet me and shake my hand.

Every molecule in the air is a color; I'm enveloped in them. They're warm and living and we're so glad to see each other, although, to be honest, I have no idea why. I've never met these molecules before and honestly don't know them personally. They call themselves Mallory and they act like they know me. I get the idea we're old friends from some other life; old friends who have come to play.

The next thing I know, I'm staring at the sky. It's pitch dark, save for a full, bright moon which turns the trees around me into dancers. The fog is coming in from the ocean and it's threatening to consume the moon: thick and soupy, it slops over the tops of trees. I see Leslie and Stoika lying close by on the ground. We're somewhere near a lake which is still and silent with only faint ripples from the air or the occasional split-second leap of a fish disturbing the glass-like water. I'm looking down at my hands. They pulse with color, but the color becomes subdued and muted and slowly fades.

The image of Burgie flashes across my mind, I don't know who it is at first. It takes me a while to realize we've left him sleeping in the van hours, maybe days or weeks ago. Slowly, I start to come down. First I feel guilty for leaving him there, then I'm paranoid that something really horrible has happened to him. What if he doesn't wake up? What if the oxygen hasn't gotten to his brain and he falls into a coma? Millions of people die in their sleep, for no reason at all. I'm beginning to feel ghastly. My head is a throbbing battleground of contradictions. Burgie doesn't know where we are and, looking around the park, I don't even know where he is.

I want to get up, but it seems to take weeks to do it. Every movement of every muscle and tissue is an ordeal. A painstaking effort at synchronous motion that I just can't pull off.

\*     \*     \*     \*

*"Mister Rivers - do you know where you are?"*
*"Mister Rivers - can you hear me?"*
*"Mister Rivers - do you know where you are?"*
*"Mister Rivers - can you understand what I'm saying?"*
*"Mister Rivers - can you hear me?"*
*"Mister Rivers - do you know where you are . . .?"*

\*     \*     \*     \*

I feel a cold, bracing wind blowing in from the ocean. I'm hearing the dull roar of engines and the far off wail of sirens from some distant fire truck, and the smell of exhaust escaping from a city bus. I look around at the others and mumble a feeble, "Hey, I think we have to go look for Burgie."

It takes twice as long to get everybody in the standing and moving position as it did me; or maybe it just seems that way, because I'm doing all the work. But we finally manage to stumble around in semi-stoned agility and set out to find Burgie.

At first we walk around in circles; the blind leading the comatose. Stoika keeps fixating on her hands, waving them in ecstatic glee in front of her face, sighing "Oh wow!" every few seconds. Leslie is transfixed by the sight of her feet, completely astonished that one actually moves in front of the other without losing balance and making her fall over. Jeanie wraps her arms tightly around herself and stares, watching every move I make. She isn't watching me out of hostility - it's something else. I try not to look back at her, but I can feel her piercing presence with every step. The back of my head feels very, very hot.

It seems like we've been walking for hours, and going nowhere. We're lost, stranded in the forest. Held captive by the Cypress and Eucalyptus trees, and the devouring, blinding, numbing fog. I can see it all now; walking in circles for days until we fall over from exhaustion. Packs of wolves run over and steal our shoes as we drop. It seems completely hopeless.

The sound of traffic is like an echo of another lifetime. I'm in a panic, but I can't say anything to the others. They are, after all, depending on me for a way out.

We keep walking. Leslie clutches my hand. "Do you know where we are?"

"Yeah, yeah. We're just about there."

"Where?"

"There."

An ominous sight appears in the fog. The silhouette of a lone figure on horseback moving slowly toward us. It sends an expedition of adrenalin throbbing through my veins. The hoofbeats become louder and louder. An immense black horse comes into view, bigger than anything in life; but the rider is still draped in darkness. I can't make out a face - oh Christ, is this what death is all about? We stand frozen on the walkway, unable to move or say a word. The horse relentlessly plods towards us.

A flash of light suddenly engulfs us. A booming voice accompanies it, coming from the horse. Oh shit - Mister Ed!

"Hey, don't you know there's no sleeping in the park? Where do you think you're going?" I can make out the jets of steam coming out of the horse's nostrils. The voice comes from the Park Ranger, who sits on top of the horse, making his nightly rounds. He isn't a particularly jocular fellow. He is, truths be known, monosyllabic and beefy, with runny blue eyes that squint and a handlebar moustache that stands straight out on either side of his oval-shaped head. He is somehow convinced he's in the lap of Carson City and we are all cattle rustlers. We snap into the innocent tourist mode and ask how far it is to the Panhandle.

He doesn't say a word. The horse blows out clouds of steam. It finally replies, "Are you serious?"

"Yes honestly, we're lost," Stoika pipes in.

Silence. We're not sure if what we're saying is the right thing or not. He flicks off his flashlight. We're now plunged in darkness again.

He lets out an exasperated sigh. "It's ten yards that way," he says, snapping the reins on his horse and slowly moving away.

"Which direction?" I ask.

He stops and turns around and, with complete annoyance, barks, "Follow me!" and puts Mister Ed into a walk.

We follow, feeling incredibly stupid, because a few seconds later, we come face to face with a traffic jam on Fell Street.

Leslie stops and points to something down the street. "Is that Burgie's van?" It is.

We race down the street with all the agility of dancing refrigerators, stumbling and staggering and feeling very, very slow.

We stand around the big Loaf Of Bread, peering in the window. Burgie is nowhere around. Maybe it really isn't his van after all. Maybe somebody's kidnapped him. Maybe he's never been there in the first place and we've imagined everything.

"Nice goin' assholes. What took you?" The voice comes from the corner, a half block away. We turn around. It's Burgie.

He's leaning against a telephone pole, watching us wander back and forth. We must've passed him several times, but didn't see him. He isn't too thrilled about being left alone. He looks hurt, pissed off and abandoned.

But we're thrilled to see him. It seems like months since we left him sleeping in the driver's seat. It becomes a chain reaction. Jeanie starts to yell and runs toward him, the rest of us follow.

Burgie's eyes widen when he realizes we aren't going to stop. We're heading directly for him. He bolts across the street to the Panhandle. We chase after him.

He begins to laugh as he runs. Burgie always laughs when he's worried what people are going to do. It's a high-pitched, modulated chuckle that's infectious when you hear it. It gets everyone laughing within earshot. We finally catch up with Burgie and fling our arms around him, trapping him in the middle. We tumble to the ground with Burgie laughing hysterically. He loves it and completely forgets how pissed off he was just a few seconds earlier. Once again, we're one big happy family; minus Buzz, who is still somewhere in the city.

# CHAPTER NINE

## HOLIDAY IN MY HEAD

San Francisco has a population of a half-million and they all seem to be stuffed into the Haight-Ashbury district at the moment. It's wall-to-wall people of every conceivable kind and type. Finding Buzz in this mob is going to take a clairvoyant. And four out of the immediate five people coming down off acid aren't really a good place to start. Burgie has lots of energy - he's rested. So we follow him with cast-iron legs down Haight Street.

Jeanie is still staring at me. She hasn't let up since we got out of the park. Staring holes, holes the size of Swiss cheese, right through me. Leslie doesn't notice, Stoika doesn't notice, Burgie doesn't notice. Only I notice.

I stand outside the Print Mint, keeping a look-out for Buzz, hoping he'll show up. Burgie, Leslie, Jeanie and Stoika have gone inside to check out posters, which they are buying by the armload.

Jeanie walks out and stands next to me. She stiffens and for once, won't look me striaght in the eye. It makes me feel like she's trying to pass a state secret. She leans over, and in conspiratorial tones goes; "You know I'm in love with you, don't you? You know I'd do anything for you." She turns her head slightly to face me and I can see from her eyes that Jeanie Nurstrom has a very large screw loose. "I want to have your baby. Nobody has to know." She shoots me a quick, piercing gaze and looks away again. "Think about it."

She vanishes back into the store and doesn't say another word. I'm stunned by this confession from nowhere. It is, after all, flattering, yet unnerving since the person giving the compliment is a complete and total whacko.

Burgie, Leslie and Stoika amble out of the store with a thick roll of Fillmore posters. We continue our search for Buzz, but not before Jeanie tosses me a half-smile with a look in her eye that reads like an old Valentine's card: "Our eyes have met. Our lips, not yet. But wait, you kid, I'll get you yet."

We continue our trek up Haight Street for several more hours. It doesn't look likely we'll ever find Buzz, with swarms of people jamming the streets. The locals have complained that the Haight isn't the same as it was a year earlier, or as magic as it was. People have died of overdoses, murders and accidents. There's been the creeping influence of heroin and speed; there's a new hostile element moving in and people are moving out. And maybe that's so, but the streets are still filled with people looking for a different life, wanting to be part of some exotic and hip scene. The incense wafting out of the stores and houses is still as intoxicating. The music filling the air is still hypnotic and I don't know the Haight from two years earlier. I'm here in 1968 and the world is a pretty beautiful place.

But when the school bus shows up, painted a mind-altering splash of psychedelic colors, and lumbers to a stop in front of the Straight Theatre, it's not such a big surprise to see Buzz stagger off with fifty other people and lurch inside the lobby. Buzz has his hand firmly planted on the ass of a young girl in a paisley, tie-died granny dress. She has short, shaggy dark hair. Her eyes are almost covered over with bangs and her nose is red from being in the sun all day. Buzz keeps rubbing her ass, running his finger up and down the crack as they float into the theater. She doesn't seem to be wearing any underwear. But she also doesn't seem to need any.

I look over to Stoika. Since our experience with Humphrey's magic beans, she seems as laid back as the rest of us and the sight of Buzz hasn't fazed her. At least, her forehead doesn't wrinkle the way it usually does when something sets her off.

Burgie decides to go in after Buzz, while Stoika stays outside with the rest of us. I keep a safe distance from Jeanie and stay close to Leslie. Stoika turns to me and says, matter-of-factly;

"I don't care who he sleeps with, just as long as he doesn't come back with the clap."

Stoika has definitely changed. A day before, she never would've said that.

After a few minutes, Burgie and Buzz emerge from the theater. He has a hickey on his neck the size of Chicago. The whites of his eyes are glazed and the color of fire hydrants and his tongue is thick and slurry. His nose is red and he's barely able to make two syllable sentences.

Since his arrival in San Francisco a week earlier, Buzz has grown the beginnings of a beard. His face is thick and stubbly. His hair is wild and uncombed. He's soaked in Patchouli oil and has several strands of beads around his neck and a small bell that tinkles quietly as he walks.

When he recognizes us, Buzz flings his arms out. He grabs me, Stoika and Leslie in one huge hug. As stoned as he is, he manages to avoid Jeanie, who inches herself further and further away from his reach. She was hoping we'd never find him.

He yells, "This is so happening, man!"

He turns to Stoika and, lifting her off the ground, swings her in the air like a rag doll. She isn't ready for the sudden show of strength and screams. But the scream quickly turns into loud staccato laughter. Buzz is just about to lose his balance with Stoika suspended in mid-air. So Burgie and I quickly prop him up from tumbling over on the sidewalk, or worse, spilling over on Haight Street and getting run down by one of the hundreds of cars driving by, with occupants leaning out, taking flash pictures, or yelling for directions to North Beach.

When the sloppy greetings die down, Jeanie puts her arm around Burgie and keeps asking when they are going back to the van. LSD has done nothing for Jeanie Nurstrom. I have the feeling she didn't take it and has been faking the whole time. Seeing her with Burgie is like seeing one of those married couples who have been together for so long it doesn't make sense. All they ever do is bicker back and forth, and it's always about nothing. Leslie and I dub it 'The Burgie and Wilma Show' every time they start up.

Buzz, being an almost-native of one week, wants to show us around his slice of paradise. In the short time he's been in the Haight, he's already managed to make friends with the locals, knows the best places to hang out, to avoid, and where to score dope from. He takes us to his favorite place; his discovery of all discoveries. It's natural for him to gravitate to where the water is. So it's inevitable that he found the bunkers.

During the war, there was a scare going on that the Japanese were planning to invade the west coast and either San Francisco or L.A. were the likely targets. So the Army Corps of Engineers constructed a series of bunkers along the beach. They were shore batteries and observation posts used by the Army and the Coast Guard to keep an eye on potential invaders.

The bunkers have long-since been abandoned. The concrete hulks jut out of the sand, bracing against the cliffs looking out at the waters. Some have already been torn down, reduced to flat slabs of concrete, dusted by blowing sand and overtaken by weeds. But those that remain are shelter to whoever finds them and pays no attention to the barbed wired and the 'No Trespassing Under Federal Law' signs. Apparently, nobody does because the fences are trampled over and the signs are hacked up to the point where all they say is a hardly menacing 'No Tre---.'

We park the van along the Great Highway and wander down some ancient wooden steps to the beach. The ocean is completely covered in fog. It's like wandering around in a mountain of cotton. There's an eerie tranquility to the place. From nowhere, waves break on the sand, then get sucked back to the still and numbing silence.

Buzz leads us up to a thick concrete building with slit-openings. There's a large iron door at the entrance. Evidently at one time it was padlocked, but the lock has long since been broken off. He knocks at the door, then turns to us and says, "A guy lives here sometimes."He knocks again. After a couple of minutes, he opens the door.

It's dark inside. The only visible light comes from the slits on the ocean-facing wall. It's grey-black versus black-black. Buzz pulls out his Ronson and flicks it.

The floor is littered with trash and bits of burned wood, but the walls are painted with intricate, colorful designs. In a corner, in a small living area, sits a straw mat, a wooden beer crate, up-ended to act as a nightstand and a candle stuck in a Roma wine bottle.

It's as cold inside as it is out. Buzz wants to stay here, but the idea of huddling together on a frozen concrete floor, doesn't appeal, no matter how stoned we are.

Then I have a flash of brilliance. I'm the one with two tons of camping gear stuffed in the back of Burgie's van. We can turn this place into a comfortable crash pad with hardly any effort at all.

So we trudge back up the hill and unload the van and trudge back down like a squad of Sherpas to set up our new-found home. With sleeping bags, cots and camping gear strewn all over, the bunker quickly takes on the appearance of a psychedelic Army barracks. I prop the radio up on the beer crate-cum- nightstand and turn it on. The only problem with the radio is that it gets only short wave. The best I can get is a Hawaiian station, or maybe it's Guam, nobody can tell.

We are lulled to sleep by music from the South Sea Islands, fading in and out. Maybe it isn't Hawaii or Guam after all. Maybe it's The Twilight Zone.

We are all comfortably encased in our sleeping bags when Buzz and Stoika get an attack of giggles. It's the first time I've ever heard Stoika laugh like that.

I wake to see tiny shafts of light starting to filter in through the slits in the wall. The Hawaiian short wave station has gone off the air, leaving only a soft, hissing emptiness in its place.

I gaze sleepily around the room as it becomes lighter from the morning sun. The iron door swings open and Buzz and Stoika appear, back from a walk on the beach.

"Good morning, campers!" Buzz announces at the top of his lungs. He digs into his velvet satchel and pulls out a fistful of Dexamyls. "Time to wake up!"he tells everybody. "Open your mouths and get ready!"He goes from camper to camper, wrapped in his Houdini cape, muttering "Domini, Domini, Salami, Baloney,"dropping a "Dexi"on each of us. Stoika follows Buzz and gives each of us a sip of mango juice to wash the pill down.

The only one not festive is, as always, Jeanie. She refuses to take her pill. Stoika stands over her, the can of juice poised to pour on her face. Burgie turns and says,

"Take it, Wilma, it might change your personality. And that might be good!"Jeanie reluctantly downs the pill, while shooting Burgie a grim glare.

We pile out of our bags and get dressed. The air in the bunker is cold and bracing. We haven't eaten anything since the day we drove up and we're starving. Also, we haven't washed in a couple of days and we're beginning to get a little 'ripe'.

We take our sleeping bags, but leave the other camping equipment in the bunker, figuring it will either be there when we get back; or if somebody needs it more than we do, they can have it; in which case, 'It's free because it's yours!'

Luckily Burgie needs gas, which entitles us to restroom privileges at the Union 76 Station. Most gas station owners are suspect of people racing into the johns and marys with toothbrushes, wash cloths and towels, especially those they consider 'hippies'. To counter the free use of the toilets, the owners have started putting locks on the doors and keeping the keys in the office. It usually means having to go sheepishly to some grease monkey, hop on one foot and beg for the key. Most of the gas station guys are cool, but there are always a few of the right thinking types with attitude problems. They're always at the stations having gas wars, waving huge banners advertising "friendly, courteous service."

When we finish cleaning up and clearing out, we head back to the van. Between the time it takes us to wash, Burgie to pump gas, clean the windows and check the oil, we've all lost our appetites. The wake up call has sounded. We decide to go exploring San Francisco, mostly on foot, mostly at ninety miles an hour.

Early in the afternoon we drive to Berkeley. Buzz knows some people who have a place there. They go to UC Berkeley and he met them during the Om Festival that happened the weekend he arrived.

It's a spacious Victorian house. Normal by Bay area standards, a mansion by L.A.'s. The three-story house is painted blue, with white trim and a red, rust colored roof. Somebody got into Americana with a paintbrush big-time. The expansive front lawn is overgrown and has been partly taken over by newly planted fruit trees. Holes have been dug all over the lawn and scrawny sticks with spindly branches. House Beautiful isn't likely to give thumbs up.

We walk up the front steps to the porch. Above the front door, a massive slab of oak with stained glass imbedded at eye-level, is a sign that simply reads Jollity Farm. Buzz rings the doorbell and waits.

"Buzz!" shrieks a bubbly voice. We don't know the voice, but we recognise the face. It belongs to the girl Buzz was wrapped around outside the Straight Theatre yesterday. Her name is Brenda, but everybody in the house calls her Misty Roses. She's responsible for the holes in the front lawn and the emaciated fruit trees. She's a little over five-feet tall and speaks with a husky whiskey-tinged voice.

Stoika isn't falling over Misty like a long-lost friend, but she isn't rolling up her sleeve to haul off and whack her either. Stoika is friendly at a distance. Misty lets us in the house.

The place is as vast inside as it is out. I have never been in a house this big. The ceiling must be at least fifteen feet high and is painted black with a display of the Southern sky on a clear moonless night. It's an immense galaxy above our heads. The walls are pale blue with painted white clouds billowing up from the floor. All around the front room are huge pieces of carved oak Victorian furniture; commodious overstuffed chairs, divans and intensely colorful Persian carpets. An old Victrola sits at the end of the room an upright model with a horn built into the cabinet. Nobody's ever played it, even though a stack of old records sits inside the storage compartment. It's all for show.

How did somebody land all this? Easy. The house originally belonged to Misty's grandmother, who died and left it to Misty in her will. Some inheritance.

Misty is twenty-one. She's been going to UC Berkeley for three years, studying Philosophy. She dabbles in art and is designing a set of Tarot cards based on Hindu mythology. That immediately strikes a harmonious chord with Stoika who, since we've known her, has been looking for a good set of Tarot cards and an equally good reader to go with them.

Stoika, Buzz and Misty wander upstairs, while Burgie, Jeanie, Leslie and I sit in the living room, stare at the ceiling and listen to Fred Neil albums on the stereo. Jeanie exchanges boozy stares with the house cat, a large grey tabby named Obelix, who sits on the window ledge in the living room, his tail slung over his shoulder like a cheap fur choker.

It's late in the afternoon and the Dexamyls we took that morning are starting to wear off. We're getting cotton-mouthed and maudlin and I keep thinking of L.A. By this time next week we'll be back there. Back to our drab, dreary, wretched, horrible, dry-as-dust, rotten, miserable lives. With nothing to look forward to but more school and, after school, the draft and the Army and getting shipped off to Vietnam and coming home in a box and why is Jeanie staring at me? She's not in love with me. She hates me. She probably wants to kill me. Worse, she wants to set me up so Leslie will think I'm having an affair with her and Burgie will find out and they'll both stop speaking to me. Jeanie wants to ruin my life; she's going to make it her goal. Divide and conquer; that's what Jeanie Nurstrom is all about. I can tell by the way she looks at me; the sly, insidious gaze, while stroking Obelix's chin. This woman is evil.

I hate speed. It's nice when you're up, but coming down uncorks every ounce of paranoia in your body. Every demon comes leaping out of the closet, clanging pots and pans.

People start wandering in. The roommates. The first one is a guy with wild curly hair parted very neatly on the side. He wears dark shades and a Van Dyke beard. He appears comfortably loose, with a wool sport coat over a black tee-shirt, loose-fitting blue jeans and oversized sandals. He steps inside the living room and regards us for a moment. He raises his arms, positioning his hands as if he's framing us in his mind's eye, and yells out "Caramba!" before vanishing upstairs. It's Andy, the self-proclaimed Dadaist, who is the author of a work entitled The Manicotti Report. As he explains it, it's loosely based on obituary columns from random newspapers, interspersed with supermarket sales ads and personal announcements against a background of Musique Concrete.

After Andy comes Mario and Pleasant. Mario is a biker-poet who restores furniture. It explains most of his handy work around the house. He is a bear of a human being whose grim and foreboding exterior belie the interior of an arch romantic. Mario talks with his hands; thick, calloused and encrusted with dirt, but completely expressive. They wave around him like wands.

Pleasant, on the other hand, isn't. In the world of contradictions, she takes grand prize. She mistrusts everybody and takes an instant and complete dislike to us. She is the total opposite of Mario. She's thin and has long, veiny hands. She has soft brown hair that runs down her back in tiny curls. She has delicate features, almost angelic in a way; with red cheeks, a slightly cleft chin and dark brown eyes. One look at her and there's no question she's lovely. But she hates everything and everybody and there's no point in even trying to make conversation with her. She has the extra bonus of a shrill and grating voice that can cut through steel, and she uses it to complain loudly about everything and everyone. She's a miserable human being who has the gross misfortune of looking beautiful. Oh well. God gives out looks and personalities; not necessarily at the same time or in any particular order.

As the afternoon drifts into evening, the house keeps filling up. More people wander in and wander past. I lose track after a while. But the house is so huge it still seems empty.

Misty, Buzz and Stoika come back down to the living room and ask if we want to spend the night. Nobody objects, so Burgie and I go out to the van to retrieve our sleeping bags.

We're walking down the driveway, past the kitchen, when a loud, piercing voice blasts out:

"You don't expect me to fucking cook for all those fucking people, do you?" It can only be Pleasant.

"You know, God has a sense of humor, doesn't he?" Burgie asks.

"Must," I answer, looking back towards the kitchen.

Dinner is a communal affair, minus Pleasant, who vanishes when we begin to commandeer the kitchen. All we see of her is a rear view, disappearing out the kitchen door, which she slams loudly in disgust behind her. So we take over and proceed to make ten pounds of brown rice, stir-fry any vegetable we can lay our hands on and open a couple of gallon jugs of Red Mountain Wine. Misty's speciality is a thing called 'Ho Chi-Minh Soup' which she throws together in a huge pot while Andy and Mario roll joints and set the table. The whole thing reminds me of Thanksgiving dinners we used to have when I was a kid. People spill out of rooms at the smell of cooking food and, before long, there are more people in the kitchen, cutting vegetables, washing dishes, boiling water, drinking wine, than there are anywhere else in the house.

It didn't occur to me how hungry I had become. We are well into our second day of not eating. When Mario wanders into the kitchen holding an immaculately rolled joint - an art form I've never quite gotten the subtle points of, being left-handed, with ten thumbs and requiring at least five hundred feet of rolling paper - we all take turns smoking it. With each subsequent hit, a strange gnawing and gurgling starts erupting in my stomach. It feels like some gargantuan vacant pit has suddenly opened and is demanding to be filled. It's not just me. Leslie, Stoika, Jeanie, Burgie and Buzz are all going through the same gastric trauma.

When dinner finally appears, it vanishes in what seems less than a minute. Like human vacuum cleaners, we consume everything in sight. I remember having a paper napkin in my hand when dinner started. Midway through, I realize it's gone and bits of the napkin are stuck to my lips. I have eaten it.

Every once in a while Andy bolts up and yells, "How does Uncle Ben convert his rice!" to which Jimmy, Velvo and a third guy, who calls himself

The Deep Frost, jump up and yell, "By the patented heat-seal process!" These guys are fellow-travellers of Andy's and they don't say another word after the Uncle Ben's episode. Dinner as art.

With everything inhaled from the table and no end to our hunger in sight, Misty remembers three loaves of Italian bread she forgot to bring out. I volunteer to retrieve them from the kitchen. I get up and make my way to the pantry, past the two-way swinging doors.

The loaves are stacked up in a large silver bowl on a counter top. There's only one problem; I have to get past Pleasant in order to fetch it. She's sitting at a small table in an alcove with her back to me. The alcove is surrounded by darkness. I step past her and reach the bowl. I don't know why, but I have this compulsion to turn and look at her. She's eating a chicken pot pie and working on a crossword puzzle in The Examiner.

I am completely enraptured by the sight of her hands. They're like porcelain as she holds the pen to the newspaper. I have no idea how long I'm standing here, but however long it is, it's too long. With all the subtlety of a land mine, Pleasant bolts around and screams,

"What the fuck are you staring at?"

I grab the bread, turn around and bolt. Not another word is spoken.

"She's a Psychology major," Mario explains. "She wants to be a social worker."

"Fascinating."

I can better picture her as the one who tosses the cyanide pellets into the gas chamber on Death Row.

After a while, a wave of stoned peace overtakes the house. Stoika and Buzz disappear. The roommates have taken their respective rooms and the guests dwindle in number to us, Jimmy, Velvo and The Deep Frost. We stake out areas of the living room floor for crash space. Obelix is having an enjoyable time leaping from sleeping bag to sleeping bag, purring loudly and scratching. Jeanie tries to convince the cat to join her and Burgie. But Burgie keeps slapping the bag shut saying,

"Wilma, that cat burps up a hairball in the middle of the night and you're sleeping in it."

Obelix decides that chewing on Leslie's hair is the thing to do, and it promptly drives Leslie nuts. She keeps tossing the cat off, who comes back for more by taking flying leaps directly at Leslie's head. Meanwhile, on the other side of the living room, Velvo has found a small toy on the bookshelf. It's a kid's toy that, when you turn it upside down, emits a whiney drone that sends everybody in the room into roars of laughter.

In minutes, the living room is reduced to a pre-pubescent slumber party with snorts, giggles, howls and the intermittent drone of the psychopathic Betsy- Wetsy.

The room eventually calms down and people drift off to sleep, even Obelix. The picture window spreading across the living room looks out to Shattuck Avenue and bathes the room in the glow of a nearby streetlamp. Outside, elm trees sway back and forth casting ominous figures on the walls and ceiling. Leslie has wrapped herself tightly around me and I desperately have to go to the toilet.

I untangle myself, peeling back the sleeping bag, and creep out. The cold air wafting in from the open living room window hits me with a jolt. I keep reminding myself that it's a lot warmer here than in the bunker at the beach. I walk slowly down the hallway until I get to the stairs leading to the second floor. The bathroom is just to the right at the top of the stairs.

The stairs creak as I walk up, competing with the snoring echoing around the house. I get to the top of the stairs and turn towards the bathroom. A faint orange nightlight points my way in the darkness.

One of the bedroom doors is halfway open; it's Misty's room. Because it faces the street, her room is filled with the same light as the living room. Even though I'm half asleep I'm still curious, so I amble slowly towards it to get a closer look. I poke my head in and peer around.

Stoika, Buzz and Misty are sleeping peacefully together. Misty has a huge four-poster bed with a canopy draped down at the foot and the sides. The three of them are snuggled together under a thick patchwork quilt. Misty is in the middle, her arms wrapped tightly around Stoika, who is sleeping to her left. Buzz is to the right of Misty, with his arms wrapped around her. Clothes are strewn all over the floor. Sticks of incense have burned themselves out, or are reduced to small glowing stubs in brass holders. I turn and quietly pad back down the hallway to the bathroom.

I have never seen two women in bed with each other before - well, at least not in that way - and I suppose I find it baffling, but Stoika seems happy. And who is anybody to say what makes a person happy or not. God knows, Stoika has enough to be unhappy about - losing the baby and all the grief that went along with it. The trip to San Francisco is the first time in ages that she's actually laughed about anything. She's also stopped drinking so much, and this is significant, because Stoika drank all the time, up until we got to San Francisco. Except for school, her job at Constantine's and her pregnancy, none of us have seen her in a social situation where she didn't have at least half a bag on. I tiptoe back downstairs to my sleeping bag and a wide-eyed Leslie who is uprooted from her peaceful sleep by the two-legged ice cube getting into bed with her. I wonder if life is going to treat Stoika right, or the rest of us, for that matter, and how is it going to wind up, in the long run? It's amazing what you think about at four in the morning when your brain feels a little like a golf ball. Your mind flies all over the place, asking questions you haven't got a clue how to answer.

I am bolted awake by the roar of a 1920s jazz tune, with shrill saxophones, muted cornets and honking clarinets playing on the victrola. I stare up at the black ceiling and the stars on a southern night and feel the warm morning sun creeping in from the picture window. I think for a moment that I have fallen into a time warp and am trapped in a Betty Boop cartoon. I peer around the room and realise I'm alone except for some strange woman who sits on the floor, sideways on to me, with 78's strewn all around her. She wears a thin silk flower print dress and bright paisley shawl around her shoulders. She taps an elegantly shoed foot of soft beige satin in time to the music; and her silk stockings shimmer iridescent in the sunlight, the seams running alluringly up the back of her leg. She is oblivious to the fact that someone, less than ten feet away from her is trying to sleep. I confess, I've forgotten. I've become absorbed by the sight of this mysterious woman.

The record comes to an end. The needle swishes back and forth. The woman gets up and takes the heavy arm off the record.

"Groovy tunes, huh?" she says as she turns around to face me.

Stoika?

At least I think it's her. Her face is covered in makeup - something I've never seen her wear before. White face powder and blood-red lipstick. She's plucked her eyebrows and highlighted her eyes with mascara. I'm speechless.

"Misty gave me some of her grandmother's clothes. What do you think?" She whirls around a few times, showing off the full effect. God, she's wearing a silk slip and garter belt, no less! It's too much.

I get up. I haven't had a cigarette since the ride up from L.A. and I suddenly feel an overpowering urge to ingest some nicotine. Mario smokes and, has fortunately left a pack by the stereo. I stumble out of the sleeping bag and weave my way over. Stoika looks at me curiously, her eyes glancing down at my crotch. I realize I'm naked and quickly retreat, fumbling around in the bag for my shorts and do a one-legged dance trying to put them on.

When I finish hopping all over the living room floor, much to my embarrassment and Stoika's giggling amusement, I resume my trek to the stereo in search of cigarettes. Sitting between the turntable and the first of three volumes of the complete Beethoven String Quartets by The Budapest String Quartet (I knew I liked these people, they have great taste in music!), is a small silver canister with the word "emergency" written on a piece of surgical tape across the top. I flip open the lid and take out a Chesterfield 101.

I look at the pack for a moment; a sailboat on a lake at sunset, pretty scenic stuff for a cigarette. I pull one out, tap it lightly and light it. I inhale deeply and feel the rush of dizzy euphoria sweep over me. I take a second drag after a few seconds and the dizziness starts to go away. I turn around to look again at Stoika, who has now selected *Boneyard Shuffle* by The Arkansas Travellers. The song starts, but I reach over to the Victrola and take the arm off the record. The room falls silent and Stoika glances at me inquisitively.

"Stoika, don't take this the wrong way but, what's happening?"

She rests her arm on the Victrola and looks at me with raised eyebrows, what little of them that are left.

"Something wrong?"she asks.

"No, no, I'm just, well . . . you've changed a lot the past couple of days. I just wanted to know what started it. I'm curious."

She sits back down on the floor, gathering up records and putting them back in their sleeves. "I don't know. I guess I decided I'm not ugly anymore."

"Stoika, you've never been ugly."

She shoots me one of those thanks-but-I-know-better looks. I press the point.

"Look, think what you want but -"

Stoika cuts me off. "All I know is what I used to see in the mirror, and it wasn't very much. I always wanted to be liked by people, but I could never figure out how to do it. Do you know it took me six months to get up the nerve to talk to you guys the first time? I guess what made the big difference was yesterday in the park. I realized that it really doesn't matter what other people think about me. And when the time comes, I know I'm going to make a good mother, but not right now, even though losing the baby was the saddest thing in my life - I think about it all the time and I will always wonder what it would've been like to have it. But it was meant to be, no matter how I felt about it - I wasn't supposed to have a kid right now. Most people think I'm crazy. The ones who know me understand, the ones who don't never will, and what's it matter to them anyway?"

Stoika glows in this new-found happiness, thanks to the wonder-world of chemicals. I guess what they say about better-things-for-better-living-through-chemistry is right.

It still doesn't explain the sudden infatuation with the 1920's and the Clara Bow makeup.

"It's the period of time I relate to the best," she says. "I think it has something to do with my last life. I have this memory of drinking gin in a white bone china teacup and being gunned down on a Chicago streetcorner. I mean, why else would I get bad vibes just from hearing the name J. Edgar Hoover?"

She gets up and puts the arm back down on *Boneyard Shuffle*. The room fills with syncopated hot jazz; a trumpet and piano blaring out loud and tinny on the Victrola. My cigarette has burned down to my finger and I'm looking around for something to put it out in. And for a second there, I thought she was normal. I smile at the floor and look for my jeans.

"I'm happy for you, Stoika. If anybody on the planet deserves it, you do," I tell her while I stuff my legs into my jeans that lie in a ball by the fireplace. They're covered in cat hair; Obelix must have decided to sleep on them. Obelix is a hairy cat.

I'm busy picking out tufts of smooth multi-colored fur as Stoika turns and cracks her mouth into a coquettish grin.

"I saw you looking in the room last night. You thought we were sleeping."

I stop and turn to her and shrug my shoulders. "Look, love is a wonderful thing and you can find it in all kinds of places."

Stoika walks over to me and lowers her head, as if she's afraid she's being watched. She looks at me as I pull my shirt sleeves out from their tangled mess.

"I, uh, never made it with another girl before. It was really interesting."

"So, does that mean you've changed over to girls?"

Stoika squints and shakes her head.

"No. It was just interesting."

I finish putting my shirt on. I reach over and put my hand around her neck and look her deeply in the eyes.

"Stoika, I really think you're okay. I like seeing you happy."

I mean it. Stoika is one of my favorite people. She seldom beams like she does on this particular morning. But then, bee-stung lips suit her and she wears her dress enchantingly.

Burgie, Jeanie, Leslie and Buzz come barelling back in. Apparently, they've been to the campus where they sat and listened to the Stone Street Swami give a lecture on life and reincarnation. Burgie's bought me a pack of Gaulois, the strongest French cigarettes on the planet.

"Here, these are for you to quit smoking."

He hands me the pack. He bought one for Buzz, too, who likes them so much he's happily lighting his second one from the stubby end of his first. The cigarettes are short, unfiltered and make me wheeze just looking at them. Buzz takes a drag and exhales, blowing out a blue cloud that, even as a smoker, almost makes me gag. I thank Burgie anyway for the thoughtful gift. Buzz eyes my pack with a grin.

Stoika's transformation puts everybody in shock. They stand in the living room dazed, unable to say anything, while she gives the assembly a look at the butterfly transformed from the caterpillar.

This is the brand new 1968 Stoika and there is no turning back. Even though school starts in three days and summer is quickly galloping into never-never land.


We spend our last night in San Francisco back at the bunker on the beach. All the camping equipment is gone: the food, the cots, the tent. Nobody, it seems, had any use for the TransOceanic radio, still tuned to the Hawaiian station, or for the fishing rods, as they've stayed where we left them.

We roll our sleeping bags out on the concrete floor and huddle close together, trying to keep warm in the darkness, gazing up at the slits opening out to the fog covered ocean, while The Voice Of Honolulu wafts over our frozen slab of stone with warm hypnotic sounds of steel guitars and voices singing in a strange language; soothing and lulling us to sleep.

Nobody has an attack of giggles tonight; we can't think of any jokes or anything funny to say. The slumber party is over and it's thinking-about-tomorrow that has everybody sullen and quiet.

Leslie seems far away. She hasn't said much to me most of the day. She falls asleep first and it's a heavy sleep, filled with sighs and sudden jerks of her feet, as if she's running, trying to escape. She tosses and turns and, in a sleeping bag ideally built for one, it becomes an uncomfortable experience for both of us.

Burgie takes the slow route back to L.A. It's a bad idea. We want to get the journey over with. We pass Monterey, Carmel, Big Sur and the endless twists and turns on Highway One. Even though the sky is blue and the ocean is spread out magnificently beyond the cliffs, it could be the Polar ice cap for all that it matters.

The silence hanging over the van is appallingly thick. Burgie keeps the eight- track playing to the point where we hear *Dear Mr. Fantasy* no less than twenty-two times by the time we reach the L.A. City limits at eight o'clock.

Pacific Coast Highway is jammed with beach traffic, and we slow to a crawl at Leo Carillo Beach. A thin line of cars spiral down the highway stretching as far as the eye can see; one big red glow of a few thousand snaking tail lights. Buzz breaks the silence and offers up the flimsy suggestion we go to The Cheetah on the P.O.P. Pier and catch The Chambers Brothers and The Paul Butterfield Blues Band. We look at him with sour, indifferent eyes. Even he doesn't really want to go.

Burgie makes the rounds, dropping us off at our respective homes. Jeanie's first, she lives the furthest west. She gives Burgie a kiss that lasts twenty minutes. They part lips long enough for Wilma to tell Burgie to come over later.

Buzz and Stoika are next. Stoika climbs out of the van looking like Gloria Swanson from Sunset Boulevard.

Buzz follows her out. He wants to see how Carl and Ludmila are going to react to their new daughter.

We stop at Leslie's house. She quickly opens the door to the van and gives my hand a gentle squeeze. She pecks me on the cheek and tells me to call her the next day, but doesn't think she can see me. Before I can say anything, she runs up the steps to her house and disappears.

We drive off and I am completely confused. During the entire drive home, she wouldn't tell me what was going on. Despite my asking her every hour if something was wrong, she repeatedly told me it was nothing; she was fine.

Great. She was fine. I'm the one feeling like a hockey puck!

Burgie pulls the van to a stop in front of my house. The lights are out, but it's not a sure-bet there won't be anybody home. He turns off the engine and stares ahead at the street. I'm about to launch into my conundrum over Leslie when Burgie suddenly blurts,

"I've gotta stop seeing Jeanie, it isn't working out. What do you think I should do?"

He's asking my advice on a subject I know nothing about. After spending much of my teenage life trying to fall in love, it's never occured to me that I would be faced with the problem of how to fall out of it. Granted, Jeanie Wilma Nurstrom is not exactly high on anybody's admiration list, and breaking up with her is the smartest thing Burgie can do. But there's still something sad about the process and I'm at a loss to tell him how to handle it.

"I don't know Burgie, why don't you just play it by ear and see what happens next semester."

My rule of thumb; if all else fails, play it by ear or pretend it doesn't exist and hope it goes away.

I have the habit of never listening to my own advice. With my two tons of camping equipment missing - probably keeping part of the population of Haight-Ashbury alive, if not warm tonight - I open the door, knowing that World War Three is about to break out. I keep thinking, one more year until freedom, as I take a deep breath and step inside.

The house is ghostly soundless. No characteristic growl from Dolores, no TV droning monotonously on in the living room. My dad's red MG isn't parked in the garage and my mother isn't in bed reading *Beyond The End Of Time* or *Travellers Of Space* as she usually does at night. There is definitely something wrong with this picture.

I wander around the house looking for clues. I turn on lights, peer into rooms and turn off lights again. I walk into my room, climb into bed and collapse.

It's the first time all week that I'm not lying on a surface that isn't concrete, dirt or wood and it feels wonderful. The only thing missing is Leslie. So I roll over and stuff a pillow next to me, pretending it's her. I try to kid myself, but it doesn't work. The pillow doesn't even smell like her, not even a trace of her shampoo. Nothing but thin air and hot, sticky blankets. I kick everything off and let the smoggy breeze from the window blow on me.

It feels like I'm trying to sleep in a bed of steel wool. I toss myself out and land on the floor, slamming my foot into my duffel bag and something hard. I clutch my foot in pain, yelling obscenities at the stupid motherfucker who left the bag lying around, before I open it and find the culprit: the TransOceanic radio. I lift it out, set it on my nightstand and turn it on. I flip the dial back and forth in the hopes of finding the Hawaiian station that lulled us to sleep in the bunker at the beach.

I finally find it, or something that at least resembles it, but the sound is dim and distant and it's lost its magic. It's no longer mysterious and tranquil.

I fall back into bed. Maybe I'm surmising things and maybe I'm surmising the same thing about Leslie. She's probably just tired from spending too much time with me. We haven't been away from each other for more than five minutes during the last week. We've been seeing a lot of each other over the past year. We've gotten to be a habit. Spending that much time together can make anybody crazy.

Still, it's lonely in bed, staring up at the ceiling. I imagine big cracks forming, cracks the size of Sunset Boulevard opening up and swallowing me, taking me somewhere; back to Golden Gate Park, to the concrete bunker on the beach. To the sound of waves hitting the sand, to foam evaporating into the fog. Six people sleeping on a frozen floor. I refuse to believe I am home.

I wake up to realize I'm certainly not anywhere else. Dolores died while I was gone. My mother goes through great pains to make sure I see the little mound of dirt in the backyard where she's buried. My dad destroyed the MG yesterday, but it wasn't his fault. He was sideswiped by a drunk in an Impala who swerved across Sunset and slammed into him and three other cars. The drunk was not hurt; drunks are made of rubber. My dad, however, came home from the hospital this morning wearing a neck brace with metal bars protruding over his head, which he's supposed to wear for at least a month. Later on in the morning a tow truck brings the MG back in bits and pieces and deposits them in front of the house for all the neighborhood to see. My father's prized possession has been reduced to broken red parts, like a kid's toy, pulverized by bad luck. It's sad.

I also learn that my Aunt Charney fell down a flight of stairs and broke her leg in eight places. She slipped on a Baby Ruth bar some kid dropped while walking down the steps of the parking structure at the California Federal Savings building on Wilshire. Luckily the bank and the parking lot are insured. It's just going to be a pain in the ass to get them to cough up the money. But Charney, the normal, fun-loving aunt from my mom's side of the family, is dating an attorney who has visions of Bel Air dancing in his head. He's filed a suit for three million dollars.

Dolores is quickly replaced by another dog. A combination Sheepdog-German Shepherd-Cocker Spaniel my mother has found in a supermarket parking lot. She names him Omar and gives him a summer haircut that resembles a fur coat rubbed with Nair.

At least this dog likes me.

Like death, taxes and the common cold, the first day of school arrives. I'm on the last leg of my high school experience. Even though I know it'll be over soon, it's the same old grind, the same old traumas, the same old waking up at six-thirty in the morning. But every now and then, I'll see Stoika wave her hand in front of her face and sigh, "Oh wow."

Some things just stay with you.

# CHAPTER TEN

## AFTER THE LIGHTS GO OUT

*"What are you going to do with that needle?"*
*"It's called a deep pain test."*
*"Shouldn't you be using that thing on a horse?"*
*"Let's put it this way - if he feels this, you'll be happy."*
*"That makes one of us."*

\*    \*    \*    \*

"She bought a box of razor blades. She's gonna go the Roman route."

Burgie's voice is shaking. He's standing in the doorway of my house freaking out; and considering the situation, he has every right to. He's been planning on breaking up with Jeanie Nurstrom as soon as she was stable enough to cope with it. Jeanie was starting to consume him. The reason is an episode between Jeanie and a fistful of Phenobarbital the weekend before Christmas. She claims it was an accident; she swears up and down it was aspirin: she had a bad headache, and grabbed the first thing she found in pill form; a whole bottle's worth.

Leslie, Stoika and I joined Burgie in the Hospital Emergency room that Sunday night, pacing the floor while Jeanie had her stomach pumped. (Buzz came up with an excuse of having to go Christmas shopping with his mother, a task none of us could imagine him doing except on acid.)

After this incident, Jeanie's mother promptly trotted her off to a shrink, but shrinks are only as good as what you tell them. So in a matter of two sessions, Jeanie was given a clean bill of health and pronounced normal. I guess Burgie was hoping she'd get shipped off to some quiet rest home in the country and fall in love with her therapist. No such luck; not in a million years, not with Jeanie.

We're talking jumbo-holiday fruitcake here, not the small box you get at the supermarket. Why she tried to kill herself was no big mystery, at least to Burgie who, in his most diplomatic way, tried to end the relationship with a well worded, well intentioned note. Not a good, bright or practical idea. Girls like Jeanie Nurstrom do not like being dumped via remote control, no matter how good or convincing the printed word is. They prefer it all happens up-front and personal, with real tears, real accusations, real threats and real, honest-to-God goodbyes.

So, the remainder of Christmas vacation, and all the way up to New Year's, Burgie's been apologizing for the letter while trying desperately to convince her not to try killing herself again. It's been working. But lately it's been Burgie's turn to contemplate offing himself. Graduation is just three months away and he's turning eighteen two weeks after that, which means, for all good boys, a trip to the local draft board. Burgie has decided the best thing to do is stop eating.

"I heard they were refusing guys who weighed less than a hundred pounds."

"Yeah, and those guys are less than five feet tall."

"So?"

"So, do you know what you would look like weighing less than a hundred pounds?"

"4-F?"

If he's going to go through with his plan, Burgie needs some portion of his life with sanity attached to it. Jeanie Nurstrom isn't exactly it.

He decides the big day will be March 15th - it seemed to work for Julius Caesar: those fabulous and groovy Ides Of March. It's a Saturday and, it just so happens, a day we're at school. The drama department has been rehearsing The Crucible, an upbeat little play about witch hunts in Salem.

While we're taking a lunchbreak, Burgie follows Jeanie down to the dressing room, believing this is the golden opportunity to break the news.

Jeanie's voice soon pierces the concrete wall and echoes into the auditorium.

"I thought you said you loved me, you fucking son of a bitch! I thought we had a fucking commitment!"

The screaming is followed by the sound of breaking glass, and Jeanie's feet clamoring up the steps and into the auditorium. Fifty dismayed freshmen, with lunchmeat breath, mayonnaise mouths and milk moustaches, watch open-mouthed as Jeanie runs like a banshee out to the foyer and off the school grounds.

I rush down to the girls' dressing room to find a pile of shattered glass that used to be a mirror, an antique lamp from France on loan from the Principal in a million pieces - and Burgie hiding, sitting on the toilet in the comparative safety of the bathroom stall, his head buried in his arms, sobbing loudly.

"Oh, did I fuck up!".

The next day he heads to her house in a frenzy of guilt. He spends the better part of three hours driving back and forth on Jeanie's block before finally parking his van and going up to her front door. She answers waving a box of Gillette double-edge blades and a device she's made for ensuring her potential suicide: two crudely fashioned planks of wood with razor blades imbedded face-up, waiting for two hurriedly slammed down arms. With a wild, cracked smirk, she informs Burgie that she hopes he'll be happy if anything really awful happens to her.

After that, Leslie and I keep him constant company. We take shifts. He sleeps over at my place. My parents are suspicious.

"Why is Burgie spending so much time over here?" my mother asks. "His parents are getting a divorce," I answer. She feels badly for him and makes sure he has pajamas to wear. She gives him motherly advice about when parents divorce and cites several statistics, but in truth, the only person she ever knew to get divorced was her sister Charney, who has been married seven times, and shows no signs of letting up. My father used to joke about Charney, refering to her as The Will Rogers Of Women, because she never met a man she didn't like. My mother's advice falls on deaf ears, of course. Burgie's parents have been divorced for a few years now.

It's about two in the morning a couple days later when my eyes pop open to the sound of a deafening crash. It's followed by a really loud car peeling off down the street. I think for a second; Jeanie got her driver's license a few months earlier, and a 1962 Lemon Yellow Buick Skylark convertible with red interior shortly after that. It needs a new muffler, which means you can hear it coming - or going - a mile away. The logic portion of my brain quickly tags her as the likely candidate.

Burgie, who was sleeping on the living room sofa when the ruckus started, races to the door. He trips over himself trying to get his pants on. By the time he's out the front door, the damage has already been done. He stands on the lawn looking at his trashed van and the cloud of exhaust trailing off, and groans.

The best we can figure, she took a tire iron to the front and side windows, smashing them handily out with one or two taps. To add insult to injury, she's dumped about ten pounds worth of bloody chicken parts all over the front seat.

"Well, look at it this way, Burgie, she isn't thinking about killing herself anymore, she's thinking about killing you."

"This is me pretending I'm lucky". Burgie scoops up decimated chicken parts that have lodged themselves in the stereo. There are shards of broken glass all over the street and the entire inside of the van is covered in a mountain of worthless diamonds.

It takes hours of cleaning to get all the chicken parts out of the van, but the *Between The Buttons* eight-track is history.

The next morning Jeanie doesn't show up for school. She's come down with a mysterious illness and probably won't be back for a while. For his part, Burgie has gone from a state of shock to a state of mourning and now headlong into a state of giddy euphoria.

I know he's on the road to recovery. Yesterday he bounced into the Rexall on La Cienega and proudly announced to the startled pharmacist:

"Give me a one- pound box of your finest rubbers, my good man, and make it snappy!"

So, Burgie's problems are over for a while. Mine, on the other hand, are just starting. Since San Francisco, Leslie has been acting increasingly distant and aloof. Every time I ask what's wrong, she smiles, rolls her eyes with a pained annoyance and says,

"Nelson, you're imagining things; I'm tired, that's all, honest."

It's two in the morning by the time we parade into Ship's, an all-night coffee shop on Wilshire in Westwood. We've been celebrating since four in the afternoon. The biggest graduating class in the school's history, we sit through a ceremony that takes three hours to finally let out. When it's over all we want to do is flee.

We've achieved instant validation; we're filled with the heady scent of adulthood; ensconced in our red Naugahyde booth, flicking ashes nonchalantly off the butts of our Marlboros and Camels, gazing smugly around the restaurant and feeling like the hottest little shits on the planet. We philosophize rhapsodic on the life we already know all about, but, clandestinely, we're scared to death of the unknown one just around the corner.

"Hey man, look at it this way," Buzz says, sinking his cigarette into the sizzling abyss of his coffee cup, which the waitress doesn't notice. "After today you don't have to do anything. You don't have to be anyplace, you don't have to get out of bed, you don't even have to answer the phone. Everything you do from now on is up to you. Is that a trip?"

Buzz has a point, even though the idea seems like a foreign one to me. After twelve years of having to do things, the idea of waking up one morning and not having to do them is bizarre.

We sit around the large table, more quiet than animated. Burgie keeps vacillating between effervescent optimism and silent terror. He has a date with the draft board in two weeks, and even though it's only to register, just the idea of having to walk into a government facility of any kind, even the post office, scares him half to death. He's beginning to resemble a refugee from Buchenwald; he's been on his starvation diet for almost four months now - nothing but lettuce, vitamins and water, and it's showing in alarming ways, mostly how far into his head his eyes are sinking.

When I first met Burgie he was a slightly chunky kid. He was never fat, but he had pudgy parts. He was more or less normal for his height which, at eighteen, is five feet eleven inches. He's now down to ninety-seven pounds. Every once in a while he'll mumble an ironic zinger like,

"Couple more pounds and I'll weigh as much as a newspaper."

He's not looking good and we're hoping he gets the ordeal over soon. It's painful trying to eat with him around. He gawks vacantly at anything resembling his favorite foods; anything chocolate, anything doughy, anything fried.

This is in contrast to Stoika who is painfully thin and has the appetite of a Great Dane. She's the only girl I know who can eat an entire large Pepperoni, mushroom, sausage, extra-cheese Pizza by herself. She instinctively raises an eyebrow at the characteristic whistle of the local Helms truck that travels the neighborhood, and, on occasion, buys herself a dozen Buttermilk glazed doughnuts which she consumes during the walk home.

One look at our table and you would never convict us of being undistinguished. Buzz finally got so many holes in his Houdini cape that he gave it up for tuxedo tails with wide satin lapels. He has two of them, which he found at the MGM Studio wardrobe sale; one black and one white. On this particular occasion he's wearing the white one, and topping the effect with an oversized black beret cocked to one side of his head. A big yellow button on the front spells in bold black letters, 'I've seen it and it doesn't work.' His Surgeon: Bellvue Hospital cap has been temporarily retired.

I spent two months allowance on a crushed blue velvet Edwardian jacket dotted with white flowers in bloom. I resemble a French bedspread. I've gone all-out for the full effect: ruffled shirt, green velvet pants and creme-colored boots. For the first time in my life, I am being mistaken for a member of a rock band.

"Hey, what do you say we drive up to San Francisco?" Buzz asks. I knew he was waiting for the right time to spring the question on us. He's been dying to get back to San Francisco ever since the day we left a year earlier.

The idea is met with enthusiasm from everybody but Leslie, who becomes quiet and subdued. She looks over at me and tugs at my jacket sleeve. She whispers,

"Nelson, I gotta talk to you for a minute?" I nod and we get up to go outside.

We stand in the parking lot, under the sickeningly yellow glare of lamps that illuminate rows and rows of Buicks, Plymouths and Grand Torismo Options. We take turns leaning against the van; pacing back and forth; folding arms, unfolding arms. Leslie looks awkward and I feel sharp, shooting pains in my stomach.

Leslie explains she's been accepted to a college in France, as part of a student exchange program she applied to the year before. She feels guilty and terrible because she's been hauling this deep-dark secret around ever since our first trip to San Francisco, when she first found out she was accepted.

"So when do you have to leave?" I ask.

"Ten o'clock tomorrow morning . . . this morning."

Some unseen group of imaginary people have just kicked me in the head. For a brief moment, I think how great it would be to drive to Pasadena to take advantage of the infamous Suicide Bridge. It seems completely appropriate, but even the sight of a self-inflicted paper cut sends me into seizures of light-headedness and I know I'd never go through with it.

Besides, Leslie assures me over and over that we'll write each other every day, no matter what, and it's only for three years and she'll be home for the holidays, and she won't look at anyone else, and she's only in love with me, and I'm always in her heart, and nobody can ever possibly take my place, and absence makes the heart grow fonder (Jesus, that one too), and she'll be back before I know it.

There is nothing I can do to convince her to stay; the plans have already been set in concrete. The only thing I can do is wish her well and accept, in the back of my mind, that this is it. After almost three years, the great teenage romance of the 60's is over.

We stay up to watch the sun rise from Griffith Park Observatory. Typical June weather: sunrise arrives as a thick blanket of fog. The air smells smoggy and damp and I feel completely hollow.

Leslie's parents are taking her to the airport. She doesn't want us to go with her; she doesn't want to go through all the goodbyes at LAX. So Burgie pulls the van up to the front of her house.

Stoika and Buzz are comfortably asleep in each other's arms in the back, while Burgie taps his feet nonstop and contemplates whether his diet will allow him one cup of coffee. Leslie and I sit on the running board and don't say a word. We hold each other close and stain each other's shoulders with tears. Leslie has gotten emotional at the last minute - even she knows this is it.

We stay that way until we hear the horn of Ken Noritake's Chrysler New Yorker blowing in the driveway. It's time to go. Leslie has been packed and ready to go for days. I feel the unmistakeable sensation that I am being quickly, quietly, politely, pushed out of the scene and out of Leslie's life, even though she keeps assuring me this isn't so. She rises slowly and squeezes my hand tightly before running off to the waiting car. She won't look back and she doesn't say goodbye.

I sit watching as she climbs into the backseat of the car, followed by Stephanie, Dale and finally Ken, who puts the car in reverse and pulls out of the driveway. Leslie buries her head out of sight, but Dale smiles sweetly and waves and, out of reflex, I wave back. I step away from the van to get a clear view of the car. I fix my gaze on the tail lights and ZOB-186 as the car moves further and further away, finally turning right on Pico, heading to the airport. The car disappears ever-so-slowly from view, as if Ken is purposely driving two miles an hour. I'm savoring every revolution the tires make on the pavement, but I can't stop it, and finally the car vanishes like a vapor trail, vanishes as though it never existed.

"You may think your life's over, but it's not,"Burgie says. He leans his head out the window, resting it on his elbow, watching me as my nose fills up again and everything around me becomes a big blur again and I start making baby noises again and stumble into the front seat of the van and get sloppy and stupid again.

"Don't worry, it hurts like a son-of-a-bitch for a while and then it goes away . . . sooner or later," Burgie adds.

Cheering me up isn't doing any good. I know I am going to stay this way for the remainder of my pathetic, horrible, unfortunate, miserable life. There is no point in continuing the charade; I am doomed.

"She said she was going to write you every day, that's got to mean something," Stoika pipes in.

She's right. If Leslie does write, it means she still has feelings for me, but the way it's been going so far I'm not so sure.

"Look . . . maybe I should stay here and you guys should go up without me."

Buzz grimaces. "You can call your parents from San Francisco and they can read you the letters over the phone."

I roll my eyes at the thought. "Oh great. I can see my mother reading a letter from Leslie and going 'I didn't know you two had sex'."

But he's right. There is nothing I can do about it, nothing I can do to stop it. I feel sorry for Jeanie Nurstrom. I'm beginning to understand how she felt.


So we set off for San Francisco. Buzz, Stoika and I have finally gotten our drivers' licenses. Buzz and Stoika take turns with Burgie driving. I, however, am voted unsafe by the rest of the passengers and relegated to the position of hurt-hopeless-vegetable for the entire trip up.

As we leave L.A., Burgie pulls to a stop in front of The Music Revolution on Sunset and runs in, bolting out a few minutes later with an eight-track of the first Spirit album. The album is significant for Burgie, because he remembers it when we were up north the year before. He heard *Girl In Your Eye* for the first time while going over the Bay Bridge at six in the morning. Funny, I was there, but I don't remember hearing a radio playing.

For the next eight hours we get a thorough indoctrination in the album, and by the time we cross the Bay Bridge, we know every word to every song by heart, and would not feel too terrible if we never hear the album again. When we finally arrive in downtown San Francisco, it's not six in the morning, it's seven at night and the tip-end of rush hour.

Things are never like they are the first time. It's true with sex, it's true with places. I'm not sure what's changed, the city or me, but something feels incongruous and strange. San Francisco has become grey and foreboding. The warm, encompassing arms aren't there to wrap us up and embrace us. It's just another place; just another claustrophobic little town.

I feel a truly creeping hostility, an unwelcome atmosphere. The people we meet on the street seem more weary, more paranoid and more contentious than I remembered the year before. Perhaps they were always that way and I chose not to notice them the first time around. Or maybe I'm feeling vulnerable, since Leslie has pulled the proverbial rug out from under me. Either way, every time a speed burnout casualty stands on a street corner and starts launching into a screaming tirade of obscenities to the world-in-general walking around Golden Gate Park, I naturally assume it's directed straight at me.

Given all these inviting circumstances, it's only natural that I decide to live here.

# CHAPTER ELEVEN

## WEATHER IS HERE

## WISH YOU WERE BEAUTIFUL

Ever since I decided that living in San Francisco would be a good idea, it's been pissing rain. I'm not sure if this is an omen, but with my new found freedom, having turned eighteen, and armed with a 2-S draft deferment, I am determined to make the best of it. The means becoming a conscientious college student.

When I graduated high school, my grandfather solemnly presented me with a $500 check for college, which I cheerfully accepted. My bank account, which has never seen more than fifty dollars at any one time, was suddenly swollen with wealth, and I pondered the possibilities of what I could do with this windfall. That was all before I realized $500 didn't go nearly as far as it did when my grandfather went to college. Then it was considered a princely sum, and World War One hadn't started yet.

I need to make things work though, because everything I do and everything I see in Los Angeles reminds me of Leslie Noritake. Also, I have this crazy idea that if I stay in San Francisco for three years, Leslie will be back from Europe and we'll pick up where we left off and nothing will have changed. I often amaze myself that I continue to believe in my skewed logic.

Buzz and Stoika are also staying. We hang out at Misty's in Berkeley until we can find a place to rent. Burgie stays with us for a week, but then leaves to go back to L.A. to face the Draft Board.

We finally get a one bedroom guest house in the Castro District, not far away from Downtown. The front house is owned by a gay couple; Ed and Miles. Ed, the ditzy one, is in his sixties and lives off a trust fund from an office building his family owns in Chicago. He looms well over six feet tall, and weighs a little over one hundred and twenty pounds. Despite a cherubic face, which bears a strong resemblance to Jiminy Cricket, he has gaunt, orange-grey features and small yellow-blue eyes, which are magnified seventy times normal size by thick glasses surrounded in heavy black frames. He rarely leaves the house. Instead, he spends most days and nights sitting in his darkened and cavernous living room, surrounded by rows of dusty bookshelves on which sit thousands of record albums of operas, his TV set;

always on, but with sound off, and an ever-present litre of Smirnoff's 100 proof.

Miles, Ed's roomate, is a cab driver in his thirties. He smokes almost as much as Buzz and drinks from the second he gets home from work to when he staggers back out the next morning. Cuba Libres are his major vice, evidenced by the enormous lime tree sitting in the backyard, the magic ingredient in mixing with rum and Coca-Cola. Miles makes a point of combing the tree clean the second anything resembling fruit appears on its branches.

The guest house is actually a garage, but it's been renovated creatively so it's a comfortable place that gives the impression of being a large Victorian doll house. Although it's very small, we're too excited by the prospects of our independence, and too enamored of the way a freshly painted house smells, to grouse about a living room whose ceiling you can easily touch by not even extending your arm, and a front door you have to hunch over to get through. We call it The minsion, short for mini-mansion. Buzz and Stoika get the bedroom and I sleep on the floor of the living room until we can find a sofa, which we finally locate at a Salvation Army Thrift Shop in San Rafael.

Buzz is studying for his civil service exam. He has it in his head that he wants to work for the Post Office.

"Man, I dig walking and that's what I'd do all day." Buzz has simple wants from life.

Stoika decides she wants go to Art School, which doesn't sound nearly as strange as it actually is. She has absolutely no leanings towards art and no indications she ever will. Still, she's applied to the Art Institute and waits patiently every day by the mailbox for an answer.

After we have settled into our new place, the letters from Leslie start coming in. At first they're forwarded from my parents and then they arrive at the San Francisco address directly from Paris. There is something very warm and reassuring about seeing the small powder-blue airmail envelope with red and white border in the mailbox. As promised, we write each other every day, whether we have anything to say or not. Most of the time we have nothing to say, so we write about what we have seen at the movies or what was playing on the radio; what the new songs are. Leslie is having a hard time adjusting to the culture over there. She feels isolated. In a way, I do too.

Although my earlier disillusionment over the city is beginning to taper off, I still have concerns and worries. For one thing, I'm beginning to wonder how long my money is going to hold out. I've opened a checking account at the local B of A and realize by the time my first semester at San Francisco State begins I'll be down to less than two hundred dollars. Stoika and Buzz are getting regular stipends of twenty-five dollars a week from home, until they find jobs. My parents aren't wild about me living in San Francisco in the first place, so anything resembling money isn't going to be easily gotten from them. The way they see it, if my grandfather considered his contribution to my continuing education enough, it was enough.

*Honey:*

*Your father and I are concerned that you use your money wisely and not spend it carelessly. Too many parents spoil their children, thinking they are doing the right thing, but all too often the money they give their children goes to buying drugs. Nelson, I hope you don't have a drug habit, as so many young people of today seem to have. Please understand our position when we tell you that we cannot send you any money at this time.*

*Love - Mom.*

I get these sort of letters every two weeks, usually around the time I need money the most. And every time I get one, it means I have to go to the bank and deplete the account a little more.

With dwindling money, every cent I have goes into school, food or sharing the rent. I have no semblance of a social life, other than Friday nights where Buzz, Stoika and I hang around the artists' entrance at the Fillmore, hoping to sneak inside. It's worked a few times, but the bouncers have gotten hip to us and we have to think of something else or come up with the necessary cash if we really want to see Santana which, to be honest, I never do.

But it doesn't seem the same without Leslie, so I find myself over at Ed and Miles', sitting in the living room several nights a week, getting sloshed on Cuba Libres, listening to the same argument, always having to do with Ed never leaving the house. He sputters and waves his arms around and cries swimming pools every time he listens to La Boheme. He never answers the door, no matter who it is and he insists they get dairy products delivered every day. Because he never answers the door or picks the milk bottles up when they arrive, there is often the unmistakable aroma of sour milk and rotten cottage cheese wafting toward the guesthouse.

Ed is heading downhill fast. He's considerably different looking than he was as a younger man. Hanging in the hallway between the front door and the living room is a framed photograph taken in 1948; he's standing with the actress Judy Holiday. He's painfully thin, as he is now, but looks eccentrically handsome in tweed suit and ascot. His face is filled with boyish assurance and his eyes are clear and direct, although it was unmistakable, even then, that he had half a bag on. He's been a full-fledged alcoholic for forty of his sixty-three years and, even though he and Miles live together, according to Miles, they've never slept together. When I asked, Miles vibrated all over, recoiling as if he'd just eaten an entire lemon. Clearly, they weren't in it for the sex.

So there sits Ed in the living room, lodged in his green overstuffed velvet chair, ears glued to the speakers piping out Tristan und Isolde and smoking Benson & Hedges regulars. The smoke fills the room, embellishing it in a permanent twilight of blue nicotine mist that clings to the red fauvist drapes and thick brown carpets, turning the beige walls caramel and the book spines a sticky mahogany. A turn-of-the-century tapestry of a young girl, with a bird's nest of curly hair, swathed in chiffon, dancing and playing a tambourine, hangs by the entrance of the living room. It was probably a colorful place once. But it's so grimy now, and stained such a deep shade of brown, that it appears to be a sepia tint.

Ed never gets out of his robe; a red satin smoking jacket. He wears a dark blue and white spotted dickie wrapped around his neck. I'm starting to think these clothes have stuck themselves to him and, if he wants to change into something else, he'll have to scrape them off like water damaged paper from a rotted binding. Ed has lost most of his hair, but insists on wearing a dark red toupee that, depending on how bagged he gets during the day, is either on straight, or crooked to the left or right, or backwards. He shaves once every three days, but manages to slice his face to shreds and spends the time sitting with torn bits of toilet paper glued to his face. He always douses himself in a quart of Old Spice aftershave lotion and a day has to go by before the overwhelming sweetness of the aroma finally subsides. It competes with the eye watering cloud of cigarette smoke for memorable room odors.

Miles, on the other hand, is compact and muscular and prone to flying off into short-fused fits, capped with "Jeeeezzzusss Cuuurrrryyysst I could go for a good screw right now!"

Miles is in his mid-thirties and has lived with Ed since he was twenty-five. He sports a full set of dentures, which he occasionally slides out of his mouth, usually as a reaction to Ed, who feigns disgust and laughs. He once said he didn't really need dentures, but decided teeth were a nuisance, so he had them all taken out, because, as he put it, "they're all gonna fall out anyway."

Miles sometimes takes off at night, heading straight to the local bath house, leaving Ed alone with Huntley/Brinkley or Lucia Di Lamermoor; to look for love, or at least a good screw in some of the wrong places. Ed isn't alone though. There's the dog; a gamy-smelling little hallucination named Highball, a Chihuahua with buggy, snot-caked eyes, who hasn't had a bath in years and whose teeth have all fallen out, except for two rank little shards of ivory that dangle malodorously from its mouth. It probably speaks volumes about his rancid temper. Nobody likes the dog, not even Ed.

"I tried killing it once, but rat poison appeals to him," Ed says, trying to stifle a sadistic chuckle, waving his arms around in bafflement that he could say, let alone think such a thing.

Ed likes me and Stoika, whom he refers to as Madame because she reminds him of an opera singer he once saw in Chicago in the twenties. He always refers to Opera singers as Madame or Maestro. Despite the fact that Ed is a mess, he has a lot of stories to tell. Most of them have to do with the Theatre or the Opera. His mind becomes clear and sharp when he speaks about seeing a particular soprano in an opera he loves. It's as though he's been transported back to the exact place and time through his own words; the real world of the present melts away to obscurity.

He's not so sure about Buzz though. He wonders if that's his real name or an alias from the police. When they first met, Ed made the comment

"Buzz. Sounds like something that runs on gasoline and needs its oil checked every thousand miles." It didn't exactly endear Ed to Buzz.

Stoika's application has been rejected from the Art Institute, while I find that most of the classes at school are full. It seems everybody wants to take Music courses of some kind and the only things left open for me are Math, History and Philosophy 21: the Principles of Aesthetics. It wouldn't be so bad if I didn't have to maintain a level of fourteen credits per semester, but these three classes only add up to eight. I can feel the cold, malicious presence of my draft board breathing down my neck. So I enroll in night school and load my learning experience with such life-enriching subjects as Urban Planning, Latin and Manual Writing.

One of the truly nice things about Miles and Ed's is Ed's piano - an enormous concert grand that sits in the living room, unplayed for the past twenty years, except for the occasional drunken foray into *Auld Lang Syne* every year or so. In exchange for doing yard work, I convince Ed to spring for a piano tuner and, when he isn't hung over I have a place to practice.

It's too late for Stoika to enroll in State or even City College, so she decides the best thing to do under the circumstances is get a job. With her experience at Constantine's during high school, she finds work at a coffee shop called The Minimum Daily Requirement in North Beach. Her job is to bake bread every day. The Twenties Vamp is put on hold, replaced by the return of the Collective Farm Worker. Ed stops calling her Madame Stoika and starts calling her Comrade. She has to get up at four every morning, but luckily she only works until three in the afternoon, since it's a breakfast and lunch place. At least somebody at the Castro District Minsion is bringing home money; Buzz and I certainly aren't.

"Hi Nelson, this is Thea Talber from the B of A. I've got some bad news." Ironically, it's the day before Thanksgiving when the bank calls to inform me my account is overdrawn by fifty dollars. Thea Talber is a teller there. Thea's always there when I go in, and she always makes sure I get her station. Thea is cute, but she's also tall; taller than me, and I'm six feet. When she sees me walking into the bank she instantly kicks her shoes off. I glance at her just as she shrinks several inches, while smiling and waving me over. She likes me. Thank God.

The fifty dollar overdraft throws me into a panic. I have no recourse other than to call my parents collect and beg for the money sent up by Western Union. They reluctantly cough up the needed cash, but not without giving me an extended lecture on the virtues of finding a job and saving money. My desire to be a full-time student, and the lack of part time employment doesn't seem to get through to them. Worse, I'm showing signs of failing miserably on the educational front, having already gotten two warnings from my Latin class that I am close to flunking out, verbatim et litteratim, and all that jazz. When I show up a few hours later, with an envelope full of cash, Thea is there as always. I get her window and we strike up a conversation. The bank is mostly empty and there's no on waiting in line, so she takes her time.

"So now that you've got all this money, you're taking me to lunch, right?"

Thea asks smugly, making no bones about the flirting going on. I smile. I don't know what to say. I think Thea's pretty. I know she's older than me by a year or two, but it doesn't bother me. I like the way she wears her hair, which she sweeps loosely back and ties into a pony-tail. Strands of auburn spill over her ears and dart across her face. She has thick, dark eyebrows, which she doesn't pluck. Thea isn't a sun worshiper; she has pale skin with a light dusting of freckles on the bridge of her nose, which she tries covering with makeup. She always wears pale red lipstick, which is barely noticeable since her lips are thin, like two horizontal afterthoughts on her face. She has dark, magnetic brown eyes. She dresses conservatively, which is understandable for a bank teller. A simple white blouse and snug-fitting black skirt, flat shoes, and the lowest of all possible heels, which in my case are never low enough. She has a small beauty-mark tucked just above her right breast. I'm curious what other beauty marks she has.

I decline the invitation to lunch of course; that would be cheating on Leslie, although God knows why she'd care; she's seven thousand miles away. I make up an excuse about having to be someplace with the money by twelve-thirty. Thea accepts the rejection in good spirit. She pretends to pout, while stifling a grin.

"Guess I'll have to eat my peanut butter and jelly sandwich all by myself then." She scribbles something on my withdrawal slip.

"Maybe you'd like to explain L.A. to me someday," she says, pressing it towards me, brushing her hand against mine, letting me feel the thinness of her fingers and warmth of her hand, while being careful to not be seen by her supervisor. The note has her address and phone number. She doesn't live very far from me; near Divisadero and Fulton.

The weather has been getting progressively colder and the days progressively shorter. This morning I walked out of the house and felt the icy wind of winter blow across my face. Leslie just wrote to say she's going to call me on Thanksgiving. I haven't heard from her in a month. Our promise to write every day has faded and it's just as much my fault as it is hers. We've arrived at the point where we have very little to say to each other, and trying to do it seven days a week is impossible. Still, I get very excited over the possibilities of hearing her voice again. My stomach fills with a jumbo assortment of knots and butterflies from giddy anticipation. It's as if she's been gone for years, not months.

Misty, who has gone back to being called Brenda, has invited us to the Berkeley house for Thanksgiving dinner. I can't go; I have to wait by the phone for Leslie, for the call which, by now, is taking on mythic proportions. Buzz and Stoika invite Ed and Miles, but they decline. Neither of them are big on holidays. Miles says that Thanksgiving and Christmas for him are usually spent in a bar and that it is, in fact, the only place one can truly appreciate the holidays. I bolt out of my sleeping bag at five o'clock on Thanksgiving morning.

A couple of days before, I figured out the time difference between San Francisco and Paris. Five o'clock here means it's one in the afternoon there and, even though I have put the phone three inches from my head, I don't want to leave anything to chance. The house is mostly dark, with only a few glints of light creeping in from outside. Stoika is usually up and on her way to work by now. I'll  hear her padding back and forth between the bathroom, bedroom and kitchen, sometimes grumbling to herself over the cold and the tiny house. But today she's peacefully asleep with Buzz and it's my turn to pace the floor.

I turn on the aging RCA 19-inch black & white TV set that Miles gave us. We hardly ever watch it, but I'm a stickler for tradition and want to watch all the Thanksgiving parades from start to finish. Besides, it gives me something to do. There's no antenna, other than the one I've fashioned from a coat - hanger and some clumps of tin foil, so I sit glued to fuzzy, snow-filled images of the Macy's parade and the J.L. Hudson parade. The phone rings at eleven in the morning and I jump up to answer it; it's Brenda calling to ask if we could bring cranberry sauce. Buzz and Stoika finally get up and get ready to leave for Berkeley around noon. I want to go, knowing I'll miss eating dinner if I don't, but I want to hear from Leslie even more, so I stay.

Twelve noon becomes six o'clock and it's dark again. It's two in the morning in Paris. The phone stays silent. I now know what Miles means when he goes to a bar on days like this. The problem is; I have to wait three more years to do that. I feel angry, hurt and very much like getting drunk. So I do the next best thing; I call Thea Talber.

I've been carrying her note around in my pocket for the past two weeks, but it takes Thanksgiving before I actually do something about it. I dial the phone and let it ring a few times, thinking she'll be out having dinner someplace, or with her family. I'm surprised when she answers.

"Thea? It's Nelson; the guy with the bouncing checks?" She knows; she can tell by the sound of my voice. She's happy to hear from me. I don't mention about waiting to hear from Leslie. She doesn't need to know that. Thea invites me over. She asks if I like red wine and old movies. I tell her I do and that I'll be over in a few minutes.

I walk up Sanchez Street and cross Market. The electric buses are moving slowly up and down the broad boulevard, lighting up the night sky and silhouetting the office buildings with sparks every time they hit a junction in the cable. The noise of the buses reverberates up and down Market Street, which is mostly empty, except for the few people who are, like me, alone on this particular holiday.

I don't mind the fourteen-block walk. It feels good to get out. The air is bracing and the wind is stiff. After a few minutes though, I begin to wonder what I'm doing. It's pretty obvious what the game plan for the evening is. And, even though I am dying from lack of sex, and the thought of making love to those eyes and that milky-white skin and those perilously long legs is tantalizing as nothing else can be, I still feel this gnawing sensation in the pit of my stomach that I'm doing something rotten. I'm lying. Thea knows nothing about Leslie, in fact she knows very little about me.

But if she knows very little about me, I know nothing about her at all. And it becomes obvious that I don't when I open the front door to her building. She's standing at the top of the stairs leading to her apartment, draped in a full length white kimono. Her hair, no longer pulled back in a pony tail, flows free across her face. The stairway leading to her apartment is

112

narrow and dim; only a single orange bulb glowing inside a Chinese lantern provides any light.

When I get to the top of the stairs, Thea opens her arms and draws me close to her. She opens her mouth and it meets mine. She clings to me tightly, as if she's still half-asleep. Her body feels warm, and I can feel her breasts pressing against my ribs. She leads me inside her apartment and closes the door behind her.

The apartment is hazily lit and mysterious. There isn't a single bright light in the place; everything glows either blue or green or orange. The air is thick with incense; an intoxicating mixture of Myhrr and Rose. She takes my hand and leads me down a pale-yellow hallway to her bedroom. It's lit by at least twenty candles. In the flickering darkness I can make out several Buddhas sitting on dressers, on nightstands and on end tables; all smiling cherubic, with their enormous stomachs drooped over small bowls of glowing incense, the smoke billowing up to the ceiling.

Thea turns to face me and unbuttons my shirt. I reciprocate by removing her kimono. All she wears underneath is a black bra and panties. I can feel my pulse racing all over, and the blood rushing to my head throbs in my ears.

We collapse on a bed piled four mattresses high and covered in sheets of black satin. The most it's ever been before this has been making love in a sleeping bag or on a simple white cotton sheet.

Thea is a biter, and it takes some getting used to, but she loves it when I slap her gorgeous ass and that takes no getting used to at all. The part of me still feeling guilty operates the lower half of my body, and it's making its dissatisfaction known. It wants to take a year to get a hard- on. It's so dark that I can't really see Thea very well. I can feel her though, and she feels soft and warm and wet and her legs seem to go on for miles.

"I want you inside me," she whispers. Those are the magic words. I spring to life within seconds. Thea is also a big believer in talking dirty. I'm thinking; 'This woman is a teller at the B of A, who, on most days, is promoting the Christmas Club or car loans, and here she is; moaning over and over, "Fuck me hard, you motherfucker!"'

We calm down after a couple of hours and Thea gets up, wrapping herself in the white kimono, and pads down the hall towards the bathroom, coming back a few minutes later with a bottle of Chianti and two juice glasses. She flicks on her TV and we watch an old Fred Astaire movie.

Thea takes a sip of wine and looks over at me, smiling. "So, do you think we conceived tonight?" I choke. Thea has a peculiar sense of humor. She starts to laugh and nudges me with her elbow. "Just kidding," she adds. "I guess I should be honest with you though." She gets up to lower the TV volume. "You're in bed with a married woman. On top of that, I have a three-year-old kid."

Thea, it turns out, is a lot of things I didn't know about. She leads me down the hallway to look in on a small sleeping figure in a bedroom; a little boy named Josh. Thea is also five years older than me; a wizened woman-of-the- world at twenty-three, and has been married for two years. Her husband is nowhere around, he isn't even in the country. He's somewhere in Canada, near Toronto, and he's going to stay there until the War is over; whenever that's going to be, maybe never by the looks of it. He's trying to get settled before he sends for Thea and Josh.

"Look, he has girlfriends too. It's not that we're uptight about it or anything. We have what you might call an open marriage. Does that bother you?"

To be honest, I'm thrilled. Considering Leslie is still weighing heavily on my mind, and other functioning parts.

Thea tells me about herself. I find out her family lives on the Monterey Peninsula and she is the youngest of five, three brothers and a sister, and has lived in Northern California all her life. She's been estranged from her mother and father and oldest brother for two years, since getting married. Josh, it seems, is an accident and, being a Catholic, Thea couldn't get an abortion. Well, she could, she'd just burn in hell if she did, or so advised the nun who counselled her. Thea likes the whole psychedelic experience, but doesn't get into the hippy lifestyle; having had a bad experience at an early version of a commune in 1965. Her sister is seven years older than her and a writer living in Montana. Her older brother, the one not speaking to her, is an FBI agent. Both of her other brothers are in the service, and in Vietnam; one in the Navy and one in the Army. I have the impression Thea is the black sheep of the family, and for that, the world should be grateful.

She knows without my telling her I am from Cleveland and that my father works in radio. She knows where my parents live in Los Angeles and that my grandfather is still alive and was born in Helsinki Finland. She knows my family name was not originally Rivers, but Riversmith, which had been changed from Roenschmidt when my grandfather hit Ellis Island. She's done some background checking on me via the Bank of America computer and I'm delighted she finds me so fascinating, otherwise it would be truly terrifying.

We talk until three in the morning and make love again until dawn. It's incredible how much Thea likes rough sex.. You could never tell by looking; she has such soft features and such a delicate air. But she goes crazy when I spank her hard or twist her nipples. At one point, she takes my hand and jams two fingers up her ass. It's as though she's trying to act out some dirty, guilty scenario that makes her feel very good, and very bad all at the same time. When we finish, she falls limply back on my arm. She kisses me softly and holds me close for fear of losing me to the thin air. And slowly, slowly we drift off to sleep.


The air is crisp and cold the next morning as it blows in off the bay; sweeping the city clean and making it almost possible to see into the next century. I'm alone in bed as the sun creeps through the bay window overlooking Fulton Street. Thea is already up and playing with Josh, getting ready to take him to Buena Vista park a few blocks away. I stumble out of bed and look for my clothes, which I find neatly folded on a wicker chair by the nightstand.

The bedroom is dramatically different in the daytime. It's changed from dark and mysterious to innocent and sublime. The walls are eggshell white and dotted with Maxfield Parish prints, framed in silver. The ceiling has been turned into a large green and Sienna paisley canopy; it gives the room its soft appearance.

The chorus of Buddhas, smiling down at me as I waffle naked around the bedroom, are a little unnerving. I get dressed and wander out to the dining room, where I am met by a small, large-eyed child, sitting at the bulky oak dining room table. He views me with suspicion. He has adult features, but they are miniaturized to suit his age. I swear the kid has grey hair. He looked different asleep, but then, most everybody does.

"You must be Josh," I say, as I sit down across the table from him. He negotiates a Bozo The Clown bowl full of Cheerios and nods that he is. Milk dribbles a small river off his chin, recycling back into the bowl.

Thea comes in with a cup of coffee in her hand. "Want some?" she asks, giving me a wide grin. I nod and she plops the cup down in front of me and returns to the kitchen to get another cup for herself.

Josh is a noisy eater, smacking his lips, slurping milk and clanging his spoon into the Bozo bowl. He must know I'm studying him, because he stops and peers sheepishly at me, while running the sleeve of his shirt across his mouth, mopping up the ring of milk. He smiles and points his finger at me and says,

"Friendy. Okay, bye-bye, see-you." I don't know what it means; but it pleases him enormously. He starts to laugh.

Thea wanders back carrying another cup of coffee and a small green Melmac plate with three pieces of Pumpernickel toast. She sets the plate down in the middle of the table and hands one to Josh and takes one for herself. "That one's yours," she says, pointing to the last piece of toast as she opens a dish of margarine and drags a butter knife across the pale yellow surface.

"You like kids?" she asks.

"You're the first person I know who has one."

"They take getting used to, but once you do, there's nothing like 'em." She leans over to Josh, playing with his hair. "Right, Bingo?"

Josh grins and points at me again. "Friendy," he says, smiling and laughing.

"Friendy means he likes you," Thea explains, "so I guess we'll be seeing more of you. Can't let the kid down, you know." She sips her coffee while resting her cheek on her hand, watching me as I negotiate the last piece of toast.

We all wind up at the park where we take turns playing on the swing, throwing frisbees and rolling on the grass with the local dogs. Thea wears the flattest possible sandals so that she just comes down to my height. I think it bothers her that she is so tall, but truthfully, it doesn't matter to me. She wears jeans and a tee-shirt underneath a bulky green sweater that keeps her warm from the chilling winds. She's let her hair down and it blows back and forth across her face and sometimes strands of auburn fall deliciously into her mouth.

Thea starts throwing me Love Eyes. I'm beginning to wonder just how legit this supposed husband in Canada really is. Maybe it's all a ruse. In case there was no magic between us, it could be an easy escape hatch. But the Love Eyes are real. I haven't noticed it before, but Thea has a lazy eye. It's the left one and, even though it's barely noticeable, I can tell that her gaze is slower from her left eye as it is from her right. I'm intrigued by that, but I don't say anything to her. It's my own private revelation and I think it's sexy.

I have to tell her about Leslie, but there doesn't seem to be an appropriate time. Especially sitting on a grassy knoll in the park with Josh on an otherwise perfect day. I'm afraid I'll screw everything up.

"Listen, I've got an extra bedroom I'm not using," Thea says, pulling her hair off her face, as she fixes a fleeting glance on me.

I haven't known her long enough to say yes, and even if I did, I'm not sure it's what I want to do. The easy excuse is, I have two roommates who are depending on me for my contribution to keep the house going. But that isn't true. Buzz and Stoika would probably be happy if I moved out because they need the room. But more important, I can't accept her offer because I'm just not in love with her. I like her; I think she's wonderful and, maybe if there is enough time, or if circumstances were different, I would move in with her in a second. But I just don't feel right about it. I could lie, but I don't want to.

"Thea, I have something to tell you -"

"There's somebody else," she cuts in.

After a few seconds of trying to figure out how to put it, I nod my head. She rests her chin on her hand, and looks at me with a Cheshire cat smile spread across her face.

"Is that for real-really or have I moved too quickly?"

"It's for real-really."

There's an awkward silence lasting a couple of minutes. It's long enough for the breeze to become stiffer and the air colder.

"She lives in Paris. She's going to school there."

Thea seems relieved. "Do you love her?"

I shrug my shoulders. "Well, yeah, of course. We've been going together since our first year of high school."

"She loves you?"

What kind of question is that? Of course she does. Thea looks over and gestures with her hands. "Well, if you two have such a great relationship, what are you doing seven thousand miles away from each other?"

I don't have an answer for that. Leslie is living in Paris and I'm moulting in San Francisco. I'm eighteen years old and want desperately to sample the world. Leslie is hanging out at the Eiffel Tower or going to the Louvre or the Paris Opera. To her, I am probably out-of-sight-out-of-mind. She didn't call me yesterday and we haven't written to each other in weeks. Our relationship is dwindling; anybody can see that. Here is an opportunity asking to be taken.

Thea is warm and bright and cheerful and we probably would be very good for each other. But I just can't convince myself that I'm not cheating on Leslie and doing a terrible thing.

"Thea, I really like you. I like you a lot. At the moment I'm not in love with you. That's not to say it can't change. I just want to take it slowly."

"Nelson, I'm a married woman, remember? I just wanted to know if you were interested in my extra room, that's all."

I can tell she's hurt by the way she's become defensive and has made it sound like I'm jumping to conclusions.

"Okay, let me think about it," I tell her.

The afternoon passes quickly into early evening. Barely five o'clock and already it's dark. Josh is tired, so I carry him on my back back to Thea's apartment, by way of a Chinese takeout place, where we order Mu Shu Pork and Josh's favorite, Shrimp Toast.

I stay over that night and the next day. I make a brief appearance at the Castro Minsion on Saturday, and put in a few hours' practice on Ed's piano. The house is uncharacteristically quiet. Buzz and Stoika aren't home, so I leave a note and change my clothes. As I leave, I notice several small yellow boxes of unopened Kodak Plus X, 24 exposure film. I don't know where they came from, but I'm in too big a hurry to investigate. I rush back to Fulton Street.

I don't resurface from Thea's until Monday morning when I have to go to my History class and Thea has to go to work. She has an extra copy of house keys made, and gives them to me just in case. I dangle them on a makeshift keychain as I sit on the streetcar, heading to school.

The more I stare at the keys, the more I picture myself spending a lot of time on Fulton Street.

# CHAPTER TWELVE

## MUMMIES IN MY CLOSET THE SIZE OF CLEVELAND

*"So what's going to happen next?"*
*"I don't know."*
*"If he comes out of this, you think he'll play piano again?"*
*"Why not?"*
*"I don't know. Maybe he forgot."*
*"How do you forget something like that?"*
*"I guess it isn't easy. Is there some way to tell if his hands are damaged?"*
*"As soon as he's conscious probably."*
*"When will that be?"*
*"When him and his brain are on speaking terms again."*
*"I knew there was a catch."*
*"There's always a catch Stoika."*

*       *       *       *

Buzz has passed his much sweated-over Civil Service exam. For his pains he has been rewarded with a cool and groovy uniform and a big leather pouch; and in celebration, he's broken down and paid cash for a lid of honest-to-God Maui-Wowie. He's been smoking dope since he got the good news this morning, so by the time I arrive back from class he is almost completely unintelligible, but happy. He's so happy his eyes are rolling to the back of his head.

Stoika comes home a little later with news of her own; she's pregnant.

"Oh wow! That's so fantastic!" Buzz slurs as he flings his arms around her, lifting her up and dragging her off to the bedroom.

That leaves me to contemplate the universe with my own joint and the TV set where Walter Cronkite, the man whom everyone in America trusts, informs me that, starting December First, mere days away, the first draft lottery since World War Two goes into effect.

The last thing I remember him saying, before blanking out, is that all draft deferments are off and everyone of draft age is eligible for one year. In that year, birthdates are drawn at random and each date is given a number. Your chances of getting drafted depend on how high or low the number is. It seems like a fair solution, unless you're born on the day they pick number one.

There's a knock at the door. My eyes focus on the small clock radio next to the sofa. It's become three hours later than the last time I looked. The knock is persistent. Not realizing my legs have become lead weights, I jump up, but nothing seems to happen. I try several times before I finally give up and yell,

"It's open!"

It's Miles. He's weaving back and forth from one foot to the other, smiling, puffy-eyed, and three sheets to the wind. "Guess what! I found a new psychic. This one's too much for television!"

Miles has made a hobby of seeing psychics; usually a different one every two weeks. But he's particular about the news he likes to hear. It always has to do with his sex life and he always wants to know when, where and how he is going to find the next great love of his life. Miles hates doing things alone.

He needs to have somebody with him so he can compare notes. He always gets tanked-up before he comes over to make the pitch, being a little embarassed that I'll say no, which I always do. I'm not a big fan of psychics. I always prefer to be surprised by the future. So when Miles stumbles over with red, pleading eyes, I usually find some excuse not to go with him, even if he does offer to pay.

Tonight, however, I decide to go.


ClareJune Abernathy lives in Daly City. The one place where you can get completely lost merely walking down the street. Every house looks exactly like every other house. The uniformity is terrifyingly charming. We finally find the place after many passes around the block.

George Abernathy, ClareJune's husband, opens the front door. He has mousey eyes that squint, and thick wire-rimmed glasses that magnify his eyes, to the exclusion of the rest of his head. He has three strands of white hair, which he plasters back in a dramatic sweep. He wears a red flannel shirt and beige slacks held up by a large black belt and an enormous silver buckle emblazoned with the Southern Pacific Railroad logo. He gives us a faintly disdainful smile. He has a jaw like a cardboard box. He doesn't say very much, but looking at him, I can feel what he's thinking. George assumes we are a gay couple; Miles isn't flamboyant, but he slips every once in a while, usually when he's surprised or when something strikes him as particularly funny and then he lets out a high-pitched shriek. I appear merely strange; with a foot- long beard, hair halfway down my back, an oversized tie-dyed workshirt and hip-hugger bell bottom jeans. George views both me and Miles with an air of passive disdain. He can't hate us; we're paying customers. But he probably dreams of murdering us in our sleep.

George speaks in a soft southern accent. "ClareJune will be right with you . . . gentlemen." He disappears into an adjoining room where the dull sounds from a TV are heard.

ClareJune comes out and motions for one of the two of us to follow her. Miles, naturally, goes first. ClareJune has two distinct features: her wig, which lurches three feet above her head in a tower of lacquered bewilderment; and her nails, which are immaculately sculpted to the sharpest of blood-red points. ClareJune, otherwise looks roughly seventy-three and barely stands erect on purple blotched twigs of legs at around four foot ten. Her house dress, a peach and floral print is draped over her like an apology. She smiles feebly as Miles walks in, waiting to hear the good news; the hoped-for encounter with Sven: ten-inch-box, big-buns and happily ever-after.

I sit in the living room alone. The coffee table is strewn with issues of House Beautiful, Arizona Highways and The Enquirer. The blonde wood bookcase standing directly across is stacked with issues of Readers Digest; every month of every year going back to 1956. The bottom row is made up of Readers Digest Condensed Books. By all appearances it's a prized collection. The walls are given over to framed posters of the Southwest; wide, expansive valleys, buttes and lots of cacti. They all have one thing in common, the image of a train; a gleaming diesel or steam engine prominently in the foreground or background of each panorama, and they are all for Southern Pacific Railroad. The room smells like a bar and reminds me of Ed's living room. The scent of stale cigarettes, mothballs and Prince Matchabelli perfume hangs everywhere. I sit and wait, listening to the soft sounds of laughter and off-key music coming from Lawrence Welk on the TV set in the other room.

After a while Miles emerges exuberant. Gunnar, his imagined love-object, is scheduled (at least according to ClareJune) to arrive by Spring. She didn't actually come right out and name names, but Miles assumes who it is, considering Gunnar is a recent addition to the cab company where Miles works.

ClareJune appears in the doorway again, and smiles, extending a spindly finger in my direction. I'm next.

I walk in and get ready to sit down at the formica-topped table. ClareJune motions me not to sit there.

"Sit in a fresh chair, hon, that one has your friend's vibrations on it."

I sit down on a straight-backed chrome and green Naugahyde chair and glance curiously around the room. It's been converted into a kind of shrine. Prayer and miracle candles fill every free surface and the lights are dim.

ClareJune holds out a regular deck of Bicycle playing cards and asks me to shuffle them. She watches me, dragging slowly and methodically on her Herbert Tareyton cigarette, studying each card as I toss it down. I have them all laid out after a few minutes. When she speaks, it's in slow, thick, measured drones, with a hypnotic lilt upturned at the end of each sentence.

"Hmm, you're a perplexing one," she admits, separating the cards with her finger for a better look. She holds her cigarette in mid-air, letting the cloud of smoke spiral to the ceiling as she gazes down at the cards and lets her mind go.

"I see an ending and a new beginning," she says - suitably vague. She continues pouring over the cards. "You're very conflicted, but all of this shall pass."

So far she's sounding like the messages from fortune cookies and I'm hoping Miles didn't have to pay too much for this non-information. She is also putting me to sleep with her voice. She looks at me with eyes a glassy mixture of milky-pink and grey. "You're going to be moving soon, maybe before the end of the month. Do you know a young woman with the first initial A? Like you, she's conflicted, but she is not what she appears to be. She loves you very much and you will spend your future together."

I pick up at hearing this. I think for a moment; who do I know with a name whose first initial is A? No one; but then it occurs to me that Thea's full name is Althea and that begins with an A, so that must be it. Maybe ClareJune is really on to something.

She stubs out her cigarette and immediately lights another one; inhaling deeply and blowing out a cloud of beige accompanied by a gurgling, phlegmy cough. She taps the cards with her blood-red nails, searching for clues.

"Do you play a musical instrument?" she asks.

I nod my head. If four hours a day of practising scales and the occasional foray into Schumann mean anything. I explain that I've been trying to get into the music program at school, but so far it's impossible because everybody else wants to.

"The cards don't lie. They see you playing a piano in front of an audience. I also see you wearing a tuxedo - maybe in a restaurant. And this woman whose name begins with A will be very supportive of you. Is she a waitress?"

I want to know if I'm getting drafted; I want to know if my life is going to end soon and if it really is going to go to hell in a handbasket. I want to know if Leslie has forgotten about me. I don't want to know about some fucking restaurant.

But ClareJune keeps asking about music. She stays on it and won't leave it alone. I don't know why.

I finally have to ask; "Does the name Leslie ring any bells?"

She looks down at the cards, trying to unearth clues. After a few moments she shakes her head and sighs.

"I see a young woman in another country. I know she is, because she stands next to a sign printed in a foreign language. I don't know what the words mean. The woman is smiling. She wears a ring of some sort. I think she's Oriental."

That's Leslie; no doubt about it.

"You won't see her again; not for a very long time, but you're going to know her the rest of your life."

I'm not sure what to make of these revelations. Never having been to a psychic before, I'm not sure how much is true and how much is bullshit. I wonder about the significance of Leslie's ring; perhaps it's something ClareJune thinks would be some clue to identifying her.

ClareJune Abernathy is right though, at least about my moving. News on that came fast. Buzz, now a member of the U.S. Postal Service, has gotten his first assignment: Sonoma, fifty miles outside San Francisco. Stoika has quit her job at the Minimum Daily Requirement and they've set out to find a new place to live. Stoika has taken up photography, having been given an old Leica from Brenda while visiting over Thanksgiving. She's running around taking pictures of everything and everybody. Even with the first batch of hit-or-miss photos, it's clear Stoika has stumbled on to something.

I don't want to stay in the house alone, even though having a free grand piano is a bargain I'm reluctant to turn down. It's too much rent to pay. Through an old friend of Ed's I've landed a weekend night job playing for tips in an upscale hotel bar from six to eleven - show tunes being the big request, with the occasional odd Puccini and Verdi tossed in. It means the hippy appearance has to go for awhile, traded in for a slightly less severe look - the hair gets trimmed and the beard goes, for better or worse. I've also landed a part-time day job, doing magazine surveys to the tune of ten dollars a day, as long as I pad out the answers and make up names of the people I'm questioning.

Luckily nobody ever asks for an address or a phone number. Still, seventy-five a month for rent is stiff. So Thea's offer to move in with her has come at the right time.

For our last day in the Minsion, Stoika takes photos of the three of us sitting together on the porch, looking like displaced kids in a playhouse. She puts the camera on a tripod, sets the timer and races to crowd herself into the picture - Buzz with his Post Office uniform; Stoika in her Collective Farm dress, oversized work boots and hair pulled into a red babushka; and me with newly shorn hair and my wrinkled workshirt, gazing off into space. I'm the only one who doesn't know why I'm smiling, but it seems like the right thing to do. Stoika cranks off a twenty-four exposure roll. I think she senses it's the last time we'll be together. Even now, with Leslie in Paris and Burgie working as a waiter in a health food restaurant in L.A., it doesn't seem likely any of us will ever be in the same place at the same time in the near or distant future.

ClareJune Abernathy didn't say anything about that.


I officially move into Thea's extra room, but spend very little time there. Instead, I spend it with Thea, sharing her satin bedsheets and her four-mattress bed, conjuring up new and wonderfully filthy words to whisper in her ear while making love. It's after falling back to semi-sleep from a pre-dawn episode that I feel the presence of someone else, standing in the doorway of the bedroom. It isn't Josh, but he bears a slight resemblance to him. He's thin and has long, stringy, dark brown hair spilling over his face and touching his shoulders. He wears a bulky grey tweed overcoat and over-sized boots. I remember something Buzz once told me to do if I was being pursued by people larger and meaner than me; pretend I was invisible;

pretend I didn't see them and they didn't see me. It isn't exactly easy to do; considering I'm naked, lying on top of the sheets and slowly losing a hard-on. So I do the next best thing; I snore. He can't possibly do anything to me asleep.

It works, at least for ten seconds. But then I feel a strange sensation; a hand wrapping itself around my dick, shaking it gently, accompanied by the soft, singsong words

"Wake up."

There is no getting around this one; I am not going to argue with somebody holding my penis in his hand. I open my eyes and see him smiling. He extends his hand.

"Hi, I'm Greg, Thea's husband." Out of instinct, I reach over to reciprocate.

The only thing I know for sure is that my face has turned the color of a tomato and a stupid smile is frozen from ear to ear. I quickly leap out of bed and realize Greg is almost half a foot shorter than me. I am a towering giant compared to him.

Thea hears the voice and instantly wakes up, letting out a yell and wrapping her arms around him.

I quickly excuse myself. "I'll let you two get re-acquainted."

I bolt back to my room, almost running headlong into Josh, who runs in the opposite direction to Thea's bedroom at the sound of his dad. Josh glances at me and says,

"Okay, bye-bye-see-you,"before he tumbles, screaming gleefully, on to his long-lost father.

I don't care what ClareJune Abernathy said, Thea and I are not destined to last. I don't care how open her marriage is; the situation just isn't going to work out.

I quickly get dressed and leave. I stuff five dollars in my pocket and go out for breakfast. My mind is torn between eggs, sausage and toast or trying out my fake ID. and getting shit-faced in some bar. I stop in a corner liquor store and buy my first pack of cigarettes in a month, Chesterfield 101's, and chain-smoke eight of them all the way to Castro Street, where I decide to pay a visit to Ed and Miles. Buzz and Stoika are way out in the country and there is nobody from the old family to talk to.

I get to Ed and Miles' house just as an ambulance pulls away. Miles stands on the porch, shaken up. He looks at me and shoots an ironic grimace.

"You must've picked up my vibes,"he says, reaching into his shirt pocket and pulling out a cigarette. "The doctor's been telling her she was going to get cirrhosis of the liver for years now, but the stupid fuck wouldn't stop drinking, the dumb son-of-a-bitch!"

It turns out Ed's had a heart attack and is going to get a thorough going-over by one of the best alcohol doctors in the business as Miles puts it. For the first time I realize that Miles, for all he claims he can't stand him, really cares for Ed.

He invites me in. I am in the presence of a man having his very own and very sudden nervous breakdown. He races through the house, flinging open drapes and unbolting windows, letting the cold, brisk breeze billow in.

"Let's get some fucking light in this dump!"

He runs down to the living room, letting the morning sun in, probably for the first time in the ten years since they bought the house.

"I fucking hate opera!" he yells as he flicks the stereo on, tuning the FM dial to a rock station and not the classical station Ed listens to. Jimi Hendrix comes blasting over the stereo, filling the room with the high-pitched wail of guitar feedback.

"If that son-of-a-bitch dies, I'm selling everything. I'm gonna have the biggest fucking garage sale you've ever seen. She's never gonna know what hit her." She, being Ed, the pretty one of the two.

Miles is too upset to go out to breakfast, so the other option of getting shit-faced becomes reality. Miles starts pouring Cuba Libres and, by nine o'clock in the morning, I am comatose.

I want to tell somebody what's bothering me about Thea. I want to talk to a sympathetic voice. But Miles is too busy being pissed off at Ed for not taking care of himself to listen to anybody else's problems. And frankly, I don't think my problems are that great, compared to having Ed in the hospital, unconscious.

I finally start sobering up around two that afternoon. Long enough to develop a splitting headache and an incredible thirst. I dose myself with aspirin and water and start feeling mildly better. I get it into my head that I really need to write Leslie a letter. I haven't written her in a long time and I want her to know I miss her and that the life I'm leading in San Francisco isn't what I had imagined. I want to explain everything to her in absolute, precise detail. I sit at Ed's ornate desk and pull out several sheets of paper and start composing. The first two tries don't go very well; my head is still pounding. By the third try I manage to get almost three pages in before I falter. Miles is busily cleaning up the house, throwing out tons of things Ed insisted on saving: newspapers, empty Vodka bottles and clothes he was never going to wear.

He appears in the doorway and hands me a large rum and Coca-Cola, starting me on the second leg of my frenzied journey. I quickly forget the importance of what I'm doing and stuff the pages into my pocket and collapse on the sofa in the living room.

Miles keeps talking about how he's going to change the house so you won't recognize it and change his life so you won't recognize that either, as if he's threatening to do it as a way of keeping Ed from dying.

I don't surface in the real world again until midnight. My head feels like a bloated grape and I'm sneezing and stink of Rum. Alcohol isn't having the same effect on Miles. He has maintained the exact level all day. Obviously he's had more practice.

I get up and start to walk out, but Miles insists on giving me a lift. I'm not sure if I want to go. I don't know if Greg is still going to be at Thea's.

But after all, I live there; I pay rent. So what if he caught us in bed; he showed up unannounced so it's his fault. I take Miles up on his offer.

He drops me off and I weave upstairs and try a few times to get my key in the front door. The pale-orange bulb glowing dimly at the top of the stairs isn't helping me see anything. After several attempts, I finally open the door and flounder in. It's quiet and still. Thea, Greg and Josh have gone somewhere. I have the apartment to myself, but I decide to go to my room and collapse on my bed.

I wake up in the morning to the sound of the phone ringing. I try to blot the noise out. But after twelve rings, it's obvious nobody is going to answer it but me. I stagger out of bed and hobble to the phone.

The apartment is the same as it was the night before: empty and quiet, except for the drone of the refrigerator and the sound of a Benny Goodman record in another apartment. I pick up the phone.

"Nelson, it's Miles. Ed died this morning. I thought you'd want to know."

He hangs up before I have a chance to say anything or react. I'm stunned. I put the phone down and become immediately awake and sober. I get dressed and call Buzz and Stoika.


I arrive at the house later in the morning, while Buzz and Stoika turn up in the afternoon. Miles is busily stacking up dishes and bric-a-brac in the living room. He's going to make good on his threat to sell everything at a garage sale. Several dealers have already been over and are carting out boxes of books and most of the opera records. Even the turn-of-the-century tapestry on the wall has been taken down. Miles wanted to throw it away, but the book dealer gave him twenty dollars for it. An antique dealer offered Miles a hundred dollars for the piano and it was dragged away before I could even retrieve my dogeared copy of Mikrokosmos from the bench.

It's obvious that Miles hasn't slept since before Ed was taken to the hospital. His eyes are red and swollen. He has a day's growth of beard and he's chain-smoking.

"I knew he hated the holidays, but Jesus Joseph and Mary, can you believe this?" Miles tries to lighten the mood, but he's miserable at it.

Highball sits quietly in a corner; the dog knows Ed is gone. Miles casts a seething bloodshot eye to the shivering flea bag.

"Can you believe it, that snaggle-tooth piece of shit lived longer than he did?" He extends his finger to the dog and yells, "You're going to the pound, like I wanted you to six years ago. I hope they turn you into a goddam wallet!"

Of the four of us, Stoika takes it the hardest. She sits on the velvet sofa and stares with lost, searching eyes at the empty walls dotted with beige squares where smoke-caked pictures and tapestries once hung. She barely says a word to anyone. She wipes her eyes occasionally and runs her fingers through her hair and continues staring, as if she's trying to find some clue, some sign from Ed.

There are no signs and no miracles and the day passes into another night. Buzz and Stoika offer to take Miles and me out to dinner. Miles is busily drinking, which he hasn't let up on since the day before. Food would just make him sick, so he declines. That leaves me to take them up on their offer, now that Buzz is getting a regular paycheck and, compared to me, fabulously wealthy.

We ride in Buzz's newly acquired 1960 white Ford Fairlane to Chinatown to a place called The Shanghai Gardens on Grant Street. It's an old upstairs joint with red velvet wallpaper and shoe leather waiters. It's the place where the locals eat. Chinese families sit at huge banquet tables and banter back and forth in such rapid fire that nobody but the locals can possibly understand them.

We're jammed into a booth in the back, away from the action, but we stuff ourselves on Broccoli Beef and Kung Pao Shrimp anyway. Stoika knows one of the waiters, a middle aged guy named Jimmy Chang, who used to stop in at the Minimum Daily Requirement every morning. He keeps smuggling glasses of Plum Wine and bottles of Tsing Tao Beer to our booth and we proceed to get plastered. It's pretty obvious we need to get a medicinal drunk this night, even though I'm still not recovered from the day before.

"Poor Ed, poor Miles, poor everybody," Stoika says sadly, lifting and draining her glass of beer. She's gone back to drinking, but not nearly the amount when she was in high school. She is, after all, pregnant.

I tell the story of how I met Thea's husband and it brings a screaming laugh from Stoika. Buzz and Stoika don't see a future in Thea the way ClareJune Abernathy does. To them it's a losing proposition and if I think Thea is going to dump her old man for me, I am heading for some serious adjustment problems.

Stoika remembers she's been carrying around a letter from Leslie for me, which has been forwarded to the Sonoma address. I hold it in my hand for a few minutes, afraid to open it, fearing it might be the dreaded Dear Nelson letter I'm convinced I'm going to get. I fold it neatly and stuff it in my jacket pocket and thank Stoika for holding on to it for me.

Jimmy brings out a brightly colored bowl filled with fortune cookies and a pot of green tea. We open up every cookie and carefully check out the phrases, but nothing seems to echo the sentiments of the day or the hopes for a happy future.

We finish and Buzz makes a grand gesture of paying the check; slowly pulling out a thick wad of cash and lovingly counting out ten dollars, including tip.

Buzz is proud of the fact that he finally has money of his own. Truthfully, it makes me feel good seeing him so happy.

We leave the Shanghai Gardens and stumble down Grant Street, past crowds of people and Chinese merchants hawking everything from slippers to Ginseng. I start to feel maudlin as we walk. It feels like old times, but I know it isn't. I glance down at Stoika's hand and notice a small silver band around her ring finger.

"Jesus Christ! You got married!" I blurt out loudly, attracting attention from almost everybody within earshot of us on the street.

Buzz is sheepishly pleased. "Yeah, it was kind of a spur of the moment thing. I just got the car and I wanted to go someplace and we figured Las Vegas seemed cool 'cause neither of us had ever been there and then we started joking and then we got married. It kind of, you know, just happened like that. No big deal."

They've been married for three weeks, but haven't told anyone. Neither Buzz's mom nor Stoika's parents know. They were embarrassed. After all, here we are, getting ready to say goodbye to the sixties; nobody's getting married, everybody is opting for living together; and these two, of all people, go to Las Vegas and actually stand up in front of some Justice of The Peace and get official. It adds fuel to the speculation that life is still, in fact, one big mystery.

Buzz and Stoika drop me off at Thea's. Ploughed for the second night in a row, I ask if they want to come up to the apartment to celebrate, but they decline. Buzz says it's parking and Stoika says it's late.

The lights are on in the living room window and someone is home; maybe the whole happy family, Buzz asks if I want to move in with them, but I can't; I still have school to make a go of and a job that barely pays the bills. Even though the lottery, and getting a number as high as 314 makes the draft deferment situation null and void, I still want to go to school to try and figure out what my life is going to amount to.

I say goodbye to Buzz and Stoika, walk up the steps to the apartment and slowly, reluctantly, open the door.

Thea and Josh are watching TV in the living room. The lights from the Christmas tree Thea and I bought are blinking and bubbling, but the branches on the tree are beginning to droop. Greg is nowhere in sight.

"He's gone. He went back to Canada."

Thea doesn't turn around. She faces the TV set, fallen under its trance.

I have the urge to breathe a sigh of relief, but walk to my room instead. There is a funny, distant feeling welling up from the living room. Even Josh is quiet and non-communicative.

I close the door and sit on the edge of the bed, flipping on the radio and filling the empty air with Schumann's fourth symphony. I take out the airmail envelope and, slowly, open it. I am afraid Leslie is going to call it quits, or worse, through some bizarre paranoid coincidence she has found out about Thea.

It's nothing like that. It's a sweet letter, loaded with apologies for not calling on Thanksgiving because she came down with the flu and was confined to bed with a 103 fever. I read it and feel terrible. I've assumed the worst about Leslie and got involved with Thea mostly out of spite. Now I'm living with this woman. I glance at the top of the letter, the carefully written date and time, which Leslie always includes. My mind spins back to the appointed hour and day and, of course, while Leslie was pouring her flu-ridden heart out to me, I was busy banging away on Thea.

There's a gentle knock at the door. I put the letter under some school books and get up to open the door.

Thea stands outside, trying on a cautious smile. She's happy to see me, but isn't sure if the feeling is mutual.

"Look . . . I have to apologize for the other day. I didn't know Greg was going to show up. I know what it must've looked like. He can't tell me when he's coming because he's afraid the FBI will find out. He says they've tapped the phone."

I rest my arm on the door frame and listen. She looks with searching eyes and whispers faintly,

"I really love you, you know."

She wraps her arms around my neck and draws me close to her. We kiss lightly several times, brushing lips softly, but then it turns more passionate and I have to stop. I slowly pull away.

"Look, I know this is kind of weird but . . . a friend of mine died this morning."

Thea's expression changes. "Oh, I'm so sorry."

She looks concerned and asks if I need anything. I shake my head and tell her I'll get over it in a day or two. She sighs, reaching over and brushing her fingers across my face.

"Still love you." She gives me a short peck on the cheek before turning and walking back down the hall.


I get a bonus check from the marketing company. They're wildly impressed with all the interviews I'm conducting for Ban Deodorant, even though it's me pretending to be seventy different people, and answering the same question seventy different ways. That isn't so much a problem as getting seventy different signatures down.

New Year's Eve is coming up and I want to celebrate. Buzz and Stoika have driven down to Los Angeles to break the news of their marriage finally to the Foley and Jordan families, so that leaves me in San Francisco with a pocketful of money burning a hole to get out.

I invite Thea to dinner and, armed with fifty dollars, we can go anywhere she wants to. Anywhere at all.

She suggests the hotel where I work - since I've been replaced for the night by a big band. I grimace at the thought; it's a little like a turkey being invited to Thanksgiving dinner but I honor her request anyway. Never having actually been to a New Year's Eve bash, I don't know what to expect.

It's corny as hell. A Guy Lombardo-type orchestra sits crammed in the corner playing pallid versions of standards and people, barely under the age of sixty, fox-trotting and box-stepping around the dance floor. This certainly isn't my usual clientele. I get the tryst and tourist crowd most nights; this bunch is from another planet.

We make our way though the Geritol habitue's on the dance floor to get to our table. Andy, the maitre-d`, has put us in the middle of the room; at the center of attention. He smiles broadly and can't take his eyes off Thea - neither can most people here.

She's beautiful tonight and full of life and has the most captivating smile. I order a magnum of champagne and we eat the chicken breast dinner that comes with the New Year's celebration. People stop staring and we get on with the process of seeing in 1970.


By eleven o'clock we both decide this isn't the place we want to welcome a new decade in. So we leave, taking the half-drunk magnum with us, and commandeer a cab to North Beach, because we heard about a big bash going on there. The streets leading to Columbus are mobbed and closed. We get out of the cab and join the several thousand people wailing, screaming, howling, dancing in the new year. This is where we wanted to be all along.

Thea and I hold onto each other tightly and walk through the crowd. Every specimen of human being is represented here. Even the cops are happy. Honest to God, a Sergeant and Lieutenant stand less than two feet away from me, drinking champagne and laughing. After all, it is the end of the decade. The sixties are over and, as That Was The Week That Was used to say, 'It's over, let it go.'

Midnight comes, bringing with it an uproar of yells, shrieks and howling proclamations. I grab Thea and shout,

"Thea, let's enjoy it while it's here."

Thea counters with, "It's not here, it's everywhere!"

Suddenly all the bars are giving booze away free. That's good news because the Magnum is gone, and so is my fifty-dollar bonus.

The biggest street party in San Francisco finally winds down around six in the morning when we finallystagger home. The sky has turned a cold drizzly grey. I feel strange walking around in a tuxedo, stained with a combination of many things I probably don't want to identify, although I'm certain at least one of them is mustard. Thea and I walk arm in arm. There's no one else on the street. We wander over to a neighbor's apartment and pick up Josh, who snores on my shoulder for the rest of the walk home.

"Nelson, life is such a pisser. I wish I met you four years ago, it would've all been different."

I turn to Thea and squeeze her hand. "Come on, don't worry about it. If it's any consolation, the psychic said I'd be with you for a long time."

Thea lights up. "Oh yeah? When did you hear that?"

"Couple months ago."

She shoots me a sly grin and slugs my arm. "And you didn't tell me. You doughhead!"

"Nelson, we have to talk." Thea sits at the dining room table across from me. She gives Josh the eye to go play outside while she says what she has to say to me.

It's June and the emotional heat generated in early December has pretty much died down to a cool breeze. The more I think about making love to Thea, the more the image of Leslie pops into my head. The guilt is starting to make me a little crazy. Thea knows something's wrong. It's only a matter of time before we call it quits. So far, my stay in San Francisco has proven to be disastrous. I've been replaced at the hotel by a guitar player who sings just like Jerry Vale and I've succeeded in flunking almost half of my classes. I'm starting to think San Francisco State and I have a mutual aggression pact going.

Thea runs her fingers around her coffee cup several times. Whatever she has to say is taking a lot of energy to get said and it must be painful for her. She finally lifts her head to face me and I can see from the pinkish tinge of her eyes that she's been crying.

"I, uh . . . got a call from a friend of Greg's last night. He finally got a steady job. He's teaching at the University in Edmonton, and he's moved into a four bedroom house . . . he wants Josh and me to join him."

It explains why Thea's been acting strange ever since getting the phone call. A few nights earlier the phone rang and Thea, as usual picked it up on the second ring. After a few seconds she dragged it into her bedroom and shut the door and didn't come out for the rest of the night, except to go in and check on Josh. She didn't say anything to me, but became distant and subdued.

I assumed Thea would be overjoyed at the news, but she isn't.

"Nelson, do you want to try and make this work?"

I've been under the impression, up to this point, that our relationship was dwindling to where we viewed each other as casual roommates, with liberal sprinklings of sex on the side. I'm not sure I'm hearing her right.

"Nelson, if you say you want us to work out, I won't go to Canada. I'll tell Greg I want a divorce. If you don't think it can work out, then I'll move."

I feel strangely powerful at first, but it quickly wears off to a feeling of anger and resentment that I'm suddenly the one making the decision over how her life is going to wind up. It doesn't seem right and it isn't my decision to make. Besides, she's five years older than me, I have to keep reminding myself, she should know what she wants.

I wonder how different my life will be if I say yes to Thea Talber. Yes, I want to work it out and yes, go ask Greg for a divorce.

But I don't.

I feel every muscle in my body tighten and the power of some unseen force take over and do the negotiating for me. My mouth opens and words fall out and I'm not sure what those words are. By the end, Thea seems relieved, almost happy in a way. And now it's my turn to feel shitty. I have this urge to blow up ClareJune Abernathy's house, since it was ClareJune who predicted this wonderful, long life of bliss with a woman whose first name began with an A.

The phone rings at a mercifully good time. Thea picks it up and hands it to me. It's Stoika. Burgie has called to tell her he's coming up for a week because he's had the gross misfortune of being picked number 4 in the lottery and his pre-induction physical is coming up. He wants to spend his last week of freedom with us.

I ask Stoika if I can take her up on Buzz's offer during Christmas and move in for a while. Stoika immediately says yes, as long as I don't mind sharing the floor with Burgie. It begins to remind me of the concrete bunker on the beach.

It takes roughly an hour to gather my belongings. It takes Thea only a few minutes more.

She has a cousin, Stacey, living in a dormitory in Berkeley who assumes the apartment while Thea and Josh pile up their car, mostly with Josh's toys and clothes, and get ready for the trek north.

"I guess this is it, huh?" I ask as she put the keys in the ignition of her VW.

"It's the best thing, really."

"Looking forward to it? It should be a nice drive."

She nods her head. "Bingo's good company."

I look over at Josh, who is rummaging around for a good toy to get started with. He's oblivious to me and to the rest of the world.

I ask her for her address in Canada and promise to write. She thinks about it for a minute and scribbles it down on a paper napkin from the hotel. Inscribed on it are the words 'Happy New Year: 1970!'

"I believe in reincarnation, you know. We'll be lovers in the next life, you watch."

I completely believe her as she breaks into a wide smile, presses her fingers to her lips and blows me a kiss. She puts the car in gear and drives slowly down the street. Josh pokes his head out and waves, yelling something in kid-language. I wave back.

Watching the car drive off, I somehow know I'm never going to see Thea Talber again in this lifetime. Maybe she's right. Maybe I am going to have to wait for the next one. I stand in the street and feel a tremendous weight of sadness fall over my shoulders. By the time Buzz shows up a couple hours later, I am a wreck on the sidewalk. I load all of my earthly possessions into the trunk and the backseat and lurch over in the front seat next to Buzz and mumble,

"Do you think I'm a particularly terrible human being?"

Buzz glances over to me, gazing momentarily at my hair, which Thea experimented on before she left.

"Naw, you're okay, but I'd dump the Bobby Sherman haircut if I were you."

I'm not okay. I'm scum. I know it. I love Thea and I never told her. I'm not having such a great time in this life so far.

"Don't worry about it,"Buzz says. "No matter how bad things get, people get over them. Thea probably doesn't hurt nearly as badly as you think she does. Listen: nobody made her decide to drive up to Canada, nobody was standing around holding a gun to her head. She could've told that guy she didn't want to, but she didn't. Stop taking the blame for things that don't belong to you."

Buzz is right. I'm blaming myself for a lot of situations I don't need to. But all the pep talk doesn't make me feel any better. I still have a dark cloud of failure hanging over me and I can't seem to shake it. The only saving grace in all of this is having Buzz and Stoika to turn to.

We leave San Francisco, heading north on Highway 101, past Sausalito, Mill Valley and San Rafael. The further inland we go, the warmer and dryer the air becomes. It feels wonderful. The air is filled with the smell of summer. We finally get to Sonoma and arrive at Casa Bob, what Buzz calls the place; a modest eggshell-colored clapboard house, with green roof, built in the 1920s. It has a porch with a wooden swing and a neatly manicured lawn with a lemon tree sprawling shade and dropping fruit in front.

The place looks like it's been plucked out of a story book. But then, so does the whole block; the whole town for that matter. For all the turmoil going on, this place makes me feel like home. It's comforting and soothing and it's good to be with old friends again.

There's only one drawback. There isn't really any room for me, unless I want to sleep on the porch. Everything in the house has been given over to baby furniture and photography equipment.

Stoika is ready to pop the baby any minute. She's puffed out three feet in front of her. "I feel like I'm carrying a Buick around in here," she says, letting out a roaring laugh. Oddly, she doesn't seem to have gained any weight anyplace else. She looks, as she freely admits, like a watermelon on toothpicks.

Stoika's passion for photography has grown since I last saw her. She's becoming proficient, although she's still, as she puts it, "trying to figure out what the hell I'm doing."

The living room is filled with her photographs, stuck to the wall with push pins; they stay up for a few weeks, while she figures out if they're any good or not. The photos run the gamut, but best of all are the people. Stoika has a way of capturing the average person on film that's magical. Everybody, no matter who they are - regular Joes on the street, guys in bars, women at the local beauty shop, kids sitting around the park smoking cigarettes for the first time - they all look like angels. It's incredible. She's already gotten an offer to work for the local paper and is thinking about re-applying to the Art Institute, but she wants to wait until she has enough confidence in her ability before she submits her stuff to scrutiny by a bunch of academics. She wants to wait until she's had the baby to see what's going to happen next. The kid will probably have to get used to being dragged around all over the place, while mom takes pictures.

One of the photos hanging in the hallway between the living room and the dining room is the one Stoika took of us the last day before we left the Castro house. I could've sworn I was smiling, but in the reality of the photograph, I wasn't; I look totally lost.


Around midnight I climb into my sleeping bag on the living room floor scrunched up between a bookcase and a sofa and look up out the window at a moonless night sky. It's so dark you can see thousands of stars. There isn't a streetlamp lit for blocks. And the quiet, except for the occasional bark of a dog or the crow of a rooster, is deafening.

My head is spinning with all kinds of thoughts and I toss and turn every few minutes, trying to get comfortable. Maybe it's the incredible silence I'm not used to because I can hear every creak and groan the house makes. Maybe I'm just feeling beaten up from the past year.

Finally I calm down.

\*     \*     \*     \*

*"Nurse - one of these monitors stopped working."*
*"How long has it been like that?"*
*"Maybe a minute. I just noticed it."*
*"Oh no."*
*"Is it bad?"*
*"I don't know yet."*

\*     \*     \*     \*

I dream I'm reading a newspaper and sitting at a white wrought-iron garden desk on the terrace of the tallest building in the world. I'm high up in the clouds. So high I can only see vague traces of the city below me. I'm busily reading an article about Cuban mansions, which are being bought up by Canadian investors. The article claims there is no cause for alarm. 'The people have a way with words,' it says. I feel a sense of urgency to call Thea, because she's going to Canada and perhaps she can put in a good word for me. I know she can, because I have the photos to prove my sense of purpose.

I turn the page and glance out of my right eye. I don't know how I've managed it, but the terrace is now very far below me and I am precariously balanced on the top of a radio transmitter tower. From where I sit, I can see the curvature of the earth and I am afraid I am going to fall.

"Oh, you'll bounce," I hear a voice say.

"I'm terrified of heights," I tell the voice.

"All you have to do is hold your breath . . . trust me."

A sudden gust of wind blows me off my chair and I fall. Only now I'm falling through outer space, heading back to earth. I am falling at a terrific speed. I look at my arms and they glow red hot. The earth is coming closer and closer, at a speed of hundreds of miles a minute. But I'm going so fast I am beginning to burn up.

There is no hope, I am a flaming torch in the sky. Like a comet, threatening to disintegrate before I fall to earth.

*    *    *    *

*"Heart rate's stabilized. Organ functions are normal."*
*"What was it?"*
*"Don't know. Equipment malfunction. With life support you have to be careful - you don't want to damage anything."*
*"You mean, in case you need a heart donor any time soon?"*
*"He has a good chance of coming out of this and you should know that."*
*"I should know a lot of things, but I don't."*

*    *    *    *

I wake up with the sun blazing through the window, turning my face into molten lava. It's going to be a hot day. It's clear and dry and the bristling air goes straight up my nose. I lunge out of bed and move my sleeping bag to a darker area of the room, but by the time I do, everybody is up and moving around the house. Buzz has appointed rounds to make. Stoika can't sleep.

In the afternoon, a VW Van pulls up in front of the house and Burgie stumbles out. It's hard to imagine, but he actually looks like he weighs less now than when I last saw him and he weighed ninety-seven pounds. He's starting to look like a pencil. Stoika's horrified. But Burgie tells her to look on the bright side; he only has a week left to go and then he'll be free.

"Yeah, if your heart doesn't stop in the meantime," she reminds him.

Buzz and I feel lousy about the lottery. Burgie is the only one who scores the low number. Buzz is in the two hundreds and I am over three hundred. It doesn't seem likely, unless a world war is declared over the next twelve months, that we will ever be drafted. Our experience with Vietnam will be largely relegated to watching it on the CBS Evening News.

For a while it's almost like old times. Only Leslie is missing.

Then Buzz comes home with a blue air mail envelope from Paris for me. When I see it I think at least she's with us in spirit.

But it turns out not exactly what I have in mind.

Leslie wasn't lying in bed with a 103 fever during Thanksgiving, she was lying in bed with a third year Economics student named Mick. They've been living together since August. She's been wanting to call me, but she was afraid her voice would give her away. She dialed the phone several times, but never got past the international operator before she froze and hung up. She thought that it was only a fling and they would have broken up by now and I would never have needed to know; but since the New Year it's become more serious than she expected and she's been spending a lot of time in London.

Well, that explains the lapse in letter writing.

I guess we're even; we both have mummies in our closets and we didn't do what we promised. It was crazy to think we would. But it hurts just the same. I'm seized with the overpowering desire to drive back to Los Angeles and start life over. I miss the old places, the old sounds and old smells. I want, for the first time in my life, to go home.


Burgie has his date with the draft board Monday morning. I decide to go back with him. We load up the van late Sunday morning with my accumulated junk, which doesn't amount to much, considering how much I dragged up the first time we stayed in San Francisco. Stoika takes several pictures of the four of us and promises that, once she has the baby, she and Buzz will be coming down to L.A. for visits.

Buzz reaches into his pocket and hands Burgie and I each a cigar. Printed on the wrapper are the words 'It's a kid!' Buzz doesn't know what sex it's going to be, so he doesn't want to commit to something he isn't sure about.

We all hug each other and Buzz tells us,

"Look, if the draft board thing doesn't work out and you get homesick for up here, let's all get a place together. I can put in a good word for you at the Post Office."

Buzz, in his round-about way, is homesick. Maybe not for L.A. but for the old times. We agree to think about it.

Burgie and I leave for the trip back south.

I'm looking forward to going back to Los Angeles for the first three hundred miles. I think of all the times and the places I've missed. I'm wondering how much has changed since I left a year earlier.

Somewhere around San Luis Obispo the bubble bursts. It finally hits me that I am heading, at sixty-five miles an hour, back to nothing.

When we get to Ventura an hour later, Burgie turns on to Pacific Coast Highway and we take it the rest of the way. The pall of doom enveloping the van is so thick you can almost choke on it. Burgie is scared to death, convinced his life will be over in less than twenty-four hours and I am convinced the best part of my life has already past me. We are hopeless, the two of us.

In my imagination I actually missed the smell of smog. I must've lost my mind - too many Cuba Libres. The brown haze sticks to the city like snot on a windshield. It seems to have been there forever. Maybe this is its way of welcoming me home.

"Look, there's worse things," Burgie says, screwing up the courage to say the first positive word in three hours.

"Like what?" I ask.

"I don't know." Burgie sinks back down in the driver's seat, like a partially inflated balloon that had been deflated again.

"Burgie, do you want me to go with you tomorrow?" He shakes his head.


It's night when we finally arrive at my house. Burgie pulls to a stop in front. The place seems a lot smaller than I remembered. The lawn is non-existent; turned into a brown and beige carpet of crabgrass and dirt. The house needs a paint job badly. Maybe it's my imagination again, but the house doesn't seem happy to see me.

I drag my suitcase out of the back and stand on the sidewalk as Burgie sits frozen in the driver's seat.

"Did you want to come in for a bit?" I ask.

"No, I'm just gonna go home and wait."

"God loves you and so do I."

Burgie glances over with a smirk. "God, I'm not so sure about."

He puts the van in gear and drives away. I turn and trudge up the walk to the front door.

I can tell something is different when I try my key in the front door lock and it doesn't fit. Denying the obvious, I assume I have the wrong key. Finally, after trying all of them, I realize none of them are going to fit; ever.

I hear a faint voice on the other side of the door. "Who is it?"

"Mom, it's me."

The porchlight comes blaring on. Two thousand watts of rank yellow glare, guaranteed to get rid of bugs, and most people standing under it. There is a shuffle of drapes and the process of unlocking the door begins. Two deadbolts and a chain and the door finally opens.

My mother looks surprised; actually more shocked, than anything else when she notices my clothes.

"Jesus Christ, you look like some old reprobate. I didn't recognize you!" She hugs me gingerly, like I'm covered in fleas or open sores.

I am always amazed at the creative use of words my mother employs. I have never been referred to as a reprobate; I feel rather pleased by it. My father sits impassively in the living room. He lowers the newspaper and gives a faint, ill smile as he sees me walk into the house.

"You should be selling pencils," he grunts, and goes back to the want ads.

"You changed the locks on the door."

Mom stumbles around for an answer. "Oh, uh, yeah, didn't we tell you? We were robbed a couple months ago."

No, she didn't tell me and, surprisingly, for a house that was robbed, nothing seems to be missing.

My mother has the habit of saying "we" when she means "I". She doesn't want to take solo blame for anything that might incur wrath.

"So, what brings you to L.A?" She looks at my suitcase like it's atomic waste.

"San Francisco didn't work out, mom. I decided to come home."

My father lets out a gasp, but quickly covers it up by coughing.

There is one tiny problem. I really don't have a home to come home to. Well, not my version of a home anyway. My parents got it into their heads that I would never grace the halls of The Rivers Homestead again, and because my father is so handy with home improvements, they've knocked out the wall between my former bedroom and the back porch, turning it into one large open space that now leaks when it rains.

My mother has christened it "The Meditation Room", but basically, it's the place where all the junk they can't bear to throw away is tossed, including a set of tires for the MG that has long since gone off to become a Toyota or a Waring Blender. My bed has vanished, as have the childhood mementoes that only I appreciated.

The only thing left of mine is the hi-fi and my records. Thank God my father has respect for vinyl, otherwise there would be no trace of my presence anywhere except for my birth certificate and I'm not so sure they still have that.

I sit in my decimated inner sanctum and know I have to get out of here. The walls I remembered being covered with beige flocking are covered over by sheets of wood panelling that don't match from one sheet to the next. Even the bare wood bathroom floor that I used to slip and fall onto when I got out of the tub is covered over in a lime-green shag carpet; frayed and stained with what looks like motor oil or spaghetti sauce.

"So it comes down to this," I tell myself, unrolling my sleeping bag.

Leslie's letter falls out. I don't know how it got there, but it stares up, waiting for me to open it and look at the contents one more time. I start to read it but give up. What's the point? I've read it so many times I already know it by heart. I decide I need to do something positive instead of pissing and moaning about lost love.

I want to be someplace that reminds me of happier times, and they don't include sitting on the floor of my former bedroom staring at a six-foot poster of two purported space aliens getting off a cigar-shaped flying saucer, being greeted by a typical smiling American family, complete with smiling dog with caption reading: 'Friends from far away.' I figure I have two choices: I can either go insane and be locked up for the rest of my life or I can take a walk and try to sort out the mess that has laughingly become my life. I decide on a walk to the LaBrea Tarpits. If nothing else, the park couldn't have changed.

Wrong.

Maybe the planets have something to do with it, but what was once an undiscovered tranquil hangout in the middle of the city is now a full-blown mob scene. A din of noise follows me. It seems like thousands of people are lining the perimeter of the park, playing tambourines, guitars, smoking dope and singing *Hey Jude* at the tops of their lungs. The only place not covered with people is the spot I remember most. The bridge that Leslie, Buzz and I once sat under, smoking dope.

The city, in the intervening years, has decided to install a sprinkler system. It's a partial deterrent to people hanging around the park all night and sleeping. The sprinkler is set on a timer; once every two hours it shoots a geyser of water over the whole grassy area, soaking everything and everyone in its mechanical wake. I arrive just as it's finishing its spray cycle, so I'm safe for two hours. The ground, however, is cold and soaking wet, but I don't care. I'm hoping for something to happen that will bring back some of the magic, even a glimmer of it, from four years earlier.

When you wish for magic, pray for it, stake your life on it, it's a safe bet it won't give you the right time of day, or may even backfire on you. Magic, like fate, is fickle and it doesn't like being demanded upon.

I look up at the sky. The clouds hang thick and unmoving; no parting into moonlit bliss tonight; it's business as usual. Fog and smog and humidity are all the air is filled with.

"You know, you're sitting in a foot of water."

I know that voice. It's Burgie. "Your mom said I'd find you here."

I peer down at myself. He's right. I am sitting in a puddle of water. It's covering my legs and ripples around my ankles. I lift my head and see Burgie smiling like he's just discovered the meaning of life.

"I'm 4-F!" Burgie beams as he excitedly holds up the letter he's gotten from his draft board.

I'm bewildered. "That weirdo diet?"

"Rheumatic Fever. Had it when I was ten. They mailed me the letter while I was up in San Francisco. Nobody told me about it until I got home."

Burgie is safe and exempt and now free to get on with the rest of his life. He stares at me sitting in the pool of water.

"What's wrong?" he asks.

"I found out I can't go home. I'm a fugitive, Burgie."

"Come on, Nowhere Man, I'll take you somewhere."

I get up off the ground. I am sopping wet and the cold air slices through me. I missed Burgie during the year I was in San Francisco. He likes my skewed vision of life and I like his optimism. We make a good team.

To celebrate his new lease on life, and the idea that life, in fact, goes on, we drive out to Leo Carillo Beach, just north of Malibu. Burgie stops the van at a deserted parking lot near the water and reaches into the back, pulling out a bottle of Mateus from a small cupboard. His father was inundated with gifts of wine the previous Christmas. Burgie took several bottles and stashed them in strategic places around the van as a sort of insurance policy for cold nights and hot dates.

One thing Burgie forgot was a corkscrew; a tragic mistake for the novice wino. We finally get the cork out of the bottle with a screwdriver.

"Here's to a new life," Burgie proclaims. He holds the bottle up and takes several gulps, before passing it over to me.

"Yeah, some future."

I pass the bottle back to Burgie, spitting out bits of cork from my mouth. The wine is sweet and bubbly and the bottle is colored a deep red with a label of green and brown with a picture of Barcelona during some deep, distant past. I'd like to be there, be anywhere but L.A., even though I've been back a few hours. After a while it occurs to me that I haven't eaten all day and the wine is going straight to my head. But I'm also feeling warm and my problems are fading into the distance.

We watch the ocean roll in and out and listen to Thelonius Monk and Sonny Rollins play *Misterioso* on Burgie's 8-track.

"What are you gonna do now?" I ask.

I wait for an answer. He slugs the wine, and rolls his window down to let in a blast of air. The breeze has become warm and dry and doesn't come from the ocean. He puts his hand out.

"Santa Ana's are blowing."

Burgie rests his chin on his arm and lets the breeze blow over his face. He stares out at the beach as the wind blows the sky crystal, pinpoint clear.

Finally he answers, "I don't know. I guess I'll keep working at the restaurant and maybe do something else. Hey, do you want to buy a car? One of the guys at work has a Corvair for sale."

It's a good idea as long as I can work out a deal to pay the car off in installments. I need a car desperately, but even more, I need a place to live, now that my childhood home is a thing of the past. Burgie can't help out there; he lives in a place in Hollywood, above the Whiskey A-Go-Go, that is so small it has a combination bathroom and kitchen. Burgie grimaces when he talks about it.

"Who says you can't shit where you eat?"

So here we are in the real world and neither of us knows what's going to happen next.

I close my eyes and try to imagine what the next six months will be like, but I keep thinking of what Leslie is doing at the moment. If my watch is right, she is probably having lunch. Or making love to that guy she met in Paris. I will be nowhere in her thoughts, not even a passing sigh, or flicker of an eyelid.

Likewise, it's undoubtedly the same with Thea Talber. But I smile and break into a laugh when I think about Josh and his catch-all phrase, 'Okay-bye-bye- see-you.'

He probably knew more of what was going on than I did.

He probably still does.

# CHAPTER THIRTEEN

## SWEET DREAMS EVERY ONCE IN A WHILE

In exchange for working in the kitchen at The Cosmic Consciousness Eatery, I've become the owner of the white 1962 Chevrolet Corvair and have enough money saved to afford a place to live while enrolling at college for the fall semester.

The best I can do, with my modest income, is a dingy flop house near Berendo and Santa Monica Boulevard, right near the campus.

Home for me consists of a threadbare three story semi-Victorian wood-frame house which has been converted into an apartment building by someone with an alternate career canning sardines. The halls are unbearably narrow and the place I call my apartment, my cell, consists of one room which the previous tenant painted a sickening shade of olive drab. I have one window and, since it came furnished, one bed that sags in the middle, one closet and a broken lamp.

Every time someone closes a door the whole building shakes violently. For no reason, the wooden beams supporting the house groan. I wake up all hours, hearing noises that convince me the house is in imminent danger of falling down. Strangely, it never does. There is one bathroom on each of the three floors and no kitchens anywhere. The house reeks of mothballs, Sterno and Franco-American Spaghetti-O's.

When I can't scam a free meal from Burgie, I have to get my meals across the street from my apartment at a place called The New Burma Inn. Like the house, it creaks and is threadbare. It's a cavernous old dump with sticky linoleum floors, sticky linoleum tables and sticky nicotine-stained walls. The tables are separated by booths; small brown rooms that are actually okay if you like dining alone. You can shut the red shower curtain that hangs over each small entrance and eat in private, usually to the strains of a Helen Forrest record piped in from the jukebox that doesn't play anything made after 1954.

The only problem with the place is the twenty-foot ceiling overhead and the flourescent bulbs that buzz and sputter and turn everything and everyone into shades of lime-tinted grey. The place is seldom filled, but there is always a thick cloud of smoke to wade through. The smoke comes from Leon Fong, a short Chinese version of Elmer Fudd with only enough hair on his head to creatively negotiate a part somewhere below his ear lobe. He owns the place. Leon continuously puffs Roi-Tan Panatellas and studies the racing form with a vengance. He has a permanent booth near the kitchen, within eyeshot of his favorite work of art: a billboard sized poster for Cerveza High Life featuring a comely Mexican babe in peasant clothing and a serape seductively draped over a bronze womanly shoulder. She holds a glass of beer while leisurely reclining on a half-moon, peering down from the lofty heights of the restaurant. He puffs away and stares at her for hours.

Two of Leon's favorite expressions are calling regulars "spud" and non-regulars "dumb bastards." Every so often he saunters by the booths to check in on customers. He sees me every other day. "Hiya Spud, want the usual?"

The 'usual' is a mysterious concoction called Student Plate, and it's my meal of the day. It costs a dollar and consists of an eggroll dipped in forty-weight oil and rolled in grease, a rotunda-shaped dome of rice that never separates, a runny brown syrup that has an object vaguely resembling a vegetable swimming inside, and three scorched balls of dough stuck to a tongue depressor, which Leon gleefully calls "chicken stick". I always have the feeling the closest this glop ever gets to actually being chicken is the picture of Colonel Sanders Leon has stuck up in the kitchen.

To complete this cast-iron odyssey, it comes with a glass of cloudy 'red drink', which Leon insists is his version of Hawaiian Punch, "Only better!", and a very soggy fortune cookie whose windfall is always the same: "BIG THINGS COMING YOUR WAY". I often think - 'An atomic bomb - a runaway train - a 707 skidding, out of control, down a runway.'

Considering Leon's fascination with the Cerveza High Life poster, it's only natural that he have a beer and wine license. The locals flock like a bevy of downtown pigeons to The New Burma Inn most nights and on weekends, and I often find myself at two in the morning, peering out my tiny second story window at police cars pulling up in front to haul off several fighting drunks who spill out into the street.

Leon chases after them, swinging a baseball bat, yelling, "Don't come back, dumb bastards!" They always come back.

For the most part, everyone in my olive-drab flea sanctuary keeps to themselves, except the times when somebody gets creative with a can of roach spray and starts using it. That single act brings many people together at once, and often not happily.

No women live at Hell House; not that there's any rule against it, but no woman in her right mind would want to live in a joint like this. No, it's just guys; smelly, horny, ill-at-ease guys. There is only one phone in the entire house, and it's always occupied by some myopic pariah trying desperately to make his love-life happen.

I don't have that problem. I'm suffering from sex-shock. Having gone through my disaster with Thea Talber and my nightmare with Leslie Noritake, I'm not dying to run out and get involved in any new adventures. I need time to heal; time to repair my mangled, botched-up psyche. It's time to give the raging hormones a rest.

I finally have the chance to enroll as a Music major and minor in Broadcasting. I'm starting to think about what I can fall back on, in case my abilities as a musician are nothing to write home about; at least I can follow in my father's footsteps and become a disc jockey. That has a certain romantic flair to it. The idea of living a vagabond existence, travelling from town to town, landing a job as a morning man at some small, out of the way 5,000 watt station, is very appealing to me on some level. Maybe, in this land of infinite possibilities and golden opportunities, I can do both!

Still, I'm lonely and out of touch. I drop by Burgie's place twice a week and we experiment with getting drunk on anything alcoholic we can find. Most of the time it's pretty conventional, but there are a few times when it gets eccentric. One night recently, Burgie bought a bottle of White Port and a bottle of Rose's Lemon Juice. We combined the two because we heard *WPLJ* by the Mother's Of Invention. They kept singing about how good White Port and Lemon Juice was and who are we to argue? Frank Zappa is God in my book.

I thought something inside of me had broken and I'd be stuck throwing up for the rest of my life.

Burgie and I decide to lay off drinking for a while.

At least Burgie is my link to the outside world. Buzz and Stoika write him, knowing I'll get the letters as well. Stoika had the baby the day after Burgie and I left; an eight-pound handful they've named Vladimir.

Word also passed along that Leslie has broken up with Mick, the Economics major. For the next few days I cross my fingers and hold my breath. But she hasn't written and Stoika warns me she's not likely to. I decide after a while that it's all over.

When I'm not in school, staring out the window of my rat-trap, listening to Leon moan about L.A. heading straight to hell, or getting drunk with Burgie, I'm hiding in a corner of the Music Library, submerged under a bulky set of headphones.

I've lately taken a liking to dramatic music; big blowsy, morbid symphonic pieces with lots of downturns and sentiments of loss. It probably has something to do with my current state of mind. As long as there is no drama in my life, there might as well be in the music I'm listening to.

"The Librarian told me to tell you that if you check out *Isle Of The Dead* one more time, you're gonna have to buy us a new copy."

I gaze with total hurt and dismay at the bearer of that news.

Audrey Piantadosi is a Music major who has a part-time job working in the library. She looks like she's just graduated high-school. She is bright, healthy and vivacious; all those things first semester students suffer from. She has full, evenly proportioned lips, a broad smooth nose and permanently reddish cheeks to go with her pale-olive complexion. Her shoulder length black-brown hair is combed to the side and she has the most mysteriously haunting gaze in her eyes.

She hands me a deadpan look at first, but realizes I'm reacting as if a close personal relative has died. She quickly opens up into a mischievous smile. "I'm kidding, but you're the only one who seems to like that piece."

It's true. I've been going through my romantic-Russian downtrodden, 'who-am-I-what-am-I-doing-where-am-I-going' phase and Rachmaninoff is sending the right chords all over my pain-wracked soul.

142

Audrey smiles. It's stunning, like a flashbulb going off in a dark room. She has the most unbelievably white teeth of any human being I've ever met. Her voice, soft, melodic and a little low, is sweet and clear and borders on hypnotic. I could listen to her read the phone book for days.

In the evening, I decide my meal of the day is going to be different. Instead of my usual one-dollar student plate at Leon's or loading up on brown rice and bean curd at the Cosmic Consciousness Eatery, I venture down the street to invest my ration of cash into a medium cheese and tomato pizza and two glasses of House Red at a place called Mama Luigi's.

Mama Luigi is a guy named Hector Mendoza whose entire experience with Italian cuisine consisted of a ride through Rome in a tank with the U.S. Army during the war, along with a healthy fixation for Gina Lollabrigida. The pizza is okay, but it's so hot it turns my mouth into a molten slab of scar tissue, which I have to keep dousing with wine.

The wine, however, is not good. It turns my lips purple and tastes like mildew. But I'm in too much agony to care at first. Five glasses later I feel very little pain and sit at my table gazing up glassy-eyed at the framed photos of Gina, Sophia Loren and hundreds of other Italian movie stars, and listen to Feruccio Tagliavini sing *Questa O Quella* from Rigoletto. Hector is an avid opera lover. Next to the cash register he has a phonograph which blasts out strains of Verdi and Bellini all night.

It isn't a bad place; it's genial and folksy and only has eight tables, all with the appropriate red check tablecloths and empty Chianti bottles serving as candle holders. My problem is strictly a monetary one. Being on a tight budget, blowing more than three dollars a day on food means I have to starve the next day.

I weave back to my hovel and stagger up the stairs to my room. Someone, a comedian of Pakistani ancestry named Hrach, who is homesick for the searing temperatures of Rawalpindi, has turned the heater up to 95 degrees and the entire house is baking.

I lay in bed, folded over like an envelope, soaking my shredded sheets in wine-scented sweat. Since morning I've been thinking, 'This is trouble, this is trouble, this is trouble,' but I don't know why. Then, in the middle of my fever-pitched delirium, it hits me; the trouble is Audrey and I am heading, on a crash course, like the fortune cookie 'Everything is coming your way' prophesy, straight to it. Since our fateful first meeting, a pattern has developed. Every day I go into the Music Library, check out several records - the usual suspects, Rachmaninoff, Vaughan Williams and Gustav Mahler, and take them over to my usual turntable. Audrey is always at the front desk by the check-out counter, facing me. I glance over in her direction and she quickly diverts her attention to a book, or homework, or cataloging new records. From the corner of my eye I know she's staring at me. And I'm sure that, out of the corner of her eye, she knows I'm staring at her.

It's a little game and we play it every day and I haven't been aware of it until this fever-induced Tuesday night.

What an idiot I am. I bolt out of bed and almost fling myself out the window, in an attempt to get cooler. It is, of course, raining outside and the temperature has now dropped several degrees.

Leon has just closed up for the night. He's locking the front door and walking off to his car, parked around the corner.

My breath erupts into clouds of steam as I exhale. I keep thinking about Audrey and realize she has been on my mind most hours of most days the past few weeks.

I start to develop fantasies about her. They run the gamut from being stuck on a desert island to being stuck on an elevator. They all end the same way; making hot, passionate, consuming love. But when the objects of my fantasy world spill over into the real one, I become painfully quiet and aloof. It's gotten to the point where I really can't be sure what's real and what's imagined. One thing for certain; I have almost unconsciously talked myself out of saying or doing anything about Audrey.

And that would be a terrible shame because I'm spending an unholy amount of time wondering about her. I spend whole afternoons, wrapped up in headphones, just looking at Audrey and watching what she does, the way she does it. The way she holds a pencil or taps her foot. You have to look at Audrey for a couple of minutes to realize she's beautiful, and once you do, she's stunning.

She always wears loose fitting clothing, so it's hard to tell if she's chunky or thin. Her legs got to me first. They are elegantly sculpted gems that bulge at her calf.

Many days find me mesmerized by the sight of her knees while the strains of the slow movement of Poulenc's harpsichord concerto play in my head. Even my choice of music has changed. It's going from weighty and moribund to frothy and optimistic.

I'm no longer in control. When I see her, a surge of liberated nerves sweeps over me and causes my stomach to do backflips. My hands turn into soggy wads of bread dough and my mouth goes the texture of a cotton ball. I am not only inarticulate and withdrawn; I am a quivering glob of ineptitude.

*  *  *  *

*"Kind of depressing music."*

*"Poulenc's not so depressing."*

*"The nurses want to know if you have anything with a beat attached to it."*

*"Burgie, we used to play this music all the time when we first met."*

*"Man, you think you know a guy . . . Can I at least request* Peaches in Regalia?*"*

*"We already played Frank Zappa."*

*     *     *     *

It's the beginning of Christmas break and I have nowhere to go. Burgie's uncle died earlier in the week and he flew to Boston for the funeral. The campus is quiet; closed down except for a few offices and a couple of events. It's the day after a rainstorm; one of those blustery, crystal clear days where suddenly the air is crisp and clean and the colors are brighter than you originally thought they were.

I've just finished four hours of piano practice in one of the soundproof rooms in the Music building. I'm sitting on a bench outside, finishing a cigarette and feeling my face get warm from the sun. A Dari-Gold Chocolate Milk carton is being pushed along the concrete walkway by stiff gusts of wind. I am fascinated by the sight.

I hear a voice coming from the right of me. "Don't you ever leave this place?"

I turn around. It's Audrey, flashing her mischievous smile. Her teeth seem whiter than ever. She's bundled in a green wool coat with a bright red scarf tied around her head. She wears a pair of brown knit gloves and she carries a violin case in her hand. She has a folder filled with sheet music under her arm.

There isn't time to build a good nervous breakdown. I am, for once, the pinnacle of calm.

"I like it when it's quiet like this. It's peaceful."

She sits down on the bench next to me.

"You know, you haven't said three words to me since the 'Isle Of The Dead' incident."

I wish I could tell her why. But I can't. All I can do is look over at her and fall into a trance. It's incredible how much she's changed once she got outside. I've never seen her in sunlight before. Her hair glistens and turns hundreds of shades of brown and dark red and auburn and burnt sienna. The cool air makes her cheeks flush and her nose turn pink.

She could have told me she was a Martian serial killer and I couldn't have cared less. I can feel that large, soft organ in my rib cage beat faster. This girl doesn't have to lift her finger; I am putty in seconds.

And at that exact moment something happens to put me on automatic pilot and say things I never would consciously or rationally say without pleading insanity afterwards.

Whatever I said, it must've hit a harmonious chord, because the next thing I know, we're in bed.

It's dawn on Saturday when I finally open my eyes and peer around the room.

Clothes are strewn everywhere. My shorts are draped across a chandelier suspended from the ceiling, and I can feel a brassiere fastened like a helmet to my head. I am lying under an enormous goose-down comforter. The room is vast. It has to be Audrey's. Thank God we didn't go back to my place; she wouldn't have stayed for more than five minutes.

Audrey lives a scant two blocks away from me, but it could be on another planet. I can't figure out if she's from a wealthy family or just a thrift shop fanatic. Her apartment is filled with antiques. Even the bed is an antique of some kind. Maybe this is normal for most people, considering every place I've stayed, with the exception of Thea's, has been thrown together by accident. Still, there is something serene about Audrey's place.

Because it's so early, the only source of light coming into the room is from outside and it's grey and murky. I imagine myself dreaming; none of this is real.

At the foot of the bed, staring back at me, is a huge wooden wardrobe with full length mirror. I stick my head up from under the comforter and see me staring back. Yes, there is a brassiere on my head and yes, I am in Audrey's apartment. I'm not dreaming after all. I wonder if she is aware I live on three dollars a day and have, as my sole means of transportation, a 1962 Corvair that leaks, has a broken rear window, no heater, and drinks oil to the tune of a quart a day. These are considerations that can't be overlooked, no matter how much love has to do with it.

Audrey stirs and opens her eyes. She yawns and gives me a sleepy smile and whispers; "I really don't want to alarm you, but you have a brassiere growing out of your head. What do you call that?"

"Arnold," I whisper back.

"Oh. . . What do you call the other one?"

"Tilly," I answer.

She erupts into laughter and rolls over and grabs me. The comforter soon goes flying to the floor.

For the first time in months, love is everywhere and the world has become a place of infinite possibilities and adventures. There is nothing that can't be achieved if I want it, and my heart is filled with an incredible sense of well-being. I'm feeling outrageously happy and satisfied. Life makes perfect sense and chaos has vanished. How can anything possibly go wrong?

# CHAPTER FOURTEEN

## THE BOAT THAT SANK ON THE WAY TO FANTASYLAND

"Nelson, I can't lie to you. There's this other guy."

The confession comes during breakfast. I've discovered Audrey likes to do things ceremoniously. Breakfast is one of those events. Next to the kitchen is a small dining room. She has two sets of china dishes that are trimmed in gold and painted with depictions of 18th century country life. She carefully lays out the table; neatly folded cloth napkins, knife, fork, spoon, china coffee cup and glass tumbler with orange juice. Each place setting is exactly like the other, something I find rather bizarre since no two things in my parents' house matched; ever.

I've also discovered Audrey likes to cook. She says it gives her time to think, to solve problems. Considering what she just told me, she busily works on a dozen-egg omelette. I can feel the blood drain from my toes as I sit, stunned, while she moves around the kitchen, wearing a burgundy-colored satin robe that opens occasionally to reveal a glimpse of spellbinding flesh.

After she tells me, the silence gripping the apartment is deadly. A pin dropping would sound like an iron lung crashing to the floor. I had the strange feeling there was going to be a catch with Audrey. This is it.

The other guy in question is an oboe player named Randall. Randall and Audrey play in the college orchestra together. I've met Randall passing in the hall in the music building; he's your average 'nice guy'; round, pudgy and a bad dresser. Randall has an adenoid problem which makes him sound like he has a permanent cold. He rarely goes outside during the day, so his skin is the color of Wonder Bread. Randall has watery blue eyes and permanently greasy reddish blond hair.

Randall is a mess. Audrey is gorgeous. This just doesn't make sense.

I don't understand her attraction to him. But if I say anything it's going to be construed as sour-grapes. So I keep my mouth shut and nod my head up and down like one of those plaster dogs sitting in the rear window of an Oldsmobile. It's all I can do. Having been a refugee of this type of thing before, I can envision my sanity jumping off the chair and running out the door. I'm going to get stuck in another one of those eternal triangles, like God's own revolving door to oblivion.

There is, however, a glimmer of hope. Audrey explains, concerned when she notices how pale I have become, that it's an on-again-off-again-type situation and that they are in the midst of their off-again phase. She is honestly trying to make me feel better, but it's hard to concentrate on what she is saying. Being a violinist, Audrey speaks with her hands. She moves them around continually when she talks and, as she does, her boobs jiggle and sway back and forth. It's a major distraction for me and the only thing I want to do at the moment is her on the kitchen table.

But I fight to listen attentively and I realize that what she's trying to tell me is I have the inside track. Even more encouraging, Randall is busy visiting his family in Portland for the holidays and that means I have three weeks to convince her I am Mister Right.

I have to clean up my act and that means making some big promises to my parents to get some cash. My mother has never forgiven me for the first San Francisco escapade, let alone the second, so when I promise unending devotion and a regular pay-back schedule for the loan I need, she laughs. "Nelson," she mutters, cocking her head characteristically to one side as she always does in the midst of saying something profound, "you don't have a pot to piss in or a window to throw it out of."

"Okay . . . look, here's the deal," I am practically down on my knees. "Loan me enough money for a car and three months rent and I'll work it off at the radio station. I'll do anything. I'll dump trash, sharpen pencils, wax floors, anything!"

My dad hands me the Rod Rivers Reptilian Gaze, where, like my mom, his eyes shrink to slits, as he ponders the fate of his hard-earned dough in my slippery pockets. Both Mom and Dad have perfected this look and there are times when I know how the mouse feels, wandering around the boa constrictor tank at the pet store.

I manage to squeeze five hundred dollars out of my dad, but not without sacrifice. I promise to paint the house, and I gleefully agree to start the day after Christmas.

I already sold the Corvair to one of the tenants of Hell House for fifty dollars; and I just bought a 1959 VW Bug for two hundred. With three-fifty left in my pocket, I look for a new place to live.

I consider it a good omen when I land the apartment on Heliotrope Avenue, not three doors away from Audrey's. It's a modest building, not particularly distinctive or quaint. It's identical to thousands of other apartment buildings from the same vintage; late 1930's California Spanish. Compared to what I've been living in two days earlier, this place is a palace.

Apartment 3. A one-bedroom, newly painted, carpeted and draped, sun-filled, spacious dwelling on the second floor, directly above a defrocked minister named George who has a passion for Cutty Sark Scotch and *The Shadow Of Your Smile*, which he plays endlessly on his Wurlitzer. Aside from the periodic serenades, which are sometimes accompanied by eerie, off-key weeping, the block is quiet. But then, anything would be quiet compared to the riot zone I've been living in before. All this, and only seventy-five bucks a month.

I have no furniture. To paraphrase my mother: I have a window to throw it out of, but I don't have a pot to piss in. So I rummage though my parents' house with the hope of finding something useful and homey that hasn't already been sold at one of their semi-monthly garage sales. The best I can glom on to, aside from the weather beaten upright piano I rescue from the alley behind the Cosmic Conscious Cookery, is a vile-looking chocolate-brown overstuffed chair with gouts of foam rubber plunging out of its sides, compliments of Dolores's replacement, Omar; the other dog of hysterical breeding and suspicious temperament, who at least likes me, but can't seem to stop humping my leg. My excuse for a lamp is an imitation brass space-age light-tree with cylindrical globes, only two of which work and one of which hangs woefully by a wire. I find a chest of drawers covered in so many coats of white enamel the drawers won't close and it feels permanently wet. It's a dismal start; it can only go up from here.

Audrey takes it as a challenge. She's a big fan of thrift shops and flea markets and knows where to go for the best stuff at the cheapest prices. We forage up and down Western Avenue between Beverly and Wilshire, where scores of junk and antique shops lay waiting for our careful scrutiny. Audrey is a shrewd negotiator, and she knows when to turn on the charm. It takes less than a day to turn my tribute to monastic renunciation of worldly possessions into a place of respectability and even borderline charm. The furnishings are tastefully sparse, but well coordinated. An antique mahogany chair with Burgundy upholstery takes the place of Bruno's throne. It's quickly tossed into the garbage, along with the space-age light-tree which has been replaced by two reading lamps that sit on oak end tables. It isn't a lot, but it makes the bare space more comfortable. Even the beat up piano manages to get a facelift, with a can of polish and some newly acquired volumes of Beethoven sonatas from the Salvation Army Thrift Shop.

To celebrate my plunge into domestic tranquility, I decide to run out and buy a Christmas tree, considering the big holiday is less than a week away.

I am amazed at how motivated I have become in such a short time. I go to Audrey's place and spend hours listening to her practise. She's a constant source of fascination to me. She has small hands, but long, agile fingers. She always cuts her nails close and has built up formidable calluses on her fingers. She plays with determination and relentless energy and she's her own worse critic. She's always stopping in the middle of a piece and repeating a flubbed passage fifty, sixty times before she's convinced she has it right.

"You've got to be bored to death," she says, taking a break.

"Are you kidding?" I answer. Although I feel somewhat left out, playing an instrument I can't exactly stuff into my pocket, I love to watch her play and I wonder if it would be different had I decided to take up the violin instead of the piano.

I manage to drag her over to my place every few days and we work on duets. Mixed in with the Beethoven piano sonatas are a few violin sonatas and we work on the Kreutzer together. She appologizes every five minutes and I hit wrong notes everywhere, but I love it when we play together, even though it's taken us three days to get through the first movement.

I want to be with Audrey all the time. Living three doors away isn't close enough; but I know if this keeps up, it'll only be a matter of time before we're living together; fingers crossed. Since that fatefully brisk day on the bench, we've spent, at the most, an hour away from each other. We are practically sewn together at the hip and if that's not enough, she has a completely incredible stereo which was given to her as a high school graduation gift. It probably cost a grand - further proof she comes from a well-heeled family. When we aren't tackling the duets, we hang out in her apartment, usually for days at a stretch, never going out except to buy food or cigarettes or to use my fake i.d. to buy wine. The past couple of days it's rained, so we've just stayed in bed, wrapped up with each other, listening to Brahms and Schumann; her favorites. All the symphonies, all the chamber music.

We trade off. I play Miles Davis or Errol Garner and then we both take turns playing favorite pop records. We both like The Beatles, The Doors, Moby Grape and Procol Harum.

There's nothing we don't say or reveal about each other that we don't talk about until dawn. The time we've spent is idyllic. Whatever is going on around us doesn't seem to matter; the real world has managed to disappear. Even if it is only temporary.


On Christmas Eve morning the phone starts ringing. Audrey and I are busy under the comforter at a particularly inopportune moment. Audrey is seconds away from having a great orgasm. She breathlessly answers the phone and I can tell by the way she tenses up that reality has come crashing through our pleasant little door.

It's that incurable dickhead Randall. He must be crying because Audrey keeps saying over and over, "It's okay, don't worry, Randall, come on."

I slowly rise to the surface of the comforter and stick my head out. Audrey faces herself away from me. Bad sign. She doesn't want to look at me while she's talking to him. I stumble out of bed, tossing on my shirt, and walk to the bathroom.

When I leave the room, the conversation becomes heated. I stay in the bathroom and play stare-off in the mirror. At the ripe old age of twenty I am beginning to develop worry lines across my forehead and I think I see two grey hairs. I scan the bathroom while the verbal pyrotechnics continue. It's fascinating how much you can find out about a person by spending some time in their bathroom. Audrey has a kid's bathroom. Fluffy pink towels and an economy-sized jar of Mister Bubble by the bathtub. Two rubber ducks, Eenie and Meenie, sit on the edge, while a Minnie Mouse throwrug sprawls between the tub and the toilet. I keep forgetting she's eighteen and this is the first time she's playing house for real.

I stand lurched over the sink until the other room falls silent, then I pad back into the bedroom. Audrey has pulled the covers over her head but I know she's sobbing because her body gyrates every few seconds and I can hear her nose running every time she tries to breathe. I lean against the doorway and watch her. I feel a sudden chill in the room. The best I can do under the circumstances is sigh and sit beside her. Women look terrible when they cry.

It doesn't matter what it's about or who they are, there's always something painfully disastrous and heart-wrenching about seeing a woman sob uncontrollably. It is one of the all-time worst feelings on earth. And they always want you to leave them alone; and to fuck off - "Why are you staring?"

But you're compelled to sit there and wait for the right moment, and you blow every one of them. I'm sitting there, trying to think of something profound to say. All I can do is rub her shoulders and mumble, "Randall, huh?"

She nods her head. "He still loves me. He wants to get back together."

Oh swell. Oh delicious. Oh son-of-a-bitch!

Audrey draws back the covers and turns to face me. She really does look terrible. Her eyes are pink runny pools and her nose is red and dripping all over the place. "Oh Jesus, Nelson, I love you and I don't know what to do."

She reaches up and pulls me close. We kiss. Her mouth is wet from salt and the tears are warm and her nose runs all over my shirt collar. She smells like a warm ocean. I wrap my arms around her and rock her back and forth. She finally stops crying and we hold each other. After a few minutes she breaks away. "I've got to blow my nose."She bolts up and runs to the bathroom for Kleenex.

I sit on the edge of the bed feeling elated and skeptical. She loves me, she said so; but she has a history with Randall and, no matter how weird he is, they broke up several times and they always got back together. You always hope you're going to be the one who changes the course of history, but you never know how entangled previous ghosts in unnamed closets are.

Audrey comes back with a box of Kleenex in her hand and stands at the edge of the bed. She's wrapped herself in a robe she hung on the bathroom door. It's powder-blue terrycloth. She wipes her nose several times. "I'm sorry, I don't mean to get like this. He's such an asshole sometimes."

She won't look at me. Her hair is spilling over her face and the part carefully arranged on the side is all messed up. It starts raining outside and the drops pelt the window pane in an off-beat rhythm.

"You're still in love with this guy, aren't you?"

Audrey raises her head and rests her chin on her hand. She stares up at a portrait of Arturo Toscanini peering down on both of us from the wall just beside her wardrobe. Even Arturo seems to be waiting for an answer. "It's not all black and white - cut and dried like that," she says, letting out a sigh and wiping her eyes for the hundredth time. "I've known Randall since High School and we were both virgins, if you know what I mean."

Audrey glances at me with one of those "It's like that" expressions on her face. Clearly, she's having doubts and I am beginning to feel uneasy. Even though she's resentful that Randall keeps hanging around and is so dependent on her, I can tell her mind isn't entirely made up. Under the circumstances, I'm just going to have to be gracious and shut up.

I put my arm around Audrey and draw her close. I sigh and stare at the floor and hope for a miracle or two. I tell her long and sad stories about Leslie Noritake and Thea Talber. I want her to know I'm no novice at this. I don't know why; it's a boring legacy. God knows what she's thinking.

We spend most of the day talking. The more we talk, the more I know I want this situation to work out. But Randall, however unsightly he is, has gotten there first. And if that weren't enough; he's coming back to L.A. for New Year's. We take turns staring up at Toscanini. I'm sure we aren't thinking the same thoughts. She's probably wondering how she can make both situations happen and I'm wondering if I pushed Randall off a tall building, would I have to prove it was an accident? Life would be so much easier if it wasn't for Randall.

Well, maybe him and one other person.

"You're not letting that hippy in here!" Salvatore Piantadosi is Audrey's eminent dentist dad. Good ol' Sal: the reason Audrey's teeth are so white.

Okay, my hair is now half-way down my back. It's parted in the middle and flies all over the place. I've grown a Fu-Manchu moustache that droops ominously over my upper lip and down the sides of my mouth. I will be the first to admit to a hippy ethic, but Sal is a dyed-in-the-wool reactionary.

Nobody but NOBODY who looks like me should be allowed to get within fifty miles of his daughter, especially on Christmas Eve. He lets Audrey in, but slams the door in my face. I know rejection when I hear it. I turn and walk back down the two hundred and twenty steps of the plush Los Feliz mansion to my Volkswagen. I think fleetingly about bombing the house or pissing on their front door, but being a peace-loving individual, I don't go past the thinking- only stage.

"Nelson! Nelson!" Audrey yells behind me. I turn round. She's racing down the steps of the house, trying to catch me before I drive off.

"I'm sorry about my dad," she pants. "I told him if he didn't let you in, I was leaving and not coming back." Common sense should tell me to keep walking.

Common sense should also tell me to do a lot of things in my life, but it never does. Christ only knows what it's good for. I take one look at Audrey and follow her back up the two hundred steps.

I'm stuck sitting next to Sal at the family dinner table, flanked by several cousins and assorted relatives. Sal says absolutely nothing pleasant to me; just glares. He's short, with straight, solid-white hair and deeply chisled features. He looks like the kind of dentist who uses Novocaine only as a last resort. He has dark beady eyes that convince me evil thoughts are running rampant in his brain. And they're all directed at me.

Audrey sits across from me, quietly dying; and Cecilia, Audrey's mother, who has tinted her hair a little too dark and uses just a little too much hair- spray, sits to the left of Sal. Cecilia is very animated, joking about anything she can think of, filling every square second of dead air with some kind of jocular comment. She doesn't want Sal to open his mouth. Too late.

"How about those little shitheads at Kent State?" he gloats over dessert, blowing a cloud of cigar smoke in my face, praying for a fight.

"What little shitheads might those be?" I ask.

"The little shitheads who burn draft cards, that's what little shiheads I'm talking about!" Sal, turning blister red, his knuckles turning white his pencil-thin nose tightening.

"Sally tell me; are you really that short, or did somebody saw off the legs of your chair?"

I hit a nerve. Sal bolts up and lunges at me with his butter knife. Audrey screams. Cecilia shrieks and almost faints and a plethora of cousins wrestle Sal to the floor. I quietly step back out of the room with the words, "Love your Dad, Audrey! Not much!"

He lets out a seething animal yell as I run out the door, not to return to Casa Piantadosi on this Christmas Eve night, or any other in my lifetime.

I drive to San-Mont Liquors on Santa Monica and Vermont and look aged enough to buy a fifth of Jack Daniels and a six-pack of Canada Dry Ginger Ale. I take it back to my apartment and drink the Christmas in. George is busy playing *The Shadow Of Your Smile* for the thousandth time and I am determined to get shit-faced drunk.

One of the few remnants of my youth still intact at my parents' house is my Zenith TransOceanic Radio. I had the good sense to bring it over to my new apartment, as it's my only source of information and entertainment. I flip it on and dial around for a station. The best I can come up with is Armed Forces Radio Service, playing Christmas music. The Christmas tree sits in the middle of the living room; barren and green, with no lights, no bulbs, just a hulk of holiday cheer. I pour and drink and pour and drink and the world slowly begins to fade away.

I fall out of my self-induced coma on Christmas Day feeling more depressed than the night before. My mouth is desert dry and furry. I have no complicated requests; I just want to hide under the covers, like Audrey when she spoke to Randall. I want to cry and blow my nose with Kleenex and have somebody rub my shoulders and say it's all right. I want to sit on the edge of the bed and look up at Arturo Toscanini and have somebody tell me they love me and everybody has a past.

I slowly put bits of myself together and crawl off to the bathroom. I turn on the shower, but there is no hot water. In retrospect it's probably a good thing, because the chill factor injects instant sobriety into me. My hangover vanishes, but I am frozen stiff in the process. I get dressed and plod over to Audrey's.

I make it to her apartment and gingerly knock on the door. There is no answer.

I knock a couple more times. Each time the knock is louder. Still no answer. I look at my watch; it's quarter to three in the afternoon. I assume she has to be at her parents' house so I turn and start down the steps.

Just then the door opens. A pudgy, round, pasty-faced kid appears. "Did you want something?"

It's Randall.

He looks glazed and half-asleep and exactly like I remembered him. He drove overnight from Portland and probably Audrey doesn't know, or maybe she really does. Maybe she's really there, hiding under the sheets until I'm gone. I'm not going to take any chances.

I shrug my shoulders. "Wrong place, sorry."

I walk down the steps and leave the building.

I leave a note addressed to Audrey tacked to the door of my apartment. It's simple and direct: *"I love you. I wish life made sense. You can reach me through my parents."* I leave the number and hope she finds it. I decide to have Christmas dinner at my parents' house.

Christmas with my parents means yams, salad with ingredients no one can pronounce, a bizarre concoction of mashed nuts in a gooey paste called Nutty- Buddy which sticks to everything, jicama and brown rice. Still, it's Christmas and I have to spend it someplace, even if it means sharing it with Friends Of The Mothership, a Vegetarian UFO group my mother has befriended in recent months.

I drive down Vermont to Wilshire, where I turn right and head west. The rain that started the day before is beginning to let up, which is good since my windshield wipers work only every thirty seconds. All the radio stations in Los Angeles have an appropriately Christmas-oriented tune playing. I make it as far as Orbach's Department Store on Wilshire, before I feel a strange gnawing sensation develop in the pit of my stomach. I'm not sick. If I was, I would've done something about it hours earlier. It's the sick I get when I know something is about to come to a screeching, grinding end; especially when it's something that matters. And Audrey really-really matters. I concentrate on the street; scanning the sidewalks, driving by shops that are, even on Christmas Day, open and having 'After Christmas' sales.

I keep drifting back to the feeling in my stomach. My upper lip is quivering and my eyes start to get wet; wet to the point where I can see nothing in front of me, even though it's stopped raining and the sun is starting to break though the clouds.

I pull the car over to the curb and sit there, rubbing my face, and staring up at the white puffy clouds that sail quickly across the sky. I rest my head on the steering wheel and wait. Maybe if I wait there long enough the feeling will go away. It doesn't - even after an hour. The sun has gone from the horizon by the time I roll my window down and let the cold breeze rush in. I start the VW up again and continue driving down Wilshire.

I get to my parents' house to find the assembled crowd has already gone through most of the courses of their Christmas meal. The house is filled with the usual gang of oddballs. Not crazy enough for strait-jackets, but not sane enough to read a road map.

"You know Nancy, the Melourians brought jicama here to Earth; not many people know that." That tidbit of inter-planetary trivia comes from Enid, a very short, fat woman with terrible skin. They all have terrible skin, and they all have 'coping' problems. The real world just doesn't seem like the place they're prepared to be part of. In addition to Enid, the group consists of a two-legged laboratory mouse named Hilary, who has an aversion to washing his hair and brushing his teeth; Christine, Henry and an Indian couple named Jupi and Mira. Christine and Henry don't appear to be part of any particular sex; they are a combination of both, but neither with parts that have any appeal to the opposite. Jupi is an Ethnomusicology professor at UCLA and Mira is a Bangalore version of a San Fernando Valley housewife. They bicker and joke at each other in Hindi and everybody eats with their hands.

My parents are surprised to see me. My father seems, in a way, relieved. "Gunther, how the hell are you?"he keeps asking, pressing his hand into my shoulder, as if imploring me not to go anyplace. He hasn't called me Gunther in years. On his breath I can smell the Canadian Club he's been sneaking all night. I have the feeling I am the sanest person he's seen all day. The traditional tin foil Christmas tree has been replaced by a tiny fake potted tree of papier mache and flocking. It was made in Korea and is painted green with a spray of silver that's supposed to be tinsel. I receive my presents; three pairs of Paisley Polyester socks, a bag of nuts and a book called Man: Know Thyself. I spend most of my visit listening to theories on flying saucers from the assembled multitude, while tossing Omar off my leg, who is showing, in his misguided humping, that he's happy to see me. My dad tosses *Exotic Village* on the hi-fi. Christmas is now complete.

My father sets me down on the sofa and shoots me an intense, but slightly boozy gaze. "Gunther, your mother and I have decided to sell the house and move to Hawaii."

They've been talking about moving to Hawaii ever since we came to the West Coast from Cleveland. But this time, my father has been collecting Honolulu newspapers and cutting out real estate ads. They have been dumping the family heirlooms at garage sales, and even more of a sure-fire indication, my mother is selling Enid her flying saucer book collection. They mean business.

"We're asking seventy-five for the place," my dad chirps enthusiastically. He shows me the ad in the L.A. Times Real Estate section. There it is, our house, on the market - definitely for sale. I feel as though the scenes of my youth are in danger of vanishing before my eyes. My home destined to become somebody else's dream home - my room, some other kid's inner sanctum.

Then it occurs to me that I've spent most of my waking hours from age twelve to seventeen trying to get OUT of this place. Why should I feel sorry if they want to sell it? Christ, they can bulldoze the place and turn it into a bowling alley if they want to!

I nod appreciatively and shove Omar and his fire engine erection off my leg.

My mother starts absentmindedly snapping her fingers. "Oh, I forgot to tell you; Burgie called: He's coming over later. He wants to talk to you about something."

I haven't seen Burgie since I met Audrey. He is the one person, aside from Buzz and Stoika, who can shed some light on the Audrey situation. He can always be counted on for sage advice, however misanthropic it might be.

"Get out of there quickly. Like now!" Burgie doesn't mince words. I run the whole picture down to him while we sit in his van, parked at Leo Carillo Beach. We are swapping slugs from three different bottles of wine he got from his father. Burgie sits swirling a small glass of red wine around in his hand and keeps shaking his head. "They make movies about that kind of stuff. The kind of movies where everybody winds up dead."

Okay, so he's pushing it. I never thought of myself as Robert Mitchum and I don't picture Audrey as Lizabeth Scott. But he has a point; this is a no-win situation, just like Thea Talber and the San Francisco fiasco.

"Burgie, all I ever want from life is peace and happiness and it hasn't happened to me since the day I hit puberty."

"Life is a pisser," Burgie answers, sighing.

"How was the funeral?" I ask, changing the subject. He's just come back from Boston the night before.

"It was okay." Burgie doesn't say anything else. He keeps sipping his wine.

"Did you know your uncle pretty well?"

"Uh, yeah, kind of." Burgie becomes quiet again.

"Burgie, is there something you want to tell me?"

"No." And this time there is long silence.

"Well, yeah. He mentioned me in his will. He wasn't from Boston you know; he was from L.A. He visited Boston once and liked it so much he asked to be buried there. He owned a lot of property around L.A. and . . . well, it looks like I inherited the Hound House."

"The what?"

"In the Valley, near Topanga, he owned this dog kennel and he left it to me with the proviso that I could do anything I wanted with it just as long as I kept it until I was twenty-five." Burgie looks distressed. "I don't know anything about dogs."

"Nothing to it," I tell him. "You feed them, you walk them, you talk to them."

Burgie nods his head and clears his throat. He always clears his throat when he is about to ask a favor. "I don't suppose you'd be interested in sharing the house with me and helping take care of the kennel?"

In the land of golden opportunities, this was about as golden as it was going to get. I grab the offer in mid-sentence. Having weathered ten years of Dolores and now Omar's hump-happy little self, I figure I know as much about dogs as anybody.

We take the Santa Monica Freeway to my parents' house and pick up my car. Burgie follows me over to my less-than-two-week-old apartment. It takes me very little time to grab the things I need and toss them into my car and Burgie's van. I'm starting to get used to quick exits; I wonder if I'm ever going to have more than the bare minimum of earthly possessions to deal with.

The way my life is going; probably not. I write an amended note to Audrey, enclosing the key to the apartment, telling her, as a going away present, she can have all the furniture if she wants.

I'll freely admit it's an irrational thing to do; running out, escaping. Leaving without so much as a face-to-face goodbye. Secretly, I feel like a coward. But I'm angry and upset and I don't want to get stuck in the revolving door again. It was bad enough with Thea. I just don't want to go through it again. I want to let Audrey know I am hurt and why I'm hurt and if she wants to talk about it, she can call me. But that's about it. I cross out my parents' phone number and scribble in the number for Hound House. Knowing Audrey, I think for certain she'll call the next day.

# CHAPTER FIFTEEN

## MALCONTENTS AND OTHER LOVE-OBJECTS

"This came in the mail."

Burgie hands me a cardboard box containing a small jar. It's about three inches around and has a black plastic lid, sealed shut. There's clear liquid inside and a strange, fleshy-looking object floating around.

"What is it?" I ask him.

"Jeanie's appendix," Burgie replies.

I almost drop the box. Jeanie Nurstrom? The same Jeanie Nurstrom he broke up with in high school, who threatened to kill herself? Who instead trashed his van with a tire-iron and tossed a sack of bloody chicken parts all over the front seat, ruining not only the front seat upholstery but the Muntz eight- track stereo tape player and *Between The Buttons*? That Jeanie Nurstrom?

"She dropped out of Cosmetology school. She wants to see me."

I know the relative calm and peace of this sleepy San Fernando Valley community isn't going to last long. I know how volatile the relationship between Jeanie and Burgie has been.

Myron, Sniffles, Butch, Ingrid and Boudou Saved From Drowning, five normally quiet and well-mannered dogs are all acting a little metaphysical when I come by to feed them this afternoon. I can tell by their plaintive barks that they know some unexplainable force of anxiety is going to be visited upon them soon; very soon.

Hound House is a breath of fresh air to me, if you ignore the heady aroma brought on by fifteen dogs milling around the backyard. Fifteen dogs and fifteen different personalities. After a while I start to feel the only difference between us and them are the two extra legs and no grasp of spoken English.

Christmas vacation has come and gone and I'm back at school, but this time making a one-hour commute each way from Woodland Hills. It's fine by me, I have grown to like driving in L.A.; it gives me time to think. Now that Jeanie has sent her appendix to Burgie, I have other things to think about besides Audrey Piantadosi who has vanished into thin air. Randall, the geek boyfriend, hasn't. I know, because I occasionally park in front of her apartment four out of five days a week and watch her window, hoping for some sign. I never see her. Only him pacing around with an oboe in his mouth.

I wonder if Jeanie has managed to change over the past couple of years. If she's still prone to manic fits and outbursts as she was in high school. So I'm a little apprehensive when we go to LAX to pick her up.

I'm expecting to find some full-blown twig-out leering at us from behind a grimy trench coat and wearing some broken, pasted together Foster-Grants. Jeanie surprises us. She acts and looks completely normal. So normal it's frightening.

She takes her customary spot in the passenger seat of the van; the very same van that, less than two years earlier, she almost single-handedly destroyed. She smiles sweetly and speaks in soft wistful tones. She reaches over and touches Burgie's leg, running her hand up to his fingers, squeezing them lightly while he drives, looking admiringly at him, telling him how glad she is to see us.

Between the airport and Woodland Hills, Jeanie and Burgie behave as if they had never broken up. Burgie is lonely and it shows. Jeanie was a major episode in his life. He often says he regretted breaking up with Jeanie in the first place. Of course, I have to remind him that he was the one who kept telling us

Jeanie was driving him insane at the time.

Jeanie's face seems different. The angular cheeks are smoothed out and rounder. Her eyes are deeper set. Even her hair has changed. It's past her shoulders now, dropping in waves behind her back. She's let her natural color come in, and light brown roots are beginning to appear. She's more relaxed and assured now. During high school, she would clip sentences and spiral into a nasal twang when she got excited. This version of Jeanie is from another planet.

So why do I get the feeling this isn't going to last?


"Don't these dogs drive you fucking nuts?" Jeanie shrieks at the top of her lungs, trying to be heard over the din of the unexplainably nervous hounds. A Dachshund named Murray, a normally docile dog who sleeps fourteen hours a day, while his owners are in Tahiti, begins the latest wave of howling. Murray doesn't have a piercing bark like the others; it's a modulated yodel. But he starts yodelling somewhere around three in the morning and it continues well into the following day. Boudou Saved From Drowning, an Irish Setter who belongs to a couple of film editors, takes up the barking cause and soon the whole kennel is in an uproar.

Since the uproar began a week ago, Burgie and I have perfected the art of counselling the dogs; we get into their cages and talk to them. The topics aren't important, just as long as we spend a minimum of ten minutes with each of them, soothing ruffled nerves.

Murray will begin his psycho-serenade at very inopportune times for Burgie and Jeanie. When he starts, Jeanie bolts out of bed and runs outside and starts screaming at the malcontents to shut up. When calm is restored, she stomps back inside and a loud argument kicks up. Jeanie can't understand why Burgie has gotten involved in something as ludicrous as a dog kennel.

It quickly becomes just like the old days. Objects start flying around the room and voices escalate to operatic levels, competing with the dogs in the sheer-volume department. I wonder what their relationship would be like if they were living in an apartment surrounded by a few hundred other people.

With the comparative seclusion of a place like Woodland Hills, which is pretty remote, they could probably kill each other and nobody would notice.

"Her doctor upped the dosage, but she ran out."

"That explains where the warm and fuzzy Jeanie came from."

Luckily, my room is at the other end of the house, away from all but the loudest of shrieks and yells. Still, I look up to the ceiling and think, no matter how much things seemed to have changed; it's how much they remain the same that counts. How long is this reunion of Burgie and Jeanie going to last?

By six o'clock in the morning the fighting has stopped. It's been replaced by something else; something bigger than me, Burgie, Jeanie and all the dogs combined: an earthquake.

Say what you want about animals being dumb. They have a good idea when disasters are around the corner, and they do their best to let you know they know. But we, the smart ones, never pay attention.

It starts slowly - a gentle rocking motion from side to side. I think it's a dream at first. Then the house begins to shake violently. By then it's almost too late. One of my new possessions is a bookcase, which I've crammed with musical scores and all the books and records I've managed to rescue from my parents' house. The entire bookcase comes careening over on top of the bed, missing me by inches.

Luckily, I am already up and running out of the room. But the force of the earthquake causes my piano, which is on wheels, to glide towards me and knock me over. I find myself crawling around on the floor, trying to get out of the house. The dogs are freaking out in the yard, trying to jump the twelve-foot fence. The only one not participating in the escape attempt is Murray, the Dachshund. He sits in a corner with a wide-eyed look of reproach on his face that seems to say, "See, I told you this was going to happen, see? But you wouldn't believe me!"

Burgie and Jeanie come roaring out of their bedroom, with Jeanie yelling at the top of her lungs, "Oh Shit! We're all gonna die!" She wraps herself in a blanket and staggers out to the front yard. Jeanie uses the earthquake as an opportunity to try some real full-scale theatrics. She collapses on the lawn, just as most of the dogs jump over the kennel fence and race towards freedom.

For some reason, Jeanie decides they are going to trample her to death so she screams, "Forgive me, Father, for I have sinned!" and crumples to the ground. The dogs run past, avoiding her, knowing a nut case when they see one. The earthquake lasts a little over a minute, but it feels like hours. The earth finally stops moving. And then it's time for the aftershocks.

Jeanie isn't going to wait around for them. When the airport reopens, she catches the next flight back to San Diego, while Burgie and I try to gather up all the escapees from Hound House who have, by now, reverted to the wild.

However, we manage to get everybody back, and several more. When the earthquake hit we had fifteen dogs; fourteen bolted and one stayed, Murray the Dachshund. With the final tally, we have over thirty dogs. We can't figure out where the other fifteen came from and none of them have any identification. What's worse, nobody will claim them even after putting up signs at every supermarket and drugstore in the West Valley. Hound House is rapidly becoming a non-profit shelter for wayward pets.


Jeanie left in such a hurry she didn't say goodbye. Burgie is convinced, and somewhat relieved, that she's gone for good. However, two weeks later Jeanie reappears at the front door, this time with a guy she introduces as Smitty. Smitty is something of a hulk and gives the impression of being one of the dimmer bulbs in the lamp shop. He looks like an escapee from boot camp, with a thin stubble of hair on top of his head and an attempt at a moustache above a thick but undistinctive upper lip. He has a heavy spray of acne across his face and a tattoo on each arm, both made in El Centro, a town where nothing happens, ever. One features a dragon spitting a shaft of fire and the other, a large heart with a dagger stuck through the middle. They look like Number Ten and Number Twenty on the list of do-it-yourself tattoos. Smitty has caricature written all over him.

Jeanie spends most of the day with Burgie, while Smitty sits on the sofa in the living room and smokes, staring at the two of them, saying very little except a few grunts when questions are asked. Jeanie is playful and in good spirits, but nobody can figure out what Smitty is.

Finally towards the afternoon, as Smitty is busy warming up the car for the drive back to San Diego, Burgie asks Jeanie who he is.

"That's my husband. We got married two weeks ago," she tells him matter-of-factly.

Burgie stops phoning Jeanie after that and, even when she calls, he won't talk to her. As Martha And The Vandellas once put it: *Love, love, love, makes me do these things.*


Summer arrives at Hound House with a vengeance. I always forget how hot summers are in the Valley until they arrive, and then I'm painfully reminded, but it's usually too late to do anything about it. This particular year is going to be worse, because the air-conditioner has broken down and business isn't good enough to fix it.

The U.S. Postal Service is capable of really good and really bad things - the bad things, which are more numerous, are audits from the IRS, dunning letters from creditors, or teary farewells from lovers. The good things, and they are few and far between, are sometimes viewed as miracles. One such miracle is the letter of acceptance I receive from Cal-Arts, a school I have been trying desperately to get into. Even more miraculous than mere acceptance is the fact that they have actually given me a scholarship to go there. This is especially good, since before I got the news I had twenty dollars to my name and was having no luck selling eight-track tapes door-to-door. It was somebody's idea of a good idea; a sort of Fuller Brush Man for Pop music. The only problem was, nobody liked what I had to sell and I was always selling to the wrong people. I would get the Country Western crowd the day I had a case of Sly And The Family Stone tapes and I would get Sly and The Family Stone fans when I had Slim Whitman tapes. I couldn't win. Cal-Arts is my first taste of legitimacy. It's a fine arts-oriented college with a sprawling campus situated at the northern end of the Valley.

I still commute to school and, after some creative juggling with my student loan, I become the proud owner of my own synthesizer. Music is making me very happy with my life. So happy that I am almost completely unaware of how lonely I have become and how it has been almost two years since I last saw Audrey.

I still drive by the apartment building on Heliotrope and gaze up at what was once Audrey's window. But she has long since moved away and even Randall is no longer there. The last number I had for her doesn't work and there is no referral. After several attempts and getting cold feet in mid-dial, I reluctantly decide to call Audrey's parents. Luckily I get her mother, Cecilia. She's cordial, but she doesn't really remember me - I'm sure she's blocked the Christmas episode out of her mind, like any other traumatic event.

According to her, Audrey is going to Moscow to study at the Conservatory and has been living in New York. If she's well on her way to establishing a career as a musician, I'm certain she has forgotten completely about me. Still, I give Cecilia my phone number and ask her to say hello to Audrey for me next time they talk. There isn't anymore I can say.

Burgie and I get our first letter from Stoika in almost a year. She's pregnant again. Buzz has quit the Post Office and left her shortly afterwards. Apparently he sent her a postcard saying he's wandering around the country 'on a quest for the meaning of life,' to which Stoika comments "Yeah, under every skirt he can lay his hands on." Word about Leslie is that she's gotten married to a French Political Science student named Alain and is living happily-ever-after somewhere in France.

I have only been asleep for a few minutes before I am catapulted into the upright position at three in the morning by intense, persistent ringing. I grab for the phone, which is right next to the bed, knocking the receiver off the hook and sending it crashing to the floor. I scramble for it and manage to hit myself in the head as the coiled up telephone cord snaps back, bringing the receiver sailing along with it. I press the phone to my ear and groggily answer it.

I hear sobbing at first and finally a nervous voice blurts out, "How the hell do you get to Woodland Hills?"

I am so used to giving directions to the place that I can do it in my sleep. "Take the Ventura Freeway to the Topanga Canyon offramp and go north four miles to Devonshire. Turn right and we're at the corner of Devonshire and Topanga. Thank you for calling Hound House."

The phone clicks. The receiver stays at my ear until the buzzing of the dial tone reaches my subconscious. I roll over and hang it up and try to settle back to sleep. And then my eyes pop open. I know that voice! It's Audrey! I rocket out of bed, flailing my arms around in excitement. I'm still half-asleep and completely confused.

I run back and forth between my bedroom and the front porch, waiting for her to drive up. I finally decide it's a good idea to put my clothes on. My stomach is spinning around like a washing machine, my hands are soggy and my mouth feels like it's packed in burlap. Maybe I dreamed it, maybe I've imagined she called. Why would Audrey, of all people, call me at three in the morning after not talking to me for two years? It was probably a wrong number. Or worse, some drunk who's not looking for me but really looking for Burgie.

Burgie has been hanging around in some dicey bars lately, and coming home with some strange versions of women.

And so it doesn't completely register when I walk back out to the front porch and sit down on the steps that Audrey is already standing there, watching me. The illusion on the porch looks exactly the same as she did the last time I saw her.

Only when she wraps her arms around me and buries her head in my shoulder do I realize I'm not imagining it.

"Jesus Christ, I missed you," she sighs.

"That goes for me, double," I sigh back.

We cling to each other tightly. The icy distance that seperated us the past two years melts in seconds. It's as if we were never apart. I know I don't want to be away from her again. Lucky for me she feels the same way.

"Who's the living doll?" Burgie whispers, as he saunters out of the kitchen to the dining room. Audrey is busy making coffee. I peer in and see her standing at the stove. She's wearing a white tank-top t-shirt and a snug-fitting pair of white cotton bikini panties. I think even she will admit she looks stunning.

"That's Audrey, remember?" I whisper back, "The one with the oaf boyfriend?"

Burgie's mouth drops three feet. "Good-night Inez! What's she doing here?"

"She's moving in."

After getting dressed, Audrey walks out to her car, a brand new gleaming green Audi, pops open the trunk and takes out three suitcases, her violin and boxes of manuscripts and books.

Randall apparently followed her even to Moscow, and it was while they were living in New York afterwards that she realized he was eventually going to drive her insane with his constant dependance on her. She began to think more and more of the times we had and regretted letting Randall monopolize her feelings in the first place. Taking a cue from my episode two years earlier, she walked out. She even left him a note telling him to keep the furniture. As far as Audrey was concerned, the world is loaded with thrift shops.

With Audrey around, Hound House takes on an air of rustic charm, even though new houses and apartment buildings are springing up around us daily. Audrey hasn't told me if her parents know we're living together - although I suspect Cecilia probably does, since she was the one who gave Audrey my phone number. Audrey disappears every Wednesday night and every Sunday morning to visit them. She comes back depressed and it takes hours to snap her out of it. I'm not sure if she's depressed by seeing them, or depressed that she's lying to them.

By the time Audrey does tell them, Sal doesn't remember me anyway. But then, he wouldn't recognize me if he did. My hair has gotten shorter; it's also gotten green and white and pink with blue tips. I'm playing keyboards in a band made up of Cal-Arts students, known as Mister Jones. I've also discovered lipstick and eye-shadow.

# CHAPTER SIXTEEN

## HIGH VOLTAGE SLACKS AND BABALU SLEEVES

The ad on the Music Department bulletin board reads, 'Keyboard Player Wanted'.

I need money.

Audrey has been auditioning for orchestras and practicing eight hours a day. I'm in my last quarter at Cal-Arts and working for my Masters degree in Music.

Burgie has started getting complaints from the neighbors about the dogs: the area surrounding Hound House has become clogged with people and traffic and, even though Burgie has promised to keep the place until he's twenty-five, fate looks like it's stepping in sooner. It's only 1974; he still has two years left to go; and already he's gotten phone calls from four different Realtors.

With all this gleaming monetary promise, we're still broke. Audrey has been reluctantly diving into her trust fund and I am ready for anything paying decent money, save donating blood. So I answer the ad.

"Can you play one of these?" Mitch 'Bender' Bernstein asks. Mitch is a sort of three-dimensional version of The Singing Skull. He's the leader of Mister Jones and he wants to know if I know anything about Mellotrons.

Mellotrons really aren't instruments, they're electronic nightmares. They look like your average organ; regular keyboard, footpedals, the whole thing. But instead of strings like a piano, or electronic impulses like an organ, the Mellotron has tapes; miles and miles of tapes, all looped around tiny playback heads. It's like having eighty-eight tape-recorders in something shaped like a Wurlitzer. Each tape has three different selections: voices, strings and horns. The sound they make is fascinating, eerie. The Beatles used them a lot and The Moody Blues made *Nights In White Satin* with one. The problem with Mellotrons is that they break down constantly. The tapes stretch and any sudden movement knocks the whole thing out of alignment. You can't get them repaired easily because there is only one Mellotron repair person on the West Coast and, if you need new tapes, you have to send away to England for them because that's where Mellotrons are made. It seems they're not destined for every household in America. Mitch can't play one to save his life; he just bought it because nobody else he knows has one.

Since buying my first Moog I've become interested in electronic music, and I now have several synthesizers in my collection, which makes me a shoe-in for the position of keyboard player. The auditions stop with me. Mister Jones has been formed.

Mitch is lead singer and also plays bass; David 'Noddy' Pine, who has dyed his hair whiter than a laboratory mouse and wears impenetrably dark glasses, is lead guitarist; and Martin 'Flash Kid' Peperno is the drummer. Martin is chunky. He has big arms and curly hair and wears tee-shirts with sequins. He sweats gallons behind the drums and takes the longest to get ready for anything because he spends two hours applying his makeup. He affects a nasal - fay way of talking and chews lots of gum. His favorite expression is "I'm bisekshall, isn't everybody?"

Mister Jones is your basic 'Glitter-Glam' group. David Bowie has been designated pop icon of the century, followed by Mott The Hoople, The Sweet, Roxy Music and The New York Dolls. Everything we play has to sound something like one of them or, even better, like all of them at once.

"Well, first ya need an image," Mitch blurts out, taking gulps of Smirnoff's 100 proof between drags on his Dunhill cigarette. I'm dubbed 'Whizz-Bang', my new pop-star name, and introduced to September Rittenberg, the ashen-grey, blue-lipped, busty girlfriend of Mitch's who does hair. She proceeds to do mine in ways I would never have imagined.

"Okay, so maybe it's not such a great idea," I tell the mirror in the bedroom as Audrey screams in horror over my transformation.

Although I grew up on Brahms, Miles Davis and Thelonius Monk and am now living with Audrey, who practises Bach and Tartini all the time, stuffing myself into a pair of skin-tight phosphorescent lime-green bell-bottom pants, three-inch white platform shoes and a gauze shirt unbuttoned to my navel seemed like the right thing to do. We are poised to play the Whiskey A-Go-Go, and the publicity machine is oiled and working overtime.

I bear a strong resemblance to a very ugly woman with questionable taste in clothing and makeup. I tower perilously above the ground in my shoes and have no idea my legs are that skinny until I wrapped them in such tight-fitting pants.

"You know, those pants are going to make you sterile," Audrey points out, looking at how intimate everything is fitting in my crotch. Thank God I've lost weight since Junior High. I'm now down to a hundred and twenty-eight pounds. Anything over that and the clothes would make me look like The Michelin Man. The things you do for commerce. Forget art - we're strictly on a money thing here, I keep reminding myself.

Mitch isn't a musician, a student or a singer. He's a self-promotion institution. In a matter of days after starting the group, we have four magazines and six newspapers visit us. Mitch pretends to be a pop-star to the inth degree. He drinks constantly, snorts too much coke and smokes nothing but Dunhill cigarettes. He spends hours in front of a mirror, trying different poses, looking deep, moody or intense and making sure he holds his bass so that it achieves just the right sexual suggestions. To Mitch, image is everything and, if we play loud enough, nobody will care if we miss notes.

He wants to be a songwriter, but he writes such undigestible classics as: *Curfew Violator*, with memorable lines like: "The deaf hear the blind see. What about you - what about me?" Deep stuff. Fortunately, most of the words and music come from David, who at least is a Creative Writing major at school.

Occasionally Martin comes up with something, but it never makes any sense, or it never goes anywhere; just one line, over and over, like his greatest hit, *I Wanna Be A Miracle* that's the line, over and over and over. I make a couple of contributions, getting into the free-for-all spirit of group unity, including a Roxy Music-influenced song called *From You Later*. We go so far as to record it, but I have big-big doubts if I'll ever see it on vinyl in my lifetime.

We've had offers to play some of the dances at school, but Mitch refuses; he wants to head straight to the big time. It's the Whiskey A-Go-Go or nothing.

After a month of more-or-less rehearsals, Mitch arranges to have publicity pictures taken. I'm happy about that because it means we're getting closer to making some money for a change.

"It's important that we all look really fabulous," Mitch keeps imploring over and over, as he alternately gulps Smirnoffs, drags Dunhill's and blows his nose. None of us can figure out how he manages to afford such expensive habits, since he has no visable means of support. We decide he's either from a rich family, a hustler or September's bank rolling him. She's mentioned race horses once or twice.

The first batch of photos are taken at a landfill; truly fabulous. The second batch has us at Frederick's of Hollywood and the last batch has us lined up in front of a chainlink fence.

I am standing. I am smiling. I am pouting. I am doing everything the photographer asks me to do. But when I get the photos back I don't see me anywhere. All I see is a seven-foot mook, wrapped up in a black feather boa, with rainbow colored hair, big red lips, eyeliner and an expression on his face that seems to ask, "Who farted?"

Mitch is a master of the con. He never takes no for an answer and manages to get a lot of doors opened which were previously bolted shut, just by perseverance. Case in point: the recording studio. We get three days of free recording time, normally had for fifty dollars an hour. We manage to lay the basic tracks to eight of the ten songs we know. Mitch has scammed another recording studio into giving us free time to lay the vocals down. Luckily, or unluckily, the second scam doesn't materialize. But at the moment it doesn't really matter.

Mitch is busy plastering our photos all over every telephone pole, record store and laundromat in Hollywood.

Maybe I don't see the possibilities, but all of his scamming must've done wonders with the Whiskey A-Go-Go management because they've booked us to play Monday night.

Historically, Monday nights are slow in the club world. Who wants to go to a nightclub on a Monday night? Monday nights are when record companies book new bands to give them exposure, usually to the press, who turn out in droves and drink like fish because it's all for free.

We're booked as the warm-up act to a Japanese group called, and I swear this is the truth, Hello Baby - Want A Kiss. They've just finished recording their latest album and their record company wants to show their appreciation for the previous four gold albums by inviting every member of the press to see their show.

Mitch spends so much time standing in front of the mirror, getting his 'image' together, and pretending he's a pop-star, that he never sings, even when we're visited by all the magazines during our rehearsals or in the recording studio. Nobody has ever seen us play; Mitch just talks about it.

And then it occurs to me, "What if this guy is nothing but talk?"

David has the solution. "Play loud and look like you're in a lot of pain."

By the time Monday night rolls around, we don't need to fake looks of pain; they are honest-to-God real.

The Whiskey A-Go-Go is jammed with Japanese press and record company honchos who have been flown over from Tokyo for the party. The club is lightly sprinkled with locals, mostly people we've invited who have to pay for their own drinks. Audrey and Burgie sit in a dark corner in the back of the balcony.

A couple of guys from the magazines who interviewed us show up. But they've been invited by the Japanese record company and are wearing Hello Baby - Want A Kiss tee-shirts - some loyalty.

A few minutes before the show starts we sit nervously in the dressing room, staring at Sunset Boulevard from our second story window, waiting for Mitch to show up. When he finally staggers in with a leather bustiered September, he's an hour late, completely, sloppily, falling-down drunk. He stands in the middle of the dressing room, weaving like a palm tree in a hurricane, perched on his five-inch blue and silver-starred platform boots, pulling his johnson out of his skin-tight blue velvet pants and trying to take a piss on the coffee table. There isn't time to worry about getting Mitch sober; the club manager comes to our dressing room door and motions us it's show time. We trudge down the flight of stairs to the makeshift tunnel that leads to the stage.

I should be terrified. I have never done anything like this before in my life. But I'm not. Strangely, the only thing I'm concerned about is the hundred dollars the Whiskey is paying each of us for the show. Hopefully, no one will remember any of this in the morning.

Mitch wanted to open the set with *Hello Susie*, a song written by The Move, another group he idolizes. When we reach the darkened stage, Mitch yells,

"Anybody know the fuckin' words!?"; then trips over the drum riser, and narrowly misses careening into the audience.

"And now, ladies and gentlemen, the Whiskey A-Go-Go is proud to present, in their first Los Angeles appearance: Mister Jones!"

Mitch is still trying to right himself when the lights come on and we begin the introduction to *Hello Susie*. Tables have replaced the dance floor, to accommodate the amount of people from the record company. I scan the audience and, to my horror, all I see are row after row of dour-faced Japanese businessmen in charcoal-grey suits, staring blankly at the stage. The place no longer looks like a nightclub; it's become a mortuary. Every one of the stiffs quietly sip double-shots of Chivas Regal Scotch, which has been specially shipped in for the show. The Whiskey A-Go-Go rarely ever stocks anything alcoholic anybody has ever heard of.

After the instrumental intro, Mitch does a high-kick to the audience and splits his blue velvet pants straight up the back. Forget that he can't remember the words; he doesn't even know where he is. He collapses to the floor, with the mike in his hand, and begins howling out something that resembles a trip to the dentist.

My worst fears are confirmed - Mitch can't sing a note. On top of that, the notes he does sing are the wrong ones; he is, above everything else, tone-deaf. The whole thing has been a scam on his part. He probably hoped it would never get as far as it has. Unfortunately for him, people have taken it seriously. Here's Mitch, rolling around on stage, unable to get up, babbling something that makes no sense, plunking away on an instrument he can't play to an audience who can't understand him.

It doesn't really matter - it's beyond mattering. Mitch finally lurches up and flails around the stage in his shredded pants with his red bikini shorts poking out from underneath. He manages to tangle himself in his guitar cord, slamming over and crashing into a stage wall in a cloud of white plaster. He picks himself up and over-ends into his bass amp, toppling it over, sending the speaker cabinet of the amp flying right into him, mercifully knocking Mitch 'Bender' Bernstein out cold in a heap of electronic debris behind the stage.

For the remainder of the set, all we see of Mitch are his blue and silver platform boots dangling limply behind us. The Whiskey stage crew surveys the carnage with alarm and offers to fish him out, but I shake my head and indicate they should leave him there; it serves him right. We carry on the set without him for what has to be the longest half-hour of my life, and turn disaster into a minor triumph of sheer willpower. David takes over singing and we quickly discover he has a good voice. We do my song and the rest of the set is made up of David's songs. No one can fault us for trying. God knows we turn in spirited, even energetic performances, but after this night there aren't going to be any others.

By the time we finish our last number you can hear hair grow. We have, in the words of our drummer, Martin 'Flash Kid' Pepperno, "eaten the big one." The lights dim up and we limp off stage to lick our wounds and die the slow death of casual indifference. We leave Mitch to the stage crew, and take the painfully long trek back to our dressing room.

We're met half way up the stairs by a gang of Japanese groupies. They have to have been imported by the record company for the headliners. They look like Catholic school girls; they giggle and wear matching white cotton blouses and look terribly sweet and don't speak a syllable of English. But they are laughing at us and not with us. We smile sheepishly and continue the endless journey to our dressing room.

The hundred dollars apiece we've been promised for the show has shrunk to fifty because the hole Mitch kicked in the wall on stage needs to be repaired. Still, fifty bucks pays many bills. David and Martin sit in the dressing room and look dejected. "I guess this is it, huh?" David muses.

"Well, maybe Mitch should be our manager and we should find another singer," I joke. I am met with immediate death stares.

"I'm going back to Urban Planning," Martin says, letting out a long, disappointed sigh and sipping his one allotted Heineken from our ration of dressing-room percs.

Audrey and Burgie tap on our door and walk in. They stop short when they see our ghost-like expressions and the pall of doom engulfing our dressing room. It's in complete contrast to the world just outside our door; the happy screams and yells greeting the headliners, dressed in matching gold lame` jumpsuits, gold platform boots and massive lacquered, teased pompadours, prancing by our door towards the stage. From what we heard about them, their big claim to fame is a medley of Elvis Presley tunes sung in a sort of broken, skewed version of English. Their opening song is called *Keeping Trucking* and it has nothing to do with anything, but the audience loves them. All those charcoal suits, leaping up and yelling like a bunch of sex-starved school girls, and those for-real sex-starved school girls losing all their reserve, becoming teenage puddles on the dancefloor.

My brush with fame came and went in a lot less than the allotted fifteen minutes. According to my watch, I still have another twelve and a half to go.

Maybe I'll be a pop-star in some other life, like the next one or the next; if they still have such things by then.

Audrey and I drive home while Burgie stays behind and tries, in vain, to get the attention of at least one of the screaming school-girls.

We head over Laurel Canyon to the Ventura Freeway, taking the curves at a reasonable forty miles an hour. The windows of my VW are rolled down and the aroma of night blooming jasmine and eucalyptus rushes in, clearing my lungs of the rotten odors of stale beer, sprayed Lysol and cigarettes smoked two years ago.

"Bugs," Audrey says, "it's only fair that I warn you, you could ask me to do anything tonight and I'd agree."

Whenever couples live together for more than twenty minutes, they adopt nicknames - secret little words that identify each only to the other, like a personal scent. Because I have the unconscious habit of sticking my two front teeth out over my lower lip when I read, I've become Bugs to Audrey and Audrey has become Otto to me, probably because I called her Aud and then added the O at the end and it just evolved into Otto.

I'm not sure what Audrey is really asking, so I call her bluff. I turn around and say, "So, how about getting married then?"

"If we leave now, we can make it to Vegas by morning."

"Otto, are you serious?"

I've never seen Audrey's eyes get so big before. Those big black dots open up and there's no question she is serious. I've hit the jackpot. "Really?"

She nods her head; big black dots and Audrey's trademark grin are all I can see from the passing streetlamps glimmering in the open window.

I stop, pull a u-turn in the middle of Laurel Canyon and drive back to the Whiskey to look for Burgie. I figure if I'm going to do this, and go through with it, I need a best-man for the occasion and Burgie is definitely my best-man. I finally manage to find him, sitting at a table in a dark booth above the stage near the dressing room stairs. He resembles a wax dummy, with an idiotic smile smeared all over his face and a trance-like stare. He doesn't notice me until I come over and wave my hand in front of his face. He snaps out of his daze and seems annoyed, as if some spell has been broken. A figure slowly emerges from under the table. It's September, Mitch's girlfriend. She smiles gingerly.

"One of my contacts fell out," she says, stuffing her boobs back into her bra and quickly lacing up her bustier.

I don't comment.

"Audrey and I are getting married tonight and I was wondering if you want to be best-man."

Burgie goes into shock. I can see his chin fall and his pupils grow larger, like a Pekinese whose eyes are going to drop out of their heads any second.

"You're gonna what?"

"I've been thinking about it for a while. You want to do it?"

He zips up his pants, shuffling nervously in the naughehyde-covered booth.

September bursts into tears and howls, "Oh that's so sweet! Can I be Maid of Honor?"

We set off for Las Vegas. Including September.

September Rittenberg is your typically good-natured, basic-values kid who just happens to have a passion for bizarre clothing. She's twenty-two and goes to Art Center studying design. She likes bondage fashions; black, shiny leather and thigh-high kid-leather boots and leather bras. She carries a pair of handcuffs around in her purse most of the time.

If she and Burgie are to become an item, it will make a bewildering combination. September has an innocent, wholesome face and, aside from her makeup, which can be anything from deep-black eyeliner to severely plucked and arched eyebrows with a massive splattering of rouge on her cheeks and purple lipstick, she doesn't look like she's capable of anything more malevolent than a tap on the shoulder. Truthfully, September is all-show. She'd have a heart attack if she ever met some real S&M folks. Burgie, on the other hand, is not part of the Hollywood scene, certainly not Hollywood circa 1974, which has become slightly more warped than it was in 1966 when we were hanging around The Hullabaloo Club and when the

Whiskey A-Go-Go had acts like Trini Lopez heading the bill. That's not to say Burgie's frozen in time; he just has his very own set of idiosyncrasies going, and they are called, Double-breasted tweed Tommy Dorsey Suits and gaudy handpainted ties.

We drive into Las Vegas at six the next morning. We think it's six, but it's hard to tell, since nobody has a watch and there are no clocks to be seen.

Time purposely does not exist here.

Marriage is popular in Vegas. The whole thing is down to a science. We are in and out of the Marriage License Bureau in less than a half-hour. Burgie and September have disappeared and we find ourselves standing in front of Burgie's van, waiting for them to show up.

"Sure you want to go through with this?" I ask Audrey.

"Oh good, Bugs, you want to back out now?" Audrey throws back, looking dim.

"No, no, Otto, I'm just checking."

To be honest, my insides are flapping around like a freshly caught Halibut.

"Still love me?" I ask.

Audrey lets out a deep sigh of exasperation. "Of course I love you, you big moron."

"Just checking," I say again, trying to conceal my nervousness.

Burgie and September come running down the City Hall steps to the van. They seem particularly elated about something.

"Guess what? We're making it a double wedding," September blurts out.

Burgie is extremely pleased. I trap him in the men's room of the Law West Of The Pecos Wedding Chapel and try talking sense into him.

"Burgie, Burgie, what are you doing?"

"I believe in miracles. I see September and I hear bells. Don't ask me to explain it - I would die for her. I want to be the father of her children."

"Yeah, and not to mention she has enormous tits."

"I don't objectify people. Personally, I think she's wholesome. She reminds me of a wheat field in Kansas."

"You've never been to Kansas."

"My mind has."

"Are you sure you want to go through with this?"

"Nothing else matters in my life."

So it becomes a double wedding. Audrey and I go first, standing in front of 'Reverend' Mel D'Amicola and his wife Beatrice. Mel is fond of Audrey because she's a Piantadosi and, well, Italians stick together. Beatrice resembles a storefront mannequin. She doesn't say anything, but she smiles a lot. Her hair is a modified Lady Bird Johnson flip which she dyes jet black.

The wedding music, *I Love You Truly*, comes compliments of the Ray Charles Singers, who have, incidentally, nothing in common with Ray 'The Genius Of' Charles.

We stand in a powder-blue room covered in fleur de lys wallpaper. A massive bouquet of flowers; golds and reds and silvers and yellows, is as plastic as the Mastercharge Card Audrey uses to pay for the ceremony with. I have fifty bucks and the wedding costs seventy-five, not to mention the ten dollars I've already spent on the license. Burgie and September pool their resources.

By nine o'clock that morning we're all married and heading groggily back to L.A.

"I have a confession to make," Burgie says, turning down *Virginia Plain* by Roxy Music on the stereo. "I sold the dog kennel."

"You own a dog kennel?" September asks, raising an eyebrow.

"Not anymore."

"Picture me relieved."

It turns out Burgie has been handed a check for a million dollars. It isn't the dog kennel that's suddenly worth the inflated amount, it's the land the kennel is sitting on: right next door they're building a massive shopping center and Hound House is square in the middle of what will become the parking lot for twelve thousand cars. In honoring his uncle's wishes, Burgie inadvertently held out and the land developers became desperate.

The trip to Las Vegas was loaded with surprises, but L.A. has its own share. Mitch has bought a gun and is looking for Burgie. Audrey's parents are threatening to disown her. Myfather is thrilled but my mother is hurt that she wasn't consulted and keeps asking, "Are you sure you kids didn't have to get married?" September's mother, on the other hand, is hysterical in joy, screaming over the phone from Albany New York, "Oh Jesus, I'm so happy - I was afraid you were going to become a lesbian!"

We all have to move; the wrecking ball is scheduled to arrive on Wednesday.

Burgie is faced with the task of taking seventy-two dogs with him; the sons, daughters, cousins and grandchildren of the '1971 Sylmar Earthquake Strays.'

Burgie gives September the hard-sell and somehow persuades her to share their new home with a pack of four-legged strangers, at least until Burgie gets them new homes, which he promises her he'll do, "Next week for sure!"

September manages to get to Mitch before Mitch gets to Burgie and calms him down long enough to persuade him to check into AA and take music lessons at night, while she and Burgie move into a sprawling bungalow up Beachwood Drive in Hollywood. Burgie, for the first time since the eleventh grade, is truly and completely happy. He has suddenly become wealthy and has a pack of dogs to look after. God only knows how long it's going to last.

Audrey and I rent a small house in Santa Monica; it's light and stucco and four blocks from the beach which means, as Burgie is quick to point out, we'll never actually go to because we live so close. We're just glad to be out of the furnace of another San Fernando Valley summer.

Armed with my Masters degree in Music, I land the first job I can find; working as the manager of the classical department of a record store. It's steady money, the first since working in the kitchen at the Cosmic Consciousness Eatery with Burgie.


"Do you know anybody who lives in Cherbourg, France?" My mother holds up a small envelope addressed to me from L. Barbier.

It's Christmas 1974, and Audrey and I have stopped in on our way to Burgie's, where September is making her first-ever Christmas dinner. I promise my parents to have a few toasts, eat some jicama and Nutty-Buddy and hear about the Christmas UFO sightings. My parents are still having their strange and non-traditional holidays. Nobody wound up in Hawaii. Martin Denny records are taking their customary place on the now-fuzzy sounding stereo and the stainless steel tree, now rusted in spots, still sits in its place of myopic honor in the living room window. My mother has finally warmed to Audrey, but my father has been crazy about her since the minute he met her.

I open the powder-blue airmail envelope and a picture falls out. It's Leslie, her husband Alain, and a little girl of two. She looks a lot like Leslie. She has Leslie's face and Leslie's smile; the open, optimistic smile that makes you believe everything will work out. The kid, however, is blonde and that's where Alain came in. They've named her Zara.

Leslie looks the same, only somehow taller and thinner. I'm convinced that, of all the people I'm going to know in my life, she is the one who is going to look roughly the same at ninety as she did at thirteen.

Alain looks like all those French guys we've seen in movies; a combination of

Alain Delon and Gerard Depardieu. It's easy to see why Leslie fell for him. He looks rugged and intense; with shocking blue eyes, chiseled granite features and long blonde hair stylishly swept back by the wind. They make a handsome family.

I gaze at the picture for a long time. Long enough for Audrey to peer over my shoulder.

"Still in love with her, aren't you?"

I glance back. She isn't expecting an answer. Even though I love Audrey very much; it's the old adage about not forgetting your first major heartbreak.

It's probably the same for Audrey, even though considering Randall, I cannot imagine why.

It's some time after Christmas when I finally fish the note out of its envelope and read it. I felt guilty about the look on Audrey's face, so I've waited until I'm back at work and sitting in the safety of my windowless office.

*Dear Nelson:*

*This was taken six months ago, before Alain and I split up. I thought you might like to see what Zara looks like. I'm moving back to Los Angeles around the beginning of the new year. I would love to see you. It's been so long since I've heard from you. I've lost touch with most everyone, except Stoika. Buzz has moved to Texas. She had another baby a year ago; a boy named Vladimir who is a year older than Zara. I've kept all your letters and read them often and smile. I hope you're doing well. I miss Los Angeles terribly and think about all the times we've had together. I will tell you more when I see you.*

*Love,*

*Leslie*

Just when you think life is beginning to make sense, God, or a reasonable facsimile, throws a curve-ball and all becomes chaos.

# CHAPTER SEVENTEEN

## THE VIEW FROM HYPERTENSION DRIVE

"How are you, Bugs?"

"Fine, Otto."

"What's happening?"

"Nothing."

"How's the tour?"

"Okay. I broke a string in Stockholm last night during the finale of the Eroica."

"Were you embarrassed?"

"I think Tulio hates me."

"How's the weather?"

"Cold . . . well . . . I have to go. Okay? . . . Love you."

"Love you."

Click.

May, 1980, is going down as a slow, boring month. Audrey, having finally landed a spot in the second violins, is in Europe with the Philharmonic, on their first world tour in years. The tour is to last eight weeks and I'm left to sit at home most days waiting for the phone to ring.

I quit my job at the record store three years ago and got involved in a production company with David, the former Mister Jones lead guitarist. We're trying to get reputations as film music composers, which means student films and industrial epics such as *Our Friend The Plano-Convex Lense*; but at the moment, work has taken a slow turn. Audrey and I speak to each other as much as we can; but after the first week the calls come less and less, and the conversations increasingly short and obligatory.

Audrey and I love each other; you can ask anybody. But there is this nagging curiosity to find out if what I remembered as being so wonderful with Leslie, really is. In the five years since she came back from Cherbourg, I've carefully avoided her. In fact, I've only seen her twice. Both times were cordial but arms-distant and awkward for both of us. Conversation doesn't go very deep and there is a lot of staring away or gazing intently down at the ground. I know she's settled into an apartment on the Westside now, a modest but spacious place near UCLA. Since her divorce in 1975 she's gotten used to being single. Zara is in elementary school and Leslie works odd jobs as a translator. Alain's family are well-off, so a nice chunk of alimony comes in each month. Enough to keep Leslie and Zara happy.

But I have this silly-ass notion there's something unresolved between the two of us; and call it a conspiracy of time and circumstances, Audrey's absence is an excuse to flirt with danger - conjuring the possibilities of acting on a taboo, and it feels risky and exciting all at the same time. So this particular Wednesday finds me just a little drunk enough and courageous enough to do something about it. However, it never really occurs to me, until she answers the phone, that I'd actually ever do anything about it.

My luck; Leslie answers on the second ring. After a few awkward gasps, fueled by adrenaline, I blurt out that I've been thinking about her and want to see her.

To my light-headed amazement, she's thrilled to hear from me and was thinking about me before I called. We agree to meet at the LaBrea tarpits; just like the old days.


It's your typical smoggy May day when I arrive at a quarter to eleven in the morning (I decide on eleven because it's too late for breakast and too early for lunch - a non-commital type of hour; perfect in case I chicken out at the last minute). I sit down on a bench facing the museum and Wilshire Boulevard and catch a few rays of warm sun. The park is empty, as it always is during the middle of the week. A couple of old codgers shuffle slowly along the asphalt path and some L.A. City School buses unload a pack of kids on a field trip to the tarpits, where they become properly indoctrinated in the ways of the cavemen, sloths and trilobites of Los Angeles.

The Cadillac billboard on Wilshire that once gazed down on the park has long since vanished. I look for the footbridge where Leslie, Buzz and I sat under and smoked dope, it's been replaced by something less quaint, but more efficient; a concrete slab.

I spot Leslie as she crosses Wilshire, walking towards the entrance to the park. After all this time she still moves like a kid; her feet bounce off the pavement, never actually seeming to secure themselves to the ground.

"You look good without a moustache," she says, sitting down next to me.

"It left around the same time Nixon did," I tell her.

Leslie smiles.

"You haven't changed a bit," I add.

She grins, staring down at her feet. "I found some grey hair the other day; I'm sure Zara had something to do with it. She's seven - she's a handful."

Conversation is hard; fits and starts and broken off sentences and one syllable agreements. We talk dumb things like weather and politics. I stare at the ground for a few minutes before finally blurting out, "Look, I really missed you. I used to tell myself you were the one person I wanted to know for the rest of my life and that one way or another, we'd always see each other. I guess life's a pisser sometimes."

"There were a million times I wanted to call you," Leslie answers. "But I felt awkward, especially with your wife."

"Audrey's known about you for the past ten years."

"Does she know you're here now?"

"She's in Germany on tour." I look down at my watch. "She's probably playing the overture to *Midsummer Night's Dream* right about now."

And then a thick blanket of silence stumbles over us. All we can do is gawk back and forth at each other. My mind has gone a complete blank again. Finally

Leslie breaks the clumsy silence and glances at my foot.

"So what kind of music do you play?"

"Jazz mostly, but I've been doing whatever pays the bills. The past few years I've gone back to playing more classical - I did a couple of recitals last year. I'm trying to get a reputation around town."

"I'd love to hear you sometime."

"Me too."

More silence.

Finally Leslie gets up from the bench and turns to face me. "I have to pick up Zara and take her to the dentist. I still think it's crazy I've got a daughter; crazier when I think how old she is. Pretty nuts, huh?" She smiles.

"Can I walk you to your car?"

She nods and we leave the park. The hazy sun is becoming warmer and the smog is thickening, with only the occasional waft of roses and cut grass scenting the air. We cross Wilshire and walk south on Stanley. Her car is parked a couple of blocks away.

"You're probably wondering why I parked in Pongo-Pongo. I almost didn't come. I figured if I was far enough away, I could talk myself out of it by the time I got to the park and turn around."

"Sorry you didn't?"

Leslie shakes her head as we stand in front of her car. She fumbles around her purse for her keys. I keep wondering to myself if what's going through my mind is a really bad idea.

"Look . . . I don't know what you're thinking, but . . ."

In a split second, the lesser part of discretion takes over and I head straight for her lips. Leslie forgets about the car door. We wrap our arms tightly around each other and fall into a trance.

It's just like the old days; just like sixteen, just like the way it felt the very first time. Magic all over, flying out of tree tops, seeping out of manhole covers. Her soft lips and her warm, delicate tongue toss me back to days and nights and smells I completely forgot about. Time stands unmistakeably still.

We pull away and look at each other and giggle nervously. Leslie pulls strands of hair from her mouth and smiles. "And you, a married man."

We both know from this moment on, everything is going to become tangled. As much as it feels like the old days; it isn't. There's Audrey. Leslie and I can't just pick up where we left off and pretend the rest of the world, and the people in it don't exist.

"You know, Nelson, this is very big trouble," Leslie whispers as we lay in bed at her apartment in Westwood. Zara, who didn't need to go to the dentist in the first place, is safely over at a friend's house, so we spend the afternoon having unbridled teenage sex.

Leslie's bedroom looks out over a block of older apartment buildings, beige stucco duplexes from the 1930's. Hers is the tallest building by one floor and it looks down on the others around it. As the afternoon presses on, the sun slowly peers in and creeps across our tangled sheets, settling on our faces.

Leslie's bed is situated right under her window. The heat of the late spring afternoon is mixed with the smell of a grilled cheese sandwich cooking in the kitchen next door and the exhaust of a Salvation Army truck, winding down the alley, picking up donations. Leslie leaves the windows open and a breeze flaps lazily against the venetian blinds. A neighbor, maybe one from downstairs or across the way, is playing *Moonglow* by Artie Shaw on his hi-fi. We lay in bed, bunching pillows under our heads and stare at each other and out the window at the apartments below. Even though music fills the air, there is a stillness that is thick and undeniable and wonderful.

For the time being we pretend it's another guilty afternoon from high school. We leave our adult worlds behind, despite logic, common sense and remorse. We fall in love with each other all over again.

Burgie keeps shaking his head. "Dumb idea, Nels. Major dumb idea. I can give you the names and addresses of a hundred people who've had affairs and they'll all tell you they don't work. They are miserable, horrible painful experiences and nobody wins in the end."

Good old Burgie; voice of reason, voice of doom. He has a right to be sour on the idea of affairs. Burgie and September are already working on separation number two, which has been going on for almost six months. The first separation occured when September bumped into an old flame at a supermarket and carried on an affair with him for almost a year. The second time was Burgie's turn. Unfortunately for Burgie, the affair was with September's cousin Julie. The bets are on that this separation is going to hold and that the old D-word is going to be bandied around a lot by the time summer rolls around.

So Burgie is dead-set against the idea of Leslie and I picking up where we left off. Even I know it's impossible, but Burgie is ruthless; he runs down the whole list: Lying. Having to remember what you lied about. Keeping your story straight. Sneaking around. Making excuses. Making sure Leslie never wears perfume. Making sure I wash my face every time I have sex with Leslie, because, as Burgie put it, "Women can smell other women; it's like radar."

Remembering not to call Leslie Audrey and Audrey Leslie. Making sure I answer the phone at all times. Dinners, presents and hotel rooms are all to be paid in cash and not with a credit card so it won't show up in print at the end of the month.

It's a great, big elaborate deception. And it's all because of love. Well, love mostly.

At first I pass it off, thinking Burgie's just being bitter and it's because he really likes Audrey and they're good friends. Audrey and I like September too. For a while we thought they made a good couple, but obviously there's more going on than we realize. This new development between Leslie and I puts him in the uncomfortable position of being stuck in the middle. So to maintain an air of peaceful coexistance, Burgie doesn't bring up the subject of Leslie and I stop asking him about Julie.

After four weeks of Leslie and I playing at being sixteen again, Audrey has finally come home. The tour was a great success. She has two months off before the new symphony season starts and she wants to spend them at home with me.

A small catch: Leslie and I are hopelessly entangled. I've been spending entire days at her apartment.

"Are you okay?" Audrey ventures suspiciously over breakfast.

I've been caught staring off into space again, the third time in a week. I'm wondering when I'll see Leslie again. She called the night before and hung up.

I left the answering machine on, but I know it was her because there was a moment of silence before she put the receiver down. Not long enough to draw suspicion, but enough so I know who called. We never set up a code for phone calls; we don't want to get into it. It seems tacky and stupid. But I haven't seen her in four days and I miss her.

"Hmm?" I answer, snapping back into consciousness. "I'm just thinking about what I'm going to play at that Santa Barbara recital."

"That's not for three months," Audrey replies. "Is there anything you want to talk about?"

I shake my head almost too fast. "No, Otto, I'm fine. Really-honest." I'm lying through my teeth and I can feel my nose grow.

"Hey, why don't we take a drive up the coast and go thrift shopping in Ventura?" Audrey says, smiling. She's testing the waters. She definitely knows something is wrong.

Four months since that fateful day in the park. It's beginning to take its toll on me. I wish Audrey would leave me alone for a while to work this out. I wish I hadn't gotten to the point where Leslie and I wanted to see each other so regularly.

"I'm sorry, Otto, I can't take any time off." My mouth creaks into an apologetic smile.

Audrey is hurt and she is starting to get angry. "Look, Nelson, we haven't gone anywhere or done anything since I got back from the tour. Would you prefer not being with me or something?"

She knows, she knows, she knows. If I just tell her, come right out and say it; I'm having this insane affair with Leslie, it would probably be a big relief to the both of us. But the hurt in Audrey's eyes speaks volumes and I'm paralyzed to say anything - I am the complete tap-dancing coward and I just can't spell it out.

Audrey spends the day in Ventura by herself and I stay home feeling like I should be taken out and shot, or stuffed and put on display with a 'beware' sign hung around my neck. I've often disliked myself for the things I've done, but on this occasion, I hate myself.

I drive to the palisades overlooking Santa Monica bay and park. I spend the afternoon sitting in my car staring out at the sun slowly dipping towards the ocean. It's a clear and hot day. The beach is jammed with people and the promenade overlooking the palisades is filled with immigrant Persian and Russian families, who picnic or sit on folding chairs or, like me, search for some shred of truth in the afternoon sky. The smell of barbecues permeates everything and competes for air space with screaming children, screaming boyfriends, screaming wives and bewildered old people who cannot make sense of America and wish to Christ it was home. So what if there's an Ayatollah?

After three years, I decide to resume my habit of smoking. I roll down the window and fire up a Marlboro Light; kidding myself into thinking that, if I'm going to start smoking again, at least I should be smoking something that doesn't really seem like a cigarette.

I turn on the stereo and pop a cassette in. The car fills with the sounds of Thelonius Monk.

I start to think about my life as a pianist, wondering why I straddle all these different musical styles and never really settle on any particular one. Next to Thelonius Monk there's Bud Powell and, after that, Artur Schnabel. The problem is I really admire these guys. But I love Jazz and Classical equally, too much to give up one for the other, and that can be a problem in a musical world that loves to pigeon hole performers. I'd be crucified if anyone I respected knew I made a living playing jingles. Maybe not; everyone has at least one mummy in their closet. Mine, it seems, is stuffed to capacity.

I get down to smoking the filter before I realize I have gone through an entire cigarette and didn't notice it. I don't know why I picked my career to feel discontented over. It's a whitewash for my real problem, which has nothing to do with pianos, but lots to do with strings. It has to do with Audrey and Leslie.

I am in love with them both. I try to convince myself that the human heart is a strong little muscle capable of feeingl love and intimacy with many people.

That line of logic doesn't work. I am married to Audrey and I am not married to Leslie and that is a fact.

As I light cigarette number two, I pose hypothetical situations to myself . One of them includes the unthinkable; asking Audrey for a divorce.

The sun starts to dip low on the horizon; becoming a large, blinding ball. I flip the visor down and a photo falls out, hitting me in the head. It's Audrey, taken when we went on a holiday to Yosemite in 1974. It's a typical Audrey photo; she's standing next to a tree stump, dressed in a pair of khaki desert shorts and wearing a white tee-shirt, holding a nut out to a dubious squirrel, who stands, poised either to accept the gift, or take off with blinding speed. Audrey's face is pointed to the camera, but her eyes are on the squirrel. She flashes that mischievous grin, those gorgeous eyes having a stare-off contest with the bushy-tailed skeptic. And those breathtaking legs.

There is no way on earth I am going to divorce this woman.

"Leslie, we have to talk." I'm standing in a phone booth on the corner of Santa Monica and Lincoln trying to carry on a sensible conversation. The beach traffic clogs the street and threatens gridlock. The noise and exhaust from a nearby bus force me to close the phone booth door and the small space becomes a furnace in seconds.

There is apprehension in my voice and she picks up on it instantly.

"So, did you want to come over?"

I arrive at Leslie's in time to watch her pull a pitcher of martinis out of the refrigerator freezer. She sent Zara to Gramma and Grandpa Noritake's house for the night to visit with some cousins who only spoke Japanese; lucky us.

Five years earlier I would never even have considered drinking a martini. Lately however, I find them to be like little music business friends, waiting happily to see me at night, but always stabbing me in the back the next morning.

I drain two glasses and slosh my dilemma out to her. None of it comes as a big shock; she's been expecting it ever since the day in the park. But even though she understands it on all the rational, adult level, she still finds it painful to hear; and I find it painful to spill out. Leslie is ahead of me in the martini sweepstakes by two doubles.

"Look, I knew it wasn't gonna work out," she says, just at the outer-most edge of slurring her words. "It's what broke me and Alain up. He couldn't keep his hands off other women."

Leslie's taking it better than me I guess. All I know is I'm not sure if I've done the right thing, even though Leslie, in her 'days-of-wine-and-roses' way, assures me I have. So we won't be lovers, it doesn't mean we can't be friends. She leans over and kisses me and runs her crazy fingers over my face.

The last thing I know, we're staggering to her bedroom.

I open my eyes to the morning light and look around the room. A sudden, strange sensation hits me: I'm not home and Audrey isn't sleeping next to me.

I roll over and come face to face with Leslie.

Getting fucked up when you're eighteen is a lot different than getting fucked up when you're thirty. The body just doesn't make the adjustment to abuse nearly as well. I try to get out of bed but get hit between the eyes by a bolt of excruciating pain, accompanied by galloping throbs in my head. I feel dehydrated and puffy and jammed full of remorse. The only thing on my mind is the desire to get home, but I have to explain why I'm not already there to my wife, and I have to sober up pretty quickly.

*    *    *    *

*"Leslie, did you see that?"*
*"No."*
*"I thought I saw his eye move just a second ago."*
*"It's probably a Muscle reflex. They say that happens a lot with people in comas, Audrey."*
*"No. I think he knows we're here."*
*"Look, Audrey . . . I think there's something you really need to know..."*

*    *    *    *

It's almost three in the afternoon by the time I finally reel out of bed, get dressed and leave Leslie's. I drive home, wracking my gin-soaked brain for an excuse to tell Audrey. It seems almost incredible; the day I decide to break off my six-month affair with Leslie, I get so drunk at her place that I pass out and spend the night. I begin to wonder just whose side in life I'm on; certainly not mine.

Audrey sits, stone-faced, in the living room when I come stumbling in.

"Where were you?" she asks.

"I got drunk with Burgie last night and passed out at his place. It was a dumb thing to do but I couldn't drive home."

Audrey nods her head, then shoots me a searingly devastated look of hurt. Did I say something wrong or worse, stupid?

"Burgie and I went to the movies last night. I called him looking for you. He came over."

Audrey doesn't say another word. It's my turn to explain.

Of course it's the worst of all possible situations to be in. Hungover, feeling like freeze-dried shit, having cold sweats, a dry mouth, and a spike

183

driven through the center of my skull, all on top of trying to explain my recently distant behavior.

I sit on the floor and put my head between my legs. I let out an agonized groan of frustration and anger at myself. It signifies that what is coming next isn't going to be pleasant.

"Look . . . I don't want to know if you're seeing somebody. I just want you to stop." Audrey says, stopping me before I spill out the gruesome truth. Her words spare potential ugliness all around and I know that I have to break the affair off for good.

"How come you don't invite Leslie over? I'd like to meet her someday."

"She's busy," I tell Audrey, "but I will. . .I promise."

It's taken a long time to patch things up, but if anything, the affair has brought Audrey and I closer together. I wonder if she ever suspects it was Leslie, or if Burgie has told her anything. She's never mentioned it. Burgie has his own set of problems and whoever put down bets that September would file for divorce by the end of the year has won.

Leslie and I meet one more time and agree it's best for everybody, especially that elusive thing called peace of mind, that we don't try to relive the past anymore. There are some things you can never bring back. We decide we're better off as friends.

# CHAPTER EIGHTEEN

## A PENNY'S WORTH OF THE BIG KIND

The phone's ringing. I open my eyes and look over at the clock. It's two in the afternoon - I didn't get to bed until eight this morning. I've been up all night working on a new album with a particularly untalented vocalist who sold seven million copies of his last album. The overtime is wonderful, but the songs are garbage and I pound out guide tracks wondering if there really is a God. Naturally, I don't feel like answering the phone. A couple of rings later the machine clicks on. It's Burgie.

"Hey, Nels, pick up the phone, it's important!"

Burgie sounds hyper and urgent. Knowing him for as long as I have, if Burgie says it's important, it has a ninety percent chance of being so. I rouse myself enough to reach out for the receiver. "Yeah, Burg, what is it?"

"Guess who's in town?"

"No."

"Buzz. He'll be here in an about an hour and he wants to see us. He's coming into town on a layover. I told him we'd meet him at the airport."

"Buzz?"

"Yeah."

"Get out of of town!"

"I'm not kidding, Nels. Honest to God!"

I haven't seen Buzz in over five years. It's exciting news. I bolt out of bed, get dressed and dump a gallon of Murine in my eyes.


It's a Western Airlines layover between San Francisco and Galveston. Burgie and I take up position at the gate and wait for him to come out. We're standing in a crowd of chubby wives, chubby girlfriends, chubby husbands, chubby boyfriends and the occasional chubby stoic in a dark suit with hand-scrawled sign searching for 'Mister Howard'.

The passengers file off, looking a combination of drunk, bored and relieved. A couple of them appear to be enthused, but it's mostly a sad bunch. Burgie and I pace back and forth. After fifteen minutes, we think Buzz missed the flight.

The door leading to the plane closes and the show is over.

We're disappointed and I'm beginning to think about the sleep I missed. We turn to leave but, sitting in a seat, less than ten feet from us, is Buzz, or a good imitation. He wears solid dark glasses, holds a white cane in his hand, and he's talking to a sweetly concerned stewardess. Lying at his feet is Stanley, a dog Burgie gave Buzz as a puppy. Stanley is mostly mutt with a small white beard, but he has some Great Dane and Dachshund mixed in somewhere and gazes around the room with two completely eerie eyes that appear to be pale blue. The dog is strange and it makes perfect sense it would attach itself to Buzz.

I figured he had changed in the five years since we saw him, but I had no idea Buzz became blind. Burgie and I exchange disquieting glances as we approach him.

"Buzz?"

The stewardess looks up at us and touches Buzz's shoulder. He does a Stevie Wonder smile and shakes her hand, telling her it's okay, She gets up and saunters back to her post. We stand in front of him, speechless.

"Is she gone?" Buzz asks, moving his head back and forth. I half-expect him to break into *You Are The Sunshine Of My Life*, but I turn and watch the stewardess disappear past the boarding gate.

"Yeah, she's gone."

Buzz lowers his glasses over his nose and winks. "Hey, what's happening?"

I lean over to Buzz and whisper, "Look uh, I don't get it."

"Just lead me around. There's a bunch of people from the airline who know me."

Buzz grabs my arm and stands up. "You want to fall by the bar and swill a few?" We continue to look confused. Buzz points his head skyward. "It's fifty percent off and I get to take Stanley for free." Stanley looks guilty for being part of the scam and won't look us in the eye.

"It's a little immoral, wouldn't you say?" Burgie suggests.

"Burgie, airline tickets cost too much."

Buzz is grayer than the last time I saw him, but he's still Buzz.

We sit at a table in the crowded lounge and manage to down four vodka tonics each. Stanley scarfs up all the peanuts we can get hold of. It's strange, talking to Buzz and not being able to get him to look at us because of the routine he has to keep up.

We run down the past couple of years, and get caught up on what each of us has been doing. I tell him about my new career in jingles for radio commercials and recording sessions for pop stars. Burgie tells him about the big divorce with September and losing the house in Beachwood Canyon. It gets even Buzz to raise an eyebrow. Buzz tells us about working on oil rigs around the world, finally ending up in Texas. But there is one subject Buzz doesn't bring up that I want to know about.

"So, heard from Stoika?" I ask eventually. I figure it's a fair question.

Stoika is a friend of ours and I figured he had to know how she was, sending child-support checks and all.

"She's okay. She's a big-deal photographer now and she sees a shrink four times a week. I don't know what those two have to do with each other. I guess it means she can afford it."

"How'd you leave it with her?" I ask.

Buzz looks down at Stanley who has an expressive face to go with his piercing pale eyes. He keeps looking as if he's going to butt in on the conversation and lay something profound on us. "So what do you think, Stan, should I tell them?"

I couldn't swear to it, but I think Stanley nodded his head. It has to be the vodka.

"Well, Nels, it's like this; we didn't exactly leave it on an up note. In fact, we left it on a pretty shitty note. She got stuck with the kids - that's got to be good for at least two lifetimes worth of hate mail. I've been writing her pretty regularly and sending the kids money. She never writes back. I don't expect her to. The kids tell me what's going on. They're pretty neat. You'd like them."

Buzz gulps his drink and rattles the ice in his drained glass to signal the passing waitress for a refill. She takes the glass and silently inquires if we all want another. We do.

Buzz plays with his cocktail napkin, running it over wet spots on the table in front of him. He lets out a sigh. "I was pretty shitty to Stoika. She liked the idea of the house and the kids and the lawn that needed mowing once a week and watered twice a day. I'm just not an Ozzie & Harriet kind of person . . . and believe it or not, Stoika was.

"She really changed a lot since she had the kids, you wouldn't recognize her. But she was getting wierd even when you were living with us. I guess maybe all the stories she used to hear from other people about my girlfriends finally got to her. I mean, what is life without being in love at least once a day. What's so crazy about that?"

The waitress arrives with fresh refills and it's my turn to pay. I hand her a fifty and it's met with an exasperated scowl. She stomps back to the cash register.

Buzz changes the subject; he doesn't want to talk about Stoika anymore.

"Man, aren't airport bars depressing? And all the waitresses are named Millie."

Burgie is smashed and missed most of the earlier conversation. He turns to Buzz after downing drink number five.

"Okay, I know about the half off part, but doesn't it get a little complicated, being blind for a whole flight?"

Buzz points down at Stanley, who is peacefully asleep at his feet, oblivious to the din of cash registers, shouting waitresses and syrupy off-tune Muzak slurping over the loudspeakers. "Stanley goes with me everywhere. He's the only sure thing in life. He's worth it."

I look down at Stanley, who doesn't seem either interested or aware of his importance on the planet.

187

It isn't easy, cramming years and previously unspoken subjects into the space of forty-five minutes. We could've spent weeks talking and not covered everything. By the time the waitress shows up with the sixth and last round, we're sloshed and emotional and Buzz is in danger of blowing his cover.

Burgie keeps asking Buzz when he's moving back to L.A. but Buzz doesn't have an answer. He figures it'll be several more years before he gets tired of working on an oil rig and he might try something else then. He carefully picks up his collection of race-horse swizzle sticks. "Stanley's not crazy about it, but there's nothing as surreal as waking up in the morning in the middle of the ocean and realizing the only thing holding you up are four stilts. You gotta admit, it puts life in perspective."

The PA system drones out a last call for the flight to Galveston boarding on Gate 67. It's Buzz's flight. We float out of our chairs and stagger down the corridor to the appropriate gate, led by Stanley, the only sober one. We get to the gate just as the flight attendants are preparing to close the door. The stewardess who sat with Buzz when he arrived, ushers him on, taking his cane and Stanley's leash.

There isn't any time to get maudlin and morose or make promises of phone calls and when-are-we-going-to-see-each-other-again. Pretending to be blind, Buzz gets out of having to deal with sloppy farewells. He waves goodbye to thin air, swinging his stick back and forth, and lets Stanley do the guiding. A few seconds later he's gone.

Burgie and I stumble into nearby chairs and watch, semi-consciously, as the plane taxies out of the terminal and down the runway to take off.

# CHAPTER NINETEEN

## TO SMILE LIKE HERBERT HOOVER

June 20, 1989; the night of our high school reunion. I'm staring at a calendar and it slowly dawns on me that it's been exactly nineteen years, eleven months and twenty-two days since Buzz, Burgie, Stoika, Leslie and I sat around the table at Ship's on graduation night and turned our collective noses up at the future.

Twenty years and nobody really knows exactly where they have gone.

Buzz and Stoika, the great love story, have been estranged since 1975. Stoika, now the mother of two teenagers, feigns illness every time his name is mentioned.

Buzz was last heard from still working on an off-shore oil rig near Corpus Christi. Stoika stayed in San Francisco for a while, working as a freelance photographer for the San Francisco Chronicle before moving back to L.A. to live with her mother after Carl died in 1986. The house remained a cowboy shrine for a while. The funeral home refused to let Carl be buried in his beloved pink Cadillac Coup deVille. The great car, with antlers and *Tumblin' Tumbleweeds* horn, would become Stoika's, and she would drive it seldom and, after a while, never.

High school reunions are either profound or profoundly embarrassing. Everybody gawks at everybody else, trying to find some "I'm ok - you're ok" from the past and we become silently horrified when we realize they aren't and neither are we.

I show up at the reunion alone. Audrey decided to pass on the experience; she doesn't know a soul except Burgie and she hates these events anyway, having been to her ten-year reunion several years earlier and weathered the whole evening listening to a shitfaced Randall bellow at the top of his lungs that she was his only true love. Luckily, she's playing a concert tonight, so she has a good excuse anyway.

The room is filled with faces; puffy, grey and surgically altered ones.

Interestingly, most everyone in the past twenty years has become one kind of alcoholic or another. There are winos, of which the camps are broken down into red and white; and the hard-core, who are broken up into the martini crowd, Scotch crowd and Tequila crowd. The Tequila crowd also takes in the fringe element which consumes Rum and 'fun-drinks' like

Daiquiris and Sloe Gin Fizzes. Subsequently, the real action takes place at the bar.

"I've never seen so many bad drunks in my life," Burgie informs me as we pick up our name tags, trying to figure out what to do with the silly-ass happy- face smiles glued over our names. They are handed to us by the same bubbly cheerleader types we avoided twenty years earlier. Only now they have skin the consistency of Doc Martens' from too much sun and too much makeup.

I'm handed two pictures of myself, neither of which are particularly good; in fact one is embarrassing: a candid shot of me falling on my ass during a rain storm in the tenth grade. We're all expected to toss one into a giant fishbowl from which a lucky photo will be drawn for a two-week vacation via Club Med to some Third World country. I toss in the prat fall photo and hope no one is sadistic enough to pick it. Burgie and I wander around the room, staring at name tags and faces. We don't recognize anybody.

It is a sea of business suits and strapless gowns; of lips as red as stop signs and enough face powder to cast a Noh Play. Wild, teased, big-frosted hair, smooth rearranged noses and abundant, perfectly formed, stretch-mark free breasts. It seems as if there isn't a single woman in the room who hasn't gotten friendly with some aspect of an implant over the past twenty years.

There is scarcely a guy in the room who doesn't have a receding hairline, an extra chin or an extra thirty pounds.

It's the shitty thing about getting older; being witness to the accumulation of unwanted mass and unwanted loss. Burgie and I are no different. We thought we were, but in the mirror of the men's john, we realize it's happened to us too. Maybe it's the fluorescent lighting. It makes everybody look fifty years older than they really are. It's the only place a paramedic can go and not be sure if the guy sprawled out on the floor is really dead yet or not.

Stoika didn't come, but sent word via Leslie who did, that she wanted to see us all at her mother's house afterwards - as long as we don't bring 'him' with us if Buzz ever shows up.

Leslie doesn't look any different from the last time I saw her nine years ago. If you pretend Zara, her now seventeen-year-old daughter, who is about to graduate high school herself, is not there, she might've gotten away with being no older than Zara herself. Zara is gorgeous and you can instantly tell by looking at her that she messes up more minds in a single day than a lot of women do in a year. She is a breathtaking combination of European and Asian; those elegantly chisled cheekbones coupled with soft exotic features. The kid turns heads everywhere she goes. And Burgie can't keep his eyes off her all night.

"How's Audrey?" Leslie asks.

"Fine. She couldn't come tonight. The orchestra season started last week."

Leslie nods her head. She doesn't really care. What she really wants to know is if we're still together or have gotten divorced. Audrey and I are still together. The brief episode Leslie and I had cooled considerably in retrospect, but there's still the unspoken bond between us.

We commandeer a table in the cavernous airplane hanger and for the evening gloss over the present and remember some of the stupid things we did in the past. Zara, not privy to the goings on of these motley adults, looks suitably bored for the whole evening and keeps asking Leslie when they're going home. Leslie shoots her kid a look that has brass knuckles tucked inside of it.

Zara and Burgie keep exchanging glances. His are smoldering and hers are curious and flirtatious; she knows how to work a gaze. She bums cigarettes off of me every ten minutes, and steals sips of wine from glasses at nearby tables. She becomes drunk over the course of the evening, and eventually stops complaining and starts enjoying herself.

I keep looking around to see if Buzz is going to show up. No one has seen him since the episode at the airport. I half expect him to wander in with Stanley at his side.

Burgie bumped into Buzz's mother a year ago and she told him that Buzz was getting seriously involved in writing poetry. Buzz as a poet is something for the mind to ponder. Even though nobody knows for certain if he's actually written anything, we all wonder if, like Buzz himself, it will actually make any sense.

The obligatory speeches and slide-show presentations and sickeningly nostalgic music - music I never liked the first time around - drags on for hours and takes up most of the evening. The unintentional hit of the reunion comes when Bobbie Weinstock, Laurie Ellenbogen and Nina Rosen prance by our table to say hi. The three friends have been close since junior high and I remember them as ones who never gave me the right time of day. They were the girls who always went after guys two or three years older, so they had absolutely no interest in me whatsoever. They have, in twenty years, achieved a unique sameness, which is remarkable and frightening all at the same time. They have the obligatory frosted blonde hair, teased and lacquered into elevated wisps and carefully adjusted to look accidental. They wear strapless evening gowns of varying shades of gloss; Bobbi in gold, Laurie in red and Nina in green. Between the three there is an acre of cleavage. It would appear they've all been to the same plastic surgeon and have emerged as identicallly rounded, lightly tanned, glossily perfect testaments to the art of Dow-Corning with matching collogen lips.

What strikes me about them, aside from the 'Stepford Wives' aura, is the fact that they are recent widows. Each of their three husbands has died of a heart attack, all roughly around the same time. They think it's funny, and laugh about it; all those poor dorks dying of coronaries. I notice Bobbi, who always sported sharp eye-teeth, never got them fixed; they remain fangs. I imagine these women with notches on their garter belts, like kills stenciled on an F-14.


It's midnight by the time we finally stumble out of the reunion and head for Stoika's.

We drive up and down Cattaraugus several times before finding the house. We don't recognize it at first. All the jungle vegetation we remembered is gone.

The towering palm trees have been cut down, the vines and lush tropical succulents dug up and torn out and everything has been replaced with regular old grass. The Foley house, once infamous for its eccentricity and inaccessibility, has become just another ticky-tacky box on another block in semi-suburbia. And sadly there are fewer houses on the block than we remembered. They've been replaced by condos; ugly little huts of cheap stucco that have miserably seedy names like Chez Venice and Belle Robertson. They sell for fortunes and everyone regrets buying them, so they quickly end up back for sale a few months later.

We finally locate Stoika's house by the sound of the stereo and the crowd gathered in and around the outside. There is a party in progress. We get to the front door and are met by a room packed with kids drinking, smoking and checking each other out. I scan the room and don't see a single familiar face, nor one that looks reasonably over twenty.

"You must be my mom's friends," the angular kid dressed completely in black says. I know it has to be Vladimir. I've never seen this kid before, aside from a baby picture Stoika sent Burgie, but I can instantly tell. He has Buzz's scraggly, curly-wavy hair, jet black, and Stoika's broad Russian nose.

The kid is handsome and it takes Zara no time to realize that. After one or two words of introduction they vanish together while Burgie, Leslie and I wander around the house looking for Stoika.

She's in the kitchen, nursing a bottle of Bardolino, smoking a Rothman and talking to some of Molly's friends. Molly is less outgoing than Vladimir but still a beauty on her own. She has Stoika's hair, or at least a variation of it; strawberry blonde, but straight as a stick, which she bobs off at her neck. She has Stoika's intense gaze and inquisitive dark eyes. Guys probably won't discover her for a couple of years, except for the ones who are as intense as she is.

Shorlty after Stoika came back to Los Angeles, Ludmilla moved out of the house to one of the condos down the street. She bought it with some of the money Carl left her. With two kids rapidly becoming adults, Stoika needs the room.

Of all of us, Stoika has changed the most. She's put on weight since our San Francisco days and is starting to develop a double-chin. There are deep lines etched on her face and her reddish brown hair is flecked with grey. But she has the spark of life that is always Stoika's. She's glad to see us and throws her arms open, letting out a loud, boozy yell. It embarrasses Molly, who quickly exits the kitchen, taking her friends with her. Even Stoikas voice has changed. It's deep, throaty and whiskey-tinged. She's finally managed to get her mother's roaring laugh.

"I was wondering when the hell you were going to show up!" she bellows. Stoika's drunk, but at least a happy drunk.

I wander around the kitchen. The last time I saw the place it was attempting to be a cowboy cookhouse. It's now a normal kitchen, with a normal refrigerator, normal food and a normal stove. The rustic shelves, the bulky pots and pans and the turn-of-the-century cans of Calumet Baking Powder are gone. Like the rest of the house, it's been met headlong by the twentieth century.

Stoika reaches up to a cabinet over the sink, pulls down three wine glasses and fills each one with Bardolino.

"Jesus, I don't know what to say . . . I haven't seen you all together since, what, 1970? Has it been that long?"

We look at each other and it dawns on each of us that the last time we were all together, including Leslie, but minus Buzz, was actually 1969.

"So how do you like my kids?"

"I think Zara and Vladimir are an item," Leslie remarks.

"Oh Christ, watch out for him . . . he's got dickhead's DNA and you know what that means."

Stoika never mentions Buzz by name. She scrupulously avoids it. To her he's 'The B Word', 'him' or 'dickhead'. It's strange, listening to Leslie and Stoika talk about kids; stranger yet to think they're both divorcees and the mothers of almost-adults.

Burgie and I explore the house and leave Leslie and Stoika to exchange war stories.

We get to the rear of the house and find the door leading to the backyard.

"Hey, I brought something to celebrate with." Burgie motions me to follow him.

The backyard as we knew it is gone; even the makeshift swing that hung on the porch looking out to the greenhouse; all of it, even the greenhouse, is gone, vanished; torn down, replaced by something, or just vacant space waiting for something else.

"It's just not the same without Cowboy Carl, is it?" I remark to Burgie as he pulls a joint out of his jacket pocket.

"I've been saving this for six months," Burgie announces proudly.

I sniff the air for a second. Somebody else is in the backyard and is already doing what we intend to. Burgie doesn't notice. He lights his joint and we take turns passing it back and forth. I haven't smoked dope in almost twenty years and I gag and wheeze like a novice.

"It's funny when you think, those kids are the same age as we were when we were last here."

Burgie exhales a blue-white cloud. "Yeah, and they're so well-mannered too . . . I don't get it. We were never like that, were we?"

I thought of something Burgie, Buzz and I used to joke about and nudge Burgie's arm as he passes the joint to me. "Remember when we said what our worst fear was? Our kids turning into accountants?"

Burgie chuckles and gasps, choking on his last hit.

"Yeah, our worst fear; we'd have kids who'd want to go to Harvard Business School. Who would, to really piss us off, wear suspenders and drag briefcases around and join the Republican party." Burgie laughs. I don't. I don't have kids. Zara and Vladimir remind me more of us than some article in a magazine.

Them, I have faith in. The '80's I don't

Two kids stumble out of the bushes. They've been smoking and are pretty high.

As they get closer we realize it's Zara and Vladimir, sheepishly slinking past.

Burgie gives Zara a hurt look, but she doesn't pick up on it and he doesn't say anything. He feels let down, especially after the inquisitive gazes they cast each other earlier in the evening.

"Shh, don't tell my mom," Zara mumbles as she shuffles by.

"Bitchin' night, huh?" Vladimir remarks. The kid's got Buzz's genes stamped all over him.

They saunter back to the house and open the door. The sounds of the party and the strains of R.E.M. spill out from the stereo. They close the door behind them and it falls quiet again.

The night air is damp, as it always is in June. The fog starts to roll in, but it doesn't touch the ground. It turns the city quiet. The glow of streetlamps and office buildings and garishly lit billboards reflect in the low clouds that spread a soft orange haze over the sky.

I look for the Helm's sign; the bulls-eye fireworks of neon that look out over Venice Boulevard. We used to see it at night from Stoika's back yard. In fact, you could see it from my parents' house. But like everything now, it's gone.

Not torn down, it just isn't lit any longer; it hasn't been for years.

Burgie and I go back to the party and stand gazing at the crowd: boys pretending to be bored, distracted by topics of weighty conversation like MBA stats or the new XTC single, try desperately to win the attention of whatever girl glances their way and smiles; the girls, wearing skintight black or baggy jeans, pretend to be wary or deeply immersed in thought, or dig in their bags for cigarettes and break the ice by asking for lights. I've never known women to carry their own lighters, even less to admit they actually have one. It's a ruse and all the boys happily oblige.

The stereo loudly throbs bass, shaking the walls. Looking at the kids around me I think about the time I looked at myself in the mirror at Audrey's apartment and how I felt, even at the age of twenty. I wonder if these kids do the same thing. Probably not.

I miss Buzz. I know he's persona non grata around the Foley house, but he was so much a part of all this. In retrospect, we haven't seen him in more years than we knew him and maybe we're really feeling badly for the passage of time and not necessarily the person. Still, it's a shame he didn't come, at least to the reunion. Burgie and I wonder where he is tonight and we inhale many toasts to him.

"Hey! What do you say we drive up to San Francisco?" Burgie drunkenly suggests to the assembled bunch.

"Fuck that! You couldn't get me near that town with a barge pole," Stoika barks.

"I thought you liked San Francisco," I ask her.

Stoika takes a big gulp of Bardolino and a drag on her cigarette and puts her arm around me and gives me a deep, boozy, forehead to forehead stare.

"Are you insane? Nobody wants to go where the lousy memories are. Nobody in their right mind, except hysterics and manic depressives, like being reminded of the times they fucked up and failed."

It occurs to me that Stoika misses Buzz just as much as we do, only she refuses to admit it, being one of the secret hysterics or manic depressives she freely mentions. But fifteen years after the vanishing act, Stoika still hurts and doesn't let anybody forget it.

The party finally breaks up around five in the morning and we stumble back to the scene of the reunion to get our cars. I leave the Santa Monica Airport parking lot at six after promising everyone we'll get together later in the week.

The sky begins to grow lighter but the fog and low clouds hang over the city like a grey sock. I make my way home and keep fighting the sadness that hovers over me. At first I pass it off as chemical; all the wine I drank, the dope Burgie and I smoked - everything is wearing off me and I can feel a hangover waiting to descend like the plague. But this feeling of sadness won't go away.

"Life goes on and nothing stays the same, Bugs. Face it," Audrey, my fountain of ever-present wisdom, explains over the coffee she has finished making.

She's up and running around the house when I get home. "You're getting older and you don't like it. Nobody does."

"Otto, you're probably right or maybe it's an ulcer, but my stomach hurts and the future scares the living shit out of me." All I want to do is sleep and hope the feeling is gone when I finally wake up.

"Guess who called me last night." Burgie has a sheepish glimmer in his eye, as he gulps a mouthful of martini before negotiating his steak.

I stare blankly at him; I can't guess. I give up. "Who?"

"Zara. Leslie's daughter. She called. She wants to see me."

"Are you serious?" I think it's funny; strange, yes; but . . . funny.

"She's attracted to me, Nels, she told me. Of course, she's old enough to be my daughter. I mean, Jesus, she's Leslie's daughter, for Chrissake!"

"Yeah, I was wondering when that was going to dawn on you."

"Sure it did, but that was six months ago. I thought she forgot about me."

"Well what do you want to do?"

"Hide," is Burgie's simple answer.

"You can't do that. You have to call her back. Go see her. You're a big boy, you can handle it."All of a sudden, I'm the one giving sage advice.

"But, Nels, she's Leslie's daughter, how does that look?"

"Like you have excellent taste. Burgie, she's gorgeous."

Burgie thinks about it for a minute, but thinks himself right back out of it.

"Nelson, it's not right. There's a moral thing."

"She's an adult, Burgie. She turned eighteen three months ago. She knows what she wants."

"That's what I'm worried about," Burgie retorts.

He is worried. He can't finish his dinner. Let's face it; it's one thing to have an eighteen-year-old girl calling an almost-forty-year-old guy out of the blue. It's something else when the eighteen-year-old in question happens to be the daughter of a high-school girl friend.

"Are you gonna call her back?"

I'm starting to get a slightly sadistic kick out of this.

"I saw her last night," Burgie mumbles.

I let out a gleeful yell, loud enough for our waiter to come to our table to check on us. "You devil!" I howl.

Burgie takes a dim view of my joyful exuberance, but it's just for show. It does him a lot of good. After his divorce from September Rittenberg, he's needed some excitement and some intrigue in his life.

"Does Leslie know?"

"Leslie isn't talking to me."

"How do you feel about Zara?"

Burgie doesn't say anything at first. He focuses on his half-eaten dinner for a long time and seems embarrassed by the line of questioning. He looks intently at his food when he finally answers.

"She is the most incredible woman I have ever met in my life." And then Burgie looks up from his plate and a sublime smile spreads over his face. "She's unbelievable, Nels."

So much for Vladimir.

"Don't worry, Leslie'll get over it," I answer.

"You don't understand, Nelson. We got married. Zara and I got married in Mexico last week."

As if somebody had planned it; two waiters with full trays collide just outside the kitchen, sending plates and aluminum platters crashing loudly to the ground. It sums up my reaction perfectly.

The idea of Leslie being Burgie's mother-in-law is a completely absurd concept. It makes total sense that she refuses to talk to Burgie now. I would too if I were her.

"I thought you said she called you last night," I ask Burgie, not entirely clear what is happening.

Burgie starts to squirm in his seat.

"Oh yeah, well, okay, I was lying. I didn't know what to say. Look, don't tell Audrey, please?" Burgie is dismayed.

"Why would Audrey care?"

"She'll think I'm a cradle robber. That's what I think I am, that's what Leslie thinks I am. She wants to have it annulled."

"I don't blame her. If it was my daughter I'd have had you arrested," I say, smiling. Burgie's face falls. He doesn't understand I'm joking. "How long has this been going on?" I ask him.

"Three months." By now Burgie is sliding down under the table to hide his embarrassment.

"Why didn't you say anything before?"

"Oh come on, I didn't know what to say."

Burgie disappears under the table. I lift up the tablecloth and stick my head under.

"Well, okay, but are you happy?"

"If I died tomorrow my life would be complete," Burgie mutters, barely above a whisper.


It takes time for everybody to get used to the idea of Burgie and Zara not only seeing each other, but actually married. I once asked Burgie why he was so quick to head to the alter and not just get into cohabitation like everybody else.

"I am always under the assumption that love is forever. So if it's forever, why not make it permanent?"

Logic. My short-coming.

Zara is a smart and mature young woman, but the operative word here is 'young', which, although she is loathe to admit, she still is. For all her poise and charm, which she has in mega-doses, there are times when she snaps into kid-mode and the mature exterior comes crashing down in tiny pieces. Case in point: the infamous Thanksgiving dinner.

"Hey fuck-head, I know who Jerry Garcia is! You think I don't know anything! You think I was born yesterday!"

"No, the day before!" Burgie snaps back. Zara stomps out of the room, slamming doors and stamping her feet.

The whole fiasco centered around a pint of ice cream; Ben and Jerry's Cherry Garcia to be exact.

The gentle and not-so-gentle ribbing has been going on all day and it's making Zara feel uncomfortable and out-of-place.

Holiday gatherings are starting to become regular events around the Rivers/Piantadosi home. We're frequently having people over and there is always a degree of bedlam present. Audrey, a big-believer in ceremonies, still loves to cook. Thanksgiving is a two-day event that starts on the eve of Thanksgiving and by the following evening when the actual carving of the turkey takes place, the house is jammed to capacity with a combination of my newly reunited friends and clients, and Audrey's friends and cohorts from the orchestra. It's always surprising to see how well everybody manages to get along; the spectrum is pretty wide. My friends being a motley group with odd quirks and tastes, and Audrey's a more genteel crowd.

On this particular Thanksgiving, even Leslie and Stoika show up. Leslie has, over the past month, struck an uneasy peace with Burgie and has finally met Audrey face to face as opposed to on the phone or via rumor. They've become friends, along with Stoika. Molly and Vladimir don't show up. Molly has decided to spend Thanksgiving at her boyfriend's parents' house and Vladimir is actively practicing anti-social behavior.

After twenty years, Audrey is finally introduced to the cast of characters who've made my life what it is. I don't know why it's taken so long for them to all meet, but once they do they become thick as thieves.

It's a shame Buzz still isn't around.

Burgie and Zara enter the kitchen, which is the place everybody seems to gravitate to during these events. Burgie's been looking haggard lately. He's developed some puffy bags under his eyes and is gaining a lot of weight. Zara has persuaded him to start going to a gym. They've been at it most of the day; swapping insults back and forth. Mostly Burgie reminding Zara that she is, in fact, still a kid. Something Zara doesn't like to hear from anybody. Zara gets back by reminding Burgie that she's been finding more hair on his comb lately than on his head and that he can no longer touch his toes without struggling.

You begin to wonder how long this marriage is going to last.

Audrey's pals from the orchestra discover the piano sitting in the corner. We take turns; me and the assistant concert master; a recent German emigre named Herbie. He sings German Lieder, and I in turn, sing Billy Eckstine. I thought I did a good Eckstine impression accompanying myself, but nobody in the room seems to know who he is, so I guess it doesn't matter; they liked the song anyway.

Zara makes a brief appearance in the living room and promptly leaves. I can see out of the corner of my eye that she's been crying. I follow her out.

"Look Zara, nobody's making fun of you." I'm trying to soothe her hurt feelings. "Nobody thinks you're stupid."

We take a walk around the block, while everybody else is getting the dinner table ready. Zara breaks into a fresh batch of tears.

"You know, I love Burgie and all that, but sometimes he really pisses me off. He tries to make me feel like a big nothing."

I put my hand on her shoulder. "Look, maybe he's the one who feels like a big nothing and has to take it out on somebody."

"He's been doing that a lot lately," she sobs.

Burgie is going through that phase known as 'here comes forty'. The inevitable, the point of departure where you are no longer considered youthful. But instead head rapidly towards middle-age and finally 'you look wonderful'.

We all hate getting older; I don't know a single human being who likes the idea. But Burgie is less enamored than most. He holds on to so many things from his youth. He is the only person I know who still has his first car, the VW van, and who still actually drives it; he's also kept his first surfboard and every letter he's ever had since he was ten; he even still has Jeanie Nurstrom's appendix. It probably explains why he got involved with Zara.

"Look, it's all going to work out; you have to believe that. You also have to believe that Burgie really loves you, but he's frustrated."

Zara smiles as she turns around and kisses me on the cheek. "Thanks, Nelson. My mom was right about you."

I laugh. If the kid only knew. We walk back to the house. We're heading up the walkway to the front door when Zara stops and turns to me. "Look, uh, can you keep a secret?" I nod and tell her yes. "I'm pregnant."

I let out a gasp; it's completely knocked the air out of me. I try to catch my breath. It isn't that she's pregnant that has me in a state of shock. It's that Leslie Noritake is going to become a grandmother.

I limp over to the curb and sit down on the concrete, gazing up and down the street and finally at a stone-faced cat sitting on the roof of a Plymouth, staring silently down at a passing Golden Retriever.

"I thought you'd be happy," Zara says as she sits down on the curb next to me.

I am busily contemplating my own mortality.

"Yeah Zara, I am, don't get me wrong, I'm very happy for you, I swear. I guess it's just that, part of what Burgie is going through is what I'm going through and thinking of your mom as a grandmother makes me feel a little weird."

I'm also worried that Zara having a baby will be the final straw and will definately kill any remaining friendship between Leslie and Burgie. First, he marries her daughter and then he turns her into a grandmother at forty. What did Leslie do to deserve that?

When we get back, the Thanksgiving table is laid-out and immense. We manage to cram twenty people around it and the starving, chatty, boisterous crowd soon subdues to the clanking of glass and silverware and quietly consuming the contents of the table.

Zara has taken the seat furthest away from Burgie just to let him know she's still upset. I keep glancing back and forth between the thinking, Jesus, Burgie a father and Leslie a grandmother. What is life?

When Burgie finally does find out about Zara, he calls me in a panic, wanting to see me. I know what it is he wants to say.

"Nels, all of a sudden I feel ancient." Burgie is nursing his third martini at our customary table at Musso's. He's in such a state that the waiter decides the best thing to do is bring over the pitcher and a small glass bowl of olives and let Burgie go at it.

"Burgie, it's important that you remember we're getting older and not necessarily getting old. There's a big difference. There are many years ahead of us and, by no stretch of the imagination, has the proverbial fat lady sung yet. We're not even forty yet and that's only halfway through.

"Halfway plus, I read the statistics."

"Burgie, we're not dead yet, knock it off."

He's squirming in his seat, feeling restless. "Hey, what do you say we head down to the beach?"

"Now?"

"Yeah, let's pick up a bottle of martinis and listen to some Tim Buckley tapes."

Not trusting Burgie behind anything more complicated than a tricycle when he drinks, I become the responsible one and do my 'designated driver' thing. Most of the places we used to hang out have long since become populated either by houses, landslides or gang-fights. I drive further up the coast and find the peace and solitude we used to have in abundance at the end of Pico Boulevard.

We wind up at Leo Carillo beach. I pull the van into a parking lot facing the water. The van doesn't sound too good. It's gone through three engines and several transmissions, but it's on its last legs this time around. I pop in the Tim Buckley cassette as promised, and Burgie busily stirs up a pitcher of dry martinis from the refrigerator he's had installed. *Dream Letter* comes on over the speakers. A wave of nostalgia sweeps over the van. I can feel the hairs raising on the back of my neck - good ones and bad ones.

"Just like the old days, eh?"

"Yeah, only I get shitty hangovers from gin," I answer. This obsession with martinis lately is beyond me. I haven't had one since my breakup with Leslie.

In pissing and moaning about becoming old men, we're getting sloshed on an old man's drink. Can prostate problems be far behind?

It's already pitch dark by six. There is nobody on Pacific Coast Highway coming in either direction. For once in many moons, we have the whole beach to ourselves. But we sit inside the warmth of the van and nurse our high-octane concoctions with two olives each which I pretend to sip but mostly stare at.

There's a storm blowing in and you can see it coming, slowly approaching the shore.

Even though it probably won't rain for several hours, there is something malevolent about the clouds. They're dark and foreboding and they remind me of the feeling I had in my stomach after the reunion. It's probably the gin. I hate gin, I don't mention it to Burgie though. In the distance you can see flashes of lightning over the water miles away. This is going to be a big storm.

"So how do you feel about fatherhood?" I ask Burgie.

"Scared shitless," he answers, sipping and draining his glass.

"I guess it means I've finally grown up. I guess you're next."

"Audrey and I never thought about having kids. I don't think she really wants them."

I pop an olive in my mouth.

"Yeah, but what about you?" Burgie asks, looking at me with boozy suspicion.

"I don't know. I sometimes think the world is too fucked up to bring kids into. I'd just be adding to the problem."

Burgie lets out a sloppy laugh.

"Nels, everybody's been saying that for years. You, me, my parents, your parents, the world in general since the beginning of time. People have always said the world is too fucked up to bring anybody new into. That doesn't stop anything."

I reach back and grab the makeshift pitcher and pour another lethal combination of gin and vermouth. I know I'm going to feel like shit in the morning. But still, we're sitting and watching the waves, like we did when we were seventeen. We spend the next few hours getting sloppy and maudlin and happy and nostalgic before we come to our senses and head home.

It's midnight when Burgie finally drops me off at Musso's to pick up my car.

The storm heading in from the ocean has finally made it to Hollywood. It starts misting at first, but then it gradually builds until the streets are turned into rivers and people vacate them in search of warm cars or dry awnings to keep from getting soaked.

I take side streets until I get past West Hollywood, and then I take Sunset Boulevard home, down to Barrington and head south to San Vicente and take that west until I get to Santa Monica and the lower-rent, but still kind-of-nice district and home. I pull to a stop and turn off the engine and run inside the house to dodge the falling rain.

Audrey is sitting in the living room. She's been waiting up for me. There is a look of confused concern on her face.

"Some woman named Mrs. Jordan called. She said she got your number from your parents. Did you know a guy named Bradley?"

# CHAPTER TWENTY

## CHASING SHADOWS

Accidents happen - that's why they call them accidents.

Buzz died in an oil-rig accident off the Texas coast. One of the platforms he was working on collapsed and fell into the ocean. He was missing for several days before the Coast Guard finally recovered his body. The thing Buzz loved the most was the thing that finally got him in the end.

When I came home from my night out with Burgie, I knew there was something wrong, just by looking at Audrey. She knew somebody named Bradley had died.

She didn't know Bradley and Buzz were the same person.

I'm stuck with the grim task of telling Burgie and Leslie. We decide it would be a good idea if we all go over to Stoika's and tell her in person.

I'm glad we do because Stoika doesn't take it well. First she goes quiet, almost stone-like, and then it builds. The news starts to settle, and as it does, so the tension mounts. The pressure cooker is about to explode.

It's the simple things in life that bring people straight over the edge. It's the cheerful phone call from the Diner's Club who wants you to enroll in their insurance program that usually does it. That happy and completely unaware voice, belonging to some student or recently unemployed office worker, making $3.25 an hour plus commission on sales, has no idea what the folksy, genial offer is going to unleash.

Stoika blows big time. She screams and keeps screaming. She rips the phone out of the wall. She vents her rage at AT&T, the Diners Club; anything and everything that isn't directly or indirectly responsible or nailed to something permanent. She destroys anything she can lay her hands on. Everything comes flying off the walls; every dish and every breakable item winds up smashed to bits on the floor. We quietly step outside and let her get it out of her system.

The sidewalk outside fills with neighbors wanting to know if they should call the police. We tell everyone what the situation is and that it should be over soon. Even when cops arrive, Leslie manages to talk them out of coming in and dragging her away in a strait-jacket.

It's Wednesday and the funeral isn't until Sunday. Burgie, Stoika, Leslie and Mrs. Jordan are to fly up on Friday. Audrey and I leave on what I call a 'Memorial Drive' to San Francisco a few days earlier. I don't know why, but I have an overwhelming desire to drive up the coast. I'm not sure if I'll ever be up this way again and don't know when I'll really want to come back.

It's the first time in years Audrey and I have spent any time out of town together. It isn't exactly a vacation and, after the first day, I'm sorry I've dragged her through all my sentimental pissing and moaning. It's hard on her, I know it. She never knew Buzz and has to put up with me getting teary-eyed at every bend in the road along Route 1.

We stop in Carmel and rent a small cottage two blocks from the ocean. The air is cold and piercing as it blows in from the water, but it's clean and it smells envigorating. The cottage was built in the early 1920's. It looks out to the coastline and has a large, warm fireplace and thickly upholstered green velvet chairs and bookcases filled with volumes of Steinbeck and Jack London, and complete bound years of Better Homes And Gardens from the 1950's. I never stayed in Carmel when I was younger; we couldn't afford it. But this is 1990 and I'm with Audrey and it reminds me of Christmas 1970 when we first met.

Maybe it's the goose-down comforter, or the warmth of the cottage. Whatever it is, it takes my mind off the thought of being in San Francisco by the weekend, and I definately need that.

It's early in the afternoon when we arrive, so we go down to the bottom of the street and take a walk on the beach. We're the only ones on the sand for miles in either direction. It's grey, overcast and threatening to rain, and the rocks just beyond the breakers are starting to fill up with barking seals.

I keep thinking how Buzz would've loved this place; all the hours he spent staring out at the water, the big smile on his face as he let the wind blow over him and cake his hair with sand and shower his face with salted mist.

It was just a fucking accident; a mistake.

Somebody forgot to tighten a bolt or forgot to wear their safety belt or had too much to drink the night before. Or somebody's girlfriend broke up with them that morning or one of the guys who was depended on came down with the flu and was busy blowing breakfast. Or maybe it was just that the sun came out of the clouds early and hit a shiny piece of metal the wrong way. Who knows why anything happens; it just does and then it's too late to do anything about it.

God has the plan and we don't.

I sit on the beach and run all the scenarios through my head while Audrey walks down the expanse of empty beach and picks up shells and interesting bits that have washed up from the sea. She's thinking about the concert she has to play in a couple of weeks; Mahler's 8th, *Symphony Of A Thousand*. Every few feet she looks back to check if I'm not sobbing or pounding the ground with my fists. I'm not. I just sigh a lot and wonder what life's all about.

After dinner we crawl under the down comforter and make love to the sounds of the ocean and the fireplace. The world, for the moment, is a distant spot, a few million miles away and I'm grateful. I begin to drift off to sleep and fall into a dream.

Burgie, Buzz and I are riding the Number Seven Bus to the beach.

"It's not all beaches and love anymore, is it?" I ask Buzz. The bus isn't going to the beach; instead it's going down an empty stretch of desert - a two-lane highway in the middle of nowhere. Burgie's watch has stopped and he's worried because he has to get home for 'the celebration,' but doesn't know what celebration it is.

Buzz holds out his hand to Burgie. It's filled with small fish, tiny minnows no bigger than a thumbnail. "Here, you can have these. I have more of them than sane people," he says. The tiny fish flap their tails.

"It would scare them if they knew," Burgie answers.

"Don't worry," says Buzz. "I know the man who makes fish for a living." Buzz turns to me. He's shrouded in his Houdini cape.

The bus comes to a stop and Buzz gets off. He's holding a surfboard and waving as the bus starts to pull away. The sun is setting on the horizon, but it looks like noon out. Buzz stands at the bustop and waves one last time before running off to a sand dune.

I wake with a start, drenched in sweat and with cotton mouth. I'm panting, like I've been holding my breath, or someone's been holding it for me. I look deliriously around the room. It's dark; the fireplace casts a dull red glow to the walls. I can hear the distant sound of crashing waves from the ocean just two blocks away. For once, the tranquility bears a resemblance to a hurricane and it scares me. My head falls back to the pillow and I stare up at the ceiling, waiting to get back to sleep. But I don't. Audrey is peacefully unconscious beside me, oblivious in her dreams that I am quietly falling apart before her closed untroubled eyes.

Friday shows up as quickly as a pause between two deranged thoughts. I've been dreading the day, but it's arrived just the same. I used to make jokes about the inevitability of things. I would laugh and remark, "Like death and taxes or the common cold!" Christ, what a wise-ass I was.

We reluctantly pack up and head north. I promise Audrey we'll come back to Carmel, just as soon as the wreckage from the funeral clears.

San Francisco has changed to the point where I no longer recognize it.

The main house is still there; turned into a Chinese Herbalist's office, but the Minsion, the miniature house we used to call home in 1969, is gone; torn down and paved over into a parking lot. The house is painted red and the picture window from what was once the living room, is clustered with displays of Ginseng Root and various other 'Wonder Herbs' along with the smiling face of Doctor Wong and his Remedies.

It's cold and rainy as we trudge down Castro Street. The city has become cleaner, more civilized and in many ways, more precious than I remembered. It doesn't look like the kind of city Buzz would want to be buried in. But then, none of us have the luxury of opening a window to the other side and asking,

"Hey Buzz, are you sure about this?" We just go with what we remember.

In a rational moment, we decided we'd have Buzz cremated. Since he hated the idea of being stuck in one place anyway, we thought the best thing to do was spread the ashes around his favorite places: Griffith Park, Mullholland Drive, Topanga and the LaBrea Tarpits. Simple. That was a week ago. Back when everyone was speaking to each other.


By the time everyone finally arrives in San Francisco, the tension is as thick as asphalt.

The score card goes something like this: Burgie and Zara are arguing and Leslie and Burgie still aren't speaking to each other. Stoika and Mrs. Jordan get into a screaming fight. Mrs. Jordan blames Stoika for Buzz's death; no small feat, considering Stoika and Buzz hadn't been living with each other for almost twenty years. Vladimir and Molly vanish after fighting with Stoika who is fighting with Mrs. Jordan because they don't know why Stoika divorced Buzz at all. They don't realize Stoika and Buzz never officially got divorced in the first place. Like any of us are going to tell them!

Audrey and I try to stay out of it, even going so far as getting a hotel on the other side of town, near Fishermen's Wharf, but it's impossible. After the first day our room has became a hospital ward for the emotionally wounded who march in and out every time a family skirmish takes place, which is usually every three or four hours.

"Can I stay with you guys for the night?" Stoika asks, standing unannounced at the doorway to our room. She's trying to get off the mental rollercoaster and land on solid ground, but isn't having much luck at it. She's shaking and can't sit still without having one leg or the other twitch in perpetual motion. Her eyes are like strawberries and framed by puffy sacks that haven't seen a full night's sleep in a week.

Having missed the great outburst a few days earlier, Audrey immediately lets her in and offers her comfort, room service - a bottle of Jack Daniels, a bucket of ice and three glasses - along with an impartial ear.

Stoika lopes agitatedly in and collapses on the loveseat in the living room. She starts to fumble around her purse for a cigarette, although she already has one lit in her right hand. "Jesus, I really hate the shit out of this town. When we first lived here I thought it was huge; it used to scare me. Did it scare you, Nelson? Christ, no wonder Buzz called her mommy-monster. She's like a fucking Stepford Wife! Nelson, we've known each since, what, the eleventh grade? Did I kill Buzz? Do I fucking look like somebody who runs around pushing people off oil rigs? Even in my mind?"

For the first time she called him Buzz. Not 'Dickhead', 'Him', or 'The B-Word'. She's stopped pretending she hates the guy.

When Stoika realizes she already has a cigarette lit in her hand, she bolts up and heads to the bathroom, carrying a steady stream of meaningful and meaningless dialogue along with her. It leaves Audrey and I to keep our end of the conversation going with a slab of off-white press-board. I try giving her the voice-of-reason pep-talk.

"Stoika, you've gotta believe you had nothing to do with Buzz's death. You weren't responsible. It has nothing to do with you. Buzz's mom has always been crazy; she's always blamed everybody for everything. It's a hobby with her."

She's doing something at the bathroom sink, but I can't make out what. She runs water and opens her purse. "Jesus Christ, I look like shit! Hey, you guys want to go out for a drink or something? I haven't been to North Beach yet!"

Stoika, in a sweeping about-face, opens the door and glides out, looking only marginally better than when she walked in. A frenzied smile is plastered across her face and she's slapped on about two tons of makeup. She bears an uncanny resemblance to her 1969 transformation, only this time I don't see it as such a hot idea.

"So how about it?" Audrey and I look at each other and shake our heads.

"Nothing personal, but I think we'll pass." I tell her.

"Besides, there's plenty of Jack Daniels here," Audrey says. "Who wants to foist themselves on an unsuspecting world?"

"Oh come on guys, I'm not that fucked up" Stoika says, weaving back and forth. Audrey counters with: "Look, it's better to get fucked in the safety of your own room than to wind up face down in some bar." Stoika glances down at the bottles on the table.

"Okay, ninny out on me." Stoika heads for the door and shuts it behind her.

Audrey glances over at me with a raised eyebrow.

"Otto, she's a big girl, she drinks like a fish and she can take care of herself."

A half hour passes by and the afternoon sky has turned cloudy and dark. It could rain almost any minute. The temperature is dropping quickly. Audrey wraps herself in a bulky black sweater and sits out on the veranda of our room overlooking Fisherman's Wharf and smokes a cigarette. She turns to me and winces.

"I hate to say it, Bugs, but I think we should go look for her."

The phone rings. It's Burgie. A cease-fire has been declared between him, Zara and Leslie. Vladimir and Molly have taken Mrs. Jordan to the funeral home to take care of last minute arrangements. Burgie wants to know if we want to go to dinner with them. He asks where Stoika is and I tell him she wanted to get drunk and is probably heading for North Beach.

"Hey man, you better keep an eye on her. Vladimir says she's been taking a lot of pills lately that don't mix well with alcohol."

I tell Burgie to get a cab and meet us at the Hotel and in the meantime I'll look for Stoika. I have hopes of finding her safely sprawled out in some naugehyde booth with a collection of swizzle sticks.

I hang up the phone just as Audrey comes out of the bathroom, holding an empty prescription bottle in her hand. "Uh . . . Bugs, what's all this?" She hands me the bottle: Percocet #30. The bottle's empty. The prescription was filled out two days earlier from a pharmacy on Market Street to Stoika Jordan-Foley.

I bolt out of the room and race downstairs. I hope Stoika hasn't got far. My worst fear is having to comb through every bar in San Francisco looking for her. San Francisco has a reputation of being a drinking town and there are no less than four bars on every corner in every part of the city. Finding her could take weeks. I quietly curse myself for letting Stoika go. I can put up with one obnoxious drunk every once in a while.

I get to the lobby and pass the Hotel bar. I stop and, impulsively, walk in.

"She left about twenty minutes ago," the bartender tells me in soft, somber tones while he dries glasses. "She kept asking when the next feed was and if she could borrow a plate and spoon." He looks at me with noncommittal, but questioning eyes, as if I am the only one on the planet who knows when the next 'feed' is going to be.

I'm relieved to find that she didn't get very far, but more frustrated, in a way, because she's now leaving cryptic messages. The lounge pianist is hiding behind a palm tree, playing a 'paint-by-numbers' version of *Autumn In New York*. It doesn't seem like the kind of place Stoika would have wanted to hang out in for any length of time anyway. I know - I used to work here.

I run through the hotel lobby just as Burgie, Zara and Leslie arrive. I tell them Stoika has disappeared to a 'feed.' Whatever the hell that is.

"Bring a plate and spoon? The feeds, remember? The Panhandle." Leslie has come up with the answer.

It's well into night by the time we get to Golden Gate Park. There is an eerie sense of familiarity to the place, but as the cab driver says as he drops us off , "Are you fuckin' nuts?"

Okay, so the park is crammed with junkies, wackos and derelicts. It's not really that much different than 1968. We're on a mission. Surprisingly, we encounter very little in the way of deranged resistance.

I will give Stoika credit for many things in this life, but I definitely think her greatest achievement is finding, almost unconscious, the exact place we all remember from our first day in Golden Gate Park. The day we dropped acid for the first time and found ourselves sprawled out on the grass gazing at the moon.

The trees around us have grown taller; the lake is dirtier and the glow from the city is just a shade more orange from the Xenon crime-lights, but other than that - if you closed your eyes and if someone whispered "Love is all you need," you'd be there.

Unfortunately, Stoika is falling in and out of consciousness. She lays sprawled out on the grass, covered in dew, singing a Moby Grape song: *"Would you let me, walk down your street, naked if I want to? - Can I, pop fireworks, on the fourth of July? - Can I buy an amplifier, on time? I ain't got no money now, but I will pay you before I die."*

Between the five of us there are five different ideas as to what to do. It runs the gamut from 'Call the Police' to 'Get her to the hospital and have her stomach pumped.'

When Audrey discovers that Stoika has a pulse too weak to defend itself, she decides it's time to dump the Socratic method of making decisions and call 911.

We take Stoika to the nearest hospital. We run through red lights and break speed records and narrowly miss becoming statistics, but we get Stoika to the Emergency Room at Harkness Community Hospital, where they proceed to pump her stomach and ask lots of questions.

"Is there a history of emotional instability in her family?" a thin, black nurse by the name of Jeffries asks.

"I'm afraid so," I answer.

"But she's never tried to kill herself before," Burgie chimes in.

"No, but she used to be a drunk," Leslie blurts in.

"She has a history of alcohol abuse?" Nurse Jeffries prods.

"Since she was sixteen," Burgie tells her.

"But she stopped for about ten years."

Vladimir, Molly and Mrs. Jordan turn up moments later. Molly and Vladimir are past upset; they're in despair. It was bad enough their father died, but now their mother has tried killing herself. Vladimir, the more reserved of the two, breaks down and cries like a baby in a corner of the waiting room. Molly is completely drained. She stares blankly ahead.

Mrs. Jordan is non-plussed; she's brought a bag of sandwiches and now proceeds to lay out an impromptu buffet on a chair in the Emergency Room.

"The company picked a nice casket for him," Mrs. Jordan remarks, unwrapping a Pastrami sandwich. "He worked for some good people, they took care of him."

She takes a bite and looks around the room. She turns to me and says in a hushed voice, "To be honest, I don't know what the hell he ever saw in Stoika. She was always so goddamn crazy. Christ, look at that family of hers, they're all fruitcakes."

I'm not in the mood to get a fight going, not in the emergency room, with three stabbing victims, a compound fracture and a domestic squabble involving frying pans and third degree burns from flying Crisco, all sitting within earshot of us. I nod my head and reach for a bag of potato chips. Audrey glances over at Mrs. Jordan and shoots her the Piantadosi Death Stare, but I squeeze her knee and silently plead with her not to get into it.

Nurse Jeffries finally comes out with the news that Stoika will be all right, but she'll probably have to stay at the hospital for at least another day. Molly and Vladimir want to see her and they're allowed a brief fifteen minutes. Burgie has taken a walk outside, looking for fresh air, so he's missed the report. I run off to find him and give him the good news.

He's standing on the corner, attempting to light a cigarette. I stop as I get near him. Burgie has never smoked before in his life and looks awkward trying to start now, especially since I've been spending the better part of my adult life trying to quit.

"It seemed like something to do," he explains when he sees my puzzled face.

"She's going to be okay" I tell him.

"Lucky her." He shuffles his feet and stares at the ground, lost.

"Jesus, Nelson, I don't get this life. I don't get a single fucking thing about it."

He tosses the cigarette down on the sidewalk, giving up after five or six attempts to light it. Burgie seems lost, trapped in a void, trying to figure his way out. "I don't think Zara and I are going to last too much longer."

"Why?"

"I can't talk to her, Nels. I have to explain everything to her. Do you know what that's like? Having to explain everything all the time?" "Well, that's what you get for cradle-robbing."

Burgie shoots me a look. I turn to him and shake my head. "Bad taste. Didn't mean it. Sorry Burg."

Now it's my turn to light a cigarette. I pull a partially crushed pack out of my pocket and search for one that isn't broken in half or ripped to shreads. I manage to rescue one and throw the rest of the pack in a nearby trash can.

With one quick movement, I light the cigarette and inhale deeply and blow out a stiff white cloud of tars and resins. I turn around, giving Burgie the all- encompassing suspicious glance. "But it's not really about Zara, is it?"

Silence.

Burgie lets out a sigh. "I don't handle this stuff very well, Nels. I never did. All we seem to do is fight. For Christ sake, Buzz is dead. We shouldn't be fighting. I wish I didn't feel like throwing up all the time. I heard someplace that smoking is good for an upset stomach."

"Old wives' tale, Burg."

Burgie and I pace back and forth in front of the hospital Emergency Room entrance and talk about Buzz. I'll admit, it's a strange place to speak highly of the dead, but the death of Buzz hits Burgie particularly hard. It's the first time we've all been smacked in the face by mortality. But Burgie, perennial youth, now fading into middle-age, is mortified.

"Who the hell are all these people?" Mrs. Jordan wonders, peering around at the faces; none of whom, aside from the immediate entourage from Los Angeles, she recognizes.

The funeral home is filled with people we assume are friends of Buzz. The memorial service was delayed until Stoika was released from the hospital. She sits in stoney silence off to the left of the casket, wearing dark glasses, while Molly and Vladimir sit in the row behind her.

At one point I notice Mrs. Jordan turn around and flinch. I turn around. The last three rows are empty but standing beyond that, near the rear entrance of the Funeral home is an older man with solid white hair, slicked back into a pony-tail and sporting a thick white moustache. He wears an elegantly tailored dark suit. He stands quietly with his hands folded and stares straight ahead.

He has a tattoo on his right hand with the word 'Tibet' spelled out in dark blue letters. He wears impenetrably dark glasses and it's hard to tell if he's been crying or laughing or experiencing any emotion at all. He's just 'the presence in the back of the room.'

Once Mrs. Jordan spots him she hunches her shoulders over and tries to push herself as far down in the pew as she can go.

Throughout the entire funeral service, he doesn't move an inch. After a while I stop noticing he's there and look back to the flower draped casket sitting in the front of the room, and let my mind wander.

Before this one I'd only been to two funerals in my life; both were for people I didn't know very well. My first, when I was four was for my Uncle Douglas. I remember people crying and carrying on, but I didn't know exactly what for. I wasn't sure if there was anybody in the casket or not. The room was filled with flowers and solemn organ music. Nobody said a word. When we went to the cemetery, I sat in the car most of the time and wasn't told anything until years later, when Uncle Douglas's picture fell out of a scrapbook. "Oh, he liked you so much!" The truth was, my Uncle Douglas didn't know me at all, but my mother always created scenarios that never existed in real life. My second experience at funerals was for the morning man at my dad's radio station. I was nine and had never met Jerry Java in person, other than hearing him once or twice on the radio. He had apparently done the popular thing that year by driving his car off a cliff near the Palos Verdes Penninsula.

I knew Buzz. We were friends since the day in 1964 when we hung out at Wallich's Music City. Even though we lost touch, I still felt a bond of family about him.

The old guy in the white suit and pony-tail at the back of the funeral home stands silently while the service plods on. A non-denominational priest who keeps forgetting who is in the casket, and refers to Buzz as Mrs. Brillman.

The mistake is understandable since Mrs. Brillman was the service just before ours. It explains all the mysterious people sitting in the funeral home. The crowd for the Brillman funeral is a lot older than us and, in fact, outnumber us by several geriatrics to one. They're holdovers and I assume the old guy in the back is one of them.

I ask Mrs. Jordan why she is trying to crawl under the pew. "That guy back there,"she says, pointing in his direction and whispering to me. "He's Buzz's father, the son-of-a-bitch. I don't want him to see me."

I bolt around in my seat and stare at him, dumbfounded. Now that she's mentioned it, he does bear a strong resemblance to Buzz - a sixty-year-old version. He knows I'm staring at him and he knows who I'm sitting next to. He gives me a faint smile of recognition, as if to say, silently, "I-know-you-know-I-know,"and continues his straight ahead gaze.

After all the years of never hearing about him and assuming he was dead, missing, disappeared, held hostage in some Middle-Eastern war zone, the infamous Mr. Jordan magically appears, alive and well.

I start to get up to walk over to him when Mrs. Jordan grabs me by the arm and practically tears my jacket sleeve off, pulling me back. "For Christ sake, don't talk to him. Don't give that asshole the pleasure of saying anything to anybody!"Mrs. Jordan is seething. She curls her lip like a Boston Terrier about to chew on a mailman's leg. Clearly, she hates the guy; it's no big secret.

But I have to admit; I see certain similarities between her and the real Mr. Jordan and Stoika and Buzz. History is being repeated here. It is, to paraphrase Yogi Berra, deja vu all over again.

"Bugs," Audrey leans over and whispers, "if I die before you, please don't do a memorial like this. I will come back and haunt the shit out of you."

Audrey never knew Buzz face to face, but she knows him well enough to imagine if he wasn't already dead, he would surely be dead after this service. Bad enough the priest keeps forgetting who is lying in the casket, the myopic organist keeps playing *On The Trail* from Grand Canyon Suite. Apparently Mrs. Brillman was a real outdoorsy type and this was her favorite piece of music.

Thankfully, after an hour of teary-eyed testimonies from Burgie, me, Leslie and a terrifyingly morose monologue from Stoika, the funeral ends with her launching into a frighteningly off-key acapella rendition of "Dear Mr. Fantasy".

Mrs. Jordan sidles behind us, managing to avoid a confrontation as we file out of the funeral home and head down the block to The Canton Gardens. It's an old Chinese restaurant Buzz, Stoika and I used to frequent back in the days when Stoika worked at The Minimum Daily Requirement in North Beach. We take over an upstairs banquet room, away from the daily customers to host the wake.

Everyone but Stoika and Audrey drink themselves into oblivion. Leslie and Audrey keep hugging each other while the bartender pours water glasses filled with straight scotch. Zara is busy holding hands with Vladimir and sneaking tongue kisses in the hallway by a phonebooth. Burgie has his turn to argue with Mrs. Jordan. Stoika is sitting out on the lawn overlooking the cemetery, tearing up blades of grass and chain smoking.

I take a breather from the rapidly disintegrating festivities and walk back to the funeral home.

Two workmen who have done this hundreds of times are methodically pulling the casket down from its pedestal and carting it off to the crematorium.

Mr. Jordan sits quietly alone in the front row, watching the workmen. I walk down the aisle and sit in a pew two rows behind him.

"Nelson, how come you're sitting so far away?"

I have no idea how he came to the conclusion it was me sitting behind him. He didn't turn around, didn't see me walk in. I get up and sit next to him. I reach over and extend my hand. He reciprocates. It's like shaking hands with a baby. His fingers feel like they've never worked a day in their lives.

"How do you know me?" I ask, feeling understandably spooked.

"Bradley mentioned you a lot, ever since you were kids."

It's hard for me to get used to Buzz being called anything other than Buzz. He just doesn't seem like a Bradley to me.

"How come I've never met you before?"

It's a fair enough request. In all the time I knew Buzz I never met this guy; never even heard him talked about.

Mr. Jordan runs his fingers over his mouth. "I left after Bradley was born, I suppose you already know that. Bradley was a dramatic kid. He probably got that from her side of the family." Looking at Mr. Jordan's white hair, his walrus moustache and his Tibet tattoo, I suspect the drama comes from both sides. Although, honestly, Mrs. Jordan doesn't look like the kind of person to walk around the streets of L.A. in a cape and think of herself as Houdini.

"Well . . . what did you do for thirty-nine years?" I ask him.

"I lived in L.A. for twenty of them. In fact, I lived less than six blocks away from Molino High."

I'm stunned.

"Well, it was a little strange for Bradley at first, seeing me with a shaved head wearing an orange robe, hawking copies of *Bhaghvad Gita As It Is* on street corners."

My mind starts reeling back to just exactly where six blocks from Molino was; it was the Hare Krishna Ashram on La Cienega. Mr. Jordan was one of those guys who used to drive people insane at the airport and on Sunset and Hollywood Boulevard. It also explains why, when we used to pass the ashram and I voiced curiosity about going to the Sunday feasts, Buzz would always change the subject or talk about reports of food poisoning there. So we never went.

Mr. Jordan, or Art as he wants me to call him, spent the goodly part of the last four decades hanging out in exotic places doing exotic things; all of them having some kind of spiritual overtone. He's been in and out of more monasteries than a brandy salesman. He finally left Los Angeles in 1970 and moved to New Mexico, settling in Taos and opening a book store, The Cosmic Eye. After scoring a big success with the 'wayless way' crowd, he decided to try his hand at publishing and made a fortune putting out anything with the words Cosmic, Pilgrim, Mind, Soul, Journey or India in the title. The biggest seller was *The Cosmic Pilgrim's Journey Through The Mind of Cooking,* which was very little more than a ripped-off version of a Betty Crocker Cookbook where recipes for Wiener-wrap were substituted with things like Trailmix For The Soul, a truly revolting concoction of dried grass, treebark and seaweed.

It sold a few hundred thousand copies.

In the intervening decades, Art has become something of a hustler. But he felt a sense of guilt over never making a real home for Buzz.

"You have to understand, Nelson, I was just back from Korea and the only perspective on life I had was going straight from high school into a war. I wasn't prepared to settle down. I needed to find out about life. Of course, Renee, Bradley's mother, didn't exactly feel the same way. She wanted to get married and settle down. But that wasn't what it was about for me, so I left."

Art stops and lets out a sigh. He's become fascinated by a small strand of blonde hair on his white jacket.

My eyes fall onto the pew in front of me. I scan the bare wood seat, shaking my head. It makes perfect sense to me. The idea that the only sense you can make out of life is that there is no sense to be made has proven to be true.

I get up to walk out. I extend my hand to him. "I better go. They were pretty drunk when I left. They must be in hysterics by now."

He gets up to hug me and starts to cry.

"He was a good kid with a good heart and I fucked everything up," he wails.

I've never had a sixty-year-old man cry on my shoulder. I feel embarrassed for him. I feel helpless. "He loved you a lot; he told me many times," I say, trying to calm the situation down.

"Oh bullshit, he hated me," Art sobs. It's true, it must be or Buzz would have talked about him to me, and I should know better than to start lying where family matters are concerned.

He regains his composure and apologizes for the outburst and makes me promise to call him when I get back to L.A. I assure him I will, then turn and walk back up the aisle to the entrance.

I assume he doesn't want to go to the wake: knowing that Mrs. Jordan hasn't let up hating him since 1951, it doesn't seem likely she would stop now. I get halfway down the aisle and stop to look back at him. He's vanished. Maybe he ducked out a side entrance or just evaporated into thin air; like father, like son.

I leave the chapel just as another cluster of mourners line up for the next funeral. I have the disquieting thought that, with the amount of funerals this place does in a day, it would be a minor miracle if we are, in fact, handed an urn containing Buzz instead of an urn containing Mrs. Brillman. I suppose it could've gone either way; Buzz being spread over Grand Canyon and Mrs. Brillman being spread over Mullholland Drive and Griffith Park.

I go back to the wake. It has turned into a free-for-all. War has broken out and hostility is everywhere.

As far as I can tell, it's Renee Jordan versus everybody, with skirmishes between Burgie and Zara, Burgie and Leslie, Zara and Vladimir, Molly and Mrs. Jordan, and Molly and Stoika. I doubt if these people are going to want to ever see each other again in their lifetimes.

When I reach her, Audrey is in the middle of laying a hot blast of screaming obsceneties at Mrs. Jordan. I fish Audrey out of the war zone and drag her away to the comparative safety of the city streets, taking her for a walk with hopes of calming her down.

"Jesus Christ, that Jordan broad is a pain in the ass. She hates everybody!"

Audrey walks gingerly, hanging on to my arm. She's taking deep breaths, trying to draw in fresh air.

"Otto, you gotta understand, she hates herself more than anybody."

Audrey snorts. "Not while I'm around!" I prop her up as we storm down the street.

Audrey looks pretty. There is something disarming about her. Maybe it's because I'm married to her, but I doubt it. The thing about Audrey is, she hasn't changed; not to me, not to anybody. She hasn't lost any of her youthful charm. She has the same look of mischief in her eyes, the same infectious grin, the same glowing white teeth. Nobody would guess in a million years she's hitting the tip-end of her thirties.

Luckily it's Sunday, so there are no stores open and the streets aren't clogged with business types. We bob and weave our way through an empty thoroughfare.

"Can we sit down for a second?" Audrey asks, panting and red-nosed.

We sit at a bustop while she catches her breath. "I have this little confession to make," she says, looking up with those mysterious eyes.

"I'm a little on the pregnant side," she blurts out.

I sit in stunned silence, glancing every few moments over to Audrey and letting the words sink in. After what feels like several minutes, I howl out laughing. I can't stop; and I don't know why I suddenly find the idea of Audrey pregnant to be hysterically funny, but I do. It's laughter out of happiness.

"When did you know?" I ask, between gleeful guffaws.

"A couple of days ago. I called the doctor when we arrived in Carmel. She announced the tests were positive. Jesus, if I had known it was this funny, I would've pushed for twins!"

I guess Audrey hasn't planned on this kind of reaction from me. I have to convince her I'm not having a nervous breakdown, but am, in fact, happy; deliriously happy. When she realizes I'm truly thrilled, a smile spreads across her face like the surface of the sun.

Audrey and I, of all people, crashing head-long into parenthood. I have no idea what the first notion of being a father is all about. Well, neither does anybody else.

And then for a moment I feel sad. How can we be having this wonderful windfall when, probably at this exact moment, Buzz is being converted into pumice, Burgie and Zara are heading for a break up, Stoika's already tried to kill herself, and Leslie will probably hate Burgie again for the rest of her life. Everyone around us is a mess. - and it goes beyond the funeral home; it's spilled over to the world in general.

"So how do you feel, I mean, you know, getting ready to do the rugrat bit?"

"A little scared; a lot scared. But happy."

I wrap my arm around her and we walk slowly back to the restaurant. The wind blows down the street and the city starts to look beautiful again. I start to wonder why we're living in L.A. anyway. And the answer, like everything else is; we have to; it's where the work is.

As we walk through the old neighborhoods, I think about all the incidents and moments that made up this part of the past. We walk up Fulton Street and I find myself gazing up at the apartment Thea Talber and I shared. I realize how relieved I am it's not 1970 anymore.


By the time we get back to the wake, the waiters are busily cleaning up the mess; everyone has gone - leaving me to sort out the bill and the damages. I try to find Burgie to tell him the good news, but he's in such a hurry to get back to L.A. he's already checked out of his hotel and left for the airport. I find Leslie, Stoika and Zara in the lobby with bags packed, waiting for a cab.

It seems Leslie got an emergency call from her parents who told her Alain has been calling from Paris almost every hour, trying desperately to get hold of her. It's a golden opportunity to hop the next flight to Orly with Zara and take Stoika with them.

"We're never going to see each other again, are we?" I ask.

"Of course we will - well, maybe not some of us," Stoika replies, glancing at the others. Leslie doesn't say anything. She looks at me and Audrey and smiles faintly.

A cab pulls up in front and the driver and doorman load up the trunk. Leslie steps off the curb and opens the passenger door, she turns to me. "I really envy you, Nelson. You've made sense out of your life. I'm a forty year-old grandmother and I don't belong anyplace."

"Leslie, that's not true."

"Audrey's a good person - don't fuck it up."

"Please don't disappear."

"I won't. I promise."

She reaches over and hugs me for what feels like twenty minutes. She buries her head in my shoulder and I feel the collar of my shirt grow warm and moist.

The others are already in the cab and waiting for Leslie. I tap her on the back.

"I think the meter's running."

She pulls back and wipes her eyes. "Jesus, I hate mascara. You'd think they'd invent something that doesn't run."

Leslie turns and wraps her arms around Audrey and kisses her on the cheek. She tells her how lucky I am and Audrey grins sheepish approval. Leslie slips into the waiting cab and, in seconds, is gone.

Vladimir, Molly and Mrs. Jordan are left to fend for themselves. Vladimir decides to stay in San Francisco for a while, leaving Molly and Mrs. Jordan to fly back to L.A.

*    *    *    *

*"Hey Bugs, listen; if you can hear me, we're waiting for you to come back. It'll be all right. Hey, if it's any consolation, the doctor says your hands are fine - didn't even break a fingernail. That's more than I can say for me right now. I'm supposed pop any day now. It'd be great if you were awake for that. We never actually decided on a name yet, did we? Me, I'm leaning towards Mallory. Don't ask me why - Talk about unoriginal. Sounds like the name of a talk show host or a Real Estate agent . . . Burgie's driving me nuts. I wish I knew what was going on in that brain of yours."*

*    *    *    *

It's three in the morning when I wake up - insomnia and a strange hotel bed working their agitated spell on me. I stare out the window at the glow of lights from Ghirardelli Square spilling across the room. Audrey stirs. I glance over and realize she's wide awake too.

"What time is it?" she asks, gazing wide-eyed at the ceiling.

I lean over, creasing my pillow, trying to get a better view of the clock radio.

"Three twenty-seven. You'll be happy to know you've been asleep for eleven hours."

Audrey groans.

"I can't sleep."

"Me either."

We get up and fumble around in the dim light, looking for our clothes. I wander into the bathroom and locate a hot plate and packets of complimentary instant coffee.

216

Audrey is up, showered and dressed by the time the water boils. I dump the tiny packets into two styrofoam cups and the air fills with the semi-plastic aroma of Folgers Instant.

We sit at the edge of the bed and sip our hot, watery bilge and stare at a brightly colored shopping bag gazing down at us from the credenza. There sits Buzz. Or maybe Mrs. Brillman.

"So, what are we going to do about that?" Audrey asks.

I don't have a clue. The original idea was to go, as a group, to Buzz's favorite places and spread his ashes around. But with the air of hostility so thick, it doesn't seem like that will ever happen.

I take the bag down and pack it with the rest of our clothes and try to forget about it for the next few hours.

We take the inland route back to L.A. and get home in less than six hours. I forget that most of Central California is not picturesque, and smells bad. The scenery sails by and is barely noticed. We only become aware of where we are when we get our first blast of smog coming over the grapevine.

We arrive home a little after noon; just in time to miss a package delivery from American Airlines. I have no idea what it is, but it's obviously something that can't be left at the front door.

We unpack and I take out the shopping bag and the urn sitting inside. It's a solid brass cylinder, capable of doing damage if dropped on an unsuspecting foot. I put it inside a bookcase in the living room and relegate it to the position of holding up a stack of Dinah Washington albums.

Homelife quickly returns to normal. The phones begin ringing and I'm getting requests for more session work. Audrey drives over to The Music Center to bone up on Mahler before rehearsals begin at the end of the week. In a matter of hours, the whole episode of San Francisco and the funeral become a dim, distant memory.

I call Burgie several times and get no answer.

There is a knock at the door around five that afternoon. I am submerged under headphones and don't hear it at first. I see an American Airlines van parked in front and get up to answer the door.

"Mister Rivers?" the smiling, but overworked airline employee asks, raising his pen to the level of his clipboard. I nod. "Got a delivery for you. Came by earlier, but . . ." I look down at a huge crate that stands between him and me. It's an animal crate. "Poor guy's been cooped up in that box for days." I kneel down and look inside.

We've inherited Stanley.

He sits in the crate, annoyed at being caged up. He's greyer around the muzzle than when I saw him at the airport, and he whimpers when he sees me. I'm not sure if he's expecting me or Buzz to peer through the holes in the box.

I sign the form and the messenger nods thanks and returns to his van.

Stanley runs into the house and immediately heads to the bookcase with the urn. He sits down in front of the urn and doesn't move. He watches it, certain that it's going to come to life any minute.

Stanley cannot be convinced otherwise.

# CHAPTER TWENTY-ONE

## I'VE KNOWN YOU SINCE YOU WERE MORNING SICKNESS

*"He's not responding - we've tried all the tests - we've done everything. I think it's time to face the situation that he's not going to come out of this."*

*"So what are you saying?"*

*"I'm sorry - but, take him off life support. His quality of life just isn't there. I know it's a terrible thing - you see him there and he looks like the Nelson you've always known, but to be honest, there's no one there."*

*"Burgie - come on, help me with this. I can't think straight - I've got a kid that's upset . . . .and I'm not doing too good myself. "*

*"I can't make that decision, Audrey. Jesus, I've known him forever."*

*"How long is it after you turn everything off?"*

*"Depends. Anywhere from a few minutes to a few days."*

*"You're sure it's hopeless?"*

*"Honestly, I would say it's ninety-eight percent certain he won't come out."*

*"Oh God . . . . . I'm sorry . . . . .all right."*

*      *      *      *

It's gotten dead quiet in here. Not to the point of hearing pins drop; there are bells and a monotone voice in the hallway is asking for someone; but the silence of the room is all I can think about for a change, and it feels peaceful and serene.

I've been picking up a lot of things the past few days; bits of conversation. Someone keeps talking about "taking him to a nice resort"; I would have suggested Twenty-Nine Palms. It's only an hour or so away. I'd like that; desert breeze and a pool. Jesus, I could use some sun, I must look like a cotton ball by now. Now they're saying "take him off life-support". I'm frightened they're talking about me.

Sometimes Audrey comes and sits next to me and holds my hand. She keeps saying, "If you can hear me, squeeze my hand," over and over. I

219

squeeze with my best vice-grip, but the desire and the end result are nowhere near each other. At first I thought I was dreaming; but I feel so lousy I've realized now, I'm dying.

It's really hard to breathe, like riding a bike up a 90 degree incline with a Buick tied around my neck. I have this strange curiosity to stop trying and see what happens next; see if it's like when I flew. It's too late for that. It's so peaceful here. I wish I could hear some Ravel; that would be nice.

I smell flowers; could be jasmine. Someone's in the room standing next to me, they don't say anything. I wish they would - 'Hi, Nelson, how are you, Nelson, you're fucking toast, Nelson' - one of those heartfelt greetings that say so little and mean so much. But instead, they leave. And the smell of flowers vanishes behind the sound of a shut door.

I guess it's up to me now.

I'm taking big gasps on my own, but no one seems to notice. I really can't keep this up. Maybe I should lie here quietly and see what happens next.

I've heard about the 'next' part. Blue tunnels and all that. I'm not quite sure I believe it. I'd like to see Buzz. I need a second opinion on this.

"Well, you're dying, what did you expect?"

"Something more profound."

"Tsk."

"What's that mean?"

"It means 'fraid not. Dying is really simple."

"Thanks. Make me feel all warm and fuzzy"

"Hey, I'm just telling you straight. How do you feel?"

"Tired."

"Wanna feel really good?"

"How?"

"Just stop fighting it."

"Easy as that?"

"Yeah."

"Then what happens?"

"You feel really good."

"And then I'm dead."

"Well . . . yeah."

"But then what happens?"

"I don't know how to explain it, pal; everything happens and nothing happens."

"Pretty vague."

"Not that it makes much difference, but you don't have a choice."

"I don't want to die."

"Hey come on, this is a great opportunity. No more pain, no taxes, no disappointments. Besides . . .we're pals. I gotta confess, I miss you man.

"Yeah, but I'm gonna miss Audrey even more. I'll miss the grin and she's pregnant with my kid."

*     *     *     *

*"Hey, I know it's hard to be still, but you have to sit on my lap and be quiet if you want to see your dad. You're . . . uh . . . not going to get too many more chances you know . . . . . Oh Christ, this is tough. Burgie, I know this is terrible to ask, but . . . can Mal and I be alone with him? "*
*"Yeah . . . sure."*
*"You'd tell me if I did the wrong thing, wouldn't you?"*
*"You did the right thing."*
*"I'm scared."*
*"Me too."*

*     *     *     *

"Nels, you're a vegetable. Get serious; you can't be too much use to anybody in your state. What are they gonna do, prop you up in a room someplace and let the kid stare at you on your birthday?"

"Hey Buzz, I just felt something."

"Kind of light?"

"Yeah."

"Sort of like floating?"

"Yeah."

Buzz raises an eyebrow and nods his head, like the kid whose science experiment is going as planned.

"You're checking out, pal."

"No, wait. I feel something else. Somebody's smacking my face."

"It's nothing. Don't pay any attention to it."

"No, I can feel it; it's a clammy little hand, really tiny. Oh shit, Buzz, it's my kid! I'm not checking out pal, I'm staying! I have to."

Buzz glances over with a look that tells me everything; he knows I can't go now. Having been there himself, he knows up and down what it's like to feel that tiny clammy hand you are responsible for and see the moon-like face that'll be a version of you someday. After a minute or so he cracks a smile and waves.

"Inhale, pal. You can do it. Think about me from time to time and take care of Stanley. He's me, you know."

"Muggi bugwy! Muggi bugwy!"

The tiny face, slapping at me, looming like a glowing white ball, gazes, stunned, and bursts into frightened tears when I finally open my eyes and look at her. To be honest, I don't know who's more terrified; the little Khruschev or me. The one really going into hysterics is Audrey. She looks wonderful.

"Who the hell is Muggi Bugwy?" I mumble in semi-legible croaks.

She stares back, her face having drained to the color of chalk.

"That's what she calls you. Don't ask me where she got it. Cereal box probably."

"So . . .what's going on?"

"Oh nothing much, we were just getting ready to harvest your vital organs in twenty minutes!" True to form, she blurts out a wisecrack answer.

"Lucky me."

Audrey shakes her head and reaches for me. In seconds I'm drenched in warm wet salt.

The kid is cute, but I wouldn't really care if she looked like Koko the Chimp. Forget the Khruschev analogy, she's the image of Audrey. She's got her mom's trouble-making grin and tiny little violinist fingers. We're all wrapped around each other like adhesive tape.

# EPILOGUE

## THE PATRON SAINTOF SMOKE AND MIRRORS

"Don't remember anything about the bus, do you?"

The way the story goes, I was running out of my managers office across Sunset Boulevard. I understand from all the cards and letters and phone calls that it had something to do with me getting my first break; a contract with a nice, small esoteric Classical label who like my photo and the fact that I can play Alkan and Bud Powell.

Six months of being in a coma, followed by therapy and rehab and a general re-aquaintance with myself have greatly improved my condition. Unfortunately, what can't be rehab'd or therapied is that I occasionally forget exactly just what instrument it is I play.

"Could be worse, you could have come to after they dragged all your important parts out."

Burgie, who will never change no matter how many times I land on my head, is being optimistic as always. I'm not exactly feeling the same way.

I keep looking at my hands. They don't look as though they load lumber, but I can't get them to play a simple scale. I sit in my room with keyboards strewn everywhere and can't figure out, even if my life depended on it, how to play them.

"Look, it isn't permanent," Audrey assures me, holding the baby in her arms, rocking it back and forth.

"Um,I forgot, what are we calling her?" I ask, pointing to the small bundle getting bigger by the minute.

"Malory."

Malory is now almost six months old. I can tell she's going to be a cute kid and most likely, a handful.

But the ordeal has been rough on Audrey. She's aged a lot. Her hair is streaked grey and she has dark circles under her eyes. She tells me she sleeps a maximum of three hours a night. I sense a distance between us; a cold veil has been drawn.

Burgie moved in shortly after the accident, keeping Audrey company and setting up shop in what used to be our den. He brought his stereo and three thousand records; all of his Prez Prado, Tito Puente and Walter Wanderly albums. He also set up a satellite dish on the roof and installed eight video cassette machines, all on timers, tuned to various news programs. "I have to be informed," he tells me. I'm not sure exactly what about. It's not clear just when he plans to move out, but for the moment I don't mind.

My first day back from the hospital and I have a lot of adjusting to do. There's an unreality to the house as I walk around. I gaze at walls, stare at doorknobs, study pictures of me taken during some deep dark past and can't quite figure out exactly what it was about those moments that were so important to keep.

"Stanley ate your shoes," Audrey adds. Stanley is laying on a rug in front of the bookcase holding Buzz's urn. He's still waiting for Buzz to appear, like the Genie from the magic lamp, and free him from his responsibilities.

He left me only two pairs: tennis shoes that reek of mildew and a pair of thoroughly disgusting boots three sizes too big for me when I first got them in1969.

My manager keeps calling, politely inquiring if I'm back to normal yet. He's made the mistake of not telling the record company what has happened to me and keeps promising the label I'll be in London to start the sessions by the end of the month. Perhaps, but in an alternative universe.

"The doctor said it's going to take time; you just have to be patient," Audrey keeps telling me. I shrug my shoulders as I step into my "clown shoes". The tips of my boots extend an easy six inches past the tips of my toes, they slap against the floor as I walk. After an hour of slapping around the house in my Bozo boots, I decide the best thing is to go shopping with Burgie.

"Man, you got hit by that bus at a bad time," Burgie confesses, driving down Melrose.

I glance over at him: "Assuming there's supposed to be a good time to get hit by a bus?" I ask.

Burgie fills me in on what I've missed and what I vaguely remembered. Aside from the birth of Malory, and not being with Audrey as she went through seventeen hours of labor, I feel relieved that I was on some other planet for most of the time. Leslie, Zara and Stoika came back to L.A. and were taking turns visiting me in the hospital and Audrey at home with the baby.

Zara and Burgie went to Mexico one weekend and decided to try being single again. However, Zara had the baby, a nine-pound behemoth named Paris. Neither Burgie nor Zara seem to know where the name came from; it was one of those wild inspirations that came as the result of a late night movie or drugs. When things went into a tail-spin and they eventually split,

Zara took Paris and got the first plane back to San Francisco to meet up with Vladimir.

Burgie took up residence at various hotels around town until he figured out what he was eventually going to do.

Alain, submerged in grief over blowing 'the best thing he ever had' with Leslie, made a dramatic plea to start over again. The timing was right because Leslie was feeling lonely and remote in her hometown and she missed life in another country. Like the rest of us, she came to the conclusion that it was never going to be the same as it was when we were convinced the world was our oyster. She moved back to Cherbourg.

Stoika moved out of the house and gave it back to Ludmila, who promptly sold it to some guy. He had it bulldozed and put a sign up where the front lawn used to be advertising "Luxury Condominiums Sometime in 1991."

"Okay, what's wrong with Audrey?" I ask Burgie.

"What do you mean?" he answers.

"I mean there's something wrong."

"It's your imagination."

"I've been living on my imagination for three of the past six months. I am not imagining this."

Burgie pulls the car over to a parking space in front of a freshly abandoned art gallery on Melrose.

"She's convinced you tried to kill yourself."

My mouth fell open. "What?"

"When the Police showed up at the hospital, they told Audrey they got a report from some bystander who saw you jump in front of the bus. Now, the bus driver denied it and the passengers deny it too, but Audrey doesn't believe them."

Oh Jesus, he's right. Maybe I was depressed. I remember waking up one morning and thinking my life was almost over and I didn't have anything to show for it except some really awful commercials and an industrial film or two. And then when I got the record deal I became terrified I wouldn't be able to come through as promised. But I wasn't depressed enough to run in front of bus. I'm crazy - I'm not stupid.

And then Burgie goes quiet. Something else is coming.

"And, I have to confess I'm in love with her. I can't help it. I've been in love with her from the minute I saw her in the kitchen at the kennel twenty years ago. I'd never come between you two, but I've been carrying this torch around and I figured you had to know. I could never tell her how I felt. She loves you Nelson. Honest, she really does, and I hated you when you had that affair with Leslie. I was afraid you were going to die and you'd never know how I really felt. Now you do and you probably think I'm less than shower scum for it. It's okay, I understand. I don't feel guilty anymore. I feel free. If anything happens to me now my conscience is clear. Life is short, but it's wide."

All this on my first day home.

"Oh Nelson, it's so good to see you back." My mother smiles, cocking her head from one side to the other, trying to figure out if I've become someone else while in a coma, having gotten it in her head that I was having a serious out-of-body experience. I found out from Audrey my parents visited me a grand total of once while I was in the hospital. My mothers excuse being "vibrations in hospitals are terrible! All that dying." However, they visited her and the baby regularly and I became worried that my mother slipped in a few chapters of the Third Eye as bedtime reading.

"Mom, I want to sit in the backyard for a while, is that okay?"

"It's kind of a mess back there."

I manage to find a partially rotted deck chair that is almost rusted shut. The brightly colored strips of nylon are worn and don't seem strong enough to support an overweight fly. But I remember this chair; it's a chair I used to sit on when I was sixteen; the sixteen I recall being maybe a week or so earlier.

A sweltering afternoon in October. It's the last gasp of summer; I've missed most of it. The sun begins to dip on the horizon and the air smells hot and thick with smog.

I arrive home in time for the two a.m. feeding. Mal is stuck to Audrey's right boob like glue. It's either post-dinner or pre-breakfast.

"What happened to you?"

I explain I've been sitting in my parents' backyard and fell asleep.

I get undressed and climb into bed and watch Mal, or 'Potsie' as I am starting to call her, have all the fun.

When Mal's had enough, she's burped and sent packing off to her crib. It occurs to me that I haven't had anything remotely resembling sex in over six months. Realizing Audrey has balooned to a 42-D has me enthused. She comes back after a few minutes and gets into bed. She lays with her back to me. After a minute I muscle up enough teenage courage to wangle a well-placed hand over a truly massive left breast.

"Uh . . . Bugs. Nothing personal, but - do you have any idea what it's like to be lugging a pair of lead-filled basketballs around?"

"Frankly, no."

"Pain comes to mind for starts. Could Penny Pontoons have a rain-check?"

"Okay."

I slowly withdraw my hand and retreat to my side of the bed.

We lay in silence for a few minutes. It's hard to start up conversation. There's so much I want to talk about.

"Otto, I didn't try to commit suicide."

She turns and shoots me a look of quizzical disgust. "I know that. The guy who filled out the accident report recanted the suicide story and said you were running down the street laughing when it happened. He just thought you were insane."

Oh.

Well that clears that up. She doesn't think I'm suicidal. Burgie is asleep in the next room and loves to listen in on other people's conversations. I lean over and, in a low, hushed voice tell her, "You know, Burgie's in love with you."

Audrey yawns. "Yes, he has been for years." She rolls back over on her side. "Don't worry about it" she mumbles. She glances back at me with half-shut eyes, squinting at the light still burning on my side of the bed.

"Leslie, on the other hand, told me all about your affair." Audrey rolls over again, leaving me with that little bon mot to comtemplate.

"I can't believe that's what's bothering you, Otto. I thought you knew about it. It happened over ten years ago. It wasn't a big deal. We made love maybe twice."

No use, she's out; snoring.

The next morning over breafast, Audrey is bright and cheery.

"Honest, Bugs, you don't have to feel guilty about having the affair. You ended it and that's that. I am not, however, going to forgive you. My mother had to put up with my dad banging every dental assistant on the West Coast. That's not to say I don't love you, but if you do it again, you'll wish you had become a science project."

And so goes love.

With Sal's contribution of Clarissa as our nanny looming from room to room, taking care of 'Potsie' during the day, and religiously reading Edgar Cayce, Audrey is back with the orchestra and spending increasingly more time away. Between concerts and rehearsals, I see less and less of her. And after a while, I see her only for short periods of time early in the morning, or very late at night.

It all happened during the Christmas season, normally the busiest time for me with office parties and club dates and a lot of socializing. This year it's lonely. I'm still trying to get back to normal and finding that it's harder than I realized. I've been practicing every day but finding it painfully slow getting my chops back; I have memory lapses where the notes on the page suddenly become hieroglyphics and five minutes later everything's fine. It's during one of those piques of anxiety that I decide to take advantage of a credit card cash advance and go Christmas shopping.

I'm on my way to Brentano's when I see something that makes me stop. Sitting at a table at an outdoor cafe, across the patio from where I am standing is Audrey. But she's not alone. There's a guy sitting with her. Out of habit, I start to walk over. It's around four in the afternoon and the sun dips low on the horizon, casting deep shadows all around. The closer I get, the more I realize she is seriously wrapped around this guy. They're holding hands and he whispers something in her ear and lightly kisses her neck. She smiles and leans towards him and they kiss. He wraps his arm around her. They look and act exactly like lovers.

I turn away. It's an impulsive reaction; I don't know whether to be angry, embarrassed or upset. I walk back, further away, joining a crowd of people in line to see a movie.

I keep watching Audrey and I slowly begin to recognize the person she's with: Randall.

I forget about Christmas and leave the crush of cheerless shoppers for home.

It's rush hour. Traffic moves at a snail's pace and it gives me time to think. I'm hurt and angry and I should've said something, made a scene, lifted Randall up by his denim Gap shirt and tossed him head-first into a trash receptacle.

But I'm not that kind of person. I feel sad that we've drifted apart this way. And I don't know if it's anybody's fault or if this is just something that happens, like taking out the garbage or getting hit by lightning.

I'm trapped behind a bus right now. It's painted like a candy cane and spewing an inordinate amount of exhaust on me. I'm struck by the idea that, maybe this is the same bus that hit me. Someone has scrawled little check marks in its grimy ass and I assume they are indications of kills the bus has made in its illustrious career.

Trying to get that idea out of my head, I roll the window of my car up and turn on the radio. The air conditioner isn't working and, after a minute, sweat begins pouring off my forehead. Clarissa has been using the car lately and she left the radio tuned to a station that isn't playing Christmas music, but for once I wish it was. It's playing a golden oldie which happens to be one of the songs I played on from a particularly rotten session in 1985.

I remember the session well. Not only was the singer, who sold several million copies of the song, extremely untalented, it was also the session I did the day before I saw Buzz for the last time. I think about him and the white cane and Stanley in the airport bar.


"I told Burgie to move out after Christmas and I want you to stop seeing Randall."

I wait up until Audrey gets home from her concert at one in the morning to say it. When I tell her she stands in the doorway looking back at me with a mixture of shock and bewilderment. Not the kind of thing one wants to hear about after playing an all-Beethoven concert for three hours.

Audrey gives me a curious half-smile, then walks silently into the room and sits down at the dressing table. She takes off her earrings and looks at me through the reflection in the mirror. She's trying to figure out if I'm bluffing or I know what's been going on. I look at her and say nothing.

The air in the room has become extremely thin. If someone inhaled, we'd fall over from lack of oxygen.

Audrey takes off her shoes; steps out of her full-length black concert dress; takes off her pantyhose; pulls her slip over her head, letting it fall to the floor; unhooks her bra and places it in the laundry basket and reaches into the closet for a bathrobe. She pulls the bathrobe down from the hanger in one quick gesture, tying the terrycloth belt around her waist securely and walks out of the bedroom to the bathroom. I hear the sound of running water from the shower.

The shower lasts seven minutes and twenty-five seconds. The house falls silent again. The bathroom door opens and Audrey pads back down the hardwood hallway to the bedroom.

She stands at the doorway for a minute. The parts of her hair that she couldn't keep dry hang in ringlets around her shoulders. Her lower lip is trembling.

"Okay, I promise."

We make love off and on until the sky outside turns a subtle shade of cobalt blue.


The holidays have arrived. And with them, a whole new batch of situations. One of them is named Zara. The other is named Stanley.

We spend Christmas eve at the Piantadosi house, amidst a mob scene of relatives I only vaguely ever met. By two in the morning we're exhausted and slowly make our way home.

As we approach our house, we spot someone sitting on the porch at the front door. It's hard to make out who it is at first. But as we get closer, it becomes clear that it's Zara holding Paris in her arms, sitting on the front steps.

Burgie becomes very quiet as I pull the car into the driveway and turn off the engine. I can see in the rear-view mirror that he doesn't quite know what to do.

"I've heard that, if you put your mind to it, you can disappear. I'm trying really hard and nothing's happening."

Audrey turns to him with a disbelieving squint.

"Burgie, she has your kid, act human."

We get out of the car while Burgie waits and agonizes, but he finally steps out.

Zara doesn't look particularly healthy. She's gaunt and her eyes are sunken and dark. She seems nervous at first and speaks in quick, choppy sentences, peppered by the continuous motion of shifting her weight from one foot to the other. We know she wants to talk to Burgie but she doesn't want to be alone with him.

We run through a list of pleasantries and Merry Christmases while I open the door to let us in.

The front door is stuck; it won't open all the way. I have to push hard before I realize there is a Christmas tree lying on the floor in front of it, and a very happy-to-see-us Stanley sitting in the hallway with tinsel draped over his head. Stanley has managed to destroy the tree and topple it over, landing wedged between the front door and the hall closet.

It's three in the morning and I don't feel like screaming at a dog who forgot what he did twenty seconds after doing it. So I grab what remains of the tree and right it, while Clarissa fetches a broom and sweeps up the broken ornaments and chewed up pieces of light bulb and tries to pretend we still have something resembling a Christmas tree.

Audrey hauls Malory off to bed while Zara stands nervously on the front porch with an equally nervous Burgie. Clarissa mutters it's the soul of his owner who didn't want to be left home on Christmas night that made him destroy the tree. I ask Clarissa if everybody else in her family is like her. She beams, for the first time since I met her, flashes a smile and proudly says:

"No, I am completely unique." Thank God for small favors.

Whenever we leave the house for any period of time without Stanley, he always makes a point of destroying something. But in all of his tirades, he's never touched the urn with Buzz's ashes. I finish straightening the tree and find myself having a stare-off with Stanley, who sits in the middle of the hallway looking ethereal. After a minute of this 'Twilight Zone' gaze, Stanley lets out a deep sigh, gets up on all fours, turns around and walks off to his bed.

"Maybe Clarissa's right, Otto. Maybe Stanley is possessed by the soul of Buzz. Nothing else can explain that dog's behavior."

Audrey is busy putting on her Christmas pajamas; red flannel with holly and mistletoe and a few well-placed Santas.

The world has achieved a certain level of madness since I came back to it. Maybe it's always been that way, and I never noticed. Burgie and Zara have taken off somewhere. Clarissa is walking through the house burning sticks of incense, muttering vague incantations and Audrey looks like gift wrap from Bullock's.. My face has been rearranged and my nose has been reconstructed with bits of my ass and my elbow and my brain has been scrambled sideways.

Somewhere in all of this is a sense of order in the universe; there has to be. How else could all of this be explained? Or is it true that God has really put us on the planet only for the big crowd scenes.

I climb into bed and turn out the light. I lay there in the darkness, staring blankly up at the ceiling. The feeling of optimism comes over me again; only this time I get the sense that everything is going to be alright after all. I have this strong urge to get up and go to the music room. Maybe this is a sign.

I sit down at the keyboard and plug in the headphones. At first nothing really happens; just scales. And then it starts. Things come back to me. I have a few lapses, but the more I play the more I remember. After a while I'm running through everything I've ever played. Everything in my body is tingling. I'm terrified and excited all at the same time - what if this is a brief respite before I forget everything for good, or what if this is God's way of telling me it'll all work out if I just trust myself. I run in to tell Audrey the good news but she's fast asleep.

Maybe it's not the crowd scenes after all.


"Hey Otto, guess what??"

I stand at the doorway of the music room and look around. The house is full of people and I'm standing, facing them in my underwear. Stoika walks by carrying a stack of dinner plates, on her way to the dining room. It looks like Stoika, but I can't be sure. She has a tan, the first tan ever in her life. Her hair is streaked blonde. "Fab legs," she comments and continues on.

I smell cooking. I smell turkey and stuffing and I hear Mozart on the stereo in the living room. Where have I been? What time is it? I gaze around the hallway into the living room and spot Leslie sitting on the sofa with Alain, who has cut his hair severely short and sports a close-cropped greying beard. Audrey's buddies from the orchestra have shown up.

I quickly make a dash for the bedroom. When I get there I notice it's been turned into a combination coat room and nursery. Jackets are piled up on the bed and Paris is lying in the middle, getting his diaper changed by Zara who looks at me deadpan and remarks, "I didn't know guys still wore those kind of shorts."

I am not particularly amused by her assessment of my phosphorescent day-glo orange bikini underwear. I quickly run to the closet and throw on my pants. I look at the clock beside the bed and I realize it's four in the afternoon. I have been sitting at the piano since five that morning.

"We tried to tell you earlier, but you were having too much fun," Zara says, slipping a fresh diaper on Paris, folding up the pee-filled one and tossing it in a plastic bag. "We decided to do dad's ashes later."

I run into the bathroom and clean myself up while mayhem takes over the house. I get quickly dressed and run into the living room to say hello to everybody before going into the kitchen to see Audrey, who is in the process of flipping the turkey over for the last two hours of cooking.

"Glad you finally made it," she says sarcastically.

Burgie is standing by the stove wearing oven-proof mittens holding a twenty-five pound bird in his hands, while Audrey rearranges the aluminum foil. "Audrey's dad beat the shit out of me in tennis," he enthuses.

"Should I pretend to be surprised?" I ask.

Audrey finishes arranging the foil and Burgie plops the bird in the roasting pan and shoves it back in the oven. Audrey flicks some loose hair that has dropped down on her face and Burgie peels off the elbow-length gloves.

"How did it go?"

"Something wonderful has happened."

"Good. You can celebrate by peeling the potatoes." She flashes me a grin and pinches my nose as she hands me the peeler. "The doctor told you it would, Bugs."

"So what happened with you and Zara?" I ask Burgie as I tackle the small mountain of twenty or so potatoes, carefully peeling each one and dropping it into a pan of cold water.

Burgie leans close to me, looking around for interested ears.

"We're gonna live together for a while and see what happens."

"Does Leslie know?"

"Not really."

"Lucky you."

Stoika and Leslie appear in the kitchen. I can't get over how robust Stoika has become. She's changed considerably since I last saw her. She is, at the age of forty, finally growing into her looks.

"So how about it?" Stoika asks. "Is everything under control?"


Stoika, Leslie, Burgie, Audrey and I pile into the limousine Stoika rented for the trip to Griffith Park, Mullholland Drive and the beach, the places we've decide to toss Buzz's ashes.

Alain declines going. He is gracious but distant from us. I can see why Leslie decided to get back together with him. He has intense eyes but a warm hand. Part of him feels the intruder and we can't dissuade him from feeling that way. Zara doesn't go, feeling estranged from Stoika because of Vladimir. They are cordial but distant, much as Alain is, and she makes excuses that Paris is coming down with something.

We are halfway down the block when Audrey realizes we've left Stanley behind. With the sun racing quickly down the horizon, we dash back to the house to grab Stanley who is properly pissed-off at being overlooked. He muscles himself into the backseat between Audrey and me, letting out a huffed sigh and a pathetic stare with a "how could you?" expression on his face.

That dog, at twelve, has become a small human. With Stanley now part of the entourage, we are safe to proceed to the hallowed grounds. The urn is balanced between my legs.

They call it magic hour for a reason. It's not night and it's not day. It's that vague interim period where the sky glows its most dramatic red and orange and its blue is the most hypnotic.

232

We arrive at the top of the highest point in Griffith Park and stop the car. We get out and open the urn, grabbing handfuls of ashes. Stoika goes first, me second, Burgie third, Leslie fourth and Audrey fifth. Audrey never knew Buzz, so she acts as Stanley's emissary.

We toss the ashes to the wind which spread like grey mist over the grass and trees and to the city below. Stoika impulsively yells out "Bon Voyage, Buzz. Have a wonderful time!"

We decide this is going to be the catch phrase for the other two places. We start saying it in unison. "Bon Voyage, Buzz, have a wonderful time!"

The last powdered grains of ash leave the urn at Malibu. The dust has scattered to the wind and blown out to the ocean; out to the setting sun. We turn and head back to the limo. Buzz is finally where he wants to be: everywhere.

The ride back down Pacific Coast Highway is quiet. I gaze out the window at the passing lights from shops and streetlamps turning on with the evening. Stoika quietly focuses on the door handle and we know it isn't the door handle she's thinking about. She picks her head up for a moment and looks at us.

"I'm glad we could do this," and we all agree.


It's dark by the time we arrive at the house. Everybody piles out of the limousine and heads into the festivities of Christmas dinner.

It's not until later when everyone finally leaves that the house becomes quiet once again. It's just me, Audrey, Malory, Clarissa and Stanley. Stanely has decided he no longer wants to sleep under the bookcase next to the empty urn, but on the floor in our bedroom.

I check on Mal. Audrey has already fallen asleep, so I wander around the house, checking locks. I glance at the partially disfigured Christmas tree in the living room. It's the end of another Christmas.

Finally I get into bed and drift off to sleep and fall, almost instantly into a dream.


We're riding in Burgie's VW Bus: me, Buzz, Burgie, Stoika, Leslie and Audrey. We're in the middle of an incredible field of flowers; there is no road, only flowers. They keep hitting the windshield of the van as we drive across. Burgie stops the van after a while and I get out to look at the flowers. They stretch as far as the eye can see; there must be millions; all yellow and red, swaying in the sun and breeze. Buzz stands on the horizon, feeding sugar to a white horse.

"You aren't going to stay?"

"I have to be there before the sun sets."

"Where?"

"Where the waves are. You can come with me, the horse is big enough."

"I look over to Audrey who holds a small puppy in her arms, wrapped in white towels.

"It's going to rain," she says.

She points her finger to the sky and a raindrop touches her fingertip; the sky becomes overcast and threatening.

"It's okay, it won't be raining when we get there. It's where summer always goes."

Buzz looks up to the sky; a bolt of lightning streaks across in front of us. The flash is blinding and we lose sight of him. Burgie, Leslie and Stoika get out of the van, looking exactly as they did in 1969. Stoika wears white makeup and her thin lace dress. She opens an umbrella and the wind from the storm sweeps her up into the sky. She roars with laughter as Buzz follows her with his eyes and mounts his horse.

"She's found the secret!" he yells, riding after her.

Burgie, Leslie, Audrey and I stand on the plateau.

"How will we know you if we lose you?" I ask Buzz as he rides away.

"I'll be around. I always am. You'll see," he yells before disappearing behind a cloud.

The sun appears, streaking across the sky, in fingers of dazzling color spilling down the field. I look back to Audrey, and the small puppy she was holding in her arms becomes a young boy standing next to her. He's nine or ten. He looks up to the sky and holds Audrey's hand. He looks like a young version of Buzz.

We are bathed in the warmth of the sun and the flowers turn a deep shade of green.


The sun creeps through the window and hits my eyes. I stir and slowly begin to wake. Groggily, I open one eye and realize Stanley has sprawled himself across our bed, something he's never done before. Audrey lies next to me, her arms wrapped tightly around her pillow, sleeping peacefully.

I'm half asleep and half awake. I lie quietly and think about the dream. I can't help wonder what it all means, if it means anything at all.

"I wouldn't worry about it," a voice says; coming from the foot of the bed.

I know I heard it. It was distinct and clear and it wasn't Audrey. And I wasn't talking to myself. I slowly raise my head above the comforter and look down and see Stanley raise his head the same time to look back at me. We stare at each other for a moment.

I refuse to believe that dog has said anything to me.

Our motto – *In order that a good story may be told* –
reflects our belief that tomorrow's literary heritage depends on investment in today's writers.

## More Great First Novels

## The Munich Sabbatical

## Pat Ann Morgan

## ISBN 0 947993 67 3  UK £15.95 USA $24.95

When art historian Viola Addison arrives in Munich to complete the
research for her new book, she is delighted at last to meet and receive
the interest of Professor Josef Feinstein. She is similarly thrilled to be
reunited with Lutz Fbenau, the handsome and wealthy lawyer with
whom she had a passionate affair when they wewe students ten years
earlier.

But right wing political extremists are active in the city, and
following a significant tip off, Detective Tom Jablonski is assigned to
investigate Viola's relationship with the Professor and with Lutz. As
violent and terrifying events unfold, the protagonists learn that
beauty has a dark side and that no one is what they seem...

A sizzling romance set in Munich's art world against the
background of the rising tide of right wing violence

'This romantic thriller has so much bite it kept me up until I had
finished it.'
*Anthea Turner*

Our motto – *In order that a good story may be told* –
reflects our belief that tomorrow's literary heritage depends on investment in today's writers.

## More Great First Novels

## Searching For Grace  Cynthia Kear

## ISBN 0 947993 75 4   UK £15.95

Played out against the backdrop of disease-ridden Eastern Africa
and the art worlds of New York and San Francisco, *Searching for
Grace* is not just a riveting portrayal of three dynamic women but
an intricate and stirring family drama.

"I have read *Searching for Grace* and absolutely love it. It is both
beautiful and engrossing and is thoroughly  involving from the
start. You have really found something quite special here."
*Michele Rubin*

'I read the book in one sitting unable to set it aside . . pleasures
and shocks on every page. I was entertained and moved, and you
can't ask a novel for more than that.'
*Lisa Alther*, author of  *Other Women* and *Five Minutes In Heaven*

Cynthia Kear is so skilled at what she is doing, she never misses
a beat. Marvelous writing. *Searching For Grace* is a winner.'
*Ruth Moose, The Pilot*

Cynthia Kear studied art history and drama as an undergraduate. She
spent fifteen years in the book and software publishing industry.
Having recently sold her software firm, she is a consultant to the
technology industry. A native New Yorker, she lives in San
Francisco where she is working on her second novel.

Our motto – *In order that a good story may be told* –
reflects our belief that tomorrow's literary heritage depends on investment in today's writers.

## More Great First Novels

### Going Away Party   Laura Pedersen

### ISBN 0 947993 77 0 UK £15.95 USA $24.95

Jess did not plan a party. She has just failed to graduate college and is
spending a week studying to retake the calculus element of her
degree. Her parents and the rest of her family have gone away for the
annual summer camping trip. When a middle aged man calls for
directions Jess asks him in, and he ends up staying for the duration.
Take a mixed up young woman just about to turn her back on
childhood and education and a lonely middle aged man who has
recently lost his wife, stir in some drinks, drama and humour and
settle down to one of the most entertaining reads of the year.

**The author**, Laura Pedersen, is well know in the United States for
her achievements; young business person of the year, the youngest
person to trade on the American Stock Exchange, a millionaire at 21,
two non-fiction titles which made the best-sellers list, her own
column in the New York Times and a regular guest on Oprah
Winfrey, David Letterman and other chat shows.

Our motto – *In order that a good story may be told* –
reflects our belief that tomorrow's literary heritage depends on investment in today's writers.

## More Great First Novels

## Celtic Fox  Richard Heygate

## ISBN 0 947993 00 2  UK £15.95 USA $24.95

A bard, an Irish warrior, a Celtic prince and an ex slave girl turned warrior are the characters who bring this Celtic drama to life. From the Dorset coast to the magic of Ireland they fight to unite the Celtic tribes and restore the ancient powers of their faith. From the hallowed chambers of McKinsey & Company to a lusty life as a Celtic Prince is a big jump for anyone, but one that Sir Richard Heygate has taken with great pleasure. Fascinated by the discovery in the eighties of the mummified corpse of a Celtic Prince that became known as 'The Bog Man' Sir Richard began to read and research everything that was available on the Celts of the period.

Scientists had concluded that the long dead prince was a willing human sacrifice, what fascinated Richard was why should a strong young prince willingly agree to be sacrificed. As Richard's research developed he discovered that the Celts were a far more sophisticated race than he had been lead to believe. They were fine artists and makers of jewellery, wove wonderful cloths and materials, worshipped life and the earth and kept their history and traditions alive verbally through the bards of the time. Magic played a great part in their lives and far from being the barbaric race the Romans depicted them to be were in many ways much more advanced than the Romans themselves.

Richard's research took him to all the known battlegrounds where the Celts had fought between themselves or with the Romans, to their settlements and their sacred, magical, places.

There is strong Celtic blood in Richard, his mother can trace her family back to the Doomsday Book and a long line of  Welsh and Scottish Kings and the more Richard discovered about the Celts the closer he felt to them until, in his own words, ' I fell through a window in time and lived loved and fought with them'

This experience will be able to be shared by everyone in the real story behind 'The Bog Man' Richard Heygate's sweeping novel, *Celtic Fox.*

Our motto – *In order that a good story may be told* –
reflects our belief that tomorrow's literary heritage depends on investment in today's writers.

## More Great First Novels

## Loose Threads Glends Burgess

## ISBN 0 947993 96 7 UK £15.95 USA $24.95

At her father's funeral, Ellen d'Ullay, aged nineteen years, decides to forsake her artistic instincts in favour of career, independence and exotic travel. She achieves everything but Ellen realizes that her dazzling lifestyle came with a high price tag. When her lover Drew chooses a more conventional wife to support his own career and Ellen discovers that Larry and Will are as transient as her other friendships she realizes she has nothing but fool's gold in her hands.

As her thirtieth birthday approaches and passes Ellen's life falls apart and she has to make some tough choices. Should she abandon her career and move to San Francisco with Jack, an older, kind man who seems to love her, and chance that a more traditional life as a wife and mother can replace her ambition? A decade later, haunted b her artistic frustrations and desperately confused, Ellen is uncertain whether she is looking for love or simply looking for herself.

Into this absorbing narrative Burgess weaves the compelling landscape of Santa Fe, and the studio of the sculptor Kit Miranda, who confronts Ellen with her uncompromising passion. New Mexico is the final thread Ellen unravels in her quest for the truth, and the courage to acknowledge it.

Ellens quest becomes a whirlwind of emotional exhilaration and danger that leaves her near death and brings this stunning first novel to a dramatic and satisfying conclusion.

Glenda Burgess lives in Northern California with her husband and two children.